"WHO ARE YOU? . . . WHAT DO YOU WANT?"

The carriage began to move and she glared at the man who was abducting her. He rubbed his thumb up and down against her palm and wrist, slowly and gently. The motion was blatantly sexual.

"So many questions, Melanie. Shall we take them one at a time?" He smiled as his fingers caressed her, exploring her neck and face.

Melanie bit her lip. He knew just how to touch a woman. Just where, too—the sensitive little hollows behind her ears, the curve above her chin, the pulse in the center of her throat . . . She shuddered, but whether it was from fear or arousal, she wasn't sure.

"Who am I? Whomever I choose to be at any particular moment. What do I want? It's not too big a list. Money, adventure, a beautiful woman. At the moment . . . you."

*If You've Enjoyed This Book,
Be Sure to Read These Other*
AVON ROMANTIC TREASURES

COMANCHE FLAME *by Genell Dellin*
FORTUNE'S BRIDE *by Judith E. French*
GABRIEL'S BRIDE *by Samantha James*
LORD OF THUNDER *by Emma Merritt*
WITH ONE LOOK *by Jennifer Horsman*

Coming Soon

THIS FIERCE LOVING *by Judith E. French*

RUNAWAY BRIDE

DEBORAH GORDON

An Avon Romantic Treasure

AVON BOOKS ◆ NEW YORK

RUNAWAY BRIDE is an original publication of Avon Books. This work has never before appeared in book form. This work is a novel. Any similarity to actual persons or events is purely coincidental.

AVON BOOKS
A division of
The Hearst Corporation
1350 Avenue of the Americas
New York, New York 10019

Copyright © 1994 by Deborah Gordon
Inside cover author photo by Bill Santos
Published by arrangement with the author
Library of Congress Catalog Card Number: 94-94074
ISBN: 0-380-77758-4

First Avon Books Printing: September 1994

AVON TRADEMARK REG. U.S. PAT. OFF. AND IN OTHER COUNTRIES, MARCA REGISTRADA, HECHO EN U.S.A.

Printed in the U.S.A.

RA 10 9 8 7 6 5 4 3 2 1

Prologue

Nevada City, California
April 1855

Melanie Wyatt was playing poker in the back room of Emerson's Saloon, disguised— quite brilliantly, she thought—as a male. A cigar was on her right, a glass of brandy was on her left, and a large pile of coins was in front of her. Her features were coarsened by theater makeup and her clothes were those of a miner—a red wool shirt, buckskin pants tucked into leather boots, and a low-crowned, broad-brimmed hat. Her expression gave no sign of the glee she felt about the three eights and two jacks in her hand.

Tyson Stone, her soul mate and good friend, was sitting next to her, studying his cards. From the moment she'd learned he was a regular in this weekly game, she had nagged him to bring her along. Her father was a regular, too, but he traveled constantly on business. If they chose a week when he was out of town, she'd told Ty, he would never find out she had come.

After months of campaigning, she had finally gotten her way. Ty had teased that she was an impetuous little tomboy, and he was no doubt right, but he didn't understand how dull it was to be a female. Ty, a miner, was the nineteen-year-old son of her father's housekeeper, and before his arrival two falls ago, she had nearly died of boredom. In a town as civilized—as tediously refined—as Nevada, a girl had to do *something* to liven up her life.

It didn't worry her that a town ordinance prohibited females from appearing in public in male attire. She had marched down Main Street in these clothes without drawing the slightest suspicious glance, even from behind. She would have sensed such speculation, sensed the danger it represented, just as she would have known if any of the twenty-odd men in this room suspected she was an impostor and meant to unmask her. This talent for divining danger had first manifested itself when she was twelve or thirteen, and the older she got, the more sensitive it became. At the moment, it provided a welcome sense of security.

Tyson sighed and threw down his cards. "I fold. My cousin Lance is holding another winner. I can smell the aces from here."

Melanie stroked her fake mustache. "You've got that one right." She tossed some coins into the pot. "I'll raise."

"On the other hand, maybe you're only bluffing," Doc Claypoole said. "I'll see your bet."

Doc had given her her only bad moment of the night, after Pete Emerson had served the brandy and she'd taken a swaggering belt to show that she was tougher than her tender years suggested. The hooch had been damned near lethal.

She had choked and sputtered. Doc had dashed to her side and whacked her on the back. Between the coughing and the pounding, she'd tumbled off her chair, sending everyone in the room into gales of laughter. Doc had knelt down beside her and reached for a button, saying she would recover faster if he loosened her clothes. A few good tugs at the bindings beneath her shirt, and every eye in the room would have bugged out of its socket. She had bolted up before any damage could be done, but it had been a narrow escape.

The fourth player folded and the final player saw. "Andy has the look of a lucky man," Melanie said, "but he's not as lucky as I am. I'll raise again."

She was tossing more money into the pot when a sharp stab of alarm tore through her. She jerked around and stared at the closed door. It opened only seconds later, and her father strode into the room.

Paling, she turned back around and raised her cards. Her disguise was good, but unlike everyone else in Pete's saloon, Thomas Wyatt was used to seeing her in male attire—the attire of a seaman or miner. He might even recognize the hat she wore, since he happened to own it.

He filled the room with his sheer physical presence. Other men liked and respected him, but they feared him a little, too. There was no shortage of stories about his shadowy past, and some of them were even true.

He had been a trader and sea captain when Melanie was a little girl, and their home had been in Hong Kong. His wife, May, Melanie's mother, had been a Portuguese beauty from the enclave of Macao. She had been quiet and frail, too sickly to take proper care of Melanie, so Shen Wai, their houseman, had looked after her. As a result, Melanie spoke Portuguese and Chinese as well as English.

She had loved Shen Wai and her mother dearly, but her life had seemed dull and gray when her father was away. One of her happiest memories was of Thomas barreling into the house after a long voyage—of a laughing giant picking her up, swinging her around, and launching into a story about his adventures. She only wished there had been more such private moments, but as Shen Wai had repeatedly told her in the years that had followed, Thomas was an important man with numerous business concerns and countless claims on his time.

Her mother had died of cholera when she was five. At Shen Wai's insistence, her father had taken her on his voyages after that, and Shen Wai as well, as her caretaker and tutor. It was unconventional, but he had owned the vessel he'd captained and could do as he pleased. They had traveled for months at a time, stopping at exotic Pacific islands and the ports of three continents, staying at the homes of his business associates.

The discovery of gold in California's American River had changed their lives dramatically. She and Thomas had read about it in the newspaper while they were docked in the village of San Francisco. Gold had been found in the region often enough for nobody to lose his head over a few stray nuggets, but Thomas was a born adventurer, as drawn to a new challenge as to the prospect of unearthing a fortune. Even before the rush began in earnest, he was taking Melanie and Shen Wai from place to place and claim to claim.

He mined more gold than most, but by 1849, he'd found a better source of income than sluicing. At eleven, Melanie was old enough to understand where he went most nights—to the local gambling joints—and to notice that he usually returned with more pouches of gold than when he'd left. He opened a string of general stores with his winnings, investing the profits in real estate and quartz gold mines.

By 1853 he was a wealthy man. Melanie wasn't

sure just why he'd quit the camps, but she suspected the Feather River incident had something to do with it. Her father seldom yelled at her when she got into mischief, merely explained with long-suffering patience why her behavior was unbecoming. But then he'd caught her paddling in the river dressed in nothing but her white work, tumbling and splashing with half a dozen male pals, and exploded for the first time in her life, raging incoherently about virtue and decency and rape. Before she knew it, they were in Nevada. Ever since, he had bedeviled her with suggestions to join this or that ladies' club or invite this or that family to dine.

He strolled around the room, chatting and shaking hands, then walked to their table. "Good evening, gentlemen. Mind if I sit in? You know how much I enjoy fresh meat."

"Sure, so long as you've got a taste for shark." Doc nodded at Melanie. "If you ask me, the boy is a ringer. Tom Wyatt, meet Lance Stone."

"My cousin from Jackson," Ty said quickly. "Lance got here after you left for San Francisco, Mr. Wyatt, but he'll be leaving very soon. Tonight, probably. You're, uh, you're back awfully early from your trip, aren't you, sir?"

"My business took less time than I thought it would." Thomas stared at Melanie. "It's a pleasure to meet you, Lance. You've been staying at my house, I presume."

Melanie took several quick puffs on her cigar, putting as much smoke as possible between her face and Thomas's eyes. Although he was tolerant of her adventures, even the most indulgent father had his limits. "Yes, sir," she mumbled.

"You're having a good visit with your family, I trust?"

"Yes, sir. Very good. I appreciate your hospitality."

"And my hat? Do you appreciate that, too?"

She reddened so much that even a double coat of makeup couldn't hide it. "Yes, sir. I hope it was all right to borrow it. Ty thought—that is, he said you don't wear it much anymore."

"True enough." Thomas sat down. "Keep it, son. Any member of my housekeeper's family is welcome to my old hat. Welcome in my home, too, for as long as he cares to stay. Anyway, you're about to return my hospitality. Double."

Thomas Wyatt lazed back in his chair, watching impassively as the game resumed. Melanie was keeping her cards up, her eyes down, and her voice low, but if she thought for one moment that she'd fooled him into believing she was Ty Stone's cousin from Jackson, she had no more brains than the moth-eaten stuffed grizzly in the corner of Pete's front room. His housekeeper's son had a lot to answer for, that was for damned certain.

Not that he took his daughter for a naive victim, of course. He didn't have to be told who had conceived this crazy prank, and it wasn't Ty. The boy was a little wild—he reminded Thomas of himself at that age—but for all his plots and schemes, he had sense enough to know that a female didn't belong at a poker game. And male juices enough, Thomas thought irritably, to be talked into most anything if the female doing the talking had a body as ripe as his seventeen-year-old daughter's. It would have been better if he had lived elsewhere, but how did you tell your pleading housekeeper that her son wasn't welcome in your home?

Doc folded a few bets later and Andy did the same, but Melanie had bluffed them into staying in longer than they should have. She grinned across at Doc as she raked in her winnings, giving Thomas his first clear look at her face. He wanted to haul her out of the saloon by the scruff of her neck. There was only one place she could have acquired that makeup, only one person who could have shown her how to apply it. It was intolerable.

Doc dealt the cards, and Thomas turned his attention to the game. An hour later, having relieved Melanie of most of her winnings, he felt marginally better. He stood and stretched. "You'll have to excuse me, gentlemen. It's been a long day. Ty? Lance? Are you ready to leave?"

Ty bolted to his feet. "Anything you say, Mr. Wyatt."

Melanie avoided her father's eyes. "I think I'll stay. My luck turned sour after Mr. Wyatt came in. Maybe it'll improve once he leaves."

In other words, she knew she was in trouble and dreaded the scolding she was about to receive. That was good. Let her worry.

"Your young cousin is a guest in my house," he said to Ty. "That makes me responsible for him. He can stay for another couple of hands, but then I want him home."

"I'll bring him," Ty said. "Half an hour at the most, Mr. Wyatt. I promise."

Thomas walked around to Melanie and put his hand on her shoulder. She stiffened and gazed at the table. He tightened his grip. "We wouldn't want your sainted widowed aunt to worry about you, now would we, son?" he said.

She finally looked up. "No, sir."

Thomas gave her a hard stare, saw a flush creep up her neck, and, satisfied, released her and left the room. It was raining hard when he stepped outside. His house wasn't far, just five blocks up

Main Street, but he was drenched by the time he got home. It didn't improve his mood.

Shen Wai, who lived in San Francisco now, had accompanied Thomas to Nevada for a visit and was reading in the front parlor. He set aside his paper and looked at Thomas anxiously. "Mrs. Stone and Miss Susannah returned some thirty minutes ago. They were at Frisbie's Theater. I'm concerned about Mi-Lan. She wasn't with them."

"Melanie," Thomas corrected automatically, though God knew why he bothered. It never did any good.

"Mrs. Stone and her daughter have gone to bed. Mrs. Stone said she had not seen Mi-Lan all evening, but imagined she was somewhere with Tyson. I find that a most disturbing prospect, Captain. That young man is not a suitable escort."

"Thank you for that remarkable bit of insight," Thomas said. "As it happens, your concern is well-founded. They're playing poker in the back room of Emerson's Saloon. She's dressed like a miner, passing herself off as Ty's cousin. A less tolerant man would have thrashed her on the spot."

"But to unmask her would have been to invite her social ruin," Shen Wai pointed out.

"Thank you for *that* remarkable bit of insight, as well." Thomas poured himself a glass of whiskey, drained half of it, and dropped into a chair. "She was wearing theater makeup, and very skillfully applied, too. My mistress must have taught her. Lila is a former actress. Owns a sporting house on Broad Street now. I had no idea Melanie even knew about her until a friend told me he'd seen them in Lila's private parlor, chatting like old friends. I ordered Melanie never to visit her again—for all the good it seems to have done."

"I can't condone her disobedience, Captain, but you must admit that if she was determined to pose as a male, it was wise to secure the help of an expert first. It increased the likelihood of a successful deception."

"The point, Wai, is that I had more control over the roughest sailor on the *Jade Princess* than I do over my own daughter." Thomas drained his glass impatiently. "I should have kept my old irons. Shackled her to her bed whenever I left town. God help me, but she's even more trouble in Nevada than she was in the mines."

Shen Wai sighed heavily. "I should have seen it sooner. It was inevitable. A thousand apologies, Captain."

"You should have seen what sooner? What was inevitable?"

"Trouble. It's the land. The *feng shui* is most unfavorable here. You must move immediately."

According to the laws of *feng shui*, certain locations were in harmony with the forces of nature, and thus lucky or favorable. Shen Wai was a talented geomancer, or interpreter of these laws, and Thomas had enough of the Orient in him to pay careful heed. "Unfavorable?" he repeated in astonishment. "What in hell do you mean, unfavorable? You're the one who told me to build here in the first place!"

"I should have studied the site during a storm before I ventured that opinion. I made an error."

Thomas rolled his eyes. "Now he tells me."

"Once again, Captain, my humblest apologies. As I believe you know, *feng shui* is more art than science. One does the best one can." Shen Wai paused. "The finest *feng shui* sites in the state are, of course, in San Francisco. I have evaluated your holdings there, and the lot you own on the corner of Hawthorne and Folsom streets is most auspicious. Given Mi-Lan's high spirits—"

"Aha! Now we get to the heart of it. I know

very well that you miss the girl. That you want her in San Francisco. *Feng shui* has nothing to do with it."

Shen Wai looked insulted. "We must be in harmony with our surroundings in order to prosper, especially those of us who are susceptible to mischief or distraction. I do miss Mi-Lan, but more important, I want what is best for her. A more favorable *feng shui* site can only help."

"So if I refuse to move, I'm a negligent and uncaring father." Thomas felt a glimmer of amusement. Shen Wai was the only man he knew who could regularly outmaneuver him. "Well done, my friend. Flawlessly argued."

"But think of your beloved Chang-Mei. She deserves grandchildren—"

"Talk about pulling out all the stops!"

"—to honor her memory. A favorable *feng shui* site will help ensure a felicitous match."

The word "match" stopped him in his tracks. Maybe Wai was right. The firm hand of a husband might be just what was needed to settle Melanie down, and there were many more men to choose from in San Francisco than in Nevada. There was more to do there, too, and the increased activity might keep her out of trouble.

"I congratulate you, Wai," he said. "You've taken an unruly wildcat and turned her into an unfortunate victim of the laws of *feng shui*. A most impressive feat of alchemy. Still, if you believe Melanie would be happier in San Francisco, I'll consider moving to the site you recommend. I do value your opinion."

Shen Wai inclined his head. "You honor me, Captain."

The front door opened, very quietly. Thomas got up. "The prodigals return," he said with a laugh. "They probably plan to sneak up to bed and try to avoid me till morning, when my wrath will presumably have dissipated into mere irritation. They don't have a prayer."

Thomas marched from the room. Shen Wai sighed as he listened to the captain's lecture. Though Mi-Lan and Thomas didn't know it, he was giving her exactly what she craved, the time and attention of the father she adored. Aware of her yearnings, Wai had done his best over the years to coax Thomas into opening up his heart, but a man couldn't be a woman, a father couldn't be a mother, and there were hurts and guilts so intense that even an old friend had no right to speak of them. He had left Thomas to his demons.

Still, the captain was an admirable man, honorable in his dealings and generous with his friendship. The day nineteen years before when Thomas had won Wai in a mah-jongg game had been the luckiest of Wai's life.

This evening had been lucky, too. Things had gone even better than he had dared to hope. He needed Mi-Lan in San Francisco, and it appeared he would have her there as soon as a house could be constructed. She would help him because the blood in her veins would demand it.

She didn't know it yet, but Thomas had deceived her about her past. He had done it to protect her from the scorn and hatred of bigots, but a shield of lies shamed one's ancestors and defiled one's honor. Now that Mi-Lan was a woman, it was up to him, Shen Wai, to tell her the truth.

She sometimes smiled when he called her that, assuming it was some pet Chinese name for her, but Mi-Lan was the name she had been given at birth. "Melanie" had only come later, after they had left Hong Kong. And the mother she called May, thinking it was short for Mary, had been born Chang-Mei.

Chang-Mei hadn't been pure Portuguese at all, but the daughter of an elderly Macao merchant, Antonio Alvares, and his Chinese mistress, Xiong-Lai. Alvares had died when Chang-Mei was seven, forcing Xiong-Lai to take a series of protectors. One of those lovers had killed her.

Chang-Mei, only thirteen at the time, had fled to a brothel in Macao. There had been no other way to survive. She hadn't been frail from birth, as Mi-Lan had been told. Her health had been destroyed by the brutality of the next three years.

Thomas Wyatt had met her when she was sixteen and he was twenty, taken her from the brothel, and installed her in a house in Hong Kong. There had been no question of marriage; men from prosperous New England families, even black sheep like Thomas Wyatt, did not marry half-Chinese whores. But he *had* loved her. Indeed, fearing for her life, he had done everything possible to prevent her from conceiving a child.

But fate had intervened. Mi-Lan was the result. Against all odds, her mother had carried her for almost eight months. Against all odds, the tiny baby had not only survived, but thrived. And against all odds, this daughter of a wealthy American merchant had been given to a firebrand Chinese peasant to raise.

Shen Wai knew that the gods didn't perform such feats without a purpose, and in time, he had come to understand what that purpose was. The emperor had lost the Mandate of Heaven and would have to be overthrown. Mi-Lan was meant to assist him in the salvation of his beloved China.

He, in turn, would have to bow to heaven's will, but only to a point. He would tell Mi-Lan that he was aiding the destitute Celestials of America, not that he was arming the emperor's enemies. No matter what the cause, her blood, her loyalty, and her sense of justice would compel her to help him as much as she could, and raising money for the poor was a good deal safer than negotiating with criminals and bribing corrupt officials.

Protecting her that way might diminish his effectiveness, but if he was punished for it, so be it. Sometimes, even the gods asked too much.

Chapter 1

San Francisco
July 1861

San Francisco loved a good eccentric, which was probably why the city was so full of them. Bankrupt merchant Joshua Norton donned a seedy uniform and anointed himself Norton I, Emperor of the United States, and everyone in town read his proclamations and honored his scrip. Socialite Lillie Hitchcock played poker and the ponies with equal abandon, chased after fires like a pyromaniac, and changed fiancés more often than a fugitive changed addresses, and the town made her its favorite debutante. Melanie Wyatt, the daughter of mining mogul Thomas Wyatt, railed against vices no lady was supposed to refer to, and the papers published her speeches; she bought and sold Oriental curios as cannily as the shrewdest Montgomery Street merchant, and the gentlemen lined up to overpay.

They had lined up to offer their hands in marriage as well, and, like Lillie, Melanie had often accepted and then changed her mind. But everyone felt her fifth betrothal, to attorney George Bonner, would stick. Indeed, with the wedding only a month away, the bookmakers had set the odds at two to three. And if some gossip claimed he had seen the bride-to-be and her pal Lillie in a Portsmouth Square gambling den, disguised as males, wagering the ceremony would never come off, well, no one put much credence in the report.

In any event, Melanie had been too busy of late to worry about her approaching nuptials. The *Aurora* had sailed into San Francisco on Tuesday, creating a need for immediate action just when Shen Wai was out of town, and it had fallen on her to cope. It wasn't the first time she had functioned alone, for Wai had a habit of vanishing for weeks at a time, often to unnamed destinations. This time, at least, he was off with her father, visiting Thomas's holdings in the Comstock, so she hadn't had to maneuver behind Thomas's back. Delays could be costly—even ruinous—in matters as sensitive as these.

The men were due back next week, several days before anyone had expected the *Aurora* to arrive. Melanie knew that the ship was important because Shen Wai had told her of a letter he'd received from a compatriot in Hong Kong, written as the *Aurora* departed that city for the Sandwich Islands and San Francisco, and sent to him aboard a faster and more direct clipper. The *Aurora*'s hold, the letter said, contained a shipment of precious articles of the type Melanie traded in, including a carved wooden tiger with a secret and vital map inside. The ship also carried eleven Chinese slave girls loaded on in Canton, and to Melanie, that cargo was the most precious of all.

These unfortunate females, some of them as young as nine or ten, had been sold by their fathers for use in the cribs and parlor houses of San Francisco's Little China. Since the day five years before when Shen Wai had told Melanie who she really was and where she had come from, she had done whatever she could to rescue girls like these—girls like her mother and grandmother— from the wretched life of the brothel. Between her trust funds and the profits from her hobby, she had bought some of these miserable creatures more promising futures—fewer than two hundred out of thousands, but the prettiest girls fetched thousands each on the flesh market, so it was the best she could do.

On Wednesday, in the dank and fog of the early morning, she donned her black and crimson cloak and matching hat and drove her gig to the Jackson Street Wharf, where the *Aurora* was berthed. The area near the docks was called Sydney Town, after the Australian convicts who roamed the place. It was a hellhole teeming with pickpockets, thieves, and burglars; rife with gamblers, whores, and pimps; and worst of all, swarming with crimps, those experts in cheating, drugging, and shang-haiing unwary seamen.

While very quiet at that hour of the day, it was hardly safe, and she was sensible enough to keep up her guard. A number of men called out to her, but their greetings were friendly. Everyone in town, it seemed, recognized the cloak and hat she always wore, even dangerous criminals like the Hounds and the Sydney Ducks.

There were no threats at all, no aura of danger, and though she was thankful for that, she wasn't surprised. She had been here twice before with the same result. She was such a singular creature, a fe-male Robin Hood who outwitted the rich in order to aid the poor, that even the basest sorts seemed to admire her.

Still, she wasn't foolish enough to count on that for protection. She was tall and strong, not some fragile flower of an easy mark. And as she re-minded her father each time he learned of one of her exploits and erupted in a torrent of paternal concern, it was well-known in San Francisco that she carried both a Colt's revolver and a bowie knife—and that, thanks to him, she could use them to deadly effect. Unfortunately, he put no more credence in her ability to protect herself than he did in her psychic gifts, which she had first admitted to several years before. Where Shen Wai had nodded pensively, Thomas had insisted that her presentiments were the product of an overly active imagination. He still thought so.

She tracked down the *Aurora*'s captain, crisply bribed him into telling her to whom his shipment of slave girls was consigned, and proceeded to the customhouse a few blocks away. Another bribe was offered, this time to an inspector, who agreed to hold up clearance of the crates containing the *Aurora*'s illicit human cargo until early Friday morning. By Thursday afternoon, Melanie had successfully negotiated with the consignee, a Dupont Street parlor-house proprietor, for the purchase of the girls, and had withdrawn sufficient funds from her bank to make the payment. She had also arranged, via telegraph, for the girls to be picked up in front of City Hall in coaches and taken to a house that Shen Wai owned in San Jose. The mistress there, Mrs. Hsing, would train them to sew, clean, and cook, then find them respectable positions.

On Friday morning, Melanie took an omnibus to Dupont Street to pick them up. The brothel was a sex-soaked haven of suffocating musk, tawdry silk wall hangings, and garish chinoiserie. It billed itself as an exotic Oriental pleasure dome, but the claim was pure illusion. The true reality of the place was degradation and violence, the only comfort, a long session with the opium pipe.

She wasn't shocked by how young the girls

were; in five years, she had come to expect it. She addressed them in Chinese, calming and reassuring them, and they understood at once. They spoke the same dialect Shen Wai did, the Chinese of the province of Kwangsi, near Canton.

The utter lawlessness and wrenching poverty of the area explained their presence here. Girls as pretty as these were valued in China where normal females weren't, because they could attract husbands above their station. If their fathers had sold them into slavery, it was because immediate cash, unlike possible courtship gifts later, put food into empty stomachs and roofs above vagrant heads.

Melanie raged at the injustice of that, but she also understood it. Family came first in China. The ten-year-old Shen Wai had faced the same desperate conditions as these girls' fathers had, and he had responded by indenturing himself as a houseboy and gardener to the merchant who had later lost him to Thomas Wyatt. Wai's father had naturally kept the bond money.

Most of the girls were heartrendingly grateful to be rescued, but one was hostile and recalcitrant. She insisted that she could earn enough as a whore to buy her freedom, then become a madam in her own right and live like a queen. Melanie argued for as long as time permitted, but to no avail. The girl wouldn't listen.

City Hall was a block away. Melanie shepherded her charges down the street, spotted Mrs. Hsing waiting with the two coaches, and sighed in relief. Things had gone smoothly today, but they didn't always. With Shen Wai away, there was no one to whom she could have turned if trouble had arisen.

She realized she was tired—not physically so much as mentally. She was seldom conscious of worrying, but deep down, she supposed that she did, and that it took a certain toll. Fortunately, the mission that remained, retrieving the wooden carving, was a simple one. Indeed, she would have completed it the previous afternoon, but when she had gone to the importer, Tobin and Duncan's Chinese Sales Room, to pick up the tiger, she had found that the clerks were still unpacking the shipment from the *Aurora*. The carving had been among the objects still in crates.

After consigning her charges to Mrs. Hsing, she started toward Jackson Street. The Sales Room was only two blocks away, and her weariness disappeared the moment she reached the entrance. She had loved this shop from the first time she had set foot in it. A fondness for Chinese things was probably in her blood.

As usual, a brilliantly costumed factotum stood guard beneath the golden dragon on the Sales Room's famous banner. He smiled when he saw her and greeted her in Cantonese. "Ah, Miss Wyatt. We have beautiful new gowns from Paris today, just right for the opera. The blue of the silk exactly matches your exquisite blue eyes."

She playfully pointed out that her eyes were more green than blue. "But perhaps I'll buy one anyway, Mr. Fong, if you think the blue silk would flatter me."

"It is surely the other way around, Miss Wyatt. You would flatter the blue silk. With your milky skin and lustrous black hair, you would make the basest rags look like imperial robes, should you stoop to wear them."

Melanie was used to such extravagant praise. It wasn't that she was a raving beauty, but that there were at least half a dozen single men to every available woman in the town. With odds like that, the Medusa herself would have been awash in effusive admirers. "Then I've spent a great deal of

money here for nothing, haven't I?" she asked
with a smile. "But I do thank you for the compliment."

She walked into the main sales hall, which contained goods from all over the world—everything
from caged canaries to French silks to Swiss
clocks. The counter displaying Chinese crafts and
works of art was to her left. A clerk was still
uncrating the shipment from the *Aurora*, inspecting, inventorying, and polishing each object
before he set it out for sale. She soon spotted the
tiger she was supposed to acquire, sitting in a
sphinxlike pose on the counter.

Joseph Duncan saw her and hurried to intercept
her. "My dear Melanie, you didn't have to rush
back so quickly. As always, it will be my pleasure
to give you your pick of the newest shipment. I
would have sent for you the moment it was completely uncrated, just as I promised. Still, if you
would care to stay and browse, it should only be
a little while longer."

"Very well, Joseph, but it's truly a hardship to
remain in your shop for any length of time." She
winked at him. "A hardship to my father's bank
account, that is."

She bought one of the new French gowns, ordering it sent to her house, and strolled over to the
jewelry counter. It had taken her over a year to es-
tablish herself as a serious collector and gain a favored position here, and ever since, she had
wondered if Duncan ever asked himself why she
hurried in so swiftly after certain shipments arrived. If so, she hoped he attributed it to feminine
impatience to see the newest goods or to a con-
noisseur's natural enthusiasm. It wouldn't do to
have him suspect the truth—that she was afraid a
key item might inadvertently be sold to another
party if she failed to come in at once. A bronze ta-

ble lamp concealing a costly jade necklace, perhaps, or a ceramic dragon with an antique ivory carving hidden inside.

She asked to see a pearl and diamond ring, slipped it onto her finger, and held out her hand to admire the luster of the gems. Then she froze. A chill ran down her spine. She felt someone watching her, not casually, but with an interest that bordered on menace. Something similar had happened the day before in the shop, but when she had looked around, she had seen nothing out of the ordinary.

She removed the ring and returned it to the clerk, then nonchalantly surveyed the room. She saw some familiar faces, but all of them belonged to tame acquaintances. If there was danger here, she couldn't identify it. And if someone had been staring, he or she no longer was.

She moved to the next counter, her demeanor casual but her senses fully alert. Shen Wai had once observed that her gift for divining trouble was much like his skill as a geomancer—as real as the five normal senses, but much more erratic. It wasn't unusual for her to feel danger or evil nearby, but it wasn't common, either. Sometimes she was right. More often she was wrong. But it was also true that when a threat had in fact existed, she had never failed to sense it.

She strolled from counter to counter, greeting the people she knew and surreptitiously inspecting the ones she didn't. Her gaze drifted past a broad male back, then returned for a second look. A bolt of recognition slashed through her. Those powerful shoulders and long legs . . . She had seen the man yesterday when she had turned abruptly and attracted his glance. She'd felt a thrill of sensual excitement when their eyes had accidentally met. He was splendidly built, with dark eyes, dark brown hair, and strong, regular features. Elegantly dressed, too, in a dove-gray frock coat and trousers, a brightly brocaded waistcoat, and a heavy gold Albert watch chain.

He turned to face her. But no. He had a humped nose and a full mustache and beard. Like his hair, they were sprinkled with gray. His suit was made of black broadcloth, the attire of a middle-aged banker. The man yesterday had been clean-shaven, younger, and more dashing.

She continued to observe her fellow shoppers as she scanned the newest goods. One could never be too careful in Little China, for it was a place of endless intrigue. According to Shen Wai, factions based on family or home district schemed and brawled continually, and secret societies called triads engaged in everything from political conspiracies to thievery and murder. Indeed, Shen Wai was so knowledgeable about these matters that she sometimes wondered if he was involved. It was possible, for example, that the tiger his confederate had sent him from China was of interest to one of his enemies—that some competitor or criminal knew of its hidden cargo and wanted it for himself.

If such a predator was prowling the Sales Room, however, she couldn't find him. Mr. Duncan soon sought her out, and they proceeded to the Chinese curios. Her eyes were drawn to the tiger. She examined other objects until Duncan left her side, then picked it up. All thoughts of intrigue and robbery flew straight from her head.

The piece itself wasn't unusual, but she hadn't expected it to be. When one was smuggling precious objects out of China and into San Francisco, the last thing one wanted was receptacles that attracted attention. The fine lines carved into the wood, however, *were* unusual, at least to an expert such as herself. The pattern was attractive but very irregular. No such markings existed in nature. She ran her finger over the darkened grooves in the wood. This feline was the work of an artist, she decided, not a hack. It was worth keeping.

Duncan gave her fifteen minutes to inspect the new merchandise, then returned to her side. "Well, my dear, does anything strike your fancy? Would you like a closer look at the porcelain vase, perhaps? Or the bronze plate?"

"At both. As usual, your taste exactly matches my own. I'll examine this tiger, too, I think. And this little statue." She listed half a dozen objects more, and a clerk set them on a wooden cart.

"If I might propose something for your consideration . . ." Duncan ran his hand over a miniature cabinet that was intricately inlaid and lacquered to a glossy finish. "When I saw this piece, I thought of your Mr. Bonner. It would be useful for holding trinkets in his office."

"And very decorative, too. I owe George a birthday gift, and this will do admirably. Thank you for suggesting it, Joseph."

"You're very welcome. If you'll come with me . . ." He took her arm. The clerk followed with the cart.

As they left the sales floor, she noticed the man with the beard standing nearby. He was facing away from her, paying her no attention, yet a sense of unease approaching alarm stole over her. She knew better than to ignore such a strong presentiment. If he was a threat, the reason was probably the tiger. If he wanted it, he could have it—but not its contents.

Duncan settled her in his office, then withdrew. She studied the curios first, looking for both age and fine workmanship. Five of the nine objects met her standards.

Her business duties concluded, she picked up the tiger and gently shook it. Nothing rattled or shifted inside. The map it contained was evidently snugly positioned.

She stared at it, trying to discover how it opened. There was no hole or obvious hasp. A closer inspection revealed that the tiger was not one piece. It was divided in a jagged line along various of the fine grooves that constituted its markings. She twisted and pulled for several minutes, her frustration increasing as success eluded her. Then she somehow manipulated it in just the right way, and it split in two. Its construction was fiendishly clever.

It was stuffed with a soft, tightly bunched cloth. She assumed the map was folded inside. She withdrew the fabric and uncrinkled it. To her astonishment, an extraordinary gold and ruby antique necklace fell out. A small piece of paper followed, and, reading it, she smiled. The Chinese characters meant, "A gift from Niuhuru."

Niuhuru was the wife of Hsien-feng, China's debauched, drug-enslaved emperor. That spoiled and selfish woman cared nothing for the people beneath her and wouldn't have donated a tael to aid them. One of Shen Wai's compatriots had obviously stolen this necklace and enclosed it with the map, knowing it would be put to good use. Melanie's smile widened at the thought of the money such a magnificent piece of jewelry would bring—tens of thousands of dollars. It was a splendid surprise.

As for the map, she soon saw that it wasn't concealed inside the cloth, but drawn directly upon it. Shen Wai had told her that it would direct him to a location in the northern half of the state where a large cache of gold was buried, but, studying it, she saw nothing that resembled a town or road.

Only natural features were shown—a stream, some trees, some rocks, and so on. A star indicated the position of the gold. She concluded that the features around the star must be unique—that the mapmaker had known that Wai would recognize the spot at once from his extensive travels, perhaps because the *feng shui* was especially fine there.

She placed the necklace on the map, folded it into a tight square, and slipped it beneath her right stocking. Then she reassembled the tiger, fetched Mr. Duncan to the office, and showed him her selections. "I've taken a fancy to this carving," she remarked as he wrote up her order. "The markings are strangely hypnotic, don't you think?"

"Hypnotic?" He sounded puzzled. "Uh, yes, perhaps they are. How fascinating."

She could have said the tiger's markings resembled the man in the moon and he would have agreed. "Has anyone else noticed? Inquired about buying it?"

"Not that I was informed of, but it wasn't on display for very long. Would you like me to ask my clerks if it attracted any interest?"

"Please don't bother. I was simply curious." As much as she would have liked an answer, she didn't want Duncan to suspect that the matter was of special importance. "If you don't mind, I'll take it with me. Would you deliver everything else to my house?"

He said it would be his pleasure and handed her his bill. She signed it, tucked the tiger into her carpetbag, and left the shop. The omnibus stop was two blocks away, the route going directly past her house on its way from North Beach to Rincon Point.

She had scarcely reached Kearney Street when

the back of her neck began to tingle. Once again, she sensed someone watching her, following her. She stopped to adjust her cloak, checking the street out of the corner of her eye. She was searching, she supposed, for the man with the beard. He was nowhere to be found.

She resumed walking. The tingling intensified, causing the hairs at the back of her neck to bristle. She hurried to the omnibus stop on Washington and looked around again, but still saw nothing unusual.

The sense of being stalked grew even stronger. It was unnerving. An omnibus came by every ten minutes or so, but after less than five minutes she was too agitated to wait. She continued to follow the omnibus track, planning to hop on a coach the moment one arrived.

She was striding briskly down Montgomery, in the heart of the city's business district, when the earth jolted sharply beneath her feet. She stopped abruptly, then looked around for a large fallen object or a heavy rumbling vehicle. That was always the Californian's first instinct, to check for a routine cause.

Then the rolling began, as if she were standing on the deck of her father's old ship. Drivers struggled to stop and control their skittish horses. She hurried to the edge of the plank sidewalk, out of range, she hoped, of any bricks or plasterwork that might loosen and fall. People rushed from the large buildings that lined the street, chattering breathlessly about the way those structures had pitched and swayed. The mood was an odd mixture of fear and giddy excitement.

It was by far the strongest earthquake Melanie had experienced, making her so dizzy she almost fell. Every now and then she heard the crash of falling stonework. Finally, after what seemed like another minute but was probably less, the rolling stopped and the mood turned festive with relief. Everyone began talking at once, congratulating one another on having escaped without harm.

Melanie inspected the damage. It appeared to be confined to ornamental features such as friezes and brackets. She was thinking how lucky they all were that the falling debris had missed them when she noticed someone lying on the ground half a block to the north. He was surrounded by a crowd, so that only his booted feet were visible. She hurried over and elbowed her way into the throng.

"Please let me through," she said. "I'm experienced in the treatment of emergencies. I help at the city hospital."

The crowd gave way. A portly gentleman was hunched over the victim's body, loosening his jacket and shirt. Melanie knelt down beside him—and got her first look at the victim's face. It was the man from Tobin and Duncan's, the one with the beard.

There was a ragged gash on his forehead, just a little below his scalp. Blood had soaked into his hair and puddled onto the wooden sidewalk, but the cut was only oozing now, not running freely. Although he was unconscious, his breathing was regular and his pulse was strong.

Melanie was inspecting him for further injuries when the color drained from her cheeks. Someone less familiar with the artifices of the theater might not have seen it, but his beard, mustache, and eyebrows were false. Paint or powder rather than years had put the gray into his hair and putty had put the hump onto his nose.

She wanted to flee, but the same compassion that had led her to volunteer at the hospital kept her rooted by this stranger's side. Disguised or not, he had done nothing to harm her. Indeed, in his present state, he was incapable of harming a fly.

She removed a scarf from her carpetbag and cleaned the blood from his forehead and hair, then held the fabric firmly against his wound. Her fellow samaritan, meanwhile, had finished loosening his clothes. The victim wore a gold chain under his shirt, she noticed absently. A circular medal dangled from the end.

The design on that medal provided an even greater shock than his identity. It was a gold rendering of the endless knot, a Buddhist motif, painted on a gleaming black background. That emblem—those colors—belonged to one of the deadliest triads in China, the Eternal Brotherhood. Only the initiated dared to wear it.

She couldn't imagine how a white man had come to possess such an article. If he had stolen it from a member of the triad and was ever caught, he was a dead man. And if someone within the triad had given it to him freely, he was both extraordinary and very dangerous.

He moaned and opened his eyes. He seemed too dazed to focus on her face, but she had no difficulty focusing on him. Those dark brown eyes . . . She stifled a gasp of recognition. He was the man from yesterday, the one she had found so attractive.

His presence here was one coincidence too many. He must have been watching her all along, both yesterday and today. He had evidently followed her out of the Sales Room, so skillfully that she had failed to spot him. Obviously he wanted something from her. That was frightening enough, but it was absolutely chilling that he was such an expert at stealth and deception. Given the medal he wore, he was either a brazen thief or a ruthless criminal. Probably both.

She jerked to her feet, hurtled through the crowd, and ran up Montgomery Street as if all the hounds of hell were nipping at her heels.

Chapter 2

Alex McClure winced and slowly sat up. A bloodstained gold and red scarf wafted slowly past his face and settled onto his thighs. He picked it up, frowning at the stains in confusion. Several seconds passed before he noticed a throbbing pain on the right side of his forehead and realized that the blood came from his own body. He pressed the scarf to his wound, then looked around.

A large gentleman was kneeling by his chest, regarding him anxiously. A crowd was clustered around, avidly watching the scene. If there was anything Alex disliked, it was attracting undue attention. He started to get up.

The gentleman put a firm hand on his shoulder to stop him. That was just as well, because the sudden movement had made him dizzy. "Please, not so quickly. You might have a concussion. Moving could cause you additional injury. How do you feel? Are you light-headed? Nauseated?"

Without thinking, Alex answered in his normal voice. The accent was upper-class English. "Fine. I feel fine."

"Then you're not in serious pain?"

"No. Not at all." To his relief, the crowd began to disperse.

"And your name?" the gentleman persisted. "Can you remember it?"

Alex had to ponder the question, which told him he was muzzier than he'd thought. He always named himself after men of the cloth, perhaps to mock his minister father, perhaps as a backward sort of tribute to the bastard's depravity, but which clergyman had he chosen? Ah, yes. Benjamin Colman, the eighteenth-century Boston Congregationalist. He was posing as an American tourist. The more ordinary one appeared to be, the fewer questions people asked.

He was about to give Colman's name when he remembered that Colman was a younger man, clean-shaven and far more stylish. Irritated that a simple knock on the head could have caused such an unprecedented suspension of his mental acuity, he answered in a flawless American accent, "Jonathan Mayhew." Another notable Boston Congregationalist.

His benefactor didn't appear to notice the change in his speech. "I'm Louis Monroe, Mr. Mayhew, and I'm sure both of us wish we had met under happier circumstances. Tell me, do you recall what city you're in?"

"Of course. San Francisco." Alex managed a smile. "A benighted place where the earth beneath one's feet has even poorer manners than the roughest crimp. I should have stayed home."

The remaining onlookers laughed and scattered, satisfied that he was completely recovered. Mr. Monroe was less easily reassured, or perhaps he simply suffered from that common American malady, excessive inquisitiveness. "Oh? And where would your home be?" he asked.

"Boston, originally. Hong Kong now."

"I've heard it's a thriving town. Growing like a wildfire. Busy and exciting. Eventual business capital of the Orient, they say. I suppose that's why you're here. On business. What do you do there, Mr. Mayhew?"

"I work for a trading firm, but this is a pleasure trip. I was curious about California."

"Ah! Seeing the elephant! So am I, from New York, and I couldn't agree more about the earthquake. It makes me want to take the first ship home. The shocks always come in clusters, you know." Monroe stood and extended his hand. "You seem to be all right. Let me help you up. I'd have a doctor attend to that cut if I were you. Clean it and bandage it, or it might become septic. Can't say I know of one, as I've only been here since Monday, but I'd be glad to help you locate one if you'd like."

Alex told himself he would sooner consult an Indian medicine man than allow some backward local to touch him. "Thank you, but I'll inquire at my hotel," he said.

He removed the scarf from his wound, saw that the bleeding had stopped, and picked up his hat, which had fallen onto the sidewalk when he'd collapsed. He pulled it low on his head to cover his injury, then allowed himself to be helped to his feet.

He shoved the scarf in his pocket. A girl had been holding it against his head when he'd come around, he suddenly remembered. A fetching, exotic-looking creature with dark, almost black hair, fine white skin, and blue-flecked green eyes that were slightly almond-shaped. The same girl who had retrieved the tiger from Tobin and Duncan's, he realized in astonishment.

"This scarf . . . I seem to recall a young woman holding it against my wound. If it belongs to her, the least I can do is return it. Did she happen to tell you her name?"

"I can't say that she did. We never got around to introducing ourselves. To tell you the truth, her behavior was very odd. First she pushed her way through the crowd to help you, and then, for no reason I could see, she suddenly left. Took off like a startled deer. I'm sure it wasn't the blood—that didn't seem to bother her at all. I suppose she might have remembered an appointment, but who would worry about keeping an appointment at a time like this? Really, I don't know what to make of how she acted."

Monroe evidently suffered from a second American malady, tiresome loquacity. "Her nerves were probably frayed by the earthquake," Alex said. "She might have imagined she'd felt another shock."

He shook Monroe's hand and thanked him for his help, then escaped down Montgomery. Given the area's history, it should have occurred to him that the strange motions beneath his feet were an earthquake, but the thought had never entered his mind. He hadn't moved to safer ground. He hadn't watched for flying stone. Instead, he had stood gaping on the sidewalk, looking upward just as a chunk of cornice had crashed from a building nearby. Then he had crumpled to the ground, out cold. It was a remarkable piece of stupidity, rarely matched in the almost thirty years of his life.

He sighed. Things couldn't have been worse if he had botched them deliberately. And to think he'd assumed the American end of the job would be child's play after the Chinese part! After all, it had been no easy feat to persuade the emperor to part with a precious necklace in the first place, much less to make sure that every thief in Peking learned that a man with sufficient daring might be able to filch it. As to the watching and waiting that had followed, the process had been lengthy and tedious.

At least the proper quarry had finally taken the bait. Unlike a normal thief, the fellow who had stolen the necklace hadn't fenced it immediately. He never did. Instead, a series of gems and antiquities had simply vanished over the years. Like the necklace, which had been sold to Jardine, Matheson, all of them had been purchased by large trading firms on speculation and disappeared en route, before those firms received them. Every foreign trading company in the Orient had sustained substantial losses in this way.

Even with all his connections, Alex hadn't been able to trace any of these costly objects to a new owner, which told him they hadn't remained in the Orient. Someone had smuggled them out of China, an extremely difficult task. A gang rather than a single individual had to be responsible, because not even Alex could have accomplished such intricate crimes without a skilled network behind him. Yet when he had checked with the established criminal triads, he had learned they weren't involved.

Then he had discovered that large numbers of weapons had turned up in the hands of the emperor's enemies six to eight months after each robbery. It had made perfect sense; if the motive wasn't financial, it had to be political. The thieves weren't only clever, but radical and dangerous. If Alex was right, their goal was to help a large and powerful group of religious zealots called the Taipings to overthrow the emperor.

Alex had always admired boldness and cunning. There was a time when he would have been tempted to join these thieves, not out of principle, but for profit and adventure. Now he was engaged in finding out who they were and stopping them, again for profit and adventure. Only a fool put his neck on the block for principle. In truth, he had little use for either side in this civil war, but the Taiping rebels had disrupted government and trade and thus threatened to interfere with his own substantial commercial interests.

The first phase of his plan, to tempt the gang into stealing the necklace after it left Peking, had succeeded brilliantly. So had the second, to follow the necklace out of China. It had been spirited to the rebel stronghold of Nanking, where a craftsman had cached it inside a wooden tiger. The tiger had then traveled to Jardine's in Hong Kong, where it was added to a shipment bound for San Francisco aboard the *Aurora*.

Alex had booked passage on the vessel in order to follow the tiger, and the necklace, to their ultimate recipient. Once he learned who was fencing the stolen valuables and using the proceeds to arm the rebels, he could put a stop to their activities. He had also agreed to see that the thieves paid a heavy price for their crimes. He'd never had much stomach for violence, but he'd always enjoyed arranging his enemies' social and financial ruin.

He had made only one mistake thus far, but it was a beauty. He had assumed that every link in the chain would be male, most likely Chinese. In his experience, females seldom involved themselves in matters such as these. They were too timid and too easily swayed from their goal. No man in his right mind would have trusted one of them with his money.

But someone had trusted the tall brunette. He had first noticed her yesterday, while he was in Tobin and Duncan's waiting for the tiger to be uncrated and claimed. Had she been smaller, he might not have seen her in the crowd; had she been less strikingly lovely, his gaze wouldn't have stopped and lingered. But it had, and she had somehow noticed, and their eyes had chanced to meet.

She wasn't the sort of fragile Oriental flower he usually preferred, but if time and circumstances had permitted, he would have bedded her. The conquest, he was sure, would have been quick, and the mutual pleasure prolonged. The women of California, both single and married, had a reputation for passion and easy virtue.

Never in a hundred years had he imagined the girl was the individual he was waiting for. He had roamed the Orient for years, sometimes breaking the law, more often skirting it, but never once had he met a female criminal who looked and flirted like a debutante. It was ironic—and lucky—that he had disguised himself that morning. He had done so because he had dawdled in the Sales Room for hours the day before and feared that another lengthy stay would attract attention, but the precaution had provided the added benefit of preventing the girl from recognizing him and becoming suspicious when she had seen him again that afternoon.

He reached Bush Street, which was two blocks from his hotel, the Oriental. The damage there was less severe, but people were still milling around, talking about the quake. He turned left, his mind on what could have caused the girl to flee. In the Sales Room, he had watched her closely only after Duncan had escorted her to the Chinese curio counter, and he was sure she hadn't noticed. She couldn't have seen him following her, either, because nobody saw him unless he *chose* to be seen.

Of course, given the way she had repeatedly looked around, she was probably wary and high-strung, the sort who might panic easily. If she had realized he was disguised, even recognized him from the day before . . . But it was unlikely. He was too fine a makeup artist. As he'd told Monroe, it must have had something to do with the earthquake. In any event, he couldn't let her see him again, at least not in an incarnation she would recognize.

Laborers were sweeping up debris in front of the hotel and tidying the crimson and gold lobby. Some pieces of gilded molding had cracked off, and numerous crystals from the chandeliers had fallen and shattered. Alex went straight to his room, which was undamaged, and removed his disguise. Then he sought out the manager, a refined young man whose eagerness to please was exceeded only by his sense of duty.

He saw Alex's wound, promptly guessed the cause, and apologized profusely. Alex assured him that he blamed neither the Oriental nor the people of San Francisco for his injury. "I do need a physician, however. As I told you when I first arrived, I live in Hong Kong. To be frank, I've learned that Chinese medicine is far superior to the Western variety. I realize it's an unusual request, but do you know of anyone in Little China?"

"As a matter of fact, I do. He's eighty if he's a day, Mr. Colman, with the foulest collection of potions and tonics it's ever been my misfortune to sniff. My maiden aunt swears by him, but she's the most eccentric female I know."

"And how is your aunt's health?"

"She's as tough as a mule and twice as stubborn. If you ask me, it's the only reason he hasn't killed her. Still, if you're determined to use a Chinaman—"

"I am. I would be grateful if you could ask one of your clerks to engage a hack and bring the doctor to the hotel." The fewer people who saw him, the better. He slipped the manager a generous sum of money. "A translator won't be necessary. I speak passable Chinese. If you'll excuse me, I would like to lie down."

"Of course. I'll see that the doctor goes straight to your room." The manager sneaked a look at the cash, then happily pocketed it. "He'll be here right away, sir. Right away. And thank you."

"Right away" turned out to be an hour and a second earthquake later, but it was worth the wait. The physician soaked the wound with curative herbs, inserted numerous fine needles into his flesh, and stitched the cut closed with a quick, light hand. Alex had tried *chen-chiu*—acupuncture—for a problem with his back with no real success, so he was amazed at the almost total absence of pain.

His next order of business was to track down his female quarry. With luck, she would still have the necklace and he could begin a circumspect surveillance. Otherwise, he would have to persuade her to tell him whatever she knew.

The usual method was psychological intimidation, and when that didn't work, physical force. With recalcitrant women, though, force was never required. Not a one of them couldn't be seduced, and if they appealed to him enough, he took them. They became exceptionally willing to talk when they were helpless with arousal and desperate for release, and once he gave them that release, especially when it was lengthy and intense and overpowering, they were so pleased and grateful he had trouble shutting them up. Now that he thought about it, he half hoped the necklace would be gone and the girl stalwart in the face of his direct threats.

He returned to the lobby, once again sought out the manager, and once again discreetly bribed him. "If we might have a confidential chat . . ." He waited for the man's eager nod. "Can you tell me anything about a fellow named George Bonner?" Bonner was his one link to the girl, the man she and Duncan had discussed at the Chinese curio counter. The name was familiar to Alex, but he couldn't recall why.

"I can tell you a great deal," the manager replied. "He's always in the papers. He came here during the rush to try his luck at mining, but didn't find much gold. Lost an eye in an accident and decided that apprenticing himself to a lawyer might be safer and more profitable."

"And was it?"

"Very much so. He's a prominent attorney now, one of the city's leading citizens. He's made a fortune on land-grant cases—the disputes that arose when Mexico lost California to the States. Those old Spanish grants were vague about boundaries. Sometimes valuable mineral deposits turned up in the hills beyond the grants, and then every landowner in sight claimed the rights to them. Even after all these years, some of those disputes are still dragging through the courts. If you ask me, lawyers like Bonner come out better than anyone. They've run up hundreds of thousands of dollars in legal fees on the biggest cases."

"So even the winners sometimes end up bankrupt?"

The manager laughed. "More often than not, that's the whole idea. The old Spanish families have their wealth in land and livestock, not cash. So if the lawyers for the other side can draw things out for long enough and cost them enough money, they have no choice but to sell off pieces of their land as they go along, to pay to keep their cases alive."

"And if their opponent is rich enough, he can

buy that same land. Win or lose, he'll get what he wants."

"Exactly. Of course, the grant cases are largely settled now, so Bonner concentrates on other types of business. Maritime, financial, criminal . . .Which reminds me—a few years ago he kept the brother of one of your Hong Kong businessmen out of our local jail. The fellow was visiting and spent too much time in a gambling den. Shot some mechanic in a drunken argument over a woman. Bonner convinced the jury it was self-defense."

That was why the name was familiar, Alex realized. The businessman was Charlie Burns, the head of the Scottish-owned trading firm Burns and Company. After the trial, Charlie had put Bonner on retainer to handle his legal needs in San Francisco.

Alex followed such affairs routinely—kept track of the personnel and dealings of all the great trading houses—but he had a special interest in Burns. His first job in Hong Kong had been as a stocktaker at the firm. He had quickly graduated to commercial spy, and then to smuggler. Indeed, Burns was where he had learned most of what he knew.

"Do you know where Bonner's office is?" he asked the manager.

"Washington and Montgomery, in the building they call the Monkey Block. It's four stories high, right on the corner. I believe he's on the second floor, Mr. Colman—the lower, the better, wouldn't you say?"

Alex smiled and handed him another couple of coins. "During an earthquake, absolutely. Can you tell me anything more? How old Bonner is? What his politics are? What sort of temperament he has?"

"He's about thirty. An intelligent, rather serious

man and a brilliant lawyer. He's originally from somewhere in the South—Virginia, I believe. I've heard rumors he's a Secesh, but if he is, he keeps quiet about it."

It took Alex a moment to remember that the term was local slang for secessionist—that the manager was referring to the American Civil War, which had broken out some three months before. Though California was isolated from the conflict, San Francisco was strongly pro-Union. Only the day before, there had been a large American Independence Day celebration on Market Street, complete with pro-Union banners and speeches.

"Why take an unpopular position in a dispute thousands of miles away when it can only lose you clients, is that it?" Alex asked dryly.

"I suppose so."

"Is there anything else you can tell me? About his private affairs, for example? His family and so on?"

"Only that he's fairly straitlaced. He's not much of a gambler or drinker, and if he's ever been spotted in a private room at Delmonico's or the Poodle Dog with a parlor-house girl, I haven't heard about it. They used to call him the most eligible bachelor in the city, but he's headed to the altar now." The manager grinned. "That is, if the lady he's engaged to goes through with the wedding. She has a habit of changing her mind."

"And her name is . . . ?"

"Miss Melanie Wyatt. She's the heiress to a mining fortune, not that Bonner needs the money, and a notable San Franciscan in her own right. Her mother died years ago, and from what I hear, her father has given her free rein ever since. Her hobby is buying and selling imported curios. She makes a tidy profit from it. Uses the money to help the downtrodden, especially Chinese whores and coolies, of all things."

And uses stolen jewelry and artifacts to help an army of Chinese rebels, Alex thought, and wondered how she had gotten involved with them and who was helping her. A bagman was one thing, but there was no way a female could be a fence or an arms trader. Bonner couldn't possibly know of her activities, either, because if he had, he would have put a stop to them. His Hong Kong clients supported the emperor. They preferred the current government to a group of unpredictable rebels who wanted to end the opium trade and limit foreign access to the Chinese mainland.

Alex questioned the manager further and learned that Miss Wyatt had been born in Hong Kong and raised by a Chinese houseman, thus her devotion to the Celestials. Her father, Thomas, had been a businessman in the Orient before striking it rich in California and now owned a sizable interest in several Comstock silver mines, which he was currently visiting. The manager even knew where the Wyatts lived—in a large house on the northeast corner of Hawthorne and Folsom streets.

The information gave Alex even more reason to keep an eye on the girl. Even if she had disposed of the necklace, she was up to her pretty neck in rebellion and must meet with her male cohorts regularly. There was no telling what a search of her house might turn up.

He excused himself, engaged a hack, and instructed the driver to take him on a tour of the local haberdasheries. There was another shock while he was out, but it was mild and caused little alarm. He purchased a number of garments and accessories, then returned to his hotel and transformed himself yet again.

He left for Bonner's office attired in a white suit,

a loosely knotted black tie, a pair of thick, gold-framed spectacles, and a silver beard and wig. The wig, which was long and lush, just covered his wound. The hunched stoop he affected and the silver-handled cane he carried added to the impression of age. He was the image, in short, of an elderly Southern aristocrat.

The Monkey Block was half-deserted after the quake, but Bonner was among those who had remained at work. A clerk ushered Alex into Bonner's private office, an impressive chamber containing Brussels carpets, velvet drapes and upholstery, gleaming mahogany furniture, and shelf after shelf of leather-bound books. Bonner himself was tall, blond, and extremely handsome. His clothes, though finely made, were austere, but the black patch he wore over his damaged left eye gave him a slightly rakish air.

"Colonel Whitefield, permit me to present Mr. Bonner," the clerk said as the two men shook hands. "Mr. Bonner, Colonel George Whitefield, from Charleston."

Alex waited for the clerk to withdraw, then said in an impeccable Carolina drawl, "Retired, of course, after the late war with Mexico, not that I didn't wish I was fit enough to fight for my city, my state, and the new Confederacy. I'm in shipping now, Mr. Bonner. I appreciate your taking the time to see me."

Bonner beamed at him. "It's a pleasure to greet a fellow Southerner and patriot, sir, a very great pleasure. Please sit down." Both men did so. "Your name is familiar. Have we ever crossed paths?"

"No, but maybe you're thinking of my famous namesake, the English evangelist from the last century. He was a distant cousin. My father was a great admirer of his." The Reverend Mr. McClure had loathed the man. Whitefield had committed the unpardonable sin of leaving the organized church to preach his own unconventional brand of the gospel.

"Yes," Bonner agreed, "I suppose that must be it. On behalf of my adopted city, let me apologize for her ill-bred behavior this afternoon. I hope you weren't too alarmed."

"Not at all. It was no worse than one of our hurricanes. I know you're a busy man—"

"Yes, but never too busy to meet with a Southern colonel, sir."

The two men began to make small talk. Thanks to the newspaper articles he had read, Alex was able to mount a scathing attack on abolitionists and the government in Washington and deliver a stirring defense of the Confederacy and states' rights. He had often observed that nothing encouraged confidences between two men like being surrounded by a common enemy, and Bonner and "Whitefield" were no exception. Still, he proceeded cautiously, nudging friendliness toward warmth and warmth toward intimacy.

"I've just been to Hong Kong on behalf of my shipping business," he finally remarked. "While I'm too old and crippled for the battlefield, there's more to war than firing a rifle, so I met with the presidents of several of the large trading houses while I was there. Taipans, I believe they call themselves. One of them, a Mr. Charles Burns, told me you'd done some work for him and suggested that I call on you." Alex lowered his voice. Nothing bred trust like a conspiracy. "To be frank, we're concerned about getting weapons and other strategic materials into the Confederacy through an expected Yankee blockade. I've conceived a plan to ship those goods into San Francisco from Hong Kong, then send them via the southern land route into the Confederacy. The taipans can get us whatever we want, but we need someone to handle the arrangements in San Francisco."

Bonner touched his eye patch and replied softly, "Like you, I would be a liability on the battlefield, but I support our cause with every dollar I can spare. I do it carefully, though, because my position here is a delicate one. I'm sorry, but if I helped you and my role became known, it would damage my career and my ability to provide money."

"I understand. The people here are blind. They refuse to see the justness of our cause."

"You're exactly right." Bonner frowned, then added thoughtfully, "On the other hand, I could quietly rent a warehouse. Secretly receive and check the goods, then have them picked up and sent south."

"Yes. Precisely." Alex was surprised by Bonner's abrupt about-face, but also very pleased. The man was in his pocket now. "We'll discuss this again once you've had a chance to think it over. In the meantime, I hope you'll be my guest at dinner tonight, along with your wife, if you're a married man. Would eight o'clock be convenient?"

"Eight would be fine, but only if you allow me to be the host." Bonner handed him the framed photograph that sat on his desk. "I'm not married yet, but I will be shortly. This is my fiancée, Miss Wyatt."

"A beautiful girl. My best wishes to you. Is she a Southerner, George?"

"No, a Californian," Bonner answered, and told him Miss Wyatt's history. He added that he looked forward to his marriage, especially to fulfilling the male obligation to teach and mold the females under his protection. Alex seconded his views, then asked how Miss Wyatt needed molding. He learned that Bonner was distressed by her commercial activities and feared that her charitable work on behalf of the Celestials could expose her to danger. When Alex hinted that he himself would put a stop to such behavior in a wife, Bonner assured him that he would deal with his bride's high spirits the moment they were wed.

"Of course, it will require tact along with firmness," he confided. "California women are very spoiled. There are so few of them that their parents indulge their every whim. Even worse, our laws give them far too much independence."

"So I've heard. It turns the natural order on its head, if you ask me. Don't the men here have the good sense to put things to rights?"

"It's not that easily done, I'm afraid. It's in our constitution, a product of the old Spanish law and the scarcity of females." Bonner explained that a man couldn't gain control of his bride's money unless she willingly relinquished it or moved with him to another state. "But she's a sensible girl. She'll defer to my greater knowledge and experience in time. I simply have to convince her—"

As if on cue, Miss Wyatt breezed through the door, interrupting him. She saw Alex and skidded to a halt. "Oh, dear. Do excuse me, George. Sam wasn't at his desk, so I assumed you were alone."

Bonner strode over and kissed her on the mouth while Alex creaked to his feet with the slow, deliberate motions of an arthritic. "Don't be silly, you know I miss you if you don't come by each day. And today of all days, I was eager to see you and make sure you weren't hurt."

"I'm fine. I wasn't far from here when the first shock hit. I've been at the hospital all afternoon, helping with the wounded. And you?"

"Fine also. I never left my office. Allow me to present Colonel Whitefield, darling. Colonel, my fiancée, Miss Wyatt."

Alex bowed low, again very slowly, and kissed her hand. Her carpetbag was looped over her arm, and he managed a peek inside. She was carrying the wooden tiger.

She smiled at him when he straightened. There was no recognition in her eyes. "A pleasure, Miss Wyatt," he said. "Mr. Bonner was just telling me what a lucky man he is."

"Was he? How gallant of you, George. The whole city knows that I'm the one who's lucky."

"I'm sure you can see, Colonel, why I'm hopelessly in love with her. The colonel is visiting here from Charleston, darling. He's joining us for dinner tonight. Where would you rather go? Marchand's or Maison Riche?"

"Either. You choose. Food is so much more important—" She reddened, stared at Alex for several seconds through widened eyes, and then jerked her gaze back to Bonner. "Once again, you'll have to excuse me. I thought I'd felt another shock. My nerves are rather on edge, I'm afraid."

Alex nodded and smiled. "Everyone's are, I expect. Mr. Bonner, I'll leave you to comfort your charming bride-to-be. Until eight, then, at . . . ?"

"Let's make it Marchand's."

Alex said he would look forward to dinner and took his leave, wondering if Miss Wyatt's stunned stare meant she had recognized him. He decided it was impossible. His disguise was too good. He already knew she had a jittery nature, and, as she'd admitted, the earthquake and its unnerving aftermath had obviously magnified it.

Chapter 3

A deep wound couldn't vanish within a few hours, Melanie told herself firmly, and a person couldn't shrink in size within a single afternoon. It couldn't have been the same man.

But if it wasn't, why had her heart begun to race? Why had her throat suddenly tightened? Why had her wrists tingled so fiercely? Was there a second man stalking her, a confederate of the first? Or was there only one, a human chameleon who could transform himself at will?

George locked the door, sat down in the chair the colonel had recently vacated, and beckoned her over. She smiled and complied, cursing the vividness of her imagination. Whitefield had been elderly, arthritic, and harmless. If she persisted in sensing danger in every corner, she was going to drive herself mad.

She dropped onto George's lap. A sinister aura seemed to linger about the chair, but she was probably imagining that, too. George unbuttoned her cloak and put his hands on her waist, and she pecked him on the forehead and slid her arms around his neck. What she'd told Colonel Whitefield was true. She was lucky to be his future wife. He had been a confirmed bachelor, and thus a delicious challenge. Every girl in San Francisco had pursued him, but she was the one who had landed him.

His mouth moved to her throat. "I was worried about you," he murmured between gentle kisses. "And with good reason. You're frightened and upset. I can feel it. I want to take care of you, darling. Let me stay with you tonight."

She stroked his hair, breathing in its scent. It was like soft flax, and she enjoyed the way it felt beneath her fingers. Then she thought about Whitefield again—or whoever he was—and tensed. "You *would* be a comfort, but . . . It's just so improper, George."

"Not if you really need me. Anyway, your father is away and your dragon of a housekeeper will never hear us from her room all the way downstairs, so no one would know I was there." His mouth grew passionate against her neck and his manhood grew turgid beneath her buttocks. "We'll simply lie together, Melanie. You know you can trust me. Haven't I always controlled myself?"

He had, but she sensed it was getting harder for him all the time. "Yes, but there's such a thing as tempting the fates." She smiled tentatively. "Let me save a little something for the man I marry, whoever he turns out to be. Please, George."

"I suppose you're right, but for God's sake, Melanie, don't remind me about the men in your past. You know I hate thinking about them." He cupped her chin. "Kiss me and touch me. Show me how much you love me."

She relaxed against his chest and slipped her hand beneath his coat to caress him through his shirt. He moaned and took her mouth, his fingers moving to her breast and lightly stroking it, his body tensing with desire. She felt no such urgency, only mild pleasure and a reassuring sense of control.

She had never relinquished that control, either to George or to anyone else. She'd only had to look at her own father to know that men had most of the power in this world and used it to their own benefit. It was only fair, then, that lust made them more amenable to a woman's wishes.

As for her own abundant passions, she had always been able to contain them, distracting herself with the Greek alphabet when all else failed. She wasn't about to hunger so much for a man's touch that she became a slave to her own desires, giving up one of her sex's few natural advantages. Not surprisingly, none of her fiancés had ever noticed she was holding back. When a man was aroused, his own pleasure was all he could think about.

She didn't really mind. She hadn't been engaged five times without learning a little about male passion, and she enjoyed putting the knowledge to use. George, in particular, adored her kisses. Wanting to please him, she gave them freely, sucking his tongue and tasting him back.

After several long, hot minutes, he tore himself away and buried his face in her neck. "God in heaven, Melanie, you turn me into a rutting stallion. I'll be worthless for the rest of the day."

She smiled at his frazzled tone. "I'm glad you enjoyed it."

He looked up. "I just wish I didn't know where you'd learned those little tricks. The thought of that woman telling you about—about—" He shook his head, unable to get the words out.

He was speaking of Ah Lan, a local madam with a fondness for frank conversation. Ah Lan wouldn't give up her brothel, but she had helped Melanie rescue prostitutes from abusive pimps and slave girls from being used as playthings by the rich. "I believe 'the finer points of kissing' is the phrase you probably want," she said.

George scowled at her so fiercely that she couldn't resist teasing him a little. "Did I mention that she's been advising me about our wedding trip? She says the right kinds of caresses can actually prolong your pleasure and drive you mad with passion. I can't wait to try them."

He blushed. "Language like that belongs in the gutter. I forbid you to use it."

"Yes, George. And do you forbid me to come to your office each day and practice on you?"

"Of course not. It's just that I wanted to teach you those things myself. If I thought you'd allowed anyone else to touch you the way I do—"

"You know I haven't, George."

"But you do things you shouldn't do," he persisted. "Dangerous things. Where I come from, a lady doesn't even talk to—to soiled doves, much less rush around rescuing them from cribs and brothels."

It had been weeks since he'd mentioned that particular subject. She wondered what had gotten him going again. "I've told you before, I can take care of myself perfectly well. I'm afraid I can't give up my philanthropy, not now and not after we're married. And the women I help aren't soiled doves—they're prostitutes and they're victims, and it's men who have used them and made them that way." She sighed and stroked his hair. "Let's talk about something more pleasant, like how happy I intend to make you after we're married. I've been reading a Chinese book about the most amazing devices and herbs. Of course, if you're too prudish to let me experiment—"

"You're a witch." He jerked to his feet, dumping her onto the chair. "Behave yourself for once."

Amused by his testy mood, she said, "But my talent for misbehaving is the chief reason you asked me to marry you. By the way, *are* you too prudish?"

"Hardly, Melanie. I'll look forward to it." He straightened his coat. "But I'm wise to you, my darling minx. You think you can turn me into a panting little puppy who'll trail after you once we're married, giving you whatever you want in exchange for being tossed an erotic bone now and then. But you can't."

Melanie knew that, but she also knew that George would work too hard and travel too much to monitor her every action, so her life and work would remain unchanged. He was healthy, handsome, honest, and intelligent, so their children would be exceptional. She wouldn't have accepted his proposal otherwise, wouldn't have pursued him in the first place. But the more she had looked after children, both at the hospital and at the Protestant Orphans' Asylum, the more she had wanted her own. And a husband was a prerequisite.

She stood and put her arms around his waist. She was truly fond of him and didn't want to quarrel. "Then I'll trail after *you*. I'll beg and plead for the privilege of pleasing you. Would you like that?"

He fondled a strand of her hair. "Will you? Wherever I go, thou shalt go?"

"Of course, George. Anywhere in San Francisco." She nibbled on his lower lip. "Didn't I set a wedding date with you when I wouldn't with any of the others? That should show you how devoted I am. I might be willing to move to the States someday, but this is hardly the best time. Anyway, you know how I feel about living in Virginia or any other slave state."

"And *you* know that I deplore slavery as much

as anyone, but that's no reason not to live in the Confederacy. I've told you repeatedly that the war isn't about slavery, which we'll abolish in time in an equitable and rational way. It's about the rights of the states under the federal Constitution, and the way those rights have been trampled on by the government in Washington."

Melanie didn't care about the legal niceties. All that mattered was that her mother and grandmother had been virtual slaves and that she deplored the institution. No matter what color or sex the victims were, she favored anything that would end it, including a Union victory in the Civil War.

It bothered her that George was on the other side, but she knew his reasons were honorable, and that he hated the handicap that kept him from fighting beside his fellow Virginians. "Let's not argue about something that's happening a continent away. I know your position is difficult. Your family is in Virginia. Your heart is there, too. I understand how you feel, because I feel the same way about China. That's why I do what I do."

He frowned. "It's hardly the same thing. You barely remember living in Hong Kong. Your only real tie to China is Shen Wai, an admirable man to be sure, but merely a family retainer. My blood is the blood of Virginia, pure and strong. Bonners have lived there for a century and a half."

He didn't know she was part Chinese, and the daughter of a kept woman. No one did. She had kept it a secret because if she hadn't, she would have been ostracized by polite society. Their balls and dinner parties meant nothing to her, but she needed her high position to assist Shen Wai with his smuggling and carry out her own rescue work.

Troubled by George's words, she asked, "Is the purity of your blood so important to you, then? For example, if you learned that one of your ancestors had Indian blood, or even Negro blood, would it disturb you?"

"If what you really want to know is whether I mind that my future wife is half-Portuguese, the answer is no." He broke into a smile. "Given your fondness for experimenting, it's obvious you've got the blood of the great Portuguese explorers in you. It's probably where your passion comes from. I can hardly complain about that, now can I?"

"Please, George, be serious about this. Do you think all people are equal, no matter what their color might be?"

"Obviously not." He caressed her nape. The hot gleam was back in his eyes. "We're all God's children, of course, but God gives some men more abilities than others, and the responsibilities to match. It's the same among the races as it is between men and women." He reluctantly dropped his hand. "Enough philosophizing, Melanie. I've got hours of work left to do, and if you don't leave, I'm going to kiss you till dinner and lose all my clients."

"Then I'll go, but if you ask me, women are every bit as resourceful and intelligent as men are. We should have the vote. I admire the suffragists enormously."

"Fine. Join them. Frankly, suffrage is a better cause than your little doves are."

"Don't call them that."

"Your victims of us wicked men, then. I'll pick you up at a quarter past seven. We'll have a quiet bottle of champagne before Whitefield comes, and you can lecture me all you like. All right?"

She raised her chin. "Don't think I won't, George Bonner."

Alex was riding down Montgomery Street in the enclosed brougham he'd hired for the evening when a distinctive black and crimson cloak caught his eye—Melanie Wyatt's cloak, which he recognized from Tobin and Duncan's. She was snuggled next to George Bonner on the driver's side of a landau, going the opposite way. Neither appeared to see him, but he turned his back as they passed him, just to be on the safe side. Things were finally breaking his way. Miss Wyatt had obliged him by leaving early, sparing him the need to lurk outside her house until he saw her depart.

His carriage crossed Market Street, traveled down Second, and stopped at Folsom. He hopped out, then handed the driver a sealed envelope. He had selected the man after numerous interviews as exactly the sort he needed.

"Remember, Ned, I want this delivered to Mr. Bonner in Marchand's restaurant at exactly ten minutes before eight. Then come straight back here and wait for me. I'll have further instructions for you then." He tossed Ned a gold coin, then removed a Colt's revolver from the holster beneath his coat and casually stroked the barrel. "I reward generously and punish the same way, depending on how I'm served. You would do well to remember that."

Ned smiled. "No need to wave around your gun, boss. I aim to please. Anything you want, I'll do."

Alex gave him another coin. "Discreetly."

"Not a word to anyone. I'll be silent as a fish."

Alex nodded, put away his pistol, and watched the brougham disappear around the corner. The Wyatts' house was a block away. Two stories high, it sat on a large lot enclosed by a stone and metal fence. There was a small flower garden in each front corner of the property, lawns bordering the driveway and main walkway, and a sizable herb garden in the back. The rest of the yard was planted with shrubs and trees.

He walked around to the rear of the house and gracefully scaled the fence. It was still light enough for him to be spotted quite easily. He circled the building using the foliage as a screen and checked the windows for signs of life. Only a single room was lit, in the right front corner of the house, but the curtains were closed, preventing him from seeing inside.

He returned to the rear of the house and slipped inside through the back door. He found himself in a hallway that ran the length of the building. There was a wide main staircase in front of him. He could hear a woman humming off-key, probably in the same room where the light was. The rhythmic squeaks of a rocking chair accompanied her song.

He stole forward, following the sound. Peeking around a doorway, he saw a handsome gray-haired woman busily knitting a shawl—an aging relative or retainer, he assumed. He'd brought along some chloroform, but he doubted he would need it for the likes of her.

He walked upstairs. Of the five rooms on the second floor, only two appeared to be occupied, one by Thomas Wyatt and the other by his daughter. The third was furnished as a bedroom and the fourth as a parlor. The final room contained tables holding curios and works of art, obviously Melanie Wyatt's collection.

Thomas Wyatt's bedroom resembled the chamber of an English lord, but Melanie's was as Chinese as the emperor's palace. The rugs, furniture, wall hangings, decorative knickknacks—all of them came from the Orient. Alex quickly searched the room, looking for the necklace, the tiger, or any other item of interest. He found nothing unusual except for some men's clothing and a large collection of what appeared to be medicines.

Melanie's carpetbag was sitting empty on the bed, but Alex doubted she'd had time to dispose of the tiger. She would have had to send a message to her contact first, then arrange a meeting. She probably had a hiding place where she stashed things temporarily. With any luck, it was here in this room.

His gaze settled on the lacquered chinoiserie armoire opposite her bed. The two large drawers at the bottom, he realized, were shallower than the depth of the chest. He removed them and inspected the interior, finding that the brace supporting the upper drawer could be removed as well. He pulled it out and tapped on the rear panel of the chest. It was a false back. There was a space behind it.

He soon determined that the panel could be moved in only one direction, upward. The floor of the upper section of the armoire was movable, too, sliding forward to make room for the ascending panel. Alex pulled it out, then slid the panel up and searched the space behind. He discovered a metal case containing expensive theatrical makeup and numerous boxes holding wigs, beards, and mustaches. The tiger was tucked behind them.

He was flabbergasted, then fascinated. The girl was no lackey, it seemed, but an accomplished gamester and actress. If it took one to know one, she might have seen through his disguises. The evening ahead looked more and more interesting.

He picked up the tiger. The craftsman who had made it had taught him how it worked in exchange for a modest bribe, so he was able to open it at once. As far as he knew, its only purpose was to conceal stolen valuables for smuggling, so he was startled when a cloth containing a diagram fell out along with the necklace.

There was also a note in Chinese, reading, "A gift from Niuhuru," the empress. It indicated what he'd assumed, that the girl had Celestial confederates who could translate it. As for the diagram, it was a map of some sort, but a very obscure one. There was no way a reader could find the terrain it described unless he—or she—knew exactly which area to begin in.

He took out his notebook and copied the diagram, thinking it probably indicated a meeting place. Perhaps Melanie or her cohort was supposed to hand over the necklace there, or receive a cache of weapons. Then again, the small star between two stands of trees seemed overly specific for such a purpose. Perhaps something was buried there—the arms themselves, for example.

He was reassembling the tiger, admiring its form and markings, when it struck him that the craftsman in Nanking had taken far more trouble with it than he'd needed to. Why had he etched an abstract design into the wood? He'd been a simple carver with a family to feed, not the sort to waste time on fancy decorations unless he was paid to. On the other hand, artists were a peculiar bunch. They took it into their heads to do all sorts of frivolous things.

With a shrug, Alex placed the tiger in the armoire. He was reaching for the box of makeup when he stopped, frowned, and pulled the tiger back out. He stared at it, turned it over, and stared a while longer. Unless he missed his guess, the design was actually a map. The markings were a net-work of roads. The darkened swirl must represent the area on the cloth diagram. But which roads? Where were they? Even if they were somewhere nearby, one would have to know the area like the back of one's hand to recognize them. For a for-eigner like Alex, the task was impossible.

Once again, he pulled out his notebook and made a sketch. By the time he'd replaced Melanie's be-longings and put the chest to rights, it was almost eight o'clock. He could spend another twenty min-utes looking around, he decided, and still make it to dinner at a reasonable hour.

Melanie looked at George's watch. "It's twenty past eight, George. I'm starving. Really, I think we've waited long enough. Can't we eat now?"

"The colonel did send a note saying he'd be fif-teen or twenty minutes late, Melanie. Please, be patient awhile longer." George handed her a roll. "Here, darling, have this. You can educate me some more about women's rights. The time will fly—at least for you."

"But you keep agreeing with me when I know you really don't. I might as well talk to the wall." She bit into the roll. "Anyway, I'd rather discuss Colonel Whitefield. You said he was a friend of one of your clients, but which client? How much do you really know about the man?"

"As much as I need to, and if you'll recall, I also said that my business dealings were confidential."

"I understand that, but I thought his visit was social. Really, why are you being so mysterious about him?"

"I'm not. A reputable attorney can't discuss his clients, not even with his future wife. You know that, Melanie."

"Yes. Then Whitefield is your client now?"

"His friend is. We've already established that." George paused. "Tell me more about your afternoon. Was the hospital very busy? Were there any fatalities?"

Melanie gave it up. When George turned into a clam, not even a crowbar could pry him open. Still, she had no right to complain. A man was entitled to his secrets.

And so was a woman, so she didn't confide that someone had followed her today and gotten hurt in the quake. She didn't mention that she'd hoped he would be taken to the hospital, or that she'd planned to question whichever physician treated him. She simply recounted the injuries she had treated, admitting that, as always, the suffering children had tugged the most at her heart.

She could tell by George's face that he was disturbed by the grislier details, but he was too tactful to come right out and say so. "You're very brave and much too generous, Melanie." He covered her hand. "You're going to be a wonderful mother."

"Why, thank you, dear. I suppose that once we have children of our own, you'll want me to devote all my time to their care." She felt a sudden chill, and shivered. "No more tending the brats of riffraff at the city hospital, hmm?"

"It's dismal and foul-smelling, hardly the place for a lady. I worry about your health, that's all. Ah! Here's the colonel now. I hope your mood will improve once you've got some dinner in your belly."

Melanie turned toward the door. Whitefield was limping toward their table, looking as ancient and decrepit as ever. Once again, he bowed low and kissed her hand.

As he straightened, his spectacles fell off and landed on her lap. Their eyes met as she handed them back. His gaze seemed to pin her to her seat, making her feel as trapped as a lamb in the clutches of a lion. She shivered again. His eyes were brown, dark brown, and they were at least thirty years younger than the face around them.

Chapter 4

⌒⌒◯◯⌒⌒

Melanie stared at the table, paralyzed by shock. It couldn't be, not when his forehead was unblemished. Not when he was gray and old and crippled. But those brown eyes of his . . . The unmistakable message they had sent . . . It couldn't be anyone else.

His makeup was perfect. Astonishing. Her psychic gifts might have led her to wonder if he was the same man—even to strongly suspect he was— but only a wizard could have known for sure. So why had he revealed himself so baldly, all but announcing who he was?

Only one explanation came to mind. He must have sensed her flashes of recognition. Decided to confirm her suspicions. But to what end?

To put her off-balance? To frighten her into doing his bidding? To terrorize her into giving him the tiger? And how could so threatening and predatory a look also radiate such savage sexual heat? What did he want from her?

"Melanie." George touched her shoulder. "I've asked you twice now if you would like the baked salmon for dinner."

She blinked at him. "You did?"

"Yes, darling. It's fresh, served with a lobster as-

62

pic. You could start with the roasted partridge, then have the oyster soup."

"Uh, yes. That sounds delicious." She gave her head a little shake. "I'm sorry, George. My mind must have been elsewhere."

"We noticed." He gave the waiter her order, then added, "We'll forgive you your distraction if you pay us men more attention from now on."

"Oh. Yes. Of course I will, George."

"It's anxiety, I suppose," the colonel drawled, drawing her gaze. He was sitting across the table from her and George, sprawled casually on the banquette. "Did you imagine you'd felt a shock, Miss Wyatt?"

"A shock?" she repeated in confusion. "Oh. From the earthquake, you mean. No, Colonel. I was just . . . daydreaming."

"About your wedding, I suppose. Marriage is a big step for a sweet young girl such as yourself. You're so innocent. So artless. So naive." He sipped his champagne, then smiled coolly. "Aren't you, my dear?"

He was baiting her, she realized, making statements with secret meanings in order to fluster her. He was succeeding all too well, too. "No. That is, I hope George finds me sweet, but he knows I'm not naive. Girls grow up quickly in California."

"Ah! So you're sophisticated and experienced. An accomplished siren. A dangerous woman of the world. Should I be terrified of you?"

She straightened and looked him in the eye. Two could play this game as well as one. "That depends on your intentions, Colonel. I can't claim to be a siren, but I'm more dangerous than you might imagine." She paused, then continued ingenuously, "A man tried to assault me on the street last year. It was a serious mistake. I pride myself on having the sharpest blade in San

Francisco. He had a tête-à-tête with my knife and now lacks the capacity to try such a thing again. When necessary, I'm also a fast draw and a crack shot."

"I'm suitably cowed. Would I be correct in assuming that when you fire, you aim for the uh, *capacities* of your male adversaries?"

"If you would like a demonstration of my technique, I would be happy to provide one," she answered tartly. "In fact, it would be amusing to use live ammunition."

George laughed. "Sheath your claws, darling. The colonel was only teasing you a little."

"All the same," Whitefield said, "I believe I would rather not duel with her, given the possible consequences. A woman's beauty has a way of distracting a man when he's trying to aim a pistol. Speaking of which, Miss Wyatt, I must tell you that you look exceptionally lovely tonight. You have the radiant white skin of an angel and the luminous black hair of a sorceress. A devastating combination. I hope you'll forgive me, George, if I confess that I'm thoroughly smitten."

George all but puffed up with pride. "I can hardly do otherwise, Colonel. I feel the same way myself."

"Why, Colonel Whitefield, how prodigiously poetic you are!" Melanie said. "I'm truly awed. Would you care to eulogize my new gown while you're at it?"

"You're a vision in blue. Like Venus, the morning star, you dazzle your admirers as you sparkle in a sea of azure."

"Such splendid symbolism, and so fast off the mark, too. An amazing talent. You do recognize the dress, of course."

He looked her up and down. "I do?"

"Yes. From Tobin and Duncan's. It was prominently displayed there. I saw you there when I bought it—and the day before, as well."

"If you say so. I've been in so many shops since arriving in this city that I really can't remember."

"But I can." She wanted him to know that she had seen through his disguises—that she knew what he really looked like. "Your suit was dove-gray. Your cravat was a gray and cranberry check. Your waistcoat was a bright tapestry of those two colors and others. It was a dashing outfit."

"That was me, all right. You have an excellent memory, Miss Wyatt, and an extraordinary eye for detail. I'm gratified that I met with your approval." He turned to George. "She's quite a woman, isn't she! You're going to enjoy married life, I'll wager. Although if I were you, I might search her for weapons before I tried to bed her. She strikes me as a little skittish. Rather like a champion mare waiting to be serviced by her first stallion."

"An apt simile," George replied with a chuckle, "but I'll be safe unless she wears her cloak to bed. That's where she keeps her knife and gun. One in each pocket, God help us, but she won't give them up. And you? Do you enjoy the pleasures of a wife and family back in Charleston, or have you opted for solitude and peace?"

"I wanted to settle down, but I never met the right filly. Now if someone as spirited as Miss Wyatt had come along . . . I would have put in my bid when she went on the block, I can tell you that much."

Melanie was tired of being compared to a horse. "And if you'd won me, you would have enjoyed breaking and riding me, I suppose."

George frowned. "Don't be crude, Melanie."

"I'll endeavor to be more refined, dear. Enjoyed

taming me, as Mr. Shakespeare put it. Will that do?"

"I suppose so. And someone certainly needs to."

"But you're exactly the right man," Whitefield declared. "Come now, be honest. Don't you relish the challenge?"

George smiled weakly, drained his glass of champagne, and instructed the waiter to bring them another bottle.

"I believe that's an exhausted yes," Melanie said. "George finds me trying at times. Much too independent and outspoken. Most men do, I'm afraid."

"But worth ten times the bother you cause," George said gallantly. "Anyway, our marriage will settle you down."

"I'm sure you're right, dear. Colonel, do tell me about your title. Is it real, or did you conjure it up out of thin air?"

George closed his eyes for a moment, seeking either divine guidance or saintly patience. "Melanie, what on earth has gotten into you tonight?"

"I simply wondered, that's all. There's something very theatrical about your new client, haven't you noticed? I can picture him on a stage in full makeup. Off a stage, as well. After all, you know what our friend Shakespeare said, and if ever a man reminded me of a player—"

"Ah. Here's our first course. Why don't you concentrate on your food, darling, and listen to the colonel and me talk? You might learn something interesting. My apologies, Colonel, but you know women and their moods."

"No apology is necessary. I enjoy women who think for themselves and say what they think. They keep a man amused. To answer your question, Miss Wyatt, I was an army officer in my younger days, but I'm retired now. I'm in shipping."

A woman could push a man only so far, Melanie decided, and George had reached his limit. She listened attentively as he and Whitefield discussed their horses, their travels, and other interests characteristic of Southern gentlemen. Only the high quality of the food and champagne kept her from fidgeting, especially the latter, which she continued to imbibe freely. The man could stay in character, she had to give him that, but if the conversation had been any duller, she would have wound up facedown in her partridge.

On the other hand, the aristocratic chitchat improved George's mood. Melanie repressed a smile when he went from relaxed to languid. Strutting evidently tired a man out. Indeed, by the time the waiter cleared away the soup bowls, he was fighting back yawns and speaking in a slurred voice.

As for her, the more champagne she consumed, the harder she found it to gaze at him in adoring silence. She wondered why women played that game. Why men expected them to. Men weren't necessarily smarter or more sensible than women, but everyone acted as though they were.

Then George's tongue twisted around, turning "Kentucky bluegrass" into "Kentuby bruegrass," and she dissolved into helpless giggles. "Poor George, as woozy as a sot. I suppose it was all that comforting this afternoon. Did I leave you frazzled?"

He reddened. "I'm sure our guest isn't interested in the topic. As I was saying, Colonel—"

"Who comforted whom?" Whitefield asked with a smile.

"George comforted me, but it was hard on his nerves. Sometimes I think I should end my visits to his office, but he enjoys them so much that I don't have the heart." She winked. "Especially the comforting part."

Whitefield laughed, but George frowned and took away her glass. "You've had too much to drink, Melanie." He stifled a yawn. "Your tongue is running away with you. Either keep it in check, my dear, or don't talk at all."

"You didn't complain about my tongue this afternoon, when—"

"I'm complaining now. For God's sake, Melanie, use a little discretion."

"Don't scold her on my account, George. If I were you, I would rejoice in my good fortune. It appears that you've found yourself a lady of staggering talent and generosity."

"What I've found is the biggest handful in San Francisco, but"—he yawned—"but she's more'n met her match in me. She'll find that out soon enough."

"Find what out, George?" Melanie asked in mock fascination. "And when?"

"How to be a proper wife. Quiet and demure. Gracious and refined. Gen'le and submissive. After—" Another yawn. " 'Scuse me, Colonel. After we're married."

If he believed that, he was even tipsier than she was. Fortunately, the waiter arrived with their main course, sparing her the need to respond directly. "Your duck looks wonderful," she said instead. "Enjoy your meal, darling, and I'll listen to our guest. Will you tell me about your shipping business, Colonel Whitefield? Do you own many vessels? Trade in many ports?"

Whitefield answered at length, handling her frequent questions with apparent ease. She was hoping to glean something of his true background from the discussion, but he seemed as conversant with the subject as a genuine merchant. Of course, that was only to be expected in a man who'd had dealings with bandits like the Eternal Brotherhood. Ships at sea were among their favorite targets.

She asked him about Charleston next, and then about his life in the army, trying to trap him into slipping and revealing himself. He never did. His mastery was maddening, his amused looks and glib replies even worse. He knew what she was up to, but far from being concerned, he was casually toying with her.

Finally, provoked past the point of caution, she remarked that his work must keep him very busy. "Do you have any time for hobbies? Painting, perhaps? Or writing?" She glanced at George, who gave her a glazed smile in return. He hadn't said a word for the past quarter hour. "Raising dogs? Collecting imported wooden animals?"

Whitefield crossed his arms in front of his chest and stared at her until she blushed and looked away. Then he said evenly, "I have a strong fascination with maps, especially arcane maps. I hear you collect things. Perhaps you know of one that might interest me."

She'd expected him to be disconcerted. After all, she'd all but announced that she knew he was after the tiger. Presumably she had cohorts. His life might be in danger if he got in their way. A normal thief would wonder if the profits were worth the risk.

Rattled by his audacity, she flailed around for an answer. None would come. It had been too long a day, too demanding an evening. She suddenly yearned to be at home, in the comfort and security of her own room.

"Drawing a blank?" he asked. "Are maps such unfamiliar territory, Miss Wyatt?"

"Yes. I'm afraid they are." She finally recovered

her wits. "But I have a great many friends, and some of them are experts on the subject. Of course, collectors are invariably jealous of what they own."

"A fascinating subject, provenance. Some say you can't legally own what was stolen before you obtained it, while other say possession is nine-tenths of the law. To which theory do you subscribe?"

"Neither. Both are oversimple." The waiter arrived with a tray of pastries. Relieved, she took George's arm. "I know what a sweet tooth you have, dear, but I'm dead on my feet. Would you mind if we skipped dessert and went straight home?"

He stared at her vacantly. "O' course not, darling. I'm tired myself. Put everything on my account, Robbie."

The waiter hesitated, then murmured uneasily, "But Mr. Bonner, you know Mr. Marchand's new policy. You'll have to give me—"

"Right, right. Sorry 'bout that, Robbie." He fumbled in his pocket and produced some money, then staggered to his feet and held out his hand. Melanie took it, but as he pulled her up, he lost his balance and stumbled toward the table. She jumped up to save him, catching him before he could harm himself.

"He's not just exhausted—I believe he might be ill," Whitefield said softly. "How are you getting home?"

George overheard him. "I'm fine." He straightened. "A li'l dizzy, but it's nothing serious. Be able to manage."

"In his landau." Melanie put on her cloak. "It's right outside. If he's not able to drive it, I can."

Whitefield shook his head. "I can't let you do that. It wouldn't be safe for you to be out this time of night with a companion in his condition. I hired a brougham for the evening. I'll give you a ride."

She would sooner have cuddled up to a rabid ferret. "That's very kind of you, Colonel, but I can look after myself very well. If you'll excuse us—"

"Ah, yes. You're lethal with a knife. A crack shot. But a female is a target after dark, and George won't be of much help to you if you're attacked. Even *you* can't control a horse and shoot accurately at the same time, especially after all the champagne you've drunk."

"You have a point, Colonel." George swayed a little and gripped the top of the banquette for support. "I am somewhat wobbly on my feet. Touch of the flu, I s'pose." He summoned the waiter back over and handed him a few coins. "Y'know my landau, Robbie. Drive it to my house after you close for the night. Rincon Hill, southwest corner of Folsom and Fremont. I'll see that you're taken home."

The men headed for the door, George leaning on Whitefield's arm. Short of making a scene, Melanie had no choice but to follow. She told Whitefield he could drop her at George's house, explaining that she thought she should stay with him until he felt better, and Whitefield agreed at once. Her uneasiness diminished a little. She would never be alone with the man, and the streets, though potentially dangerous, were still busy at this time of night. He couldn't harm her and get away with it. Besides, she was very well-armed.

Whitefield's brougham was in the alley behind the restaurant. He exchanged a few terse sentences with his driver as they settled George in the carriage. Melanie waited nearby, shivering in the cold night air. It was very dark out. Dank and foggy, too. And the alley was eerily deserted.

Her heart began to race. Things felt wrong. All

askew, somehow. Not dangerous, she realized in confusion, just—disturbing.

Whitefield hopped out of the brougham. The driver followed, closing the door behind him. "We made Mr. Bonner as comfortable as we could," the hackman said.

Whitefield, meanwhile, was casually grasping her wrists. He folded them into a single large hand, so quickly that she was captured before she had the wit to back away. She immediately tried to free herself, but he adjusted his hold to keep her where she was.

"Relax, Melanie. Bonner will be fine once he's had a good night's sleep." The Carolina drawl was gone, replaced by the flat speech of New England. "I'm not going to hurt you, I promise. Now come along."

"No. Are you insane? Let go of me!" She pulled as hard as she could, trying to yank her wrists from his grasp, but she couldn't. "This is outrageous. What do you think you're doing?"

"Protecting my capacity to produce an heir." He reached into the right pocket of her cloak, grabbed her gun, and flipped it to his driver. Her knife quickly followed. "Nice choice of weapons. Compact. Accurate."

"I'm thrilled you approve." She tugged and twisted, all but wrenching her arms from their sockets, but it was no use. She couldn't escape. "You're hurting me, you lout. But I suppose it gives you a great deal of satisfaction to manhandle a woman half your size." She began squirming like an imprisoned cat. "I said let go of me, you lily-livered bloodworm, or I'll scream so hard I'll shatter every window in sight."

He gathered her close against his chest, trapping her between the coach and his body, and clapped his hand over her lips. She tried to bite him, but couldn't get her mouth open. She wriggled and kicked at his shins, but she might as well have battled an oak tree. Despite what she'd said earlier, the only pain came from her own ineffectual struggles. He was so strong that he didn't have to hurt her to dominate her completely.

She felt something hard beneath his coat—a gun in a holster, she realized. The fact that he was armed should have terrified her into submission, but she decided it was only to be expected in a man of his type. She kept fighting.

He tightened his grip for several seconds, applying just enough pressure to cause her discomfort, and then eased up. She took it as a warning, a sign of his impatience with her resistance. "Settle down, Melanie. If you don't cooperate, you can kiss Bonner goodbye for the next six or eight months, because I'll put you out with chloroform and then deliver him to a crimp I know in Sydney Town. Believe me, he'll be shanghaied out of here on the next ship to leave port."

She froze, suddenly as frightened as she was angry. He meant it. He would actually do it. Her heart began pounding in her ears, all but closing up her throat.

Chapter 5

Whitefield gingerly removed his hand from Melanie's mouth, but it was clear that he would clap it back in an instant if she dared to raise her voice. "Who are you?" she asked hoarsely. "What do you want?"

He nodded to his driver, who opened the door to the carriage and then stepped aside. "Thank you, Ned. We can get going now."

Whitefield lifted her into his arms, climbed into the carriage, and sat down, settling her on his lap. Ned closed the door. She scrambled away, pressing herself into a corner of the brougham. Although Whitefield permitted the withdrawal, he kept a light hold on one of her wrists to prevent her from fleeing through the opposite door.

George was on the seat across from them, half-sitting and half-lying down. She squinted at him, trying to determine his condition in the dim light of the nearest gas lamp. He appeared to be fast asleep.

The carriage began to move. She glared at Whitefield, who looked back impassively. "What have you done to him. Where are we going?"

"So many questions, Melanie. Shall we take them one at a time?"

He rubbed his thumb up and down against her palm and wrist, slowly and gently. The motion was blatantly sexual. "Bonner doesn't appreciate you, you know. Not the way he should. But I do." He kept stroking her hand. "I enjoyed myself tonight, Melanie. You made me exert myself. It doesn't happen often. In fact, with a woman, it's never happened before."

She pictured him as he really was, dark and handsome and compelling, and a hot flush rose up her neck. Wretched champagne, she thought. "Am I supposed to be honored, you miserable blackguard? Or flattered? I assure you I'm not. And stop doing that, damn you. I don't like it."

He smiled. "I know you don't. It arouses you too much."

"It makes my skin crawl." She tugged at her hand. To her surprise, he released her. "You're the most arrogant swine it's ever been my misfortune to encounter. You said you would answer my questions. Did you lie about that, too?"

"No." He tucked a strand of her hair behind her ear, then started to caress her, exploring her neck and face with light but firm strokes of his fingers.

He knew just how to touch a woman. Just where, too. There were those sensitive little hollows behind her ears, and the curve above her chin, and the pulse in the center of her throat, and the outline of her upper lip . . . She shuddered, but whether it was from fear or arousal, she wasn't sure.

"Who am I? Whoever I choose to be at any particular moment. What do I want? It's not too long a list. Money, adventure, a beautiful woman . . . At the moment, you. You're very beautiful, but I believe I've already told you that. The amazing thing is, I actually meant it."

He moved closer, so that their thighs and shoul-

ders were touching. She began to tremble. His caresses were making her hot and languid, as if they
were driving through a steamy and sensual tropi-
cal jungle.

She bit her lip, fighting the urge to offer her
mouth. He was an accomplished deceiver, she reminded herself, a ruthless criminal. His words
meant less than nothing. But everything about him
heated her blood, even the danger. Especially the
danger. She couldn't seem to cool the fever.

"What have I done to Bonner? Nothing perma-
nent. Just a slow but thorough soporific. He'll feel
fine when he wakes tomorrow morning. Cheerful
and well-rested." He massaged the nape of her
neck. It would have felt soothing if it hadn't been
so blasted erotic. "As for where we're going, the
answer is nowhere in particular. Just riding
around, getting to know each other better."

The prospect was much too intriguing. She took a
deep, desperate breath. *Alpha, beta, gamma, delta*. No
man got the better of her. No man. *Epsilon, zeta,
eta, theta*. She never lost control of herself. Never.
Iota, kappa. Men were all the same, slaves to their
loins. Even this one. *Lambda, mu*. But not her. Not
Melanie Wyatt. *Nu, xi, omicron*. She had handled the
biggest Don Juans in San Francisco, and she could
handle him.

Ice crept into her blood. She rushed to embrace
it. "So you're glib and evasive in addition to being
a liar and a bully," she said crisply. George
snorted, shifted onto his back, and began snoring
peacefully. "Frankly, I prefer honesty and sub-
stance in a man, Colonel White—but you're not a
colonel at all, are you? What *is* your name, anyway?"

"I've had three or four of them during the past
week. You can call me whatever you want." He
put his arm around her shoulders. "Most women

in your position would be terrified. Hysterical. You're not. You're levelheaded and brave, and you fight like a tigress. I like that very much."

"It's all you're going to like, you contemptible villain, so savor it while you can. You've gone to a great deal of trouble to arrange this—this ridiculous abduction, or seduction, or whatever it's supposed to be, but you'll find it's a complete waste of your time. It won't get you a thing."

"But I didn't decide to abduct you until eight this evening, and it was very little trouble at all." He nuzzled her neck, unbuttoning her cloak as he kissed her.

His fingers grazed her chest, perhaps inadvertently. Her breasts were cradled and pushed upward by her corset, leaving her nipples exposed and vulnerable under the thin silk of her gown, and they puckered and hardened at once. It was starting all over again, she thought in dismay. *Pi, rho, sigma*. She couldn't seem to catch her breath. *Tau, upsilon, phi*. What in the world was happening to her?

"As for what it will get me, that remains to be seen. Seduction is always nice, but accepting what a woman offers eagerly is even nicer. Admit it, Melanie. We wanted each other from the first moment our eyes met. Both of us saw it. Felt it in our blood."

He was right. "Very well, then," she said irritably. "I found you somewhat handsome, I suppose. But the rest is sheer invention on your part. And even if it weren't, Mr.—Mr. Smith, I happen to be engaged, so unless—"

"It's Alex. My name. What the hell."

"So unless you plan to rape me—"

"Don't be absurd, Mellie." He kissed his way to her earlobe, then gently sucked it. A warm curl of pleasure spiraled through her belly, then slowly snaked lower.

Chi, psi, omega, she recited silently, and then paled. Dear Lord. She'd never reached the end before. This was a crisis. A full-out emergency. What was she going to do?

She forced down her panic and tried to think rationally. She needed a plan of action, that was all. Perhaps if she went backward. Forward was hard enough, but backward would be close to impossible. It was sure to distract her.

"Let me spend the night with you," Alex whispered in her ear. "I'll devote myself to pleasing you. Has Bonner ever done that? Made you moan and bite and scratch? Made you shake with pleasure? Made you scream with every climax, again and again and again? Because I could."

Backward did the trick. It took intense concentration to begin with, and she made it even harder by picturing a desiccated tutor looming over her, drumming Greek and Latin into her head. God, but she had loathed the lessons her father had insisted on providing. Especially classical languages.

"Incredible," she said aloud. "Simply incredible. Honestly, Alex, you're the most—is it really Alex, by the way?"

"Umm. You smell delicious, Mellie. Like jasmine and lilies."

"And *you* have an extraordinarily high opinion of your skill as a lover. It's not an attractive quality, you know."

"Not my skill. Skill is for mindless automatons. I prefer passion. I would take the time to feel what's in your heart. To listen to your body sing to me. To sense what you want and need." He kissed her on the mouth, biting gently on her lower lip. "You're exquisite. Intoxicating."

He reminded her of herself. Pretty words, ardent lovemaking, total control. An immense threat, in short. She had to defeat him. To neutralize the threat. If she didn't, the lives she planned to save with the necklace and the gold would be lost to slavery and degradation.

She turned away from him, then buried her face in her hands. "Don't talk to me that way. It confuses me. I've made a promise to someone else—"

"Who doesn't deserve you."

"But Alex—"

"Hush, sweetheart." He covered her breast with his palm, then found her nipple and lightly kneaded it. She wanted to shy away—she wasn't used to such caresses, even from George—but she didn't dare. "I can make you happy. He never will. Leave him, Mellie. It's no sin to change your mind."

She faced him, hesitantly putting her hands on his shoulders. "But I don't know anything about you. Who you really are, where you come from, why you want the tiger—"

"Later." He kissed her hard on the mouth. "I'll tell you everything later. I promise."

She parted her lips and let him kiss her passionately. He was very skillful, his tongue nimble and provocative in her mouth, his fingers playfully erotic on her breasts. She had never experienced such intimate, seductive lovemaking, and it stirred her as much as it embarrassed her. Still, a wall had gone up and she wasn't going to permit him to tear it down. She coiled her arms around his neck, got as close to him as she could, and forced herself to rub her breasts against his chest. His control slipped a little, his breaths coming more quickly and his mouth growing rougher.

She kissed him for another minute, felt his tension mount and his body begin to burn, and knew she was going to win. She gave herself a stern lecture about the exigencies of the situation, then climbed onto his lap. He groaned and thrust himself against her, moving his hips in slow, rhythmic circles. His manhood was hard and swollen and demanding. A fiery wave of desire surged through her, and she moaned softly. A man's arousal had never affected her this way before, but she couldn't help it. He was such a magnificent physical specimen that even a nun would have desired him.

She fought the urge to succumb even as she moved sinuously against his groin. The wall stayed precariously in place. "Alex, no," she whispered urgently. "We have to stop. It's not right."

He took a deep, ragged breath. "It's perfect. You're perfect."

"But George—"

"Even another earthquake wouldn't wake him." He took her mouth again, kissing her with almost savage need. Then he pushed aside her skirts, slipped his hand underneath them, and ran his fingers up her stockinged leg. Any farther and he would reach her knickers, which were loosely fitted with openings at the crotch and back, in the latest fashion.

She stiffened. She had already permitted him unthinkable intimacies—invited more and more of them with each passing minute—but she couldn't let him do *that*. Touch her in a way that only a husband should. Not even for the tiger or Shen Wai or a fortune in buried gold.

His fingers crept under the edge of her knickers. Her womanhood was utterly open to him now. Burning with a mixture of excitement and shock, she started to push away his hand—and then stopped. So many lives were at stake. If she refused him and he cooled off, and it all fell apart . . .

She was still agonizing about what to do when

he gave her thigh a gentle squeeze and withdrew his hand. "Easy, Mellie." His voice was raspy with frustration. "Just relax. I won't rush you."

She was immensely relieved, but also a little guilty. He could be tender and sweet, and she had teased him half to death. It was a low thing, to tempt a man so unmercifully, making promises only a trollop could keep.

Still, war was war. "I know. I'm sorry. It's just that—"

"I understand."

"No. You don't. The thought of you inside me . . . It frightens me, Alex. You're so big." She didn't know if he was or he wasn't, but Ah Lan had once told her that all men loved to hear that they were. "It excites me so much I can barely stand it, but I know you'll hurt me. You won't be able to help it."

"Mellie . . . sweetheart . . . Of course I won't hurt you. I'll enter you gently and slowly. Stretch you to take my size. It'll be fine, I promise."

"Let me touch you first," she whispered. "Let me feel your shape. Then I won't be so afraid."

He shuddered. "God, yes. Whatever you want." He eased her off his lap, then unfastened his trousers.

She couldn't see him in the dimness of the carriage, a fact for which she was devoutly grateful. The prospect of touching him was unnerving enough without having to watch what she was doing.

She leaned against his chest and put her left hand on his thigh. Her right hand clutched his jacket. Ah Lan had also told her that men liked to conquer their women in bed. Control them. Make them burn.

"I want you to take me," she whispered. "Force

me to submit to you. Make me beg for your touch. Kiss me again, Alex, harder and deeper. Please."

He did, but his mouth was more frenzied than forceful, and his body was shaking fiercely. She kneaded his thigh, then inched her fingers toward his manhood. He groaned when she finally touched him and abandoned her mouth to nip her ear and neck. She grasped him more firmly, and was stunned by his warmth and size and thrusting male strength. As she tightened her grip, her right hand darted beneath his coat and extracted his pistol from its holster. A second later the muzzle made contact with his rapidly deflating male shaft.

She released him with considerable relief, cocking the hammer of her pistol at the same time. "First you're going to tell me your name, and then you're going to tell me who you work for."

He leaned back in the seat, breathing hard. A good ten seconds went by. "You're a blockhead, McClure," he finally muttered in disgust. The accent was English now. "A total and complete idiot. Hoisted on your own petard. Your stupidity is unbelievable."

Melanie fought the urge to smile. "It's Alex McClure, then?"

"Hmm? Oh. My name. Yes. I never really got to you, I suppose. Not for a single minute."

"No. You're English, I presume?"

"Half-English, half-Scottish, and dumb as a dodo." He sighed heavily. "Do you think you could point that thing somewhere else, Mellie? I don't mind dying, but I'd hate to survive as a eunuch."

She ignored the request. "Why not? Given your self-described lack of intelligence, you would be doing us all a favor if you failed to reproduce. What's your connection to the Eternal Brotherhood?"

"The what?"

"The Eternal Brotherhood, Alex. You wear their medal around your neck."

"Do I really? Tell me, who are they?"

"A very dangerous Chinese triad, but I'm sure you already knew that." She wiggled the gun for effect, but he didn't even flinch, must less tremble in abject fear. "Come now, no more pretenses or evasions. What's your connection to them?"

"I don't have one." He crossed his ankle over his knee, seemingly at ease. "One picks up the damnedest things in curio shops, doesn't one. Please, Mellie, have pity on me and point the gun somewhere else. It's making me very nervous."

"Is it? It doesn't show."

"Take my word for it. It is."

"Good," she said, but drew the pistol back and raised it a few inches.

"Thank you. You're a woman of singular compassion." He stretched. "God, it's been an exhausting day. My wound is throbbing like a drum. I can't wait to get this damned wig off."

"You're a good actor, but you can't be as calm as you seem. I'll bet you're quietly terrified. And if you're not, you should be, because if you don't answer my questions—"

"You wouldn't really shoot me, would you? After all we've meant to each other?"

"I certainly would, but I would try not to kill you. A fractured bone here, a useless limb there . . ."

"Right. I get the idea. Could I button up my trousers? It's downright unpleasant, flopping around in the dank night air this way."

"Tell me who you work for, Alex. If I believe you, I'll give you my permission to dress."

"Hmm. I don't have much choice, I suppose. Myself. I'm a free-lance. Thieves usually are, you know." He looked at her hopefully. "Was that good enough?"

"No. There's the matter of your medal to clear up. One doesn't find such things in curio shops. A member of the triad must have given it to you. How did you earn it?"

"If you know who they are, you know I can't answer that question. Blood oaths and all that. By the way, how *do* you know? That is, I assume you saw the medal when I was unconscious, but how did you know what it was? Very few people here would recognize it, and virtually no one outside Little China."

She rolled her eyes. "I have the gun, you thick-brained dolt. That means I ask the questions and you answer them. How did you earn the medal?"

"I don't care *who* has the gun, I still can't tell you. Enough is enough, Mellie. Go ahead and shoot me if you feel you have to, but I won't be badgered." He buttoned his trousers. "Will you look at that? I'm getting hard again. You have the most amazing effect on me. I see you and I spring to life. I haven't been this randy since my schooldays."

"Can we leave your excessive sexual appetites out of this?" Melanie stroked his belly with the muzzle of the pistol for emphasis. "Are you working for them? Did they order you to get them the tiger?"

"No. I'm a free-lance. I've already told you that. And no more questions about the bloody triad."

"Then how do you know about the tiger? Why do you want it?"

"One hears things here and there. Gossip and rumors."

She gnashed her teeth in frustration. The man should have been sweating blood and squealing like a pig, not coolly fobbing her off with meaningless generalities. "Very well, Alex. Sit up straight and hold out your arm. We'll start with a simple flesh wound to your wrist. If that doesn't do the trick, we'll progress to more painful injuries."

He did straighten, but very languidly. "I believe I'll leave my arm where it is, Mellie. You see, you're forgetting Ned, my driver. If you fire, you'll attract his attention, and he still has your knife and pistol. You can't hold off both of us, not for very long."

"But I can *kill* both of you," she said impatiently, "then say it was self-defense. Under the circumstances, no jury could convict me. I'm not playing a game here—"

"I know you're not. You've got the tiger. I respect you as a fellow professional. But you're not a murderer, either, any more than I am."

His hand shot out with lightning speed and chopped down brutally on her wrist. She started and winced, but she didn't drop the gun. Still, her grip on it loosened a fraction, and that was enough. Alex grabbed it, uncocked it, removed the bullets, and tossed everything on the seat.

Her mouth went dry. Whoever or whatever else he was, he was no angel, and he was no doubt furious with her. She had humiliated him sexually. Threatened him repeatedly. Forced him to reveal his secrets.

She retreated to a corner of the carriage. She wanted to apologize, but no words would come out. She thought about placating him with sex or bribing him with the necklace, but her pride wouldn't allow it. He couldn't shoot her, not without reloading the pistol. As for the other possible punishments, at least they weren't fatal.

He put down a window, then stuck his head

outside. "Ned, take us to Mr. Bonner's. Rincon Hill, southwest corner of Folsom and Fremont."

So he was taking George home. That was something, she supposed. "And after you drop him off? What do you plan to do with me?"

"Drop you off as well, naturally. You did say you wanted to stay with him." He sat down close beside her. "Have you changed your mind? Would you rather remain with me?"

"No, but—"

"Hmm. A pity." He took her hand. "You'll have a nasty bruise tomorrow." He raised it to his lips and kissed the back of her wrist, very tenderly. "Right there. I'm sorry, Mellie, but you didn't give me much choice."

She stared at him in disbelief. "I take it back. You're not a thick-brained dolt. You're a total madman."

"What did you think I would do? Beat you? Rape you?" He put his arm around her and cupped her chin, bringing her lips to within inches of his mouth. "I don't operate that way especially when someone only gives me what I probably deserve. Although you have to admit, castration and mayhem are rather severe penalties for a harmless bit of drugging and attempted seduction." He traced the outline of her upper lip with the tip of his tongue. "God, you taste sweet. You know, I've been thinking about what I said before, and I suspect I might have been wrong. Shall we find out?"

He began kissing her again, but not the savage way he had kissed her before. He nipped and sucked her lips, and when she refused to part them, nuzzled her face and throat, over and over again, cajoling and stimulating her with infinite patience and determination. She sat motionless, reciting the Greek alphabet forward and backward— once, twice, three times. The exercise enabled her to ignore the lightning that slashed through her body and control the yearning in her tongue and lips, but he wasn't discouraged by her stoicism.

"If you were any hotter, you would burst into flames," he said with a grin. "Come, sweetheart, open your mouth for me."

She didn't reply. She didn't even move.

"No? Very well, then, we'll try something else." He bent his mouth to her breasts.

Her hands flew upward, grabbing both sides of his head and trying to push it away. He grasped them with languid self-assurance, forced her arms behind her back, and gently shackled her wrists. She wriggled frantically, trying to free herself, but he wouldn't release her.

He lowered his head again, then found a nipple and took it between his teeth, right through the fabric of her high-necked gown. He nipped it sharply and a stunned little gasp of pleasure escaped her lips. Laughing softly, he sucked and nibbled until it was hard and engorged. Then he abandoned the first and played with the second, alternating gentleness with roughness until she moaned in surrender.

Resistance was now the farthest thing from her mind. Her breasts ached. Her nipples throbbed madly. The most feminine part of her felt like liquid fire. She writhed against his mouth and groaned his name because she couldn't stop herself, because she needed something she'd never needed before. And all the Greek letters in the world couldn't change that.

He took her in his arms and kissed her again, teasing her exactly as he had earlier, but she was susceptible to it now, desperate for his mouth, and she offered herself almost at once. He whispered something against her lips, but she couldn't make out the words. Then the torture began again, even more exciting than before.

Finally, frustrated to the brink of tears, she began to plead with him. "Oh, God, Alex. Please. Don't do this to me . . ."

"Gently, Mellie, gently. I'm sorry. I thought—hell, never mind." He gave her his tongue, sweetly at first, then with drugging, dominating thrusts that aroused her even more wildly. She felt his fingers on her breasts, caressing and gently pinching, and began to moan again, making odd little noises that sounded as if they came from somebody else's throat. She wondered if he would slip his hand back under her dress, and if she would stop him if he did. She didn't think she could bear to, although she would probably die of shame afterward.

She was shaking uncontrollably by the time he released her and moved away. "That answers *that* question," he said evenly. "We're at Bonner's house. Do you still want to go inside? Or would you rather come with me and finish what we started?"

She didn't understand what he was asking. He was so cool, so relaxed. She stared at him through glazed eyes, vaguely aware that the carriage had stopped moving.

"Finish . . . ? Oh." She blushed fiercely. "No. I can't do that." She hugged herself and tried to stop trembling.

"You mean you won't. Stubborn to the very end, even if it means suffering the torments of hell, eh, Mellie?" He stroked her cheek. "So soft and sweet and hot. Maybe I should have taken you here in the carriage and put both of us out of our misery, but I have an odd streak of romance in me. I want fireworks the first time I make love to you, and having your unconscious fiancé snoring a yard away put a bit of a damper on things. Ah, well. We'll have other opportunities. By the way, I hope you'll have divested yourself of Bonner by the next time we meet."

Her head began to clear. She shook it in denial. "No. This was—I don't know what it was. Madness brought on by the earthquake or too much champagne. Or my fear of you somehow transmuting itself into fleeting desire. But it won't happen again."

He smiled. "If you thought that was fleeting, I can't wait for sustained. And it will happen again, because you want it to, and as a gentleman, the least I can do is oblige you." The smile turned crooked and teasing. "All night long, Mellie. I'll give you climax after climax until you collapse in blissful exhaustion. Sound tempting?"

"No." It did, actually, but she wished that it didn't. The man was a swaggering lout. "Anyway, if you were the gentleman you claim to be, you wouldn't boast about—about your alleged prowess as a lover."

"I wasn't boasting. There's nothing 'alleged' about it. I was simply stating a fact."

"A fantasy, you mean. You weren't that impressive."

"No? And here I thought you were stunned. Overwhelmed. Are you telling me I was wrong?"

She glared at him. "Oh, shut up."

"Hmm. I didn't think so. You can't imagine how much I look forward to our next meeting." He opened the door of the carriage. "Tell me, sweetheart, are you sufficiently recovered from your unbridled passion to be able to walk, or should I carry you?"

"Damn it, Alex, will you stop being so bloody pleased with yourself? I told you, there won't be a next time. There won't be any future meetings."

"On the contrary, given our mutual interest in maps, future meetings are inevitable. The map on the tiger is especially ingenious, wouldn't you say?"

"*On* the tiger?" Melanie repeated, and then pictured the markings and realized he was right. She was stunned. She'd never suspected, never would have seen it without his help. "Oh. You mean the map etched *into* the tiger. Yes. Very ingenious."

"So you didn't realize. I had a feeling you might not, but I assume your compatriots would have. Actually, I missed it myself at first." He hopped out of the carriage and held out his hand. "The darkened swirl, I suppose, indicates the position of the cloth diagram. Do you concur?"

"Uh, yes. Of course I do." Reeling from what he'd just told her, and even more from what he'd done to her and made her feel, she numbly took his hand.

Chapter 6

An hour later, George's valet Hackett turned to Melanie and delicately suggested, for the third time, that it was safe for her to leave. "Mr. Bonner's pulse is strong and his color is good. Whatever brought on his attack, he's obviously much better now. You need your rest, Miss Wyatt. Please, let me fetch Mrs. Winchley"—George's housekeeper. "She can keep an eye on him while I walk you home."

Melanie felt George's forehead. He had stirred briefly when McClure had carried him inside, then fallen into a sound but normal sleep. "Hmm. Still no fever." She yawned. "Maybe you're right. I am rather tired, but leave Mrs. Winchley be. At her age, she needs the rest more than I do." Melanie patted the pocket of her cloak, which was lying across her lap. "I don't need an escort—other than my Colt's revolver, that is."

"Excuse me, miss, but things can happen this time of night, even in only four blocks, and even when a lady is as good with a gun as you are. I'll come with you."

She was about to argue when the image of Alex McClure popped into her mind. True, he had returned her weapons, but he was also dangerous and unpredictable. For all she knew he was lurking outside, plotting another round of kidnapping and seduction. She felt herself redden. Given how good he was at both, it wasn't the sort of threat she could disregard.

"Very well," she agreed, "but please, Hackett, do stay with Mr. Bonner. I'll get Mullins to walk me home." Mullins was George's head groom. A huge bear of a man, he would provide much better protection than the diminutive valet. "He'll have to get up anyway, to see to Chestnut when Robbie shows up with the landau."

Hackett reddened a bit himself, then fixed his gaze on George's chest. "Mullins doesn't—I'm afraid he won't be able to help you, Miss Wyatt. I'll go get Mrs.—"

"He won't? Why not?"

"He, uh, he isn't here right now."

"Really?" Mullins, a bachelor, had been with George for years. His rooms were above the carriage house. "Where is he, then? Not injured, I hope, or coping with some sort of emergency."

"No." Hackett looked more uncomfortable than ever. "It's just—he doesn't work here anymore."

"He doesn't? Whatever happened?"

"Mr. Bonner had to let him go." Hackett stood. "The less said about it, the better, especially to Mr. Bonner, if you know what I mean. I'll get Mrs. Winchley now."

Melanie took Hackett's arm to prevent him from running away. "Wait a minute, Peter. What's all the mystery about? Did Mullins commit some grave indiscretion? Filch a piece of the family silver or gossip about an important client?"

"No. It was nothing like that. He's a fine man—I wouldn't say he's not. But he got a better offer and he took it, and Mr. Bonner isn't happy about it. It's a touchy subject, miss. Surely you understand."

Melanie nodded and Hackett hurried away, returning a minute later with a yawning Mrs. Winchley. Then, pistol in hand, he led Melanie down the stairs and out of the house. From the way he swaggered, he probably saw himself as a brave sentry protecting a defenseless maiden. She didn't have the heart to remind him that the maiden was the better shot.

In any event, she was glad to have his company. Her hand closed tensely around her gun as he opened George's gate. She was shaking slightly as they started down the street, but there was no sign of McClure and no aura of danger. It was only after a block or so, when she was sure no one was watching or following, that her nerves began to steady.

To her relief, the area around her house felt as secure as the street. Once again, no sense of danger or agitation filled the air. If McClure was watching—if he had lingered there during the evening—she couldn't feel it. Given the intensity of the aura he invariably radiated, even after he had left a spot, she was almost certainly safe.

She opened her door and stepped inside. "I'm still a little worried, Hackett. Promise you'll send for me if Mr. Bonner isn't up and off to work at the usual hour. I'll fix him a tonic and bring it right over."

The valet smiled. "I'll tell him you said so, Miss Wyatt. No offense, but the prospect of drinking one of your Chinese potions will have him up and about in no time."

"You see? They truly work wonders." Smiling back, she bid Hackett goodnight and headed up the stairs.

In truth, she doubted George was in danger. She had remained at his bedside that evening out of duty and a concern for appearances, not because she was worried about his health. When she hadn't been chatting with Hackett, she had been thinking about McClure—wondering who and what he was, for whom he worked, and what he wanted. George had barely existed for her.

Her behavior suggested a reality she didn't want to confront, so she told herself it was a question of priorities. At the moment, nothing was more important than her mission. McClure stood between her and success, so naturally he had filled her mind.

He was no doubt extremely dangerous, but her instincts told her he'd been honest about the drug he'd administered to George being a harmless soporific. He had knocked George out for only one reason, to manipulate her into accepting a ride in his brougham and then staying there until he was ready to let her go. Given how quickly he'd begun to caress her, his goal must have been seduction. That puzzled her, because he didn't seem like the type to put himself out for the sake of a passing conquest. He must have had a deeper reason for making love to her.

Unsettled, she dropped onto her bed and chewed distractedly on a fingernail. She'd suspected from the start that he was clever, and his actions this evening confirmed it. Spur of the moment or not, his plan had been perfectly executed. She was no patsy, so it was no small feat for a man to disarm her and then force her to do his bidding, but McClure had managed it quite easily.

Even worse, he had demolished her defenses, arousing her into a state of such mindless abandon that her continued virtue was a technicality. If he had persisted, she might have given herself. It was horrifying. She had betrayed George and acted like a harlot, and the fact that she'd been frightened and a little drunk was no excuse. It didn't matter how handsome and virile a man was, or how expert a lover, or how fiercely she desired him. She should have been able to handle Adonis himself by now.

McClure's only mistake, in fact, had been to succumb to the passion he'd felt in return, and he hadn't made it twice. When he'd made love to her the second time, he'd been cool, determined, and as lethal as a shark. She was on her guard now, but even so, she dreaded the prospect of another encounter.

She slowly changed for bed. Someone as shrewd as McClure would do nothing without a reason, she suddenly realized, so why had he sought out George that afternoon? Invited him to dine? Suggested that she join them? And what should she make of his precisely timed note saying he would be late for dinner? What had delayed him? Where had he been?

She paled in alarm and dashed to her armoire. If she had been McClure, she would have searched this house for further information at the first opportunity, and the absence of menacing vibrations didn't negate that. She was the one who interested him, the one he'd been following since yesterday afternoon. George had probably been nothing but a means to an end—a way to meet her, to gain information about her, and to lure her out of her house so he could inspect it.

She yanked out the two bottom drawers and the brace between them, removed the middle divider, and shoved up the back panel. At first glance, the objects in her hiding place looked exactly as she'd left them, but she was always precise about where she put things, planning for exactly this eventuality. After a closer inspection, her stomach knotted up. Her belongings had definitely been disturbed.

She pulled out the tiger and fumblingly opened it. She knew at once that McClure had managed to unlock it; she had positioned the Chinese note in a corner of the folded cloth map, and it fluttered out far too quickly. To her astonishment and relief, the gold and ruby necklace fell out as well. She put everything back and reassembled the tiger, thinking that he was the oddest thief she had ever encountered. The necklace was worth thousands. Why hadn't he stolen it? What sort of game was he playing?

Thinking hard, she set the tiger aside and put the armoire to rights. McClure must have been in this house for close to an hour. She should have sensed such a long occupation immediately—should be shivering from the danger even now. For the first time in her life, her clairvoyance had failed her miserably. For all she knew, he was near her right this moment.

She pictured him stealing into her room as she slept, drugging, binding, and gagging her, and then sneaking her out to his carriage. After all, he could hardly have failed to learn how rich her father was. Maybe he hadn't bothered with the necklace because he'd decided to kidnap her. Even the costliest piece of jewelry was worth a pittance compared to Thomas's mines.

She imagined herself waking up his prisoner, and shuddered. He would probably conceal her in a small, clammy cave or a tiny, sweltering shack. She hated confined spaces.

Thoroughly shaken, she unsheathed her knife and carried it into her father's bedroom, along with the tiger. Thomas's door was the only one upstairs with a lock. She turned the key, then pushed a small chest in front of it. After placing the tiger under the bed, she slipped between the covers and stared into the darkness.

If McClure broke into the room, the noise would surely wake her. She would be muzzy from sleep and blinded by the night, her gun of little use against an attacker who was accustomed to the darkness. But once he got close enough to strike, she would feel the position of his body and attack him first. She fell asleep with her hand under her pillow, her fingers wrapped firmly around her knife.

She awoke the next morning with a start, having slept far more soundly than she'd intended or thought possible. After a few seconds, images from her dreams flooded back—hotly erotic flashes of Alex's mouth tasting hers, of her nipples hardening against his teasing fingers, of her hand grasping his aroused manhood and slowly exploring it, and enjoying it as much as he. She flushed deeply. It should have appalled her that she'd had to touch him last night. She shouldn't have wanted to repeat the experience in her dreams.

Forcing the pictures from her mind, she looked at the clock on the mantel. It was almost eight. She never slept this late. Had Alex drugged her, then, just as he had drugged George? Administered an even slower-acting soporific?

She swung her feet to the floor. Given the way she had behaved the night before, perhaps he'd slipped her an aphrodisiac. It would explain her unprecedented susceptibility. On the other hand, she hadn't felt the least bit muzzy or unusual. Still, one could never be too careful. It would be a cold day in hell before she ate or drank again in his presence, that much was certain.

She glanced at the door. The chest was where she had left it. She checked beneath the bed. The tiger was still there. He hadn't come in during the night.

Even so, the knowledge that he might have tried made her heart race in alarm. She sat down on the floor, crossed her legs, folded her arms across her chest, and breathed slowly and deeply as she counted silently back from fifty, exactly as Shen Wai had taught her. Her panic subsided, and she was able to think more logically. Her fears of the night before, she told herself, were absurd. If Alex had wanted to kidnap her for ransom, he would have knocked her out with chloroform, dumped George in the alley, and carried her off to his hide-out.

Whatever he was after, then, it wasn't only money. He'd been much too indifferent to the value of the necklace for a simple thief, and he'd let her go when a man of his intelligence would have understood her worth as a hostage.

It all came back to the tiger, she decided. The carving seemed to be his chief interest, yet he hadn't stolen it when he'd gotten the chance. Instead, he had made a point of commenting on the map engraved on its surface, deliberately dropping a vital clue into her lap. It was likely that he knew the tiger and the cloth diagram led to a fortune in gold, but couldn't decipher them. He probably assumed that she could, and planned to follow her to the treasure, then snatch it from under her nose. Robbery, after all, was a far less risky endeavor than kidnapping.

Still, there was the continued presence of the necklace to untangle. Alex evidently had complicated goals, but in the end, what they were made little difference. The treasure would save countless lives. She had to retrieve it.

She couldn't wait for Shen Wai to return, either. Having found the maps, Alex would certainly have copied them. If she lingered in San Francisco, he might lose patience with the delay and search for someone to interpret them—someone who could lead him to the gold, probably in exchange for a healthy share of it. His connections were probably as extensive as they were unsavory, so he was likely to succeed.

She pursed her lips in irritation. She had no idea where the wretched gold was buried, and, unfortunately, she couldn't very well wave the maps around San Francisco and ask if anyone recognized the terrain. The wrong sort could get wind of her plans and try to beat her to the cache. Or George could hear of her activities and try to put a stop to them. Honesty was an annoying liability in matters such as these. Unlike Alex, she didn't know a single reliable criminal, much less a clever and discreet one. She was on her own.

Frowning at the injustice of it all, she opened the tiger and studied the map inside. She had traveled widely in California, especially in the northern part of the state where the gold was supposedly buried, so perhaps something would strike her. After a minute or two, she realized that the geological features shown had to be in the mountains. Where else would you find a stream, numerous stands of trees, and outcroppings of rock?

She reviewed what Wai had told her. The Celestials who had mined the gold had buried it for fear of having it stolen, partially milling it before putting it into crates. Then as now, the Chinese were fair game. Few white men cared if some thief took their property, even if he killed them in the process.

But her people were patient by nature. The miners had returned to China, sneaking out enough treasure to live comfortably for years. In time, they had known, the rush would end and gold-laden miners would become a thing of the past. They would be able to bring out their cache more safely. But before they could return, they had heard of how their compatriots were suffering in America, and had decided to donate their remaining riches to Wai's rescue efforts.

Partially milled or not, the gold was cumbersome, so Melanie doubted that the miners had moved it very far. The cloth map might describe the range by the coast or the one across the north, but the foothills in the east were the likeliest possibility.

She broke into a smile. If so, she was in luck. Her old friend Tyson Stone, who was a newspaper editor in Nevada now, had roamed the Mother Lode for years. If anyone would recognize the markings on the tiger, which she assumed were stage roads and Indian trails, Ty would. And unless he had changed drastically since they had last met, he would refrain from asking questions she didn't want to answer and look upon the quest as a grand adventure.

Short of going on horseback, there was only one way to reach her old hometown. One took a steamer to Sacramento, then a stagecoach up to the foothills. The boat sailed at four each afternoon, which didn't leave her much time to prepare. She jumped to her feet. She had a great deal to accomplish in the next eight hours.

Back in her room, she pulled out Ty's most recent letter, which had arrived a few weeks before. She studied his handwriting, then practiced copying it. Within an hour, she had produced a splendid forgery. Delighted with her ingenuity, she pulled on some clothes, packed her carpetbag, and tiptoed down the rear stairway.

She was about to slip out the back door when Mrs. Dibble ran her to ground. In accordance with the wishes of her employer, the woman didn't so much keep house as keep tabs on Melanie's health and whereabouts, or attempt to.

"Oh, no, you don't," she clucked. "Not without eating something, Miss Wyatt. Lordy, you're always rushing around so, you would waste away to nothing if I didn't force a good meal down you now and then."

"I'm hardly wasting, Mrs. Dibble. In fact, some people consider me rather strapping, including my fiancé. Anyway, I'm not hungry. I need to drive to the post office and—"

"You need to put something in your stomach, and no arguments, missy." She frowned. "Why are you wearing that dreary old hat and coat? I thought you saved them for storms and funerals."

Because black was harder to spot and follow than black and crimson. "Just a whim," Melanie said. "I'm in a dreary sort of mood, I suppose."

"And little wonder, seeing as your belly is completely empty. Come along now. I'll have Artie see to the gig while you eat, so it won't cost you a moment's time. I made some apple tarts this morning, especially for you. Doesn't that sound tempting?"

Melanie yielded, but she was so agitated she had to force down the pastry bite by bite. By the time she took the reins of her gig, she was praying that the inevitable jostling wouldn't have disastrous consequences. It was a crisp and sunny morning, though, and the clean sea air soon settled her stomach.

She assumed that Alex would try to tail her—it was what she would have done in his place—but if he was anywhere nearby, she couldn't sense him. That was cold comfort given the way her clairvoyance had deserted her the night before, so she glanced at the sidewalk and street as she drove into town, searching for someone of his height and general build. Nobody fit his description, either on foot or in a carriage.

The post office was on Washington Street. She was crossing Market when her neck and ears began to tingle. She slowed and looked around. Within two blocks, the sensation grew from a soft quiver to an alarming throb. There were numerous vehicles on this section of Montgomery, but none of the passengers looked familiar, and neither did any of the pedestrians. Businessmen, matrons out shopping, families taking the air, plainly dressed mechanics, elegantly garbed Celestials, an occasional drunk and tramp . . . Still, Alex was out there somewhere. She could definitely feel him.

The sense of menace was stronger than ever. She couldn't understand it. Now that she was thinking more clearly, she couldn't believe that the man who had kissed her injured wrist so ruefully the night before would deliberately harm her. The worst he could do was steal her gold or perhaps her virginity. Why did she have such an intense sensation of danger? Was it all the lives that would be ruined if she failed to retrieve the gold?

She coaxed her horse into a trot, driving as fast as the traffic allowed. The activities she'd planned for this morning were innocuous and unrevealing, but she couldn't have Alex tailing her this afternoon. He would learn too much. She would never forgive herself if she led him to the treasure.

She parked her gig in front of the post office, then went inside to the ladies' window and got in line. Some ten minutes later, the clerk handed her a magazine from New York and a letter from a friend in Stockton.

Her next stop was George's office, about a block and a half away. She could feel Alex's presence as she walked down Washington Street, but when she stealthily looked around, she couldn't spot him. It set her teeth on edge.

The sensation diminished only after she'd entered the Monkey Block and climbed to the second floor. Sam was working, poring over a ledger. He greeted her warmly, adding that Mr. Bonner was at his desk.

"He was a trifle under the weather last night, Sam. How is he this morning?"

"He looked fine, Miss Wyatt. Why don't you see for yourself? He won't mind the interruption. He's researching precedents."

Melanie nodded and went inside, then closed the door and walked to where George was sitting. "You look much better. I'm glad." She pecked him on the cheek. "I was a little concerned."

"Is that all the hello I get?" He took her hand and pulled her toward his lap, but she refused to sit down. "What's the matter, Melanie? You're acting as if I'm contagious."

She smiled. "Don't be silly, George. I can see that you're fine. It's just that—"

"Then give me a proper good morning kiss." He ran his hand up and down her hip. "If you remember, I was severely deprived last night."

"Which is why you'll want more than one kiss, but I don't have time for anything else. I have a million things to do." Besides, she felt as if Alex were watching her. She could remember her response to his touch and knew George would never make her feel that way. It was exactly what she'd thought she wanted—the safety of perfect control—but suddenly, the thought of a life without real passion was terribly depressing.

George smiled indulgently. "What things, darling? Shopping for a new gown? Reading to a group of restless children? Meeting your friends for lunch?"

"Getting ready for a trip to Nevada. Nevada City, I mean." In March, the area including the Comstock had separated from Utah Territory and pilfered the name "Nevada," making it necessary to add the clarification. "I've just come from the post office. I had a letter from my old friend Tyson Stone, begging me to visit as soon as possible." She opened her carpetbag, removed her mail, and put it on the desk. "Here. You can read it if you'd like."

George picked up the letter and perused it. According to its contents, Ty was worried about his sister, Susannah, who was gravely ill with pneumonia. He implored Melanie to come to his home immediately and stay for as long as she could. Melanie's presence would cheer Susannah up, he said, while her skill with Chinese herbs would hasten the girl's recovery. In a burst of creativity, Melanie had even added a heartrending bit at the end about how much Ty missed his late mother in difficult times like these, and about how hard it was to be the sole guardian of a sixteen-year-old female. He desperately needed the gentle touch of someone like his dear friend Melanie, he'd allegedly written.

Frowning, George put the letter aside. Melanie was perched on his desk by then, attempting to avoid the perils of his lap. "Our wedding is only a month away," he said. "You don't have time to run off to the mountains. You have too much to do in town."

Mere minutes ago, he'd labeled her a lady of frivolous leisure, but she tactfully refrained from saying so. "Not really, George. Almost everything is arranged by now. But if it will reassure you, I won't stay more than two weeks."

He shook his head. "I still don't like it. Stone is a bachelor. It isn't proper."

"But his little sister is there."

"Yes. Half-delirious with pneumonia. She's hardly a suitable chaperone."

"There's nothing romantic between Tyson and me," she pointed out. "We're simply old friends. Like a brother and sister."

"Then prove I have nothing to worry about." He stood, putting his hands on her waist. "I missed making love to you last night. I woke up aching for you. Now that you're here, the pain is worse than ever. If you want me to let you visit your friend, you'll have to give me some reassurance."

He bent his head to kiss her on the mouth, but she turned away, so that his lips landed on her cheek instead. "I was at your bedside for a whole hour last night, George Bonner, ready to kiss you for as long as you liked. It's not my fault that you were in no condition to take advantage of it."

He laughed softly and cupped her breast. "Is that why you're so out of sorts this morning? Because I had the bad form to become ill and disappoint you?" He stepped forward. "I suppose Colonel Whitefield bored you senseless on the ride home. That you mean to make me pay for *that*, too."

She wiggled backward on the desk, trying to forestall any closer contact. "It would serve you right if I deprived you until the wedding. The old coot went on and on, blathering about horses and farming. I was lucky to stay awake."

"But he's a Southerner of the old school, so it's only to be expected." George tucked his finger under her chin, then continued, "You may find him tedious, but he's entirely harmless. You're my future wife. I expect you to be polite to my clients and friends. I trust you managed an enthusiastic show of interest."

Melanie was about to suggest that he skip the

unnecessary lectures when she realized there
might be information to be gained by holding her
tongue. "Of course I did, George. I hope the same
is true of him—that he'll have the manners to send
you a note asking how you feel. After all, you
wouldn't have taken sick last night if he hadn't
kept filling your wineglass."

"It was the waiter who did that, not the colonel," George said with a laugh, "and it was likelier
flu than too much wine. In any event, Whitefield's
manners are flawless. A letter arrived first thing
this morning."

Alex didn't miss a trick, Melanie thought, and
leaned forward a little. "Did it?" She fiddled with
George's cravat, adjusting it in an affectionate and
wifely way. "What did it say?"

"Nothing important. Just that he hoped I was
better, and that he's leaving town for a week or
two to attend to some business down to the south.
He wants to take us to dinner when he returns."
George took her hands and pulled them toward
his neck, but she stiffened and tugged them away.
"So the idea of seeing him again makes you cross,
does it? Well, my dear, if you kiss me sweetly
enough, perhaps you can convince me to let you
beg off."

He slid his hands under her buttocks, pulling
her to the edge of the desk with a quick, hard insistence that brooked no resistance. Bending his
knees to fit her to his groin, he rubbed himself
gently against her softness and kissed her throat
and neck. She was no stranger to the feel of his
aroused manhood, but never like this—never
when she was so exposed and helpless. She stiffened even more and tried to close her legs.

"Oh, no, you don't." Openly amused, he grasped
her thighs to keep them apart. "Kiss me, Melanie.
Press yourself close to me. Come, darling, open

yourself up to me." His tone was coaxing, even pleading. "I'm going to be your husband soon, remember? You should want to give me whatever I ask."

But she didn't. For the first time since she'd accepted his proposal, she didn't even want him to touch her. The thought of it made her queasy. But the change was within her, not him, so she could hardly blame him for being confused. She was confused herself. She had no idea why she had turned so cold.

"Now who's in a hurry? Can't we talk awhile first?" She grasped at the first unpleasant subject that came to mind, hoping it would cool him off. "Hackett mentioned you let Mullins go. I was sorry to hear it. I always liked him. What happened?"

"Hackett should learn to keep his mouth shut." George nibbled her lips and pressed her close again. "It was unpleasant. Let's leave it at that."

"Tell me, George," she said a little desperately. "I'm curious."

"He was stolen away," he mumbled. "The Vanderbroecks offered him a fortune." He sought her mouth, but she turned her face away. "Damn it, Melanie, let me kiss you."

"But he's a genius with horses. Surely you could have matched—"

"No more questions. No more talk." He began thrusting himself against her. She went rigid with shock—he'd never been so wild before—but he didn't seem to notice. "You're torturing me. Denying me to make me desperate for you. And I am. I'm not made of stone. I can't stand it anymore." He worked at her mouth and rode her faster and harder. "I need to finish," he panted. "Please, Melanie, kiss me. Move your hips. You're got to help me finish."

But he didn't need her help at all. Seconds later he buried his face in her neck and jerked violently, again and again and again. Then he turned on his heel and walked away, stopping in front of the draped window and standing in stiff-necked silence. Thanks to Ah Lan, Melanie understood what had happened. Desire had made him weak. Frenzied. Mindless. He had spilled his seed.

Shaking a little, she slid off the desk and packed her bag. She didn't blame him for being angry and humiliated. She had sensed more than once that he was embarrassed by the strength of his own passions, and her rejection couldn't have helped. It had to be galling to a man to lose control of himself so completely—to plead and beg when a woman was as cold as ice.

Half a minute went by. He didn't move. "I guess I'll be going now," she finally murmured. "I'll write to you from Nevada City."

"No." He turned abruptly. "You're not going anywhere, Melanie. You're my future wife, and I won't have you living with another man."

She felt guilty enough not to object too strongly. "Be reasonable, George. I'm not going there to live with Ty, just to visit him and care for his sister. I'll be back before you know it."

"Don't tell me to be reasonable," he replied curtly. "If you're going to be my wife, you'll have to abide by my wishes. I expect you to stay home."

"Even though Ty is just a friend?"

"Don't be naive. He's dying to be more. He can find someone else to play nursemaid if he really wants to. If he insists on you, there's only one reason."

She prayed for patience and tried again. "But I want to go, and I promise I'll be perfectly safe. Regardless of what you think, they're old and dear friends, and they happen to need me. Can't you understand that?"

"What I understand is this," he bit out. "You don't care what I want and you don't have the sense to know what's best for you. If your father were here, he would put a stop to this nonsense. Since he's not, I will. You're to go straight home and stay there until I pick you up for dinner."

That did it. Her eyes narrowed and her chin went up. "I'm not a child, so please don't speak to me as if I am. I've always been independent and I don't intend to change. If making decisions for me and ordering me to obey them is your idea of marriage, then perhaps we should forget the whole thing."

His jaw clenched in apparent fury, but he shook his head after a couple of seconds and sighed deeply. "Damn it, Melanie, you know it's not. I've never interfered with what you do, but I have the right to hate the idea of your going away. I love you, so don't ask me not to be jealous of Tyson Stone. Don't tell me not to worry about your health and safety. And don't expect me not to miss you dreadfully."

"Then come with me." But she knew he wouldn't go. His law practice came first, and he had court dates to keep.

"I wish I could, but I'm too busy." He stepped closer and put his arms around her. "I still don't like it, but if it's really so important to you, you have my blessing. Promise me you'll be careful during the trip—"

"Of course I will."

"—and that you'll lock your door when you retire each night."

"It's not necessary, but if it will ease your mind, then I promise."

"Good." He brushed his lips across her mouth.

"Off you go, then. Write to me as soon as you get there. I want to know your plans."

Melanie agreed and left before he could change his mind. As she reached the stairs, it occurred to her that he hadn't offered to come to the wharf to see her off, even though it was only a few blocks from his office. Deep down, he was probably still annoyed with her. That should have bothered her, but it didn't. She dismissed him from her mind.

George walked to the window and parted the drapes, watching the street until Melanie had left the building. Then, unable to stop himself, he picked up a heavy brass ashtray and hurled it viciously to the floor. All women were trouble, but Melanie Wyatt was the devil's own sorceress, a wanton little witch who had beguiled him with her wiles and turned him into an impotent puppet.

He cursed his own passions. For years, it had been enough to spill his own seed when the urges overcame him. He'd managed without a female very well. He'd never even been tempted to buy one.

And then he had met *her*, and she had addicted him to her taste and touch, and his member had done the rest. Made him desperate to possess her completely. Led him to the altar before he'd had the sense to see her clearly.

It betrayed him repeatedly now, hardening and throbbing insanely whenever she came close enough to give him pleasure. He turned into a rutting animal, a lust-crazed beast. And now she was deliberately withholding her favors, torturing him even more. She'd made him so desperate for release that he had totally lost control, moaning and panting and pleading like a mewling child. It was appalling. Intolerable.

He dropped into a chair. If he despised himself for wanting her, he despised himself twice as much for needing her money. He wished he could have ended their engagement just now when she'd given him the chance to, but he'd had to hedge his bets. So he had played the spineless worm, backing down at once when she had challenged his rightful authority.

But circumstances could change. He pulled out the letter he'd received that morning and quickly reread it. It contained information about a new investment. He'd had a long run of bad luck with his speculative ventures, but this one was a sure thing. All he had to do was raise enough cash and he could corner the market in Asian spices and make a fortune.

It was a brilliant scheme, faster and even more lucrative than helping himself to a portion of Whitefield's Confederate supplies. If he could collect in advance from enough clients and sell enough of his belongings, he could recoup his previous losses. And then he would finally be free.

Chapter 7

A lex was still out there. Melanie could feel the cold prickle of danger along her spine as surely as she could feel the rough wood of the sidewalk beneath her feet. She looked around as she made her way down Washington Street, but as usual, failed to see him. While logic insisted he wouldn't hurt her, her instincts said otherwise. Unable to help herself, she increased her pace to a panicky trot.

She was breathing hard by the time she reached the post office. The scene there couldn't have been more normal—people chatting, bustling to and fro, and looking at their mail. She felt for her gun, rummaging in the deep pocket of her old black coat, relaxing when her hand closed around the familiar wooden handle. Not for the first time, she reminded herself that she could defend herself better than most men could.

She hopped aboard her gig and snapped the reins, and her horse bolted forward. Feeling safer now that she was riding, she grimaced in self-disgust. She was acting like a sniveling chicken, a spineless coward. Alex could try to bend her to his will and use her for his own ends, but he wouldn't succeed unless she allowed him to. No man would. Hadn't she learned that yet?

She turned down Sansome Street, thinking irritably that it wasn't so much being followed that unnerved her as her failure to spot her pursuer. It felt like a deadly game that she was losing badly, a dangerous match of hide-and-go-seek.

She frowned. Now that she thought about it, she'd made it awfully easy for him. She always took the most direct route she could, all but marking her trail with crumbs.

Smiling slightly, she turned west onto Clay Street. Two blocks later, she changed direction again, checking the street and the sidewalk as she drove. She altered her course every block or two after that, sure she would eventually spot him, cheered by the notion of besting him. She would give him a haughty nod, she decided, silently indicating that she'd been toying with him all this time, leading him on a wild-goose chase through the streets of San Francisco.

Once again, however, the victory went to him. Though she could feel him, the only men she recognized were a pair of finely dressed Celestials in a chauffeured carriage. She had seen them on her way to the post office, or two gentlemen very much like them, but since it was obvious that neither could be Alex, she took no notice of them as they followed her down Stockton Street. When she turned a few blocks later, they continued straight ahead.

She wasn't sure when she first suspected the mourner. It was only natural to ignore a female, after all, even one who had been behind her for quite some time. And then it struck her that the woman was a virtual giantess. Even more suspicious, she was swathed in drab black clothing from her veiled hat to her old-fashioned cloak, concealing her body and face.

Melanie turned down Market Street; the mourner followed. She entered Third Street; the mourner did the same. She doubled back on Mission; so did the mourner. She was sure now that it was Alex. Her pursuer had the shoulders of an ox, and, besides, who would take such a circuitous route without a questionable reason?

His disguise was a work of art. She was proud of herself for penetrating it—too proud, in fact, to settle for a simple nod when she could deceive him about her plans and throw him off the track. And if she postponed the coup de grâce for a few minutes in order to savor the sweetness of her victory, well, who could really blame her?

She stopped her gig and got out. Alex stopped as well, watching her as she strode forward. He was too heavily veiled for her to see his features, but his cloak rode up his arm as he reined in his prancing horse, giving her a clear view of the narrow strip of wrist above his glove. It was covered with dark hair.

"You appear to be lost," she called up to him. "Can I help you find your destination?"

He answered in a deep, husky voice that seemed to rumble out of his mouth. "I am sorry to trouble you, miss. It vas a mistake to follow you, I zink. Please, to forgive me."

His accent, a bold creation of indeterminate European inspiration, was so unusual that Melanie had to bite her lip to keep from laughing. "It's no trouble at all, si—I mean, madam. Where were you trying to go?"

"Ze cemetery. Alone Mountain, I zink it is called. My dear brother—"

"*Lone* Mountain," Melanie corrected. "It's out Bush Street."

"Boosh Street? I do not know of it. Ve vill come to it soon?"

"Actually, we passed it quite some time ago."

"Did ve? Again, please to forgive me. It was ze clothes zat you vear . . . Like mourning, I zink. I decide zat you go zere, too, but maybe I vas vrong. Still, you have had a loss recently, yes?"

He was quick with a likely story, she had to give him that. "No. Fortunately for me, I haven't. Bush Street is several blocks north of Market Street." She pointed. "The one up there. You were about to say something about your brother, I believe?"

He nodded. "Yes. My poor, dear Fritz. He vas a saint, miss, a saint."

"*Vas?*" She cocked up her eyebrow. "Is he dead, then?"

"Yes. Vith ze anchels, for sure. Zat is vy I go to ze cemetery. If you vould direct me—"

"But you really must tell me about your brother first. I wonder, was he as large an individual as you are?"

"Oh, yes, even larcher. Strong like a bear. He mined ze gold und sent it to ze family, und zen, ven ze rush vas over, he vorked on ze ships. Such a hard life he had. Und now . . ." He shuddered with apparent grief, then sniffled loudly. "Gone forever. A fever of ze brain."

Melanie resisted the urge to congratulate Alex on his performance. "Such a pity. Still, it happens to the best of us in the end. It's nothing to whine and moan about. You really must get a grip on yourself."

He stiffened. "I beg your pardon, miss?"

"Surely you've read the Bible, madam. You know. Ashes to ashes and dust to dust. Besides, given Fritz's illness, he would have been demented if he'd lived, so it's all for the best." She smiled encouragingly. "Don't you agree?"

"Ach. You Americans. No sentiment." He shook his head in seeming dismay. "As for me, I have made a very long trip to say goodbye und must be on my vay. Ven I come to zis Boosh Street—"

"Indeed you have. From where, I wonder? Hong Kong, perhaps? Or Macao?"

He hesitated, then answered uncertainly, "No. I do not know zose places. I live in Chicago. My people are from Bavaria."

"Ah, yes, Bavaria. It's not much of a country, is it? Small, poor, and exceedingly dull. Even lower than England, in fact, and the English are the scum of the earth. Don't you think so?"

His tone went from uncertain to chilly. "I vould not know, miss. I have never been zere. I am sorry to have taken up your time. I vill leave you now."

"But you mustn't go yet. We've only just met." Melanie hopped into his gig before he could drive away. "I do hate conversing with someone I can't see, don't you? Really, it's a terrible impediment to communication."

As she raised her hand, he recoiled in apparent alarm and grasped the bottom of his veil. She attacked from the top, grabbing his boater hat and sweeping it off his head, then tossing it onto the seat. He'd made himself into a gloriously ugly woman, complete with bushy brows, a hawklike nose, a protruding jaw, and a mottled scalp that peeked through his thinning black hair.

He stared at her, visibly stunned. She stared back in slowly dawning horror. Her hand rose up, seemingly of its own accord, and touched his nose. It didn't feel like putty. Blanching, she firmly tweaked it. There was no question about it. It was real.

Her nose, she thought. It really was a woman. Dear God.

Her cheeks turned scarlet. "I-I'm so sorry. I

don't know how to apologize. I thought you were someone else, but obviously you're not, are you? That is, you're not who I assumed you were."

The woman edged away from her, looking at her as if she were a total lunatic. "I see. I have to go now—"

"But we were playing a sort of game, and he kept disguising himself—brilliant disguises, really—and you were all covered up, so naturally I assumed he was you. I mean, I assumed you were he. But I was wrong. And I said such horrible things to you, too. Believe me, I'm sorrier than I can say. I hope you'll forgive me."

"Yes. Of course." The woman put her hat back on. "It is getting late. I really must be going."

Melanie gave it up. There was no recovering from such a staggering social disaster. "When you get to Bush Street, go that way," she said with a sigh, and pointed toward the west. "The cemetery is fairly far—about thirty blocks." She jumped from the gig and trudged away. She'd had enough of trying to outwit Alex McClure, at least for one morning.

Grinning from ear to ear, Alex clutched his belly and tried desperately not to laugh. He was lounging behind a hedge, dressed as a prosperous but slightly out-of-fashion older gentleman, but the disguise hadn't really been necessary. It was easy to avoid detection in a busy city street. All you had to do was scoot from vehicle to vehicle and doorway to doorway and your quarry hadn't a prayer of spotting you.

He had excellent hearing, so he'd caught almost every word of Melanie's conversation with the Bavarian mourner and enjoyed the tangle immensely. Indeed, with the exception of having a gun held to his manhood, there was little he *hadn't* enjoyed in his dealings with Melanie Wyatt. Her opposition had turned a routine if diverting adventure into the most fun he'd had in years.

She was clever, dangerous, and beautiful, and, most exciting of all, determined to resist him. After last night, he knew that she was passionate by nature and strongly attracted to him. When a woman like that surrendered, as Melanie inevitably would, her previous recalcitrance made the fires burn all the hotter.

Not that he still expected her to drop into his lap, of course. He'd learned better over the past few days. She was devoted to her cause, so she would fight him as hard as she could. She was an experienced seductress, so a routine session in bed wouldn't turn her head. If he wanted her to help him destroy the Chinese theft ring, he would have to overwhelm her with fleshly delights. Provide her with unprecedented physical excitement. He might even have to induce her to fall in love with him. It was a formidable challenge, but one he relished.

When it was over, he knew, she would thank him for opening her eyes. She would come to understand that her activities were both criminal and harmful to the best interests of China, and she would realize that her fiancé was as wrong for her as a man could be. True, he had looks, wealth, and position, but he was also conventional, self-important, and patronizing. He didn't appreciate her wit and intelligence and didn't deserve her passion and spirit. A marriage between them would be a disaster.

She climbed into her gig and spurred her horse forward, and Alex straightened and followed. If she believed herself to be in love with the fellow, he mused, she was wrong. A woman who loved a man didn't walk in to see him, as Melanie had that morning, with such a grim expression on her face, or emerge from the encounter looking relieved to have it behind her. In the end, then, Bonner would be irrelevant. If Alex handled her right, she would forget all about him.

She continued down Mission Street, and he stealthily tailed her. She drove to Second Street and turned right, then took Folsom to Hawthorne Street. She never looked back, not once, so his prudence wasn't necessary. After she turned into her driveway, he settled himself behind a tree across the street to wait for her next move.

Mrs. Dibble was knitting in her favorite rocking chair when Melanie entered the house. She hurried to the housekeeper's side, holding out Ty's alleged letter. "I've had some terrible news," she said in a tear-choked voice. "Remember the Stones? Our dear, dear friends in Nevada? Poor little Sukey is at death's door with pneumonia, Mrs. Dibble. Her older brother is begging me to come and help. I plan to go there as soon as possible with my most potent curative herbs. I know I can save her life if only God will give me the chance to."

Mrs. Dibble took the letter, reading it with the pursed lips and narrowed eyes of the confirmed skeptic. That was only to be expected. Time and again, Melanie had spun tales worthy of Dickens and sworn to them without compunction, on the Bible or even her mother's memory if the mission was important enough. Everyone knew it didn't count if you crossed your fingers behind your back. Afterward, though, she'd invariably felt compelled to confess. She was cursed with an honest nature.

Mrs. Dibble handed the letter back and emitted a dubious snort. "Humph. This paper looks awfully familiar, miss. Seems to me that you have some just like it in your room."

"Uh, yes. That I do." The blasted woman had the eyes of a hawk and the memory of an elephant. "Isn't it lovely? It's from Mr. Bancroft's shop. I liked it so much that I sent some to Ty last Christmas." Her eyes filled up and a tear or two escaped. "And now, that he should use it to deliver awful news like this . . . Oh, Mrs. Dibble—why Sukey? She's such a sweet, gentle girl."

"It's the will of the Lord. It's not our place to question it." The housekeeper fixed her with a searching stare, then abruptly softened. "Come now, child, dry up your tears. We all have our troubles. It's the human condition."

Melanie pulled a handkerchief out of her carpetbag and dabbed at her eyes. "Yes. I suppose you're right."

"Of course I am." Mrs. Dibble sighed deeply. "I'm not a well woman, but if the girl is at death's door, then it's our Christian duty to help her. If we hurry, we can catch the four o'clock steamer. I'd best get to work."

Our, Melanie repeated silently. *We*. Damn. It was a wrinkle she hadn't anticipated. "It's kind of you to offer to join me, but it's really not necessary. I've made the trip before, if you'll recall, and nothing untoward has ever happened."

The housekeeper paid her no attention. "Sorting and ironing our clothes, packing, closing up the house . . . Lord, but I've a lot to do."

Inspiration struck. "You're always telling me how lucky I am to be marrying Mr. Bonner, and he approved of the trip, so you see, you've got nothing to worry about."

"He did, did he? And when, might I ask, did you find the time to speak to him?"

"I went straight from the post office to consult with him."

"And he didn't object? He didn't try to stop you?"

"I swear he didn't. He knows what old and dear friends the Stones are. He would have accompanied me if he weren't so busy, but I promised to write him each day with my news. What with the wedding, we decided I shouldn't be gone for too long. Two weeks, perhaps." Mrs. Dibble was greatly attached to her own bed, which was double-sized in order to accommodate her propensity to toss and turn. "Three at the most."

"Three weeks?" she repeated in dismay. Duty, however, won out. "Well, I've coped with greater hardships than that. Mr. Bonner is much too permissive, if you ask me. Besotted by love. The fact is, you have a talent for getting into trouble. Your father would want me to keep an eye on you."

A change of tactics was obviously called for. Melanie managed a sheepish smile. "Very well then, no more arguments. I have a confession to make. I only put you off because I felt guilty about imposing. Actually, I'm relieved that you're coming. You'll be a great help to me in the sickroom. With the cleaning up, I mean."

Mrs. Dibble wrinkled her nose. Whenever possible, she avoided both bodily fluids and the babies and invalids so likely to spew them forth. "What cleaning up?"

"To cure an illness like pneumonia, we have to drive out the dangerous humors with expectorants, enemas, and emetics, and replace them with curative tonics to prevent dehydration. With luck, fetid humors pour out of the body continually. From every possible opening, often with no warning. The poor patient can't help it." Melanie paused. "Really, this is going to work out splendidly. With two of us taking turns at Sukey's bedside, cleaning things up, it won't be bad at all. I admit I was concerned about how you would cope with the poor accommodations, but as you yourself said, you've experienced far worse."

"Poor accommodations?" Mrs. Dibble repeated uneasily. "What do you mean?"

"There are no beds. No extra ones, that is. Ty has boarders now, so both spare bedrooms are taken."

The housekeeper's enthusiasm for the expedition was diminishing rapidly. "Then what will we sleep on?"

"The sofa in the parlor and the hammock on the porch. The hammock is rather narrow, but I expect you would still prefer it. You know how uncomfortable a house can be when the temperatures reach the nineties, and it will be cooler outside than in. You'll sleep more soundly."

"The nineties? I didn't realize it was that hot in the mountains."

"We'll be in the foothills, not the mountains, but don't worry. It's a dry heat, so it's not too bad. Of course, I do remember a stagecoach ride where it soared into the hundreds and two of the passengers vomited on the floor, but that was mostly the driver's fault. He was a demon with those horses. I thought he was going to pitch us over a cliff." Melanie frowned thoughtfully. "You know, Mrs. Dibble, my father won't like the idea of returning to an empty house. We should get Janine to come and stay."

"I don't know." The housekeeper was beginning to look dazed. "The way she prattles on . . . I try to keep them apart, but even so, he's taken to locking himself in his study on the days she comes to clean. Have you noticed?"

"Well, yes, but at least she's a good worker. She

would do his laundry, pick up after him, and fix him any meals he wants to take at home."

"And drive him mad with her chatter. And I would get the blame, you can count on that. A body can't win. He expects me to watch you, but he'll grumble about being abandoned." Mrs. Dibble scowled at her knitting. "You can't find decent help in this city."

"Umm. The good ones all get married." Melanie waited a few seconds, then snapped her fingers. "I have it. He can stay in a hotel."

"But he hates them, miss. With all the traveling he does, he gets sick of them. He's always saying so."

"That's true." Melanie pretended to mull things over. "Maybe I could share you. Papa's due back on Thursday, so you could stay in Nevada until that morning. The worst of the purging should be over by then, so I won't have the constant mopping up. By the way, how are you at administering medicine? It goes in at both ends, you know."

Mrs. Dibble turned a subtle shade of green. "Not very good, I'm afraid. I won't be much help to you there. In fact, I'm thinking that it hardly pays me to go. All that hard travel for such a short visit ..."

"But any help is better than none. The trip won't be so bad. The steamer is more stable and less noisy than it used to be, and the stagecoach ... We'll have the usual dust and jostling, I expect, but nothing truly uncomfortable."

"Not for you, maybe. You're young and healthy with a good strong back. But I have my delicate stomach and weak spine to consider." She shook her head. "I don't know, miss. If I fell ill before I even got there—"

"Oh, dear. You're absolutely right. You can't risk it, Mrs. Dibble. It was selfish of me to even ask you." Melanie leaned closer, adding in a tone of utmost confidence, "If I drag you along and cause you to become sick, Papa will be angry with both of us. I think I should write him a letter. I'm good with words. I could explain everything and head off his objections in advance. That way, neither of us will get into trouble."

Mrs. Dibble allowed herself to be persuaded, and Melanie went upstairs to pack, returning some twenty minute later with enough summer garments for a month. She asked the housekeeper to mend them, press them, and put them into a trunk, then helped her carry everything into the sewing room. The task would occupy her for hours.

Back upstairs, she wrote Thomas a letter and left it on his pillow, then finished packing, tucking her medical kit into her valise along with her makeup box, her toiletries, and various sundries. Next, she wrote a note to Mrs. Dibble on the most common paper she owned, to be delivered by one of Shen Wai's servants later that day. Finally, she prepared an account of the week's activities for Shen Wai and slipped it into an envelope along with tracings of the two maps. She planned to search for the gold at once, she told Wai, and felt he should do the same. That way, with luck, one of them would find the cache before Alex McClure did. She slipped the tiger into her valise, placed the bag on her bed, and went back down to the sewing room.

After chatting with Mrs. Dibble for several minutes, she remarked that she had some last-minute errands to run and made her way to the carriage house. Her purpose wasn't to collect the gig, but to fetch young Artie, who was almost exactly her size. He was always game for adventure, so he didn't utter a peep of protest when she asked him to exchange clothing. She fitted them both with wigs afterward, then applied the proper makeup. By the time they left the house, each could pass perfectly for the other, at least from a distance.

They climbed into the gig. Melanie, the apparent groom, did the driving, while Artie, playing the lady, sat by her side. As usual, it wasn't long before she sensed Alex following her, but this time, it was exactly what she wanted. She drove to the bank and the telegraph office, waiting in the gig while Artie conducted her business. Her next stop was a clothier's, where she left Artie to browse. She took herself to a candy shop in the meantime, then a stationer's. She could have crowed with glee when she realized that Alex had remained at the clothier's. She had done it. She had fooled him into watching the wrong person.

She picked Artie up about half an hour later. Their final stop was the Mercantile Library on Montgomery Street. As usual, playing the servant, she helped him out of the carriage. "Now remember, you're to go inside and remain for a full hour. You can look through magazines to pass the time. When you come out, you'll find the gig waiting in front. Drive it straight home and change into your usual clothes. You mustn't say a word about our activities to Mrs. Dibble, do you understand that?"

"Sure, Miss Wyatt." He looked troubled. "All the same, I don't like it a bit. You're up to something dangerous again, aren't you?"

"On the contrary, Artie. Thanks to your help, I'll be completely safe."

"But your pop would kill me if he found out. If you would tell me what you plan to do, I could—"

"No, Artie. If you knew, it could get you into a great deal of trouble. That's the whole point. The less I tell you, the safer we'll be. But if a stranger should stop you and question you, I want you to tell him everything we've done. No lies or evasions, all right?" Alex wouldn't harm the boy. He was astute enough to know when he was hearing the truth and too measured by nature to indulge in pointless violence.

"Then you expect someone to question me?" Artie persisted. "Who? The man you're trying to fool by pretending you're me? Why? What does he want from you?"

"Never mind that. Just take yourself into the library and stay there. You'll find some gold coins under the seat when you get back in the gig."

The bribe did the trick. Artie strolled into the library as gracefully as a debutante, and Melanie drove away. Shen Wai's house was near Dupont Street, seven blocks away.

She could have pounded the seat in frustration when the hairs on the back of her neck promptly prickled. She'd been so clever, so careful. She'd fooled him so completely. How could he possibly have realized? He wasn't human, damn him, but the demon spawn of a seer and a chameleon.

She was about to return home to devise another plan when she remembered that Shen Wai had a secret exit from his house, a tunnel that began in his cellar, crossed beneath the street behind the building, and emerged into a basement-level laundry owned by this cousin, Shen Li. She could enter Wai's house through the laundry and exit through his side door. Alex would wait in the street in front of the laundry and miss her completely.

Some ten minutes later she emerged from Wai's cellar into his kitchen and began calling to his majordomo, Fou Ning. Ning knew very little English, so she spoke in Chinese. "Ning, it's Mi-Lan." She began walking through the house. "Ning, are you home? Hello? Ning? It's Mi-Lan Wyatt. Where are you, Ning? I have to speak to you."

As she entered the front hallway, he trotted down the stairs, saw her, and did a comical doubletake. "A fine disguise, Miss Wyatt. One of your best efforts, I think. May I give you a cup of tea?"

"Thank you, but I don't have time. I leave for Sacramento at four." She removed an envelope from her pocket. "Please give this to Shen Wai the moment he comes home. It will explain everything."

She hadn't bothered to seal the envelope. Not a thing went on in this house or in Wai's life that Ning didn't know about, but Wai didn't mind at all. Ning was loyal to a fault, and thanks to his inquisitive nature and remarkable memory, a great asset to their cause. He was able to repeat exactly the gossip he continually heard and describe with perfect accuracy the intriguing events he so often witnessed.

She grinned at him. "You can read it after I leave." She would have written it in English if she'd wanted it kept a secret. Wai wasn't as fluent in reading the language as in speaking it, but he could cope when he needed to. "Then put it somewhere safe, all right? It's very important."

"Don't worry, Miss Wyatt. I will." Ning took the envelope. "So you're off on another adventure, eh? Can I be of service in any way?"

"Yes, in several ways. My gig is parked in front of Shen Li's laundry. Will you ask one of the servants to drive it to the Mercantile Library and leave it out front? He should depart in, oh, about thirty minutes."

Ning nodded. "I'll see to it. What else can I do?"

"I'll need you to send someone to my house, pick up a trunk and a valise from Mrs. Dibble, and bring them to the Sacramento steamer. I'll wait outside the ticket booth." She removed a second envelope from her pocket and handed it to Ning. "He should give her this letter. She won't be pleased that I've gone directly to the boat, but she'll do as I've instructed."

"Also in thirty minutes, miss?"

"No. As soon as possible. Actually, one man could take my gig and do both."

Ning pulled a bell cord and a servant quickly appeared. As Ning rattled off instructions, it struck Melanie that he had been in the Mother Lode for three or four years and might be able to assist her in yet another way.

After he had dismissed the servant, she asked him to take out the maps she'd traced and study them for a minute. "Does anything look familiar? The roads or the terrain?"

He reluctantly shook his head. "I'm afraid not. I'm sorry I can't be of more help to you."

Melanie put her hand on his shoulder and smiled. "But you've been of enormous help already, my friend. I'll let myself out the side door. And thank you for everything."

She hugged the wall of the house when she first got outside, but this time no one was watching. She was sure of it. Still, she walked more rapidly than usual once she'd reached the street. She was anxious to reach the safety of the steamer. The four o'clock departure couldn't come quickly enough.

Fou Ning hadn't read more than half of Mi-Lan's letter before he was scowling with disapproval. The lady was clever and brave, but careless with her own life. Emergency or not, she shouldn't have undertaken such a dangerous mission. He wanted to haul her from the boat, drag her back to the house, and lock her in the cellar until Shen Wai returned, but he couldn't. She was a wealthy white woman, or appeared to be, while he was only a Chinese servant. One scream—and she *would* scream, she was as stubborn as a mule when it came to her causes—and the authorities would be all over him like fleas on a mongrel dog. They would beat him up, throw him in jail, and forget he even existed.

By the time he'd finished reading, the disapproval had turned to naked fear. Like his master, he loved Mi-Lan dearly, and she was in terrible peril. He'd heard rumors recently that one of the triads might have learned about the buried gold and sent men from China to retrieve it, but that was mere gossip, unsubstantiated whispers. This Alex McClure, on the other hand, was very real. He sounded extremely dangerous. A female was no match for him.

Feeling sick, Ning studied the two maps, trying to recognize something—anything—that would help him determine the locale. Then he could go to the steamer and tell Mi-Lan what he knew. Warn her about the triad, too. But he drew a blank.

Someone pounded on the door. Sighing, he returned the maps and the letter to their envelope and walked over to the sideboard. But before he could activate the mechanism that exposed the secret compartment beneath the middle drawer, the door was forced open and two men barreled through. Both were Celestials, a servant and his master judging by their dress, and both were holding pistols. He quickly shoved the letter under his tunic.

"Mi-Lan Wyatt!" the master barked. "Where is she?"

One glance at the man and Ning knew he belonged to a triad. Such men had a certain look about them, a ruthless, swaggering air that warned people to do as they demanded. "Who?" he asked, looking puzzled.

The master nodded at the servant, who struck Ning viciously across the cheek with his closed fist. His head snapped back and he grimaced in pain, but he didn't speak.

"Mi-Lan Wyatt," the master repeated. "We're watching her, not that it's any of your concern. We know your master raised her. Someone entered the laundry across the street, then disappeared. The proprietor admitted there was an underground passageway to—" He noticed the envelope protruding from Ning's tunic. It had slipped when the servant struck him. "Give me that."

There was no use trying to withhold it. These men would only kill him and take it anyway. Ning held it out.

The master removed its contents, then quickly read the letter. "I was right," he said to his servant. "Mi-Lan was disguised as the male. The female was actually her groom." He chuckled. "I can't wait to see Chung's face when he learns he was watching the wrong one. He was so certain *he* was right."

He glanced at the maps, then glared ferociously at Ning. "You! These diagrams! What place do they lead to?"

The rumor was obviously true, Ning thought. This man and his compatriot Chung had been sent from China by their triad to locate the buried gold. "As the letter mentions, to a cache of gold. I don't know where it is. Like Mi-Lan, I can't interpret the maps."

"Try harder. Perhaps the answer will come to you." The master snapped his fingers, and the servant grabbed Ning from behind and pinioned him.

Ning didn't struggle. It was foolhardy to challenge these men. Submission was the only path to survival.

The master punched him brutally in the stomach. He doubled over, gasping and coughing. "I swear to you, I don't know what they mean. I don't know where the gold is."

"I don't have any patience for liars. Mi-Lan came here to consult with you. You must have helped her." The next blow was a kick in his groin. He fell writhing and retching to the floor. "Talk, coolie! Now!"

Ning remained silent. Both men kicked him savagely. He curled into a tight ball and buried his head in his arms in a desperate effort to protect it. The master yelled at him about the diagrams, demanding to know where they led, but he couldn't tell them what he didn't know. And even if he had, he wouldn't have said a word.

The last thing he felt was the toe of a boot slamming into his right temple.

Chapter 8

Alex was beginning to wonder if he'd been duped. In the forty minutes he'd been standing in the Mercantile Library, watching Melanie from the far right, her behavior had grown increasingly odd. She had helped herself to a sheaf of magazines, then buried her nose in one after another, never once looking around the room. Where was her usual vigilance? She had turned the pages so quickly that he doubted she'd done more than look at the illustrations and glance at the headlines. Had nothing caught her interest in all those articles? And then there was the way she kept tapping her foot. It wasn't like her to fidget.

He emerged from his position behind a pillar and slowly approached the table. Her hands were covered by gloves, her face was blocked by her hat, and her cloak was draped casually around her shoulders, so the closer view was of little help. If he wanted to verify her identity, he would have to talk to her.

He walked to her side. He was still disguised as an older gentleman, but he doubted she would be fooled for very long. Not from so close a distance.

He cleared his throat to get her attention. "Excuse me, miss. I wondered if you were finished with that magazine."

She didn't ask which one, but gathered them all up. "Yes. You can have them." She held them out, avoiding his eyes.

Alex took them. It hadn't been Melanie's voice, but he bent down for a better look at her face to confirm his initial impression. She turned away, but not quite quickly enough. Scowling, he straightened. Unless he missed his guess, he'd been watching a boy all this time.

He considered dragging the lad outside and grilling him, then decided against it. The boy would probably howl like a banshee. It would appear that he was assaulting a woman. He didn't want a scene, much less a run-in with the local authorities.

"I only wanted *Hutching's*, miss," he murmured. "You can keep the others." He placed them on the table, then nodded politely. "Have a pleasant afternoon."

He tossed the issue of *Hutching's* on a chair as he strode from the room. Melanie had probably consulted with her cronies and left the city by now, but if he was lucky, he would be able to track her down. She was several moves ahead of him, though, so he had no time to waste. Fortunately, an omnibus came along just as he started down Montgomery Street. A short time later, he was standing in front of the Wyatts' door.

The woman who answered his knock was the knitter he had glimpsed the night before, but she was younger than he'd realized, probably about fifty, and unexpectedly handsome. She opened the door a fraction and poked her head outside. Her stern expression made her look as formidable as Mount Diablo.

"Yes?" she asked crisply.

He simply gazed at her, apparently dumbstruck.

"Yes?" she repeated impatiently. "Did you want something, sir?"

"I—I'm sorry," he stammered. "Please—I hope you'll forgive me for staring. It's just that you're the image of my dear late wife. And when I saw you, it—it startled me. I still miss her very much."

She opened the door halfway. He smiled shyly. She flushed a little. Looking in the mirror that morning, he'd told himself he made an attractive older gentleman. The lady obviously agreed.

"I understand," she said. "My own dear husband passed away six years ago, and I pine for him whenever I see someone who strongly resembles him. Is your loss very recent?"

He gazed at her for several seconds more, then lowered his eyes in apparent embarrassment. "A year and two months. Really, I must apologize again. I don't usually go on this way."

"Don't be silly. It's perfectly natural. Were you looking for Mr. Wyatt?"

"For Miss Wyatt, actually." He looked up. "She's his daughter, I believe. I was told that she trades in Oriental curios. My favorite niece is getting married soon, and I wanted a special gift. Something unique. Do you think Miss Wyatt will be able to help me?"

"I'm sure that she will, but she's not at home at the moment. How soon is the wedding? A few days? A few weeks?"

"Next weekend. I could come back later, if you would tell me what time you expect her."

The woman looked sympathetic. "I'm terribly sorry, Mr., uh—"

"Seabury. Dr. Samuel Seabury." An Episcopal bishop of the last century. "Forgive me, ma'am. I should have introduced myself at once."

"And I'm Mrs. Dibble, Mr. Wyatt's housekeeper.

It's a pleasure to meet you, Doctor." She opened the door all the way. "I wish you had come by earlier. Miss Wyatt left a short while ago. She'll be gone for several weeks."

Alex's face fell. It wasn't entirely an act. His instincts told him it would be difficult to get additional information out of this woman.

"What a disappointment!" he said. "I so rarely get to San Francisco, you see. I've been visiting my cousin here, and he mentioned the other night that he'd bought something from Miss Wyatt for my niece. He said she had exceptionally good taste. I don't, to be honest. It's something of a family joke. I was hoping she could help me select something." He suddenly brightened. "If she can't, perhaps you can. Does she have prices on her merchandise? Or, if not, do you know what she charges?"

"I'm afraid I don't. She keeps it all in her head." Mrs. Dibble hesitated, then beckoned him inside. "Perhaps I have a solution. We could go upstairs and look at her collection. If we find something we like, we can set it aside. When Miss Wyatt returns, she can let you know the price. She can mail it to you as soon as she receives your payment. I'm sure your niece will forgive you if your gift is a little late."

"Your plan sounds perfect. You're extremely kind." Alex closed the door and directed a smitten stare at the lady. "My late wife was the same way. Thoughtful and kind. And, uh, very pretty, too. Like you."

She blinked at him, visibly flustered, and turned toward the stairs. "If you would come this way ..."

He couldn't afford to move too fast and scare her off. Touching her arm to get her attention, he mumbled, "I've annoyed you. I'm sorry. I've behaved like a bumbling fool."

"Of course you haven't, Dr. Seabury. You were caught unawares by the resemblance, that's all. Come along now."

He smiled in feigned relief and followed her upstairs. "Well, here we are," she said bracingly. "I'm sure we'll find something your niece will like."

As he inspected the merchandise, he told her that he treated patients in the State Lunatic Asylum in Stockton, painting a subtle picture of kindness and dedication. She warmed to him. He asked her opinion continually and kept murmuring how grateful he was. She warmed to him even more.

"I'm leaning toward this ivory dragon," he finally remarked. "What do you think?"

"That it's a beautiful little piece. As I mentioned before, the workmanship is impeccable." She picked it up. "Your family is wrong about your taste. It's excellent. I'll put this away for you."

"Thank you, Mrs. Dibble. I only hope I can afford Miss Wyatt's price. If I could just be sure—" He was ready to move in for the kill now. A light seemed to go on in his head. "It just occurred to me ... If we could conduct our business by telegraph, I could pay for the dragon before I leave and take it home with me. Could you tell me where she's gone? Is she visiting friends?"

The housekeeper considered the matter for several seconds, then replied, "I think it would be best if I sent the wire. That way, she'll know you're on the up-and-up. And I'll get a faster answer out of her than you would."

It wasn't what Alex had hoped to hear, but he still had an ace or two up his sleeve. "Wonderful. I don't know how to thank you." He lowered his eyes and fixed them on his feet. "I, uh, I believe I'll be visiting your city again soon. There's so much to do here." He finally looked at her, pausing as if he were afraid to go on. "I still have another two days here. I wonder—that is, I was thinking that it would add to my enjoyment immensely if, uh, if I had a knowledgeable guide."

"And I thought you were much too shy to ask such a thing!" She blushed and smiled. "I have a thought of my own, Dr. Seabury. Miss Wyatt is on the steamer to Sacramento. It leaves at four. Suppose I write her a letter describing the ivory dragon and asking the price? You could track her down on the boat and have her put her instructions in writing." She blushed even harder. "We could complete the transaction over dinner, if you would care to be my guest."

Pay dirt, Alex thought triumphantly, and beamed at her. "I would be delighted. It's been years since a beautiful single lady has offered to cook me a meal."

She walked to Melanie's desk, quickly scrawled a note, and held it out. "And now, I believe I have some shopping to do. Both of us had best be on our way, wouldn't you say?"

"Yes." He took her hand in both of his, held it for a moment, and then brushed an awkward kiss across the back. "I'll provide the champagne and the flowers." He removed the note from her fingers. "Until . . . six, shall we say, Mrs. Dibble?"

"Harriet," she replied.

Melanie was fast asleep in her stateroom on the *Crysopolis*, the newest and most luxurious sidewheeler in the California Steam Navigation Company's fleet, catching a much needed nap before sailing time. She awoke with a start, her fingers tensing convulsively around the knife she was clutching under her pillow. It was only a moment later, when her sixth sense assured her that Alex was nowhere about, that she relaxed and smiled.

The boat would depart in under an hour, and she would finally be safe.

Feeling refreshed and alert, she tossed aside her covers and stretched like a cat. Her trunk and valise were sitting in the middle of the floor, both of them still locked. She thought about stripping off her groom's clothing and putting on a dress, but decided against it. The boat held up to a thousand passengers, most of them male. Some would be drunkards, braggarts, or worse. It was silly to change when she could stay as she was and avoid the flirts and showoffs.

She left her room, locking the door behind her, and made her way to the starboard side of the top deck. The fog was rolling in, adding a damp chill to the air. She took a deep breath, savoring the dank feel of the breeze and the salty scent of the bay. As she'd told Mrs. Dibble, it was the last cool day she was likely to enjoy for weeks.

She leaned over the railing. From her vantage point near the stern, she could see the comings and goings along the entire length of the wharf. The steamer to Stockton was berthed directly behind the *Crysopolis*, and numerous masted vessels were anchored nearby. A colorful array of carriages, wagons, and gigs raced to and fro, some full of passengers, others laden with cargo. Their numbers grew steadily larger as sailing time approached, making Melanie wonder if they would be able to avoid hitting horsemen, pedestrians, and one another. Miraculously, they did.

Most of those approaching the ticket booth appeared to be business or professional men, but every sort imaginable took the steamers—adults and children; males and females; upper class and working class; Mexicans, Celestials, free Negroes, and even a group of Kanakas from the Sandwich Islands. By ten minutes to four, the wharf was swarming with last-minute arrivals impatient to get on board. A few of the more nervous sorts even tossed their valises on deck before hurrying to buy their tickets, so they could embark as quickly as possible.

It was a habit by now to watch for Alex, but Melanie didn't expect to see him. She was so confident she had eluded him that she planned to remain on deck after they sailed and watch the sights along the way, especially the islands in the bay and the incomparable Golden Gate.

Then, only minutes before four o'clock, the sense that he was somewhere close by struck her from out of nowhere, circling her throat like a garrote. She gulped for air and frantically searched the wharf, but it was hopeless. The chances of finding him in the tumult below her were almost nil.

There was no point leaving the boat. Even if she could make it down to the main deck in time, he would only spot her on the boarding bridge and follow her off. He must have questioned Artie and realized they had exchanged clothing. He had probably described her to everyone in the area after that, eventually finding people who had seen her and told him which way she had gone. The man was a human bloodhound.

She hurried back to her stateroom and locked herself inside. She would have to evade him in Sacramento, that was all. The wharf there was a madhouse when a steamer came in. Hundreds of passengers milled about while carters, porters, tradesmen, stagecoach drivers, and hotel clerks loudly solicited business. With a good enough disguise, she could lose herself in the throng and slip onto a coach for Nevada City before Alex had a clue she had even debarked.

She shuttered up her porthole. She was too

jumpy to be hungry, but she had missed lunch and knew that her appetite would eventually triumph over her nerves. She couldn't risk a trip to the dining cabin, though. She couldn't leave her stateroom at all. Feeling trapped, she removed some chocolates from a paper sack, a gift she had purchased for Sukey. Looking at the candy, she felt a wave of nausea roil through her stomach. Perhaps she wouldn't need them after all.

Alex finished his dessert, a slice of succulent apple pie, and contentedly sipped his coffee. He had enjoyed both his dinner and his companions, a pair of middle-aged sisters who were returning to the capital after visiting their elderly parents in San Francisco. Both had husbands, but that hadn't stopped them from flirting outrageously. Women in this state, whether married or single, collected male admirers like lepidopterists collected butterflies, but Alex—or rather, Dr. Seabury—didn't mind being a specimen. He had discovered years ago that mature women had a confidence and sauciness that younger females lacked.

Most younger females, he corrected silently. Not Melanie Wyatt. He told his companions he would see them later, at the concert in the main cabin, then went upstairs. Having strolled around the steamer for hours after he'd boarded and failed to run Melanie to ground, he was impatient to learn if Ned had been any more successful.

The young hackman had proven himself to be so quick-witted and reliable during their first evening together that Alex had assigned him to watch Melanie's house that night. He had taken Ned on this voyage for much the same reason, to spell him while he slept. But he had soon found more challenging services for his clever new assistant to perform, including trying to learn which stateroom

Melanie was in. His own disguises never deceived her for long, but she had glimpsed Ned only briefly the evening before and was unlikely to recognize him, especially after Alex had aged him a good twenty years.

The hackman was lounging on his berth when Alex entered their stateroom, still dressed in the smart steward's uniform Alex had borrowed, for a generous price, from one of the steamer's employees. "I had no luck at all," Alex said. "And you?"

"Let's put it this way," Ned replied. "I knocked on twenty or thirty doors and took orders for eleven meals. I should have started up here instead of down below, because she's just up the passageway, in 216. There are now ten starving souls on this steamer, wondering what's become of their dinners—and one well-fed lady who's pleased as punch about the helpful new service they've started to provide."

Alex grinned at him. "Then you actually took her a meal?"

"Sure I did. She was jumpy enough as it was. I didn't want to arouse her suspicions."

"Good thinking. The lady has a wary nature, Ned. She would probably suspect a choirboy. Do you think she recognized you?"

Ned shook his head. "No. She greeted me with her Colt's revolver, then stared at me for a good five seconds before she decided I was harmless enough to talk to. I coaxed her into trying the roast duck. Marched myself into the galley afterward and helped myself to a tray, then piled on a duckling with all the trimmings and took it up to her room. She was glad to see me again, I'll tell you that much. I'll bet she ate every bite."

"And nobody questioned you?"

"Not a soul. I guess they took me for a real steward. By the way, boss, she was still done up as a boy, just like you described, and downright fetching she was, too." Ned winked at him. "I especially liked those snug black breeches she had on. I have to admit, if I was a sodomist and I saw that tight little bottom twitching at me—"

"Believe me, I plan to enjoy it to the fullest." Alex burst out laughing at the way Ned's mouth dropped open. "I wasn't talking about buggery, you scoundrel. I meant caressing her. Making love to her. You're to keep your hands off the girl, do you understand? She belongs to me."

"Anything you say, boss. Can I ask whose bed you plan to sleep in tonight?"

"My own, more's the pity. I might have staked my claim, but it's a little premature to work it." Alex removed his wig. "Not that I expect to—" He cut himself off. Ned was gaping at him again. "What are you staring at now?"

"Your forehead. That's a nasty cut you've got."

"Oh. That. It happened during the earthquake. I was hit by some falling stonework." He began stripping off his trousers. "As I was saying, I don't expect to get much sleep tonight. I've heard there's an exceptionally rich poker game in the captain's quarters later this evening. Given how generously I compensate you, I believe I had better attend."

"And exactly who'll be playing in it, boss? Not Colonel George Whitefield, obviously, and from the way you're undressing, not Dr. Samuel Seabury, either."

"Benjamin Colman," Alex said.

"That's your real name, then? Benjamin Colman?"

"Yes."

Ned laughed. "And pigs can fly."

"Do you like Alex McClure any better?"

"Now, that one may even be real," Ned drawled. "Can I offer my services as a valet?"

Alex accepted, admitting with a sly smile that Colman was something of a dandy. Ned, he found, was a man of many parts. Not only did the hackman efficiently remove the makeup and gum from his skin and hair; he also brushed Alex's hair into the latest style. Half an hour later, having donned a double-breasted brown reefer jacket and checked trousers, Alex departed for the concert in the main cabin.

All of the boat's upper staterooms opened onto an inner passageway that ran down the center of the deck, so Alex's trip to the main staircase took him directly past Melanie's door. He paused in front of it, remembering the homage Ned had paid to her bottom, thinking that if her coat hadn't concealed that particular asset when he'd seen her that afternoon, he would have realized at once that something was amiss. He smiled, telling himself that he envied Ned the view.

The thought led him to recall the warmth of her stockinged legs when he'd fondled them in the brougham, and to wonder how her bare skin would feel beneath his fingers. Soft but delightfully firm, he decided. The women of San Francisco, like those in Hong Kong, appeared to be in excellent physical condition. It was probably from walking up and down the many hills in the two cities.

His hand tingled at the thought of caressing her. There was something very tantalizing about the prospect of undressing a woman who was clothed as a boy—unfastening her buttons one by one; slowly unraveling the bindings that flattened her breasts, teasingly grazing each white strip of newly bared flesh along the way; sliding down her breeches very gradually, kissing her ever more intimately as he went lower ... The tingling grew hotter and spread throughout his body, centering itself in his groin. He smiled ruefully at the way his hardened manhood began to throb. As much as he enjoyed the way the girl affected him, it could be bloody frustrating at times.

He started to turn away, then hesitated. He could knock on her door and say he was a steward, there to collect her dirty dishes. She was sure to let him in, and once she did, he could have her in his arms within seconds, his mouth on hers to stop her from crying out. He had overwhelmed her once and could do it again, giving her no time to think or object—not until much later, anyway, after he'd kissed and petted and teased her into submission, then pleasured her so thoroughly she ached. Then, if she protested, or even if she didn't, he would do it all again. It beat spending the night with Ned. Hell, it even beat lining his pockets at the card table.

He stared at her door, picturing her naked beneath his body, moaning and writhing and clawing at his back as his thrusts grew faster and deeper. Sweating a little now, he lifted his hand to knock. It was only at the last possible moment that his common sense reasserted itself and his hand froze in midair. He was dealing with Melanie Wyatt, and she was no ordinary female.

She would probably answer the door with a loaded pistol, and even if she didn't, she would strike at him the moment he tried to touch her— kick and scratch and bite, just as she had last night, only this time they weren't in a deserted back alley and he didn't have a drugged fiancé handy with which to blackmail her. People were all around them and would hear her struggles and cries. Would-be rescuers would fly to her aid, encountering what appeared to be a dandified gentleman raping a working-class lad. They would beat him to a pulp and enjoy every moment, then hold him for the sheriff in Sacramento.

Grimacing at the disaster he had almost invited, he dropped his hand and turned toward the stairs. He was too hot for the girl, that was the problem. Not in total control of himself. A man made costly errors in this state.

That was all the more reason, he decided, to adhere to his original plan and simply follow her. Sooner or later she would resign herself to having him around, and then it would be easy to gain her good opinion. All he would have to do was listen to her views and pretend to help her. Then, when she began to soften, he would arrange an opportunity to rescue her from harm. By the time he was through with her, she wouldn't just yield to his advances and melt in his arms; she would steal into his bed and plead to be taken. The Chinese theft ring, he thought with satisfaction, would be as good as destroyed.

Down in the main cabin, he located his dinner companions and told them that his friend Dr. Seabury was ill and wouldn't be joining them. They promptly asked him to fill in, then flirted just as expertly with Colman, who was under thirty, as they had with Seabury, who was more than twenty years older. Colman confessed he was charmed.

The three then listened to the concert, which featured patriotic music played by a six-piece band. Alex, who had high standards after his many trips to Europe, was pleasantly surprised by the quality of the performance. Since his last visit to California some six years before, the state had grown enormously in sophistication as well as in population and creature comforts.

As soon as the concert ended, he sought out Captain Whitney and introduced himself as a former sailor who was now a Hong Kong merchant. Like most seamen in the state, Whitney had sailed the Pacific extensively, making numerous voyages to China. It was hardly surprising, then, that he and Alex had many acquaintances in common and shared fond memories of many of the same places. After a nostalgic conversation, Whitney invited him to drop by his cabin around eleven for what he termed a friendly little game of poker.

"And the stakes?" Alex asked.

"Twenty and thirty. Bring coins only, no bills."

So much for little and friendly, Alex thought. "And an extra shirt," he said with a laugh, "because from the sound of it, I'm in danger of losing the one I'm wearing. In half an hour, then, Captain. I'll look forward to meeting my fellow players."

He went upstairs for his money, once again passing Melanie's door. This time he ignored the way his loins tightened at the thought of her in bed and walked briskly to his room. When he came back the other way, her neighbors from across the corridor, a pair of Celestials, were talking beside their open door. Their presence quashed any temptation he might have felt to try to bluff his way into her room.

He stayed on deck until eleven, enjoying the stars and the mild night air. Where San Francisco was gusty and cold at this hour, the valley was at its most pleasant. The temperatures, which could soar into the hundreds during the day, cooled down thirty degrees or more at night.

By a quarter past eleven, he had met his fellow gamblers, all prosperous business and professional men, and was gazing impassively at his first hand. It was an ugly sight, all low cards and not a pair among them, so he folded. The others didn't, betting exuberantly and rapidly. They were tossing down fancy whiskey and savoring fine cigars, but Alex did neither. He didn't smoke, and he'd learned long ago that nursing one's liquor was far more conducive to winning than pouring it down one's throat.

The excitement in the room mounted as the pot increased. Then, just as the betting ended, the entire boat jerked so violently that everything on the table jumped and skittered. The steamer lurched a short ways forward, scraping and bouncing, then came to a dead halt.

The captain, who was observing rather than playing, sighed deeply. "Feels like we hit a bar. I'll need to direct us off, gentlemen, but you're welcome to stay here without me for as long as you like."

They took him at his word. Alex didn't play as well as he usually did, but he was still up over seven hundred dollars when the boat resumed its voyage and the captain reappeared. Luckily for him, his fellow players were rich enough and drunk enough to have lost both large sums of money and their proficiency at poker without missing either one.

It was half past midnight by then, but the game continued unabated. Perhaps it was the suggestive time of night, perhaps it was the thought of Melanie sleeping so close to his bed, but his concentration and judgment lapsed and he lost heavily over the next five hands. He finally forced the girl from his mind and recouped some of his money, but all the fun had gone out of the game.

Restless now, he yawned and excused himself, saying he'd had a long day. Ned was sleeping quietly when he returned to their stateroom, but he doubted he could do the same. He stripped off his jacket and cravat and unfastened the buttons at the throat of his shirt, then went outside to the stern of the boat. Everyone seemed to be asleep. The outside lanterns were all burning, but not a single light shone through any of the windows. It was very peaceful, the only noises the chug of the engine and the splash of the wheel.

He leaned against the railing, his back to the river, and gazed at the starboard row of portholes. His stateroom was the second from the stern, Melanie's the sixth. He pictured her asleep, snuggled beneath the covers in a light cotton nightdress, or perhaps in nothing at all. A sleeping woman was the most enchanting creature on earth. Soft, vulnerable, and completely irresistible.

He especially enjoyed seducing them awake. More than one lover had told him that his caresses had stolen into her dream, so that she had responded while she was still asleep, kissing him and moving against him as much as in her mind as in real life. By the time she'd awakened fully, she was aroused and ardent and compliant.

His groin began to ache fiercely. That was how he wanted Melanie Wyatt, sweet and fiery and submissive. And there was no reason not to have her that way.

Chapter 9

A few minutes later, Alex walked down the lantern-lit inner passageway to Melanie's stateroom and inserted a slender picklock into her keyhole. He was skilled enough with the instrument to have defeated even the most difficult of locks, but this one yielded quite easily. The door, however, failed to do the same. There was something blocking the way.

He bent down a little, braced himself against the door, and pushed gently with his arm and hip. There was no ardor in him now, only coolness and concentration. His entire mind was focused on the task at hand, especially on the need for extreme quiet.

The object, a trunk, wasn't bulky enough to present a serious obstacle and gradually gave way. As soon as the door was sufficiently ajar, Alex slipped sideways into the room and waited motionless by the trunk until his eyes had grown accustomed to the dimness. He soon spotted a china-laden tray on the floor and realized that he had missed stepping on it by inches. Luck, it seemed, was with him.

Melanie's berth was in the most shadowed area of the room, but he could see well enough to tell that she was lying on her side facing the bulkhead. Her blanket was pulled above her shoulders and stirred slightly with each breath she took. He crossed to the porthole, a matter of several steps, and opened the shutter slats halfway. Enough light came into the small room to provide him with better vision, even after he had closed the door.

He approached the berth. Now that the dangerous part was over and he was on the verge of reaching his goal, his body abruptly caught fire. His manhood grew rigid and swollen, his heart began to pound in his throat, and his hands started trembling like a schoolboy's. He prided himself on being an inventive and generous lover, but when he looked at Mellie Wyatt, he wanted to strip her naked, plunge his unsheathed member inside her, and plow her until he exploded, again and again, all night long. It wouldn't do.

He forced himself to relax, breathe deeply, and think about the delights of slowly seducing a woman. There was the pleasure of investigating the contours of her body and the challenge of discovering which spots were the most sensitive. There was the satisfaction of coaxing her from sound sleep to dreamy desire to reckless abandonment. And there was the sweet torment and wild excitement of knowing she was his for the taking but making himself wait to enjoy her. He smiled and shook his head. Far from cooling him off, the inventory was only making him hotter.

He eased himself down on her berth. She was curled up like a child, her knees pulled halfway to her chest and her hands resting protectively near her head, one of them nestled under her pillow and the other almost touching her lips. Her hair was plaited into tight braids, probably so she could pin it close to her scalp in the morning and cover it with a boy's wig. It was a crime to confine something so beautiful.

He edged forward until his thigh just grazed her back, then inched her covers down to her hips. She hadn't undressed for bed, but was still wearing her groom's shirt and breeches. Ned was right about her bottom. It was so delectable that he couldn't keep his hands off, and so warm and lush that he removed them almost at once. If he hadn't, he would have begun to undress her.

She hadn't scrubbed off her makeup, either, though some of it seemed to have rubbed off in her sleep. It was difficult to be sure, but he thought her brows looked lighter, and her thready mustache and goatee even wispier than before. To his amusement, he didn't much care if they weren't.

He bent over her, putting his left hand on the mattress in front of her waist to brace himself. That left his right hand free to cup the back of her neck, then lightly caress it. Her skin was hot and a little moist, and the downy hairs on her nape felt like silk. His member started aching and his gut twisted. He stopped for a minute, sternly lecturing himself about the need to take his time.

She murmured something but didn't move. Enticed by the sound of her voice, he lowered his mouth to the crook of her neck and breathed in her jasmine and lily scent. The perfume affected him like an erotic potion, heating his blood and making him reel. He wanted to turn her lips to his mouth, then tease them open with his tongue, but forced himself to refrain. It wouldn't be long before instinct led her to part them and seek him out.

His fingers grew restless on her neck, moving teasingly along her nape and back. She tensed a little, and he smiled. She was beginning to wake up. Knowing how much it aroused her, he planted kisses across her shoulder and down her arm, sucking and nibbling her flesh through the fabric of her shirt.

Melanie hadn't heard Alex come in or move around. She hadn't felt him sit own on her berth or stroke her bottom. She hadn't even roused when he had positioned himself over her body and cupped her neck. She had tossed and turned for far too many hours that night, assailed by a sense of menace that had waxed and waned all evening with unnerving irregularity. Then, just before eleven o'clock, it had grown so intense that she had burrowed beneath her covers in fear, trembling so hard her teeth chattered. In the end, she hadn't so much fallen asleep as passed out from exhaustion.

She finally began to wake when Alex stroked the back of her neck, but quickly incorporated the sensation into a dream. The muscular thigh against her back became a bulkhead in the hold of a ship, and the fingers teasing her neck became the feet of a rat scurrying over her nape. She was hiding from someone and didn't dare move, but the rat revolted her so much that she couldn't stop a hoarse cry from escaping her throat.

The rat kept prancing around her head, rousing her until she was halfway between sleeping and waking. Irrational panic gripped her, a sensation that had nothing to do with the rat and everything to do with the menace she'd endured all evening. She tried to get up and run, but she couldn't move. Her limbs were paralyzed.

Something touched her shoulder—tickled her, pinched her, bit her. The next second she came fully awake. She didn't know where she was, only that she was terrified. Her eyes flew open, but she couldn't see a thing. Then she remembered that she was in a berth aboard a luxurious steamer. Whatever was touching her, it wasn't any rat.

Her reaction was pure instinct—fight or be killed. Her hand tightened around her knife, and she jerked herself upright, slashing out blindly in an arc as she rose.

Alex never even felt her jerk awake. He was so muddled by desire that his entire world began and ended with the feel of Melanie's body and the hunger inside his own. He finally realized she was moving, but it took him a deadly extra second to interpret the action as threatening and snap out of his trance. The image of her Colt's revolver flashed into his mind. It struck him that she might have slept with the weapon nearby—that he needed to be out the door or flat on the floor, and *now*. He twisted away from her, turning his back to her hand as he bolted from the bed.

He wasn't fast enough. Melanie felt her knife meet something solid, then slice through it. She heard the soft rip of material splitting as the knife slashed sideways, but knew from the amount of resistance she encountered that more than fabric was being cut.

The knife sprang free. She could make out a retreating form, a hulking monster, and it frightened her into abject panic. She opened her mouth to scream, but she was panting so hard that she couldn't catch her breath and make her vocal cords work. Nothing came out but air.

Then the monster turned and spoke to her. "Jesus, Mellie, are you trying to kill me? Put the damned knife away."

She recognized his voice—it was the one with the English accent—and stopped trying to shriek. Anything was better than a nameless fiend, even a dreaded enemy. "Alex?"

He walked to the porthole and opened the shutter. More light came into the room. "Who the hell else would it be?"

She tensed when he turned to face her, but he was apparently no more eager for physical contact than she was. Moving to the corner diagonally across from her, he slowly raised his hands. "See? No weapons. I'm harmless. I won't try to touch you again. You win this round, okay? Just put away the knife and try to calm down."

It was the first time since Thursday that she'd seen him undisguised, and she had forgotten how very handsome he was. She felt a churning warmth in her belly, but ignored it. Several seconds went by. Finally she demanded, "What are you doing here?"

He lowered his hands and rolled his eyes. "What do you think I was doing?"

Now that her panic had subsided, it was easy to guess the answer. The "feet" on the nape of her neck must have been his fingers, and the "teeth" on her arm, his mouth. He'd been caressing her awake. Trying to seduce her again. "I really don't know," she said. "I care even less."

"God, but you're hard on a man's ego." He shoved his hands into his pockets and took a few steps forward. "I'm sorry I frightened you, Mellie. I truly didn't mean to."

She glanced at the door. It hadn't been forced, but her trunk had been pushed aside. "How did you get in here? Did you pick my lock? Bribe someone to give you a passkey?"

"The first. It wasn't difficult."

And she had slept right through it. Precautions seemed to be useless against the man. The thought should have scared her senseless, but instead, it merely annoyed her.

In fact, far from being afraid, she felt safer now than she had all evening. It was probably the knife, she decided, and raised her hand in a threatening way.

Alex groaned. "You wouldn't, Mellie. Not again." He retreated to the corner. "Would you?"

She wiggled the knife. "I certainly would, unless you leave this very moment and see to it that you don't—" She stopped in midsentence. There were several small spots on the carpet that hadn't been there before. Bright red ones, right in front of his feet. Only seconds ago, the area had been directly behind his back.

Frowning at the stains, she scooted to the end of the bed for a better look. A large droplet splashed onto the floor behind him, and then another. "You're bleeding," she said. The thought made her queasy and faint.

"Well, of course I am. You stabbed me in the back, remember?" He shifted his weight from one foot to the other and awkwardly stretched his neck, then added in a disgruntled tone, "It stings like fire, too, I can tell you that much."

"It does?" Another few drops stained the rug, and her knife fell limply to the floor. Despite the story she had spun the night before, she had never wounded a man in her life. She was appalled by the damage she had done and the pain she had caused. "God, Alex. It's really bad. You're dripping all over the carpet."

"I suppose it's only to be expected. Sharpest blade in town and all that." He glanced over his shoulder. "Hmm. Very impressive. And it was a new shirt, too. A pity." Flashing her a grin, he laced his hands together in front of his groin. "Then again, I'm probably lucky it was only my back."

She was suddenly blazingly angry. Scrambling off the bed, she charged to within a yard of his chest, planted herself squarely in front of him, and glowered at him. "You're bloody right you are! For heaven's sake, Alex, I've told you I make a point of being armed. After following me for two days, you must have known my frame of mind. Didn't it occur to that tiny brain of yours that it might be dangerous to break is here in the middle of the night and scare me half to death? Never mind castration, you witless dolt. I could have stabbed you through your heart. Slashed your miserable throat. You could be dead on my floor right now."

He smiled again. "Then the thought that you might have killed me bothers you?"

Her hands clenched into fists at her sides. "Yes, damn you, although God knows why it should. You've caused me nothing but trouble since the first moment I saw you." Trouble and terror, she suddenly recalled, and took a wary step backward. "I know you're my enemy. I'd have to be a fool not to fear you and try to protect myself. It's obvious that you're extremely dangerous."

"True enough, but not to you." He looked at her reprovingly. "I would never hurt you, Mellie. Haven't you figured that out yet?"

She barely heard him. "But you don't *feel* dangerous," she mumbled to herself. "Not anymore. And I'm not even holding my knife now. I don't understand it."

"Feel?" he repeated. "What do you mean, 'feel'? Can you sense that sort of thing?"

"Uh, no. Of course I can't." It was stupid to reveal one's strengths to one's opponent. "It was a figure of speech, that's all."

The stains on the floor were even larger now, she noticed. If she didn't do something soon, he could faint from loss of blood. "Turn around and take off your shirt, Alex. I want to have a look at your back."

Alex didn't budge. His back was as painful as

he had claimed, and not just from the wound Melanie had inflicted, but he wasn't going to let her inspect it. A man could handle only so much embarrassment in a single night, and he had exceeded his limit.

It had been a mistake to come here in the first place, of course, but he could forgive himself the error. He hadn't enjoyed a woman since Hong Kong, and Melanie was as desirable as she was challenging. He was only human, as susceptible to temptation as the next man, and his hunger for her had routed his common sense. But to let passion turn him into a careless idiot twice in as many nights . . . That *was* unforgivable.

He wasn't about to bare his back and add baring his soul to the list of his humiliations. "Thank you, but I'll treat the cut myself." He started toward the door. "Good night, Mellie."

She quickly blocked his way. "And how will you manage that? The wound is on your back, and fairly high up from what I could see. You'll never be able to reach it."

She was right. He would need help, but if he accepted it from her, she would ply him with painful questions. He considered lying—he always did, with women—but for some reason, he didn't want to. Not to Melanie.

"I'm traveling with a servant," he finally answered. Ned would mind his own business. Men always did, unlike women. "I'll wake him and have him take care of it."

"A servant?" Melanie frowned reflectively, then nodded to herself. "Of course. That's how you found me. The steward who took my order for dinner was no steward at all. That was very clever of you, Alex. I fell for it completely." She raised her chin. "Now stop arguing with me and let me doctor your back. I never go anywhere without my medicinal Chinese plants. You've traveled in the Orient—perhaps you even live there—so you must know how efficacious they are. They'll heal you far more quickly than anything your henchman can apply."

Alex was startled into temporary silence. The girl never ceased to amaze him. He had assumed it might be days before he could secure the proper treatments, and here she was, carrying them in her trunk.

He pondered the two alternatives. He enjoyed excellent health, so a delay was unlikely to harm him and would spare him an unpleasant grilling. On the other hand, all knife wounds were susceptible to infection, and this one would almost certainly slow him down. The herbs would prevent complications and hasten his recovery.

He sighed. Melanie was far too formidable an opponent to fight at half strength. Every time he underestimated her, he paid a heavy price. It was ironic, but to do his job, he would have to put himself in her hands.

Then, just in the nick of time, a third alternative suggested itself. "The man is my valet, not my henchman, and accustomed to seeing to my needs. If you would give me—"

"He may dress you and patch you up, but he's still your henchman. You told him to find out which stateroom I was in, and he did. Playacting and deceit are hardly the duties of your average servant." Her eyes suddenly widened. "Good grief. His voice. It was Ned-the-hackman-and-accessory-abductor, wasn't it? Leave it to you to find such a gem-of-all-trades right in San Francisco. If he serves you well enough, will you keep him with you and make him an honorary member of your triad?"

Alex gave her his severest look. "I told you last night, Melanie—"

"I know, I know. You bought the medal in a curio shop and I'm not allowed to question you about it." Undaunted, she tugged at his shirt, trying to free it from his trousers. "I'll make a deal with you, Alex. We'll pretend it's a meaningless trinket if you stop acting like a recalcitrant child and let me—"

"No." He grasped her wrists and placed them firmly at her sides. "But I do know the value of the herbs, so I would be obliged if you would give me the proper substances and tell me how to use them."

"It's not that simple. We're talking about extremely powerful medications—"

"Then I'll listen extremely carefully. For a witless dolt, I have a surprisingly good memory."

Melanie stared at him, trying to figure out why he was so reluctant to have her treat him. He had schemed like Iago to touch her and have her touch him in return, so he should have relished every pat and stroke. "Are you afraid I'll deliberately hurt you? I admit to having a vengeful streak, but I would never let a patient suffer. I'll be as careful as I possibly can, Alex. I promise."

Scowling, he folded his arms across his chest. "So I'm a coward as well as a simpleton now. How charming. If you're finished insulting me—"

"But I didn't mean to. It's just that I don't understand—" Unless it was stupid male pride. Men hated to show weakness in front of females. "Ah! Now I see. Your enfeebled condition has made you so hopelessly delusional that you think I'll swoon at the sight of your naked flesh and beg you to make love to me, and you're afraid you won't be able to perform." She fought the urge to smile, not entirely successfully. "Once again, Mr.

McClure, allow me to put your mind at ease. It will take every ounce of fortitude I possess, but I'll somehow manage to control my lust for you. Now take that blasted shirt off and lie facedown on my berth before you collapse where you stand and I have to treat you on the floor!"

"Enfeebled and delusional, hmm?" A dangerous gleam appeared in his eyes. "You may finally have a valid point, but weakened or not, I'm confident I would perform more than adequately." He began toying with one of her braids, putting a firm hand on her shoulder to prevent her from moving away. Her throat went dry and she stiffened defensively. "If you want proof, invite me to come back here after Ned fixes me up. But do me a favor first. Remove the fuzz from your chin and lip. I like you better without it."

He touched the two places he'd mentioned, then ran his fingers over her throat and neck. She flushed and tried to turn away, but he simply cupped her face and continued to stroke her. Then he felt for her pulse, and she reddened even more.

"Hmm. Unusually rapid, isn't it? Tell me, sweetheart, exactly how lustful are you? And just how hard do you find it to control?"

She finally managed to pry away his hands and back away from him. "It was only to tease you into cooperating, Alex. You know that as well as I do." Except that the more he touched her, the closer it was to being true. "Now tell me why you refuse to let me doctor you. I swear I'm an excellent physician, much better than Ned could possibly be. You'll heal faster if I treat your wound. Isn't that what you want?"

It was exactly what Alex wanted, and the sooner the better. Being knifed was bad enough, but the muscles in his back had knotted up, and it wouldn't take much to send them into spasm.

Then, if he turned the wrong way or moved too abruptly, the resulting stab of pain could force him to his knees and leave him helpless on the floor.

He began to reconsider. Melanie was sorry she had hurt him and anxious to make amends. If she was even half the physician she claimed, she would help him immensely. She might have some herbs to relax his spastic muscles, too—might even be willing to give him a therapeutic massage. And afterward, given the way she blushed and jumped whenever he touched her . . .

He stepped forward, captured one of her braids, and pulled off the twine at the end. She backed away, but he simply followed her and released another two braids. She was flush against the berth by then, panting in a way that made her flattened breasts rise and fall suggestively.

He stopped only inches short of her chest. "The truth?" He dealt with the fourth and final braid. "I have an aversion to being touched intimately by a woman who looks like a boy."

She swatted away his fingers, leaning backward a little to avoid any further contact. "Keep your hands to yourself, Alex McClure. And the way I look didn't bother you before."

"It was darker in the room. Clean off your face and brush out your hair, Melanie. Then you can do whatever you please with me."

Melanie darted around him and dashed across the room. She had never met a man who could rattle her so completely or arouse her so easily. He was stalking her as if he meant to eat her, and instead of putting him in his place with some well-chosen lashes of her tongue, she was sizzling like a piece of barbecue.

She straightened to her full height. "Listen to me, you overbearing ox. You brought that knife wound on yourself, and both of us know it. I don't feel the least bit guilty about stabbing you, so—"

"Yes, you do." He grinned at her.

"No, I don't, so stop trying to play me like a fiddle. It's just that I hate seeing people suffer when I know I can relieve their pain. I'm willing to help you, but only if you're a perfect patient. No chasing me around the room or trying to fondle and kiss me. I don't want to hear a single pretty compliment or provocative phrase. Is that clear?"

"You drive a hard bar—oh, Jesus, Mellie." Alex swayed like a drunkard and groaned pitiably, acting for all he was worth. He knew it was unsporting of him, but the thought of Melanie with her hair down and her makeup off was too tempting to resist. Blinking in apparent confusion, he dropped onto the bed and sat weaving back and forth.

Melanie rushed to Alex's side and got her first good look at his back. The wound was about six inches long, and the clinging fabric around it was soaked with blood. Horrified, she murmured, "Just take it easy, Alex. Everything will be fine. Tell me your symptoms."

He raised his hand to touch her face, then dropped it like so much dead weight. "I feel weak. And the room keeps dimming and spinning."

He was either up to his old tricks or on the verge of fainting. Melanie felt she had little choice but to assume it was the latter. "It's nothing that won't pass if you let me take care of you. I want you to lie down on your stomach, all right? I can't treat your wound if you're sitting up."

He gave her a glazed look but didn't reply. More concerned than ever, she grasped him under his arms and coaxed him down. He wound up on his side rather than his stomach, but she decided it would have to do.

"Lie quietly, Alex. Try to relax." She picked up his legs, which were as heavy as water-soaked logs, and dragged them onto the berth. "I'm going to get my medicines now."

"I'd rather you got Ned." He tried to sit up, but some light pressure on his arm kept him where he was. "I don't like your braids. Are we moving, Mellie? What's all that noise?"

"We're traveling on a steamer to Sacramento, remember? The noise is the steamer wheel turning." Alex was becoming increasingly irrational, Melanie thought, increasingly agitated. "I'll brush out my hair," she added soothingly, continuing to hold him down, "but only if you quiet down and stop trying to move. Please, Alex. You could hurt yourself if you don't keep still."

He nodded and stopped fighting. Relieved, she crossed to her valise and hurriedly unlocked it. From behind her, she heard him moan again. She glanced over her shoulder. He scowled, muttering something about her goatee.

She'd encountered this sort of behavior before. Agitated patients could fixate on a topic, becoming dangerously upset if the annoyance wasn't removed. She pulled out a brush and yanked it through her braids, then took a handkerchief and a jar of cold cream out of her bag and hastily dealt with her face.

She removed her box of medicines next. The light shining in through the porthole was adequate for most purposes, but not for mixing ingredients accurately or treating a grievous wound with the necessary gentleness. Fretting about the additional delay, she fetched a lantern from the room's storage cabinet and struggled to get it lit. It seemed to take forever.

Finally ready to begin, she turned toward the berth. Alex was propped up on his elbow, gazing at her. She'd rarely seen a man look so intent—or so lucid.

"That's much, much better," he said. "I'll look forward to brushing your hair more thoroughly. After you finish saving my life, that is."

She wanted to crown him with the lantern, but settled for slamming it down on the table beside the berth. "You—you conniving liver fluke! I'll never believe another word you say. Another thing you do. It would serve you right if I stabbed you all over again, twice as deeply, and let you bleed to death in the passageway."

"But it *is* painful, Mellie. Very painful. I couldn't endure it half so stoically if I didn't have your beauty to distract me. Why do you think I improved so dramatically?"

She snorted in disbelief. "And you followed me onto this boat because you can't live without me. Now pull off that shirt and lie down on your stomach before I change my mind and throw you out of my room. I'm going to apply a styptic poultice to your wound, and don't try to win my sympathy by groaning about how painful it is, because the medicine won't sting a bit."

He held her gaze for several seconds, then abruptly looked away, staring at the far bulkhead. The playful gleam in his eyes faded, and a grim wariness took its place. "Yes. All right." He paused. The next few words seemed to be dragged out of him. "I might need some help, Melanie."

She tapped her foot impatiently. "Well, you won't get it from me, Mr. McClure. Leave your performances for the theater and get on with it."

"Right." He struggled to sit up, wincing a few times as he rose, then pulled his shirt out of his trousers. When he tried to raise it over his head, though, some invisible force seemed to stop him halfway. He grimaced and shook his head. "I don't think I can do it."

If he thought he was going to trick her into a virtual embrace, he was crazy. "I said get on with it, Alex. I'm not going to stand here forever, you know."

He tried again, but abandoned the effort almost at once. To Melanie's disgust, he even gasped dramatically, as if she had stabbed him all over again. "It's no use," he mumbled. "You'll have to help me. I'm sorry."

She put her hands on her hips and regarded him with total exasperation. "Don't you ever stop?"

"Please, Mellie." He stared at his lap. "It's, uh, it's an old injury. The muscles in my back—they go into spasm sometimes. I suppose it's from fighting the pain."

He looked embarrassed, even anguished, but she'd been hoodwinked too often to fall for it. "Very well, Alex. Raise up your hands, and see that you keep them high in the air, because if they come anywhere near my body, your supposed back spasms will be the least of your problems."

He gingerly inched up his arms, moving as if he expected a hellish seizure to fell him at any moment. Unimpressed, she grabbed his shirt and pulled it carelessly over his head. He didn't say a word, just flinched and sucked in his breath.

She assumed it was more theatrics until she saw the ashen strain on his face. You couldn't fake that sort of sickly sheen. She had really hurt him.

Feeling guilty and contrite, she started to apologize—and then glanced at his chest. It was crisscrossed with weltlike scars—dozens of them. It was an appalling sight, but she couldn't tear her eyes away. Having spent a good part of her childhood aboard a ship, she recognized the marks as the lingering remains of the punishment that would be inflicted by a lash or a cat-o'-nine-tails, but no bos'n she'd ever met would have whipped a man on his chest, much less thrashed him severely enough to leave such noticeable and multiple scars.

She finally inspected his back, swallowing hard when she saw how badly she had cut him. She had come perilously close to slicing more than flesh. The wound was deepest at the beginning and needed stitching, then tapered to a bloody scratch. It was clean and even, though, so there wouldn't be much of a scar, not that he was likely to care. He already had a backful to match the ones on his chest.

The horror didn't even end there. Some of the scars on his torso trailed downward into the area covered by his trousers. She suspected he'd been whipped on his thighs and buttocks, as well.

He hadn't simply been punished now and then, perhaps for misbehavior aboard a ship, or beaten soundly by an enemy issuing a warning. He'd been coldly, brutally, and repeatedly tortured.

Chapter 10

Alex was tense and unnaturally still, as if he was trying to erect an invisible barrier between his body and Melanie's senses. She understood now why he hadn't wanted her to tend him. He hadn't wanted her to see his scars. He had assumed she would ask questions he preferred not to answer. She peeked at his face from out of the corner of her eye. His expression was completely blank.

She felt a surge of compassion. "I, uh, I lied to you before," she said softly, and gently stroked his hair. He didn't react at all. "The poultice will sting at first, but the discomfort shouldn't persist. I'll use roots containing an analgesic and a muscle relaxant. They should numb you almost immediately, then provide deeper relief from the spasm and pain. Let's get you onto your stomach, and then we can begin the treatment."

She slid her arms around him, supporting his neck and back to prevent any further trauma. She was acutely aware of his size, his muscular strength, and his nakedness. Other than her father, she had never seen a man to match him, and she had seen more than her share. Between the ship

167

and the camps, her girlhood had been anything but sheltered.

She tightened her grip, praying she could handle his weight. "Let yourself go limp and fall. Don't worry about moving too quickly and getting another jolt. I'll hold you and ease you down. I'm a lot stronger than I look."

Gritting her teeth with the effort, she slowly lowered him to the berth. While he still didn't speak, he cooperated fully. But far from relaxing, he was as taut as a drum.

"You're doing very well," she said as she straightened, "but it would be better if you weren't so tense. Breathe deeply. Try to relax your muscles each time you exhale."

She fetched some towels from the cabinet, inadvertently stepping on her knife as she tucked them around his upper body. She absently picked it up, noticed the dried blood on the blade, and paled. "That should take care of any spills. Are you reasonably comfortable now?"

Alex nodded. Melanie had meant his body, and his body was doing fine, but he couldn't say the same for his mind. Never in his life had he been treated with such tender concern, but he wasn't enjoying it. A man wanted to feel vigorous and commanding, not impotent and helpless. It was embarrassing to have to rely on a woman for every little thing, especially one as beautiful and desirable as Melanie.

He wasn't looking forward to her therapy, either. As she had said, the herbs could be extremely potent, capable of killing as well as curing. He only hoped she knew what she was doing. And then there were the scars that covered his body. He almost wished she would ask about them and get it over with, except that he had no idea how he would answer.

She stroked his hair again. He would have liked that very much, but he knew she saw him simply as a patient, or perhaps as a pitiable victim. It made him feel like a lapdog.

"Would you like me to put a pillow under your head?" she asked.

"No. I'm fine." He hesitated. "Uh, Mellie?"

"Ah. Finally talking again, are you? So what's on your mind, Alex—besides the pain you're in and the fact that you hate being indisposed, especially being obliged to take orders from some mannish, knife-wielding female?"

The scars. His own uneasiness. Melanie's gentleness. He smiled at the way she had described herself. Her keen wit, too.

"Just—I wonder if you could explain what you're doing as you go along. Tell me what herbs you're using and what effects they have. I'm interested in Chinese medicine. It's the only kind I trust."

"In other words, you aren't sure that you trust *me*." She put the knife on the table and sat down beside him. "Don't worry about a thing. You got yourself stabbed by the right woman."

"Did I?"

"Yes. I'm very proficient. Shen Wai—he was my father's houseman when I was a child, and he more or less raised me—he showed me the common folk remedies when I was nine or ten. I developed a strong interest in the subject and began to study it on my own. When I was eighteen we moved to San Francisco and Shen Wai introduced me to a physician named Chang Wei, who taught me still more. He's very old and very wise. I've consulted with him often over the years."

Alex was greatly relieved. "I know the man. He treated the cut on my forehead. I asked the hotel manager for someone Chinese, and Chang was the one he recommended."

Melanie brushed Alex's hair back from his forehead to get a better look at the wound. "He did his usual splendid job, I see." Her fingers drifted to the back of his neck and absently massaged it. "It's healing very nicely. Another few days, and you'll be able to snip out the stitches."

"He was good with a needle. Used acupuncture to deaden the pain." Her touch was very soothing. Some of the tension drained from his body. "Are you? Good with a needle, I mean? And will I need one?"

"I'm afraid you probably will. I don't know acupuncture, but I can numb the area with herbs. In all honesty, though, I'm not as skillful as Dr. Chang." Not nearly as skillful. She carried the proper supplies for emergencies but had never been obliged to use them.

"But you do know how to do it."

"Of course I do." She had assisted. It was close enough. "I promise you, you have nothing to worry about."

"No. I suppose I don't." After the life he had led, pain was the least of his worries. If it hadn't been for his anxiety about the scars, he would have relaxed completely. "Why do you keep petting me that way? As if I'm a wounded Chihuahua?"

"Surely not a Chihuahua, Alex. You're much too strong and large. Perhaps a Great Dane." She tousled his hair and rose from the berth. "Because it's therapeutic, that's why. According to Dr. Chang, the laying on of hands channels curative energy into a patient's body."

"I can believe it. I'll bet it would work even better if you stroked me somewhat lower," he said, mustering a grin.

"Don't press your luck." She crossed the room and removed a bottle of oil and a large bowl from her valise. Alex watched intently as she poured some oil into the bowl and placed it on top of the lantern. She was preparing the poultice, he realized. She wasn't going to bring up the scars, at least not yet.

He didn't know whether to be astonished by her discretion or irritated by her refusal to act the way a female was supposed to. He knew the sight had appalled her. She had studied him forever. He couldn't believe her silence would continue indefinitely.

The subject felt like the sword of Damocles by then, poised precariously over his head. Unable to stand the suspense, he finally muttered, "All right, Mellie. You win. Why haven't you asked me about it yet?"

She knew exactly what he meant and didn't pretend otherwise. "I wasn't playing a game. I didn't ask because I suspect you hate talking about it. That you hate even thinking about it. I'll bet you would have taken off your shirt much sooner, but you were afraid I would badger you for an explanation. Am I right?"

He was embarrassed it had been so obvious. "Yes. So?"

"So nothing. I won't. Let's talk about something else."

Perversely, he no longer wanted to. "But why didn't you? People always do."

"You mean your women always do, but I'm not one of your women." She shook the bowl a little. "I was raised by men. I've been surrounded by them all my life, first on my father's ship—"

"He took you to sea?"

"Yes. I was born in Hong Kong. He was a trader and a captain in those days. My mother died when

I was five, and Shen Wai persuaded my father to take us along on his travels after that. In '48, we read about gold being discovered and settled in California. We spent the next five years in the camps, then moved to Nevada City." She gave the bowl another couple of shakes. "Until I was fourteen, I was the tomboy to end all tomboys. After the childhood I had, I suppose it's only natural that I sometimes think and act like a man. For example, I like poker. I like fast horses, too, both riding them and betting on them. And I enjoy a good story, both telling one and hearing one. So if I haven't asked, it's because I was brought up to mind my own business. Of course, I have a lot of female in me, too. I doubt—"

"Hear, hear," Alex said, and let his gaze drift to her bottom.

She burst out laughing. "Talk about being male to the core! Why do you even bother to look? Force of habit? Wishful thinking? Given the shape you're in, you couldn't bed me right now if I offered myself on a plate."

"And it's extremely unfeeling of you to remind me of it, too," he grumbled. "You were saying . . . ?"

"Hmm. Oh, yes. That I doubt a man would be as curious as I am, or listen with the same tenderness if you chose to confide in him." She stuck a finger into the oil. "Or chatter away like a squirrel, for that matter. This is coming along well, all things considered."

He stifled a yawn. "What is it supposed to do?"

"Heat up. The poultice works best when it's warm. The point is, I'm probably nothing like the people you're used to, Alex. Male or female."

"Nothing at all," he agreed. "I keep discovering that."

He pictured himself playing poker with her and decided that the only stakes that interested him involved her clothing. Still, if she had been a man, he might have enjoyed having her as a friend. It was damned unsettling. Mistresses were for sex and amusement, not fellowship. He put it down to the male clothes she was wearing and the shock of being stabbed.

Melanie fished out her measuring spoons and two bottles of herbs. Alex looked so sleepy and harmless that it was hard to remember he was a hardened criminal who was plotting to steal her gold and a conniving Lothario who made love to advance his schemes. She had never expected to find herself talking so comfortably with him, but if she had learned anything over the years, it was that life took some strange turns. You played the hand you were dealt.

"This is *niu-xi*," she said, measuring some into the bowl. "Achyranthes in English. It's especially useful for knife wounds. It cuts the swelling and lessens the pain. It's also effective in relieving muscle spasm." She opened the second bottle. "And this one is *dang-shen*. Bonnet bellflower. It's a styptic, primarily, and also a general tonic." She remembered another principal property of the root as she put some into the bowl. "A powerful aphrodisiac, too." She cocked up her eyebrow. "Interested, Alex?"

"I've already admitted how much I would need one," he said irritably. "And to tell you the truth, the way I feel right now, even that wouldn't help."

"I'm vastly relieved." She stirred the mixture. "My virtue is obviously safe for the time being, not that the poultice would put me at any risk. The *dang-shen* has to be ingested for that purpose."

"Virtue is an overrated virtue, sweetheart. I wish I'd had some of that *dang-shen* earlier. I would have slipped it into the duckling Ned brought you. A few caresses and you would have torn off my clothing."

"But I did, Alex—and some of your skin along with it, if you'll recall." She put some gauze into the bowl and saturated it with the medicinal oil. "Anyway, you're not supposed to be provocative, remember?"

"You started it." He yawned and closed his eyes. "All that talk about aphrodisiacs. You were teasing me. Making sport of my lapsed virility. You do have a vengeful streak."

"I was simply describing the plant's properties, just as you asked me to." She carried the bowl to his side. "I'm going to put this on now. We'll leave it for about two hours, then clean and stitch the wound." She paused. "Uh, Alex? It *will* hurt at first, so if you want to grumble and curse, go right ahead. People usually do."

But when the gauze made contact with his skin, he merely flinched and clenched his jaw. She massaged his neck and shoulders to calm him, and he murmured that the pain was easing. Relieved that the analgesic was working so quickly, she prepared a dose of oral medication and knelt by his bedside to administer it.

"This is *bai-shao*. Peony root. It's dissolved in rice wine. You'll be taking it three times a day. It's especially good for knife wounds. It prevents infection and bleeding and lessens pain and swelling. I've dissolved some *dang-gui* in the wine as well. That's Chinese angelica. It's an excellent antispasmodic and painkiller. And both drugs have a strong sedative effect."

"So you plan to keep me drugged," he mumbled. "Escape from me while I'm staggering around like an opium smoker."

"It hadn't occurred to me, but it's a definite plus." She held the glass to his lips. "Come, Alex, drink up. That's it. I have to admit, you're a much better patient than I expected. I want you to get some sleep now."

He muttered a woozy "Yes, ma'am" and promptly nodded off. Yawning, Melanie extinguished the lantern and put it in the cabinet, then pulled a watch out of her valise and checked the time. It was a quarter past two. She needed some sleep herself.

She closed the shutter and lay down on the floor. She was fruitlessly trying to get comfortable when it struck her that she would be perfectly safe on the bed. Alex was bound to sleep longer than she was, but even wide awake, he was harmless. She tugged at the bindings around her chest. They were horribly restricting, even worse than her tightest corset. She would have to change disguises in the morning in any event, she realized, so why continue to suffer? She slashed through the strips with her knife, then pulled them away. It felt wonderful to breathe freely again.

She slipped into the berth with her back against the bulkhead. She and Alex touched here and there, but she knew the contact would soothe him as he slept. After a few seconds, she put her hand on his shoulder and lightly stroked it. Her last thought before she fell asleep was that he looked remarkably innocent for a seducer and a thief.

Alex woke up first. He felt Melanie's hand on his arm even before he opened his eyes, and his manhood responded ardently. He was relieved that it was working properly again. The pain came a moment later, but it was much less severe than before.

He saw Melanie's shirt billowing free, then noticed the outline of a firm, high breast against the heavy cloth. He wanted to cup it, to tease the nipple to life, but his conscience wouldn't let him. After the devoted way she had nursed him, she deserved gentleness and affection, not calculating lust.

He pushed her hair off her face, then stroked her cheek. She awoke with a start, tensed like a compressed spring, and stared at him in wild-eyed panic. For once, he was fully prepared. He grabbed her wrist and firmly held it down.

The panic turned to wincing confusion. "Alex, please . . . You're hurting me. It's the same wrist—"

"I'm sorry." He eased his grip. "The look in your eyes—I was sure you were going to scratch me." He brought her hand to his mouth and nuzzled her palm. "Or dig your nails into my wound."

Melanie screwed up her face. "Ugh. What a gruesome thought. I was startled, that's all. I'd forgotten you were here." His kisses were sending warm waves of pleasure through her body. She tugged at her hand. "Stop that. Let go of me."

He gave the flesh at the base of her thumb a sharp little nip, and desire lashed through her like a whip. Her arm went limp, and she shuddered. A part of her didn't want him to stop, but the rest had more sense. Unfortunately, she couldn't decide which would be more effective, reciting the Greek alphabet or raining down threats on his head.

"Ah. You like that. I'll keep it in mind for the future." Smiling, he released her hand and slapped her on her rump. "Well, Mellie? Are you going to loll around panting for more or are you going to stitch up my back?"

The fog cleared abruptly. "The latter, you priapic egomaniac, and without the benefit of anesthesia if you don't keep your hands to yourself." She crawled off the berth with as much dignity as she could muster and checked her watch. It was almost four. It would be dawn before long.

She lit the lantern, then removed the gauze from Alex's back. Whatever inclination she might have had to keep scolding him disappeared when she looked at his scars. She couldn't conceive of such savagery—or such suffering.

She gently cleaned the wound. "The swelling is almost gone. It should close up nicely. How is the pain?"

"Not too bad."

"And the muscle spasm?"

"Much better."

She took a bottle of medicine out of her box. "This is fresh *da-huang*. Root of rhubarb, finely minced. It won't numb you completely—you'll still feel the needle—but it's the best I can do."

"Don't worry about it."

She prepared a mixture of oil and *da-huang*, covered the cut with fresh gauze, and worked the medicinal liquid into the wound. The preparation always smarted at first, but he didn't even flinch.

She sat down beside him on the berth. "Ten minutes, Alex. You're as tough as an old boot, do you know that?"

He laughed, but the sound was bitter. "I've had to be. I'd be dead otherwise."

"Yes." She ran her hand over his lower back. "I can see that."

He closed his eyes, all but announcing that he regretted raising the subject and wanted it dropped. She knew she should hold her tongue, but when she looked at his back, she simply couldn't do it. "I wish I had known you when it happened," she said softly. "There are herbs to lessen the pain. Hasten healing. Prevent scarring."

He didn't reply. She bit her lip in remorse. "I'm

sorry, Alex. That was the female in me talking—
and the sedative in you, I suppose. How are you
coming along?"

There was more silence. She cursed her runaway mouth and squirmed with guilt. "I, uh, I
was thinking . . . Would you like me to give you a
massage after I stitch you? It would loosen your
muscles a bit more."

He still didn't answer. Another minute went by,
then two, then three. She could feel the anger radi-
ating out of him and it wounded her heart. That
was crazy—the anger was for whoever had hurt
him, not for her, and anyway, he was her enemy,
or at least her adversary—but she couldn't help it.

She checked the time. "Five more minutes,
Alex."

There was no reaction. She grimaced, twisting
her hands together in misery. Another few minutes went by.

Suddenly he spoke. "How old are you?"

Something inside her leaped back to life. "Twenty-
three. Twenty-four in October."

"Then you couldn't have helped. I'll be thirty
next month. You weren't even born when it
started."

"Dear God." He'd been a child of less than six
or seven. Her body got clammy and cold, and she
fought the urge to retch. "How long did it go on?
And who—"

"Maybe later, Mellie." He sighed heavily. "I
never should have told you. You're trembling.
You'll probably lose your dinner and stab me full
of holes."

"Don't be absurd." But between her horror and
her lack of experience, she was afraid she probably
would.

Alex bit back a curse. Sedated or not, he couldn't
understand why he had raised the subject in the

first place, much less returned to it ten minutes later. God knew he didn't make a habit of indulging feminine curiosity, or even feminine anguish. He had anguish enough of his own, and he preferred to keep it private. It was as if some demon had taken hold of him and compelled him to start babbling.

He glanced at Melanie. She looked shaken clear to her marrow. Grim-faced, she fetched the materials she needed, then removed the gauze from his back and sat down beside him. The first prick of the needle was extremely tentative. It was a bad sign.

He focused on a spot on the wall and tried to retreat from his body, to pretend he was floating above the mattress. If she had done this before, he was mad old Emperor Norton. As he had expected, the insertion of the first suture was a lengthy ordeal. He struggled not to move, and luckily for him, succeeded. Her hands shook through the entire procedure.

"You're doing fine," he said afterward.

"I was slow and clumsy." Her voice was strained. "I'm sorry, Alex. I've never done this before. I was afraid to tell you the truth."

"I figured that out on my own. Maybe you should think about all the times you've wanted to strangle me. That should help you jab me with real authority."

"That's not funny. Was it very painful?"

"Not compared to being stabbed." Or whipped, but he didn't dare say so. "I'll survive, Mellie, although a little more speed might be nice."

Melanie nodded. The second suture went in more quickly than the first, and the third even quicker than that. Alex groaned when she said there would be five or six more, but the whole group together took less time than the first two.

"We're almost done now. I just have to clean off

the oil so the plasters will stick." She put the medicated gauze back on his cut. "It's a strong solvent, so I'll let you get numb again first, in case some creeps into the wound."

"Thank you." He stretched and relaxed, then rested his chin on his crossed arms. "You've been wonderful, Mellie. You're sweeter than I deserve."

She was pleased by the compliment, but also a little guilty. "But if I hadn't stabbed you . . . Of course, you never should have come here in the first place." She shook her head reproachfully. "Conquest and pleasure. It's all you men think about. And look what it got you." Still, the punishment had greatly exceeded the crime. "About your spasms, Alex . . . I could mix up some liniment and give you a massage. If you would like me to, that is."

"I believe I would like it very much." He paused. "Do you feel that? The boat is slowing down. We must be near the dock. Where are you going next?"

"Sonora."

"Obviously I can cross the town off my list."

She sighed. "I should have told you the truth. It would have thrown you completely off the track. Why do you persist in following me, anyway?"

"Helpless infatuation," he said. "And why are *you* so generous? Are you trying to lure me into a false sense of security so you can brain me with the lantern and escape while I'm out cold?"

"No. As eager as I am to elude you, I'm much too nice a person to leave you bleeding and concussed on the floor."

Alex didn't reply. She *was* a nice person, much nicer than he was. Soft, compassionate, and forgiving, just as a woman should be. It made him desire her all over again.

He pictured her with her head thrown back in

excitement as he suckled her breasts and rubbed a teasing finger between her legs. He enjoyed a hard-won conquest as much as the next man, but there was nothing quite as sweet as pleasing a woman you were fond of. The way she trembled and clung, then opened herself completely ... He would take Mellie slowly, he decided. Inch by agonizing inch, employing the torturous self-control of Shakta Hinduism. It would be splendid.

He suddenly realized she was talking to him, and stopped daydreaming. "I'm sorry. My mind was ... somewhere else. What did you just say?"

"I asked you how your back was coming along."

"Oh. I can't feel a thing." It wasn't true, but his member was throbbing. He wanted her closer.

She gave him a puzzled look, then went to work. As she had feared, some liquid seeped into the cut, overpowering the anesthetic and collapsing him like a deflating balloon. He might have suspected she had seen the heat in his eyes and intentionally cooled him off, but she applied the plasters too gently for that, then slathered the liniment on his back with fingers as light as snowflakes.

Her touch grew firmer, massaging rather than stroking, and he groaned with relief. It hurt a little when she hit the sore spots, but even the pain felt good. His bones turned to jelly. If there was such a thing as being paralyzed by contentment, he was.

"You're a marvel," he mumbled after a few minutes. "An angel."

"Actually, it might be better if I worked you harder and deeper," she said. "You're very tight, Alex."

In other circumstances, he would have teased

her about double meanings, but you didn't tease a madonna. "Whatever you say."

She leaned over him, putting her full weight into her hands. She was surprisingly strong for a woman, even better at working out the knots than his man in Hong Kong because her fingers were smaller and more dexterous. As the muscles loosened and the pain faded, an overwhelming sense of gratitude surged through him.

It was followed almost at once by an urge to talk, and not just about his childhood. He wanted to tell her why he had come and why she should help him, but that was a recipe for disaster. It was too soon for such confidences. She wouldn't have listened. On the contrary, given her beliefs, she would have tossed him to her friends the Taipings, who would have treated him a lot less gently than she just had.

Still, the urge persisted. He found it a difficult one to fight. He cursed the sedatives for addling his brain, but somewhere deep inside him, he knew it wasn't only the drugs.

Chapter 11

Melanie pressed her thumbs into the small of Alex's back and probed the muscles around his spine. "You feel the tightest right here. Is it the focal point of the spasms?"

"There are no spasms anymore, just soreness." He unfastened his trousers and drawers and nonchalantly eased them down, stopping just sort of his buttocks. "The pain is lower." He touched a spot a few inches below the waist. "Right here. I've been thinking, Mellie . . . the two of us have a lot in common."

Melanie barely heard him. She was too busy trying not to gape. She often gave massages in the hospital, but only to women and children, never to men. Her sole experience with males was with her own father, and touching one's father was nothing like touching a virile stranger.

Alex's body was hard and lean and strong. His skin, though damaged by scars, was firm and supple. She found him as splendid as a classical statue, but looking at a statue didn't make her pulses race. And touching one didn't heat her blood or make the backs of her wrists and knees tingle madly.

"The harder you can knead the area, the more

relief I'll probably get," he said casually. "My masseur in Hong Kong uses his elbows. *Yah-hsueh*, he calls it. Acupressure."

"Yes. I've heard of it." She took a deep breath to settle her jumpy nerves, then leaned forward and dug her elbows into his back. As she had expected, the scars went as low as the eye could see. Another wave of compassion surged through her.

She pressed and kneaded, and he moaned softly and mumbled something about how good it felt. A minute or two went by. "That's one of the things we have in common," he suddenly remarked. "Hong Kong. I live there."

Hong Kong, she repeated to herself. That was a good, safe subject. "I thought so. Isn't that where your triad is based?"

"It's not my triad. How many times do I have to tell you that?" He glanced over his shoulder, scowling at her. "Hell, you're hard to confide in. Do you want to hear about the damned scars or don't you?"

Her mouth almost dropped open. "Well, yes, of course I do, if you truly want to tell them about them." But the prospect made her uneasy. It was bound to be an awful story. "It's just that I wouldn't want to push you."

"Why not? You aren't the least bit reluctant to push me about the triad."

"That's different. I do it to tease you. I enjoy the way you stiffen and bluster."

"I'm thrilled that you find me so amusing." He was silent for such a long time that she was afraid she had annoyed him into keeping the tale to himself. But just as she was about to apologize, he started speaking again. "I was at sea for several years. That's another thing we have in common. So when women ask me about the scars, I say I had a brutal captain. But given your background, I doubt you would have believed it."

"No. There are too many of them, and they cover you too completely. You would be dead if it was a single beating, and you wouldn't have tolerated such abuse more than once. You would have deserted—or died trying to defend yourself." A chill raced down her spine, and she shivered. "But a young child doesn't have those choices, does he?"

"No." There was another long silence. She switched back to her thumbs and palms, soothing him now, encouraging him to continue. "My father—he was a fanatic, Mellie. A Scottish minister who called himself a servant of Almighty God and saw demons wherever he looked. My mother died when I was six—another thing we have in common. I was their first child. It was a hard birth, and she never really recovered. She lost every other baby she conceived, and believe me, my father planted a horde of them inside her. It never occurred to the bloody bastard to exercise a little self-control. Sexual congress was his holy right, condoms were a tool of the devil, and my mother's bad health was the fault of his firstborn son."

Melanie's hands lightened still more, consoling him tenderly, conveying emotions she barely knew she felt. "But how could he have blamed you? You were an innocent baby. Was he totally insane?"

"On the contrary, he was coldly logical. He said I was born possessed—that the birth took two days because the evil inside me wanted to cause pain. I cried continually for the first year. My mother blamed colic and my father blamed Satan. The older I got, the more of a hellion I became. I had endless energy and a rebellious nature. And according to my father, that was the work of Satan, too. My first memory is of him paddling me, saying that the evil in my body would flee from the pain. I was three or four. I can recall my mother arguing with him after that, trying to protect me. It was the only area in which she stood up to him, and he was so obsessed with her—so in love with her—that he let her have her way. But of course, she lived only two more years."

His tone was so flat and detached that if Melanie hadn't known better, she would have thought all the emotion had been wrung out of him years ago, leaving only a cold void behind. "And then there was no one to stop him," she said. "No family friends. No other relations."

"No one at all. He remarried a year later. He'd gone from paddling my bottom to thrashing my back with a rod by then. When I still didn't improve, he switched to a lash. Once, during a particularly severe beating, my stepmother tried to intercede. He dragged her into their room and slammed the door. I could hear him whipping her—hear her screaming with fear and pain. He said he would send her to the madhouse if she challenged him again. She didn't. I told her not to. I was only nine, but I couldn't be responsible for her being hurt, or for my little sisters losing their mother."

So he had been brave as well as tough. He'd had a big heart. The Reverend Mr. McClure must have beaten out all the trust and innocence. "Then he didn't indulge her the way he indulged your mother?"

"No. He married her for the use of her body, and because he wanted a son to preserve the family name. A good son, not a bad one like me, but my stepmother kept giving him daughters. He always protected my private parts when he whipped me, but if he'd had another son, I doubt that he would have bothered. He used to yell at me between lashes—tell me I had killed my brothers and sisters and murdered my mother, say I was possessed by the devil, explain that if he didn't purge the evil with pain, I would be damned forever. I was always in trouble—accidentally breaking things, talking in church, taking food I wasn't allowed to have—but the punishments were unpredictable. He would make me pray with him for four straight hours for running away, then beat the tar out of me for making a mistake in my grammar."

Melanie felt faint and nauseated. "So even when you tried to be good—"

"I still got punished. Not that I tried very hard. I told you, I was rebellious. Strong-willed and stupid. I ran away a few times, but people always found me and brought me back. Finally, when I was ten or so, I tried to fight him physically. I was big for my age, but my father was a giant, and my resistance enraged him. He spread-eagled me to my bed and thrashed me with a cat until I passed out. I never fought him again."

"Oh, God." She fought the urge to gag. "It's a miracle he didn't kill you. What did you—? How did you—?" She couldn't go on. Sympathy and horror had closed up her throat.

"Escape?" He hesitated. "Late one night when he was sleeping, I picked up one of his pistols, and I realized I didn't know which of us I wanted to shoot more. I can't remember a time when I didn't hate him, but somewhere deep inside me, I thought he was right about what I was—something evil that deserved to die. If it hadn't been for—" He stopped abruptly.

Concerned, Melanie put her hand on his shoulder. "Alex? Are you all right?"

"I'm fine." His voice was tight. "There's nothing more to tell. A month later, I ran away again, but

I was luckier than before. Nobody saw me. I escaped to England."

She was still reeling from the hell he'd endured when he gingerly turned over and slowly sat up. In the process, he exposed a good deal more of the male anatomy than she had even seen before. Prominent pelvic bones, dark brown curls, and, most disconcerting of all, a considerable expanse of soft dusky skin, not tumid and thrusting aggressively as she had come to expect from the male member, but nestled softly and innocently against his loins. She stared at him in helpless fascination, and his flesh began to lengthen and swell.

She turned beet-red and quickly looked away, but out of the corner of her eye, she could see him tug up his trousers and button them halfway. She sneaked a look at his face. Incredibly, he was smiling slightly.

Still blushing, she forced herself to meet his eyes. "But you can't stop there, Alex. If it hadn't been for what? What else happened that night? What did you do in England?"

"Nothing happened." He tucked a pillow behind his back and leaned against the bulkhead. "I put the pistol away and went to bed."

"I don't believe it. Something extraordinary took place. Something inside you changed. Tell me the rest of your history."

He gave her an artless look. "Mellie . . . my stomach feels as if it's caught in a vise. Do you suppose you could perform the same magic on my chest as you did on my back?"

She knew what he was up to, and it wasn't going to work. "I would be happy to—if you answer my questions while I'm massaging you."

"An interesting proposition." He raised his brows. The eyes beneath were cool and a little mocking. "That's the female in you bargaining with me, I presume?"

His arrow hit its mark, and she flushed again. "Yes. I'm sorry. It's just that when you talk to me that way, I feel so—" She bit her lip. She'd felt emotions she had no business feeling, like closeness and warmth and concern. "So curious about your life. Are your stomach muscles truly sore, or was it just a ploy to shut me up?"

"They're sore." He grasped her hands and settled them on his belly, placing her thumbs about an inch below his navel. "Right here."

She probed a little, finding that his gut was as tight as he'd said. Softening instantly, she poured some liniment on his stomach and gently worked it in. He slid down a little, and she began making gentle circles on his belly with her thumbs, soothing, loosening, and stretching him.

Alex closed his eyes. When Melanie touched him that way, he could almost forget the humiliating details he had divulged and the pity they had evoked. Drug-induced or not, the lapse was as mortifying as it was unprecedented, but at least he hadn't babbled about his mother. He hadn't lain his whole miserable life at Mellie's feet. His manhood and his dignity were diminished, but at least they weren't in shreds.

Her fingers gave him more relief than pleasure at first, but it wasn't long before a distracting heat suffused his groin. He felt his nipples harden ... his heart speed up ... his forehead grow damp. His member, just barely awake when she'd begun, was soon straining against his trousers. He fought the urge to follow where it wanted to lead. Her therapy had a sweetness all its own. He hadn't felt so indulged, so pampered, in longer than he could recall. He didn't want her to stop.

He opened his eyes halfway and studied her

through his lashes, finding pleasure in simply watching her. She was nibbling her lower lip in concentration, her head bent forward, her hair swirling around her face like a wild dark cloud. She moistened her lips, leaving them slightly parted afterward, absently licking and rubbing them with the tip of her tongue. A jolt of sexual hunger tore through him. She was moving in time with her hands, and whenever she swayed forward, her shirt slapped gently against her body to provide a tantalizing hint of the curves beneath. He pictured her sitting naked on top of him with her knees clutching his thighs, circling the base of his shaft with her slender, exquisite fingers and slowly impaling herself, then rocking in the exact same rhythm to take him deep and then withdraw, over and over, while he quietly lost his mind.

The image was his undoing. It made him want her with a fiery need that destroyed his delight in any tenderer pleasures. He quickly decided there was no reason to wait. The boat was in port, but everything was quiet. Dawn had broken and the passengers would be waking soon, but few of them would hurry to debark. They would breakfast on the boat. Nothing in town would be open this early—no shops, no offices. The first stagecoach wouldn't depart for more than an hour.

Under the circumstances, he could take all the time he wanted. All the time Melanie deserved. He realized he very much wanted to please her, but it wasn't for the usual male reasons— masculine pride, masculine domination. It was her compassion. Her generosity. He felt affection toward her. Admiration and gratitude. He wanted to show her those things by the way he made love to her.

"A little higher," he murmured. He knew he would have to coax her. Every woman he'd ever desired had expected to be pursued, especially the first time he took her. "If you could rub my ribs ..."

She slid her hands upward and pressed down hard with the heels. He moaned in contentment, and she laughed softly. "You're not a Great Dane at all, but a cougar. You're big and ferocious, but when you're content, you go limp and purr."

"Remember that if I ever frighten you again. Your hands are the best weapons you have." He grasped her thumbs, pressed them flat against his nipples, and rubbed them slowly back and forth over the erect nubs. She tried to pull away, but he refused to release her. "Right now, they have me at their mercy. You make me ache for you, sweetheart."

Melanie ached as well, but she didn't want to. It was wayward and very dangerous, the way his nakedness heated her blood. She hadn't missed the evidence of his arousal bulging against his trousers, and the knowledge that he desired her had stirred her even more. Worst of all, the feel of his skin had sent the most shocking pictures through her mind, the images even more lurid than the ones in Friday's dream. Alex kissing her hotly, touching her in forbidden places, slowly undressing her ...

"You have to stop that. It isn't right." She was trying to sound firm, but her voice came out breathless. "I belong to another man—"

"That's absurd. No man will ever own you, least of all Bonner. You're far too independent. Besides, I assumed you had cut him loose. You're not wearing his ring."

She embraced the subject like a long-lost lover. Any topic was safer than Alex's male appetites. "It's in my pocket. I could hardly leave it on my finger. I was disguised as a groom, remember?"

He gave her a lazy, knowing smile. "I don't believe it. I saw the look on your face when you left his office yesterday. I'll bet the two of you quarreled—that you broke things off and gave the ring back."

"I didn't." She tugged at her hands. "If you would let me go, I would be able to show you."

"Fair enough." He released her right hand, but kept the left one imprisoned.

She dug the ring out of her pocket and waved it under his nose. "See? I'm still engaged and I intend to remain faithful."

He snatched the ring away, then turned it this way and that, studying it at length. "Paste," he finally announced. "In addition to all his other faults, the man is cheap."

She looked at him skeptically. "I don't believe you. That's a real diamond. Real emeralds. The ring is from Shreve's." She held out her hand. "Give it back to me, Alex."

"If that's what he told you, he's either a liar or a dupe. I know gemstones, and—"

"I'll bet you do," she interrupted with a sniff. "After all, you've stolen so many of them over the years."

"Just a few, actually, and only from people who deserved to be robbed. Among other things, I'm a trader. Gemstones are one of my specialties."

She didn't want to listen, but her instincts said he was telling the truth, and so did the gentleness in his eyes. "And you swear the stones are fakes? You're absolutely sure of it?"

"Yes—but very good ones, if it's any consolation."

It wasn't. She kept telling herself that her doubts about George were nothing but cold feet, but this was very different. Shreve's was the finest jeweler in town. They didn't cheat their customers. George had presented the ring in a Shreve's box, but obviously he had bought it somewhere else. Gotten it on the cheap. She hoped he'd believed the stones to be real, but even if he had, it was still the behavior of a liar.

Alex sat up and put his arm around her shoulders, then eased her against his chest. His body was warm and comforting—and much too hard and exciting. "I'm sorry you had to find out this way. Are you very upset?"

"No," she murmured, knowing she should have been. She had accepted George's proposal. He should have meant more to her. "Disillusioned and even offended, but not upset."

"Then you realize you don't love him. Good. I was afraid you might think you did." He tossed the ring onto her trunk. "Can I allow myself to hope that you've finally decided to get rid of him?"

"I don't know. Maybe there's a reasonable explanation." But she slowly shook her head. "If there is, though, I don't know what it could be."

"Financial problems?"

"Impossible. He's a successful attorney. He has tons of money."

But Alex wasn't so sure. There had been that business with the bill at Marchand's, and even before that, Bonner's puzzling turnaround about sneaking in goods to the Confederacy. He might well have realized that he could steal a large share of the proceeds of such an operation with little or no chance of discovery.

At the moment, though, it was Bonner's fiancée that interested Alex, not his finances. He pulled Melanie's shirt from her breeches with a quick flick of his wrist and slid his palm against her belly. Her skin was perfect, like the softest imperial silk. She stiffened and jerked away; he tightened his grip on her shoulders and pulled her even closer. Then he moved his palm back and forth across her stomach, slowly and firmly. To his immense satisfaction, she flushed and began to tremble.

She pressed on his arm and hand, trying to push them away, but he was much too strong for her to succeed. Her excitement was enchantingly obvious. She was breathing much faster now and her nipples were fully erect, thrusting enticingly against the fabric of her shirt. He ran his palm over her breasts in a quick, light caress, then returned his hand to her belly.

She shivered. "Don't, Alex. Please, no more. You have to stop touching me."

"Why? I'm enjoying it and so are you. Believe me, I can feel just how much. And surely you're finished with Bonner now."

He was right on all counts. The pleasure was so intense that she could barely think, much less talk, much less resist. As for George, she only knew that she couldn't respond like this to one man and then marry another—could she? "That's the whole point," she said a little wildly. "You're ten times worse than George is. A pirate, a thief, a liar, a rake—"

"No. I'm nothing like him, Mellie." His hand stilled. "I'm not an outlaw, either. I admit I've skirted the rules—even broken them a few times—but that was years ago. I also admit I've lied to you, but not since last night, and I won't lie to you again. That's a promise. As for your final accusation . . ."

He cupped her chin and lifted her face to his. He looked sober, earnest. "One final admission. I enjoy making love. I like women and they seem to like me back. I've had my shares of offers. So I plead guilty to having the instincts of a rake, but

I'm far too selective to have lived the life." He smiled warmly, and her resistance began to melt. "No man in his right mind wouldn't want you, sweetheart. You're brave and sweet and clever—and very beautiful." His expression turned quizzical. "Your hair and eyes ... You mentioned you were born in Hong Kong. Are you part Chinese?"

She had been taught to lie about her mother, told that she had no choice, but she couldn't lie to Alex. His scars demanded the truth. Her pain was nothing compared to his.

She steeled herself for the inevitable rejection. Though he lived in the Orient now, he was still a white man, a European, and her alien blood would make her lower and cheaper in his eyes. "Yes," she mumbled. "My mother was Portuguese and Chinese."

His smile returned at once, even warmer than before. She let out a breath that she hadn't been conscious of holding. It shouldn't have mattered what he thought, but it did.

"Ah." He unbuttoned the top two buttons of her shirt. "That explains it." And then the third and final button.

"Explains what? And why are you fiddling with my shirt?"

"Why I couldn't stay away from your room tonight. I tried very hard, but it was hopeless. I have a weakness for Oriental women—and a hunger for *you* that turns me into a witless wreck whenever I see you or even think about you." He took a side of her shirt in each hand. "As for your second question ..." He tore it down to her waist with a single, fluid movement. "So it would be easier to do that." He sucked in his breath. "God, you have beautiful breasts."

She flinched and froze, stunned by what he had done, shocked to find herself exposed. By the time she came to her senses and grabbed the tattered shirt to pull it closed, it was too late. His left arm was around her shoulders and his right hand was on her breast.

"Such soft, white skin," he murmured, "and such exquisite nipples. Like rich brown jade on Sung porcelain." He took a nipple between his thumb and forefinger. "But warm and alive, Mellie. Not cold." He rolled it rhythmically back and forth, applying a little extra pressure at the end of each rotation. Every gentle pinch sent a delicious burst of heat through her body. She felt herself growing hot between her legs, and disturbingly damp.

His fingers roughened a little, kneading her breast and pulling at the throbbing nipple. She threw back her head and fought for air. How did you tell a man to stop something like that? The pleasure was paralyzing, overpowering. But if she allowed him to continue . . .

"Alex . . . please . . . don't," she finally choked out. He gave her nipple a sharp little squeeze, and she flinched at the shock of arousal that tore through her. She suddenly wanted to submit to whatever he asked, but she knew that was madness. "Oh, God. What you're doing . . . You make me so hot, and I can't think—"

"Hush, sweetheart." He nuzzled her neck, then murmured in her ear, "Don't worry. I won't do anything you don't want me to." He nipped her lobe. "You're an angel. I would kill myself to please you."

She would be long dead by then, the victim of too much ecstasy. He explored her ear with his tongue, and she closed her eyes and relaxed against this body in silent surrender. He moved his hand from her shoulder to her other breast, gently covering it, teasingly withholding his caresses, and she thought she would burn up with longing. She arched her body feverishly and rubbed herself beseechingly against his palm.

"That's good. Very sweet. Don't be afraid to show me what you like. To tell me what you want." He gave her what she craved, stroking her tenderly one moment and masterfully the next, and her arms went helplessly around his waist. She wanted him to kiss her the way he had in the carriage—the playfulness, the passion, even the torture. Especially the torture. She turned her face and blindly sought his mouth.

He plunged a hand into her hair and gently pulled up her head. She opened her eyes. His gaze could have scorched ice. "If it were up to me, I would taste your breasts very thoroughly now, but if you would prefer me to taste your mouth . . ."

She blushed and lowered her eyes, embarrassed by the thought of him biting and sucking her nipples as he had in the carriage, but directly on her bare flesh. "Whatever you want, Alex. Whatever pleases you."

"'You do. Immensely." He ran his fingers down her cheek, then grasped her chin. "Would you like me to tease you with kisses, Mellie? Like I did last night?"

She managed a whispered yes.

"Then that's what I want, too. Tell me when you've had enough. And touch me back. Caress me. Please, sweetheart."

She would have obeyed his orders willingly, but that final "please" turned her into his eager slave. She moved her thumbs to his nipples and stroked them as he'd taught her to before, and he murmured his approval. A moment later, his fingers recaptured her breast and his teeth closed over her bottom lip. He gently nipped her, then lazily sucked and tasted her. She opened her mouth for him, but he ignored the sweetness inside and began to explore, planting kisses on her throat and jaw and eyes. She adored that—his patience, his tenderness—but it wasn't long before she wanted more. Much more. She raked her nails over his nipples in passionate frustration, and he shuddered and returned to her mouth. But his lips were as playful and provocative as before. Torture and bliss.

Her hands grew restless on his chest, kneading and stroking wherever they could reach. Somewhere on the fringe of her senses, she heard the sounds of the awakening boat—soft footsteps, quiet voices—but she paid them no attention. Nothing mattered except Alex and how he was making her feel. She tempted him with her tongue as he nibbled her lips, and he pulled her roughly into his arms and buried his mouth against her neck. She slid her hand over his heart. It was racing so fast, it should have exploded out of his chest. He was excited, she realized. Very excited.

He was also incredibly controlled. He straightened after a moment, then brushed his mouth chastely across hers. "Mellie?"

She clutched his shoulders and looked at him through glazed eyes. "What?"

"I've a mind to tease you awhile longer, since you like it so much." He smiled. "Assuming I can manage to hang on. Would you enjoy that?"

"God, Alex. I don't know. I guess so." She pressed her lips to his closed mouth and kissed him frantically.

So it started all over, and after a minute or two she wanted him so desperately that she simply snapped. She didn't say a word. She couldn't even think. She just bit his lip. Hard. And then she went rigid, appalled by her loss of control, afraid of what he would do to her.

He slid a hand into her hair and eased back her

head. She saw the blood of his lip, and winced. She noticed the beginnings of a smile—and then, a second later, she realized he was flat-out furious. It didn't show on his face, but she knew that he was, because a wave of menace slammed into her with such stunning force that the terror almost stopped her heart. She jerked herself out of his arms, thinking only of escape. She had to get out of this room. She had to get off the boat.

But he was faster than she was, and much stronger. She didn't get more than an inch off the bed before he pulled her back down and dragged her onto his lap. She lashed out wildly, pushing and kicking and scratching, and he cursed under his breath and tumbled her backward onto the bed. She wound up trapped beneath his body with his hand clapped over her mouth and her arms pinned over her head, her wrists imprisoned firmly but gently in his other hand.

"Jesus, Mellie." He was panting as hard as she was. "You're either going to kill me with pleasure, or kill me, period." He gingerly removed his hand from her lips and supported himself on his elbow. "What the hell happened just now? What went wrong?"

She could still feel the danger. It was vibrating through the room in rapid, powerful waves. She cringed away from him, trembling uncontrollably. "Don't hurt me, Alex. Please. I didn't mean to. I'm sorry."

"You're sorry you bit me?" He looked astonished. "Hell, Mellie, I loved it. It was damned exciting. And even if I hadn't . . ." He sighed. "Look at my chest, for God's sake. My back. After what was done to me, how could you think I would hurt someone else?"

Her head was in a muddle. He wouldn't. It didn't add up. "I—I don't know. But you've admitted that you're dangerous. You must have enemies—"

"Yes. And if they attack me, I fight back. But I don't enjoy violence and I certainly don't hit women." He loosened his hold on her wrists. "All right? If I let you go, will you promise not to scratch out my eyes? Can we talk about this calmly?"

She nodded uneasily, and he released her. The menace was still out there—she could feel it—but she suddenly understood that it wasn't coming from Alex. She shuddered at what that implied. There was someone else. It wasn't Alex. Maybe it had never been Alex.

She put her arms around his neck. "I'm frightened. Please, just hold me."

He slowly lowered himself until his chest was grazing her breasts. "Hold you? You're half-naked in my arms and you expect me just to hold you?" He nuzzled her lips, murmuring against her mouth, "I'm sorry, angel, but I'm not that much of a gentleman."

"Oh," she said, and slid her tongue between his teeth.

He let her taste him for several seconds and then took control, giving her a slow, deep kiss that burned away the fear.

Then someone pounded on the door.

Chapter 12

Alex jerked awake and reached for his gun, wondering why the private coach he and Melanie were traveling in had stopped. He was preparing to do battle with one of the local outlaws when he saw that it was only the driver changing horses. He checked the time. It was ten o'clock already, more than three hours into their journey.

He gingerly stretched, testing the condition of his muscles. Thanks to Melanie's therapy, they were flexible and only slightly sore. He stared at her for a long moment. He had hired this coach so they could get some sleep during their trip to the mountains, and she was curled up on the seat across from him, doing exactly that.

Five hours ago, he had been sure he would possess her secrets as well as her body by now, but he had been wrong on both counts. He had Ned to thank for that or, rather, the fact that the hackman had pounded on her door like a stamp mill just as victory was within his grasp. Alex didn't give a damn that Ned meant well. If he had wanted a retainer who fussed and fretted when he didn't turn up, he would have hired an old maid.

Ned had admitted to searching for him everywhere—on deck, in the main cabin, in the captain's quarters, and finally in Melanie's stateroom, calling out that he was a steward and needed to retrieve her tray. Alex had gotten rid of him almost at once, but to no avail. Melanie's mood had changed to one of embarrassment and anxiety by then, and there was no changing it back. She had informed him that she was traveling to Nevada City and suggested that he come along, then ordered him from her room in no uncertain terms.

He still hadn't forgiven Ned the interruption. He had even banished the hackman from the coach, telling him to ride outside with the driver. Knowing how softhearted Melanie was, he had resigned himself to being scolded for his harshness, but she hadn't said a word. On the contrary, only moments before their departure, she had slipped out of the carriage, handed Ned her pistol, and told him to stay on his guard. Alex hadn't bothered to ask her why. The shuttered look in her eyes had told him it would be a waste of his time.

The carriage began to move again, and he yawned and lay back down. He was still very tired, and their journey would take until late afternoon. He intended to get some answers, but there would be ample time later to drag them out of her.

He slept until their next stop, Auburn, where they changed horses again and dined. The meal was tense and silent at first, but he exerted himself to be charming and cajoled her into a more talkative frame of mind. She admitted she had once lived in the town, in the very hotel where they were eating, then spun a wonderful yarn about how her father had played cards with the notorious local highwayman Tom Bell and walked off with eight thousand dollars in stolen Wells Fargo gold. Wyatt had kept every dime, too. Alex decided he was a man worth meeting.

Back in the coach, she opened her valise and took out a shot glass and a jar of liquid. She filled up the glass, then held it out to him. "It's time for your next dose of medicine. I want you to drink every drop."

He frowned at it. "I don't think so, Mellie. I'm still trying to recover from the first dose."

"Nonetheless, you're going to do as I say." She sat down beside him and shoved it under her nose. "Come, Alex, don't be difficult. It will help keep you well."

"Me? Difficult?" He snorted. "I'm not the one who kisses like an angel and turns men into—"

"That has nothing to do with—"

"—quivering, panting wrecks. I'm not the one who chases around town and steals onto boats and leaves men exhausted from trying to follow. Who—"

"Then stop trying. Anyway—"

"Who held a gun to whose loins, hmm? Who stabbed whom in the back? Who got bitten, for God's sake? Compared to you, I'm the most easy-going human on the planet."

She gave him a long-suffering look. "All of which you deserved, and none of which has anything to do with taking your medicine. Are you finished complaining yet?"

"I suppose so." He paused. "For the moment."

"Then drink." She pressed the glass to his lips. "Right now. No more arguments."

He sighed and complied. "There. I hope you're pleased. I believe I've earned a reward for being so cooperative. Specifically, I deserve to know why you told me where you were going and begged me to come along."

She set the jar on the floor. "See that you keep taking that, Alex. Three times a day until it's gone. And I didn't beg you; I simply invited you."

"I stand corrected. Why the sudden change of heart, Melanie?"

She returned to her own seat. "Helpless infatuation."

Alex roared with laughter and Melanie reddened and looked away. She had flung out the first excuse that came to mind, tossing his earlier words back at him, but they weren't so far from the truth. She *was* infatuated with him. He was dangerous and fascinating and exciting, and when he touched her she burst into flames. But their night together had been madness. She shuddered to think what would have happened it Ned hadn't interrupted—and if the growing aura of danger in the room hadn't terrified her back to reality. But it was over now, and she wasn't going to repeat it.

Alex stretched out his legs and placed his feet beside her on the seat, easing them against her thigh. "Tell me something, Mellie. Why do you keep treating me like a dimwit?"

"I don't." She inched away from him. "I'm still very tired, Alex. I'd like to lie down, so if you would remove your feet—"

"Do you think I haven't noticed the fear you keep sensing? The way it materializes from out of nowhere and grips you by the throat?" He shook his head impatiently. "I'm not so thick-brained that I can't add one and one and come up with two. You've got an enemy out there. You're clairvoyant, so you know when he's close by. That's why you were so surprised last night when I didn't feel dangerous anymore—because you thought it was me. But it isn't, and you fear whoever it is even more than you once feared me. That's why you told me where you were going after trying to elude me for two straight days. Why you asked me to come along. You wanted some extra protection. That's also why you gave Ned your revolver."

He was exactly right, but Melanie wasn't going to admit it. The more he knew, the easier it would be to steal her gold.

"I'll take your silence as a confirmation," he said coolly. "Since you're using me as a bodyguard, the least you can do is tell me what you've gotten me into. Why are you going to Nevada City? Who else could be following you, and why? For the necklace? For the maps? Where do they lead?"

She raised her chin. "If I wanted to tell you, I would. I don't."

He leaned forward, put his hands on her waist, and hauled her onto his lap. She squared her shoulders and looked pointedly out the window, but she didn't struggle. It would have been fruitless.

"Obviously I didn't make myself clear enough." He grasped her jaw and turned her head. "I want answers, Mellie, and I want them now. It was an order, not a request."

She glared at him. "And if I don't obey it? Will you beat me, Alex? Borrow the coachman's whip and rip off my clothes and—"

"No, damn you." He dropped his hands in disgust. "You have a tongue like a razor, Melanie. Don't ever accuse me of that again."

Melanie retreated to her own side of the coach, so appalled with herself that she wanted to sink through the floor. "I'm sorry. I didn't mean to compare you to your father. I didn't stop to think what I was saying. But you have no right to order me around. No right to manhandle me." She took a deep breath. "And no right to demand answers when you won't give any yourself. You haven't exactly been forthcoming, Alex. You won't tell me who you're working for or why you're following me, and when it comes to anything more intimate, your response to my questions is to scold me for prying or refuse to speak at all."

"That's absurd. You know more about me than I do about you, not that I see what difference it makes."

"I know about your scars. That's all, and it's not enough to induce me to trust you. I've told you about my childhood—"

"So did your friend Bonner. Hell, so did the manager at the Oriental. Your childhood is obviously common knowledge in San Francisco, so if you consider what you told me an intimate confession, you have an unusual definition of the phrase."

She was stung by the charge. "And what about the fact that I'm part Chinese? Do you think that's common knowledge, too?" The words were no sooner out than she tensed and paled. It had been stupid to bring up the subject. She had reminded him of something with which he could blackmail her.

"No. You would have been ostracized if people knew. I promise you, they won't find out from me." He sighed deeply. "Look, Mellie, I want to help you, not hurt you. You trusted me enough to let me make love to you last night, so why can't you trust me a little now? Tell me what you're involved in and let me do what needs to be done."

"Because you're my enemy. Sh—I mean, my cohorts would have mentioned you if we were on the same side, and they haven't. Anyway, I'm perfectly capable of handling things myself."

"You can't seriously believe that. My God, if I were the villain you keep claiming I am, I could have kidnapped you three times over. Stolen your maps, tortured you into talking, used your body however I pleased ..."

Her stomach turned over, but she didn't let it show. "Are you threatening me with those things if I refuse to do what you want?"

"Hardly. I'm insulted you would even ask. The point is, you aren't handling things nearly as well as you would like to think." He suddenly smiled. "If you were, I wouldn't be in this coach right now, playing escort. What happens when we reach Nevada City? Are your cohorts waiting for you there? Are you counting on them to help you? To protect you from whoever is following you?"

"Yes—and to dispose of *you*," she said. Ty was bound to know someone who could get him off her tail.

"Not a chance. Wherever you go, I'll be right behind you." He lazed back on the seat. "Give it up, Mellie. This isn't a game you can win."

"To me, it isn't a game at all," she retorted. "Since it means so little to you, why don't *you* give it up?"

"Because I always finish what I start. And because I'm enjoying myself too much. You've bewitched me, sweetheart. Why do you think I've been so patient?" He yawned and closed his eyes. "Still, my tolerance has its limits. You would do well to remember that."

Ty and Sukey Stone lived in the same house on Main Street where Melanie had lived in the early fifties. Thomas had given the place to the Stones after he'd moved to San Francisco, but Mrs. Stone had died of a stroke a few months later, leaving the two children alone. Thomas had quickly offered Sukey a home, saying that a twenty-year-old lad who gambled and caroused shouldn't have charge of an eleven-year-old child, but Ty had promised to quit the mines and settle down, and he had kept his word. He had even taken two different jobs to save for the future, one as a hotel clerk and the other on a local paper. The owner had hired him to sell subscriptions and advertisements, but it wasn't long before he was operating the press and writing stories. He had a real talent for the work, especially uncovering a good scandal.

It was only when Sukey reached thirteen that he'd begun to doubt his ability to cope. He'd felt she needed feminine guidance and a more cultivated life, and their great aunt in Philadelphia had offered both. In the end, though, they had stayed in the States for only two years because Sukey had a tendency toward fragile health that the Eastern heat and humidity had exacerbated.

Ty owned his own business now, printing everything from handbills to books and publishing a weekly paper that he wrote and edited himself. Sukey often helped at the shop, especially when school was out of session. As far as Melanie knew, they were content with their lives.

Artie, the groom, had wired Ty from San Francisco that she was coming, so Melanie assumed he would be home when she arrived. As for Alex, he slept on and off throughout the trip, probably due to the medicine he was taking. Whenever he was awake, she made a point of studying the scenery avidly. It discouraged uncomfortable questions.

The tactic succeeded until they approached the outskirts of town, and the coachman asked her where to go. She hesitated, thinking it might be better if Alex didn't know her destination. Why make it easier for him to tail her?

He saw her uncertainty and broke into one of those knowing smiles that made her want to kick him. "I told you, Mellie, this isn't a game you can win. There are two of us and only one of you, so someone will be watching you every moment. If you were planning to go to a hotel first, then sneak off to a friend's house during the night, you might as well save your money. You'll only be seen and followed."

It was exactly what she'd been planning. Vexed, she stuck her head out the window and gave the coachman directions. "The house is on Main just north of Cottage." She added, "I'll point it out when we get there."

"And whose house would we be talking about?" Alex asked.

There was no point in refusing to tell him. Anyone in town could provide the answer. "Ty and Sukey Stone's." She smiled sweetly. "Obviously you're convinced I have some deep, dark reason for this trip, but you're wrong. They're old friends. I thought it would be fun to visit."

"If you say so. All the same, I want to know more about them. Who they are, how you know them, what Stone does for a living . . ."

"I fail to see why I should satisfy your curiosity."

He pointed out the window. "Because if you don't, I'll carry you into those woods, tie you and gag you, and leave you to cool your heels while I sit in a saloon in town and coax the information out of the local residents."

It was a persuasive argument. "You'd better pray you never need stitches again," she said with a scowl, and told him what he wanted to know.

They reached the Stones' house ten minutes later. The building next door was a boardinghouse now, and several of the upstairs windows overlooked the Stones' yard. Melanie grumbled that Alex led a charmed life and resigned herself to being watched. There would be time enough tomorrow to figure out how to elude him.

In the meantime, she allowed herself to enjoy the pleasures of seeing old friends and catching up on their lives. The three talked so easily at first that Melanie could hardly believe it had been over two years since her last visit. Sukey had turned into a beauty in that time, a chestnut-haired siren with curves Melanie envied, who looked twenty if she looked a day. Ty was as handsome as ever, a blond-haired, blue-eyed god of a man, but Melanie thought he looked tired and a little tense. He was trying to relax and enjoy himself, that much was clear, but he wasn't succeeding. She decided he was probably working too hard. A man had little choice when he started his own business.

By the end of dinner, though, she was wondering if it wasn't more than that. The meal itself had been splendid, a veritable feast prepared by a girl Melanie had rescued a few months before and sent to Ty and Sukey, but the conversation was a near disaster. Melanie had tried to be amusing, telling Ty yarns about her romantic misadventures, and Sukey had done the same, offering tales about their eccentric Eastern relations, but he had barely laughed. Indeed, stories about practical jokes and social blunders that once would have had him rolling on the floor evoked only weak smiles that seemed to mask his disapproval. Melanie even caught him staring blankly into space a couple of times. This rigid, distracted man wasn't the Ty she knew. It was dismaying.

Sukey finally stood and began collecting the dishes. "Why don't I give Suk-Ling the rest of the evening off? After all, she worked so hard all day cooking. I'm sure you two want to be alone—to talk without a little sister being around—so I'll clean up." She gave Ty a sidelong look. "I could go over to Betsy's afterward. Get out of your hair for a while."

He shook his head. "No, Suke. You know what I said last week. Not until Friday."

"But it's only twenty past eight. I won't stay long—"

"That's what you said the last time. Have you forgotten what time you strolled in?"

"No, but I've told you a hundred times, I didn't do it on purpose. I just didn't realize how late it was. Please, Ty. I said I was sorry. I won't be long. I swear it."

"I would say no in any event, Sukey. We have a busy day at work tomorrow. You should be getting your rest, not gossiping with your friends."

"But I'm not the least bit tired," she insisted. "I'm dying of boredom, staying home all the time, and I don't see what difference an hour—"

"I said no. That's final." Ty got to his feet and gave her a hard stare. She was as tall as Melanie, but at six foot three, Ty towered over both of them. "Since you're so bored, you can go straight to bed after you clean up."

Sukey's eyes got watery. "No! You're a damned tyrant. I hate working for you. Just because *you* don't have any fun—"

"We have company," Ty interrupted curtly. "I expect you to behave like a civilized young lady. If you use that sort of language again, I'll wash out your mouth with soap. Now clear the table and go to your room."

Sukey burst into tears and protested bitterly. Ty bellowed right back at her. Finally, after three or four heated exchanges, he picked her up and slung her over his shoulder. He marched from the room to the sound of her yelling.

Melanie dismissed Suk-Ling and cleared the table, then took out a bottle of brandy and carried it into the parlor along with some glasses. As she sat down on the sofa, the door at the top of the stairs slammed shut. A series of loud thuds quickly followed, as if someone was trying to kick it down, and then wild sobbing.

Ty reappeared, dropped down beside her, and gratefully accepted a glass of brandy. "I don't know what to do with her, Melanie. She's so emotional. She giggles one moment, sulks the next, then screams like a fishwife or bursts into tears. And the things she accuses me of . . . You would think I was Torquemada. I've disrupted my life for the girl, not once but three times, but you would never know it. I'm not complaining—I love her and I did it willingly—but there's no gratitude from her, no obedience or cooperation. I had to lock her in her room, can you believe that? She would have sneaked out through the back if I hadn't."

"She's simply growing up," Melanie said gently. "Spreading her wings and trying to fly. Sixteen is a difficult age for a girl. She's trapped between childhood and womanhood, and her emotions are running sky-high. And of course, you're her brother, not her father, and you were wild as a young stallion at her age, so she thinks you've forgotten how it feels to be sixteen—turned into a stodgy old man who doesn't understand her." She sipped her brandy. "Haven't you, Ty, maybe just a little? Couldn't you let her go to her friend's house for an hour?"

"No. She was an hour and a half late last Thursday and she's being punished. She knows that. She wouldn't even have asked to go if you weren't here." He drained his glass, then refilled it. "And that's not even the half of it. You saw how mature she looks. For a year now, men have been dancing attendance on her, and she encourages them for all she's worth. She flirts and leads them on, and she won't listen to me when I tell her how dangerous it can be. At least twice last spring, she went to Betsy's house and then slipped out to meet some actor. I got rid of the man—I told him I would beat him to a pulp if he went near her again—but suppose she's taken a fancy to someone else? I'm afraid to take my eyes off her. I can't trust her to be sensible."

"Not until her juices stop bubbling, anyway." Melanie grinned at him. "Poor Ty. Talk about getting your just deserts . . ."

"Damn it, Mel, it's not funny. People are beginning to gossip about her." He took another swig of brandy. "What am I going to do? It's like a war zone around here."

She thought for a minute. "Maybe you need a break from each other. Have you considered sending her to boarding school when the new term begins? The girls' academy in Benicia is supposed to be excellent."

"So I've heard. She's mentioned it at least six times. But she could sneak out there just as well as here, and I wouldn't be around to beat off the snakes."

"I doubt you would need to. The whole point of misbehaving is to challenge your authority and show you she's growing up. So let her go away. Give her the independence she wants. I'm sure it will solve your problem. After all, she's smart enough to know she'll be sent home if she breaks the rules."

Ty finally unbent a little and smiled crookedly at her. "Oh? Do you speak from personal experience?"

Melanie mulled it over, then shook her head. "No. It was different with me. My father was so permissive that there was nothing to rebel against.

I simply had a wild streak. I was raised in a man's world and I didn't see why I shouldn't be able to do everything that men did."

"And besides, Thomas ignored you most of the time. You wanted to make him pay you a little notice, so you behaved outrageously. Better a lecture than nothing at all."

"I don't think so, Ty." But she thought about it a little more, just to be sure. "Really, that's not what I was trying to do. It was simply youthful high spirits."

Ty was quick to disagree. "On the contrary, you were desperate for your father's attention, and that was the only way to get it. Shen Wai could see it. So could my mother, but when she tried to talk to Thomas about it, he insisted he was home more than most men with his business interests were—"

"But he was. That was true."

"Maybe, but you needed more. And I'll tell you something else about your father. He's a rake. He uses women until they bore him, then cuts them loose. You've watched that all your life, and it's made you distrust every man you meet. So whenever you let one too close, you get scared and run away." He took her hand. "I don't see the diamond and emerald ring you wrote me about. I didn't want to say anything in front of Sukey—I doubt that she even noticed—but I take it that Bonner is the latest casualty."

Melanie's head was spinning. She couldn't ignore what Ty had said—he knew her too well—but she couldn't believe it was true, either. She'd had a wonderful childhood. Her father had tolerated her pranks and spoiled her with gifts, and Shen Wai had given her his time and affection. What more could a girl have wanted?

"Yes," she finally murmured, "but it's a long story. Maybe later . . ."

"Is that why you came up here? To get away from Bonner?"

"No, but that's a long story, too." And under the circumstances, it was the wrong time to tell it. "About Sukey—"

"I won't abandon my responsibilities toward the girl," Ty said sternly. "I'm all she really has, and whether she knows it or not, she needs me right now."

"I agree. You're a wonderful brother, Ty. She's lucky to have you." Melanie put a gentle hand on his shoulder. "But sometimes a girl her age needs the sympathy of an older woman. Maybe I can help. She and I have a similar nature, so why don't I try to talk to her? See if I can help you two understand each other better?"

"Sure. Why not?" Ty handed her the key to Sukey's room, then poured himself another brandy.

Melanie knocked on Sukey's door, then let herself into the girl's room. She was lying on her bed, reading a book. She glanced at Melanie indifferently, then returned to her novel.

"Men are definitely the weaker sex," Melanie said lightly. "Female emotions totally unnerve them. Your poor brother is sitting on the sofa, brooding about his ability to cope, drowning his sorrows in brandy."

Sukey threw down her book and tossed her hair. "My poor brother is a damned jackass. A bloody fool."

"Language like that doesn't shock me, Suke. Not after a ship and all those camps. So use it or don't, I really don't care." Melanie sat down beside her. "Do you want to talk? I know I was Ty's friend first, but we're both women now and we have a lot in common. I can't promise that I'll take your side, but I'm sure I'll understand your feelings. I was considered a real handful in my day, and all because I wanted to live my own life and have a little fun. Sound familiar?"

Sukey simply shrugged so Melanie kept talking, relating some of the pranks she had pulled as a girl, telling comical stories until a reluctant smile appeared on Sukey's face. Then she spun a trio of yarns about her years in Nevada City and the escapades she'd embroiled Ty in, usually against his better judgment, and Sukey finally surrendered and dissolved into giggles.

"I had no idea," she said. "I missed everything, being so young. You were lucky, Mel. You got away with tons."

That was when Melanie knew Ty was right. It hit her like a bolt of lightning and left her dazed. "Only because my father couldn't care as deeply as Ty does. He has a cooler nature than your brother. I know he loves me, but his business dealings come first. So he didn't spend much time with me when I was a child, and as long as I was physically safe, he never really worried. Except about my virginity. *That* always made him hysterical." Because of her mother and grandmother, she suddenly realized. He was afraid some taint in her blood would make her like they were. "But it's different with Ty. You're the most important thing in his life. I doubt he gives a fig about goodness and purity for their own sakes, but he doesn't want to see you hurt, either by some man or by people's bad opinions. He's only trying to protect you."

Sukey sighed dramatically. "But that's so stupid, Mel. Like you said, all I want is a little fun. So what if I like to flirt and tease? I know what I'm doing. I haven't met a man yet whom I couldn't outthink and outsmart."

The girl was young, foolish, and impossibly romantic. She needed to hear a few home truths. "But they *are* out there, and when you tangle with one, you're playing with fire. Take my word for it, Sukey. I've learned about them the hard way."

"Really?" she breathed. "You mean you met one? Did he try to—? Did the two of you—? Are you still—well, you know."

"He did, we didn't, and I am, but I came much too close to being the reverse."

Sukey's eyes widened. "Gosh. Was it incredibly thrilling? Did you want him desperately? Is he the reason you broke your latest engagement? Are you going to keep seeing him?"

So much for Sukey not noticing. The blasted girl was fascinated by the whole affair, the last thing Melanie wanted. "Men like him know how to thrill you. They know how to make you want them. But you could be anyone and they would do the same thing. The cold truth is, I have no future with the man. He's not the domestic type. He's not even respectable. I'm just grateful I came to my senses in time, because he's the sort who could break your heart, and believe me, no amount of excitement is worth that. Ty knows all that. Why do you think he's so worried about you? Would it be so terribly difficult for you to settle down a bit and do what he thinks is best?"

"Even if I did, it wouldn't solve anything." Sukey twisted her hands together in her lap. "I can guess what Ty told you—that I'm disobedient and ungrateful and temperamental—but that's not really fair. There's a whole other side to it, but whenever I bring it up, he says I'm just a child and refuses to discuss it."

"Then discuss it with me," Melanie said. "I'm sure I can make him understand."

Sukey did, saying that after their mother's death her brother had changed from a sunny, fun-loving rogue to a sober model citizen who was a slave to his work. She knew he had done it for her and was grateful, but she also felt guilty about costing him his youth. He seldom went out in the evenings, seldom enjoyed himself as he had when she was a girl. He would have married by now if it weren't for her, but there weren't even any women in his life, at least not any respectable ones.

Sukey resented all that, resented the fact that Ty had made huge sacrifices on her behalf that he needn't have made at all. He could have led a full and happy life, but he had allowed his duties as a guardian and an editor to become obsessions. And now that the war had broken out, it was worse than ever. Back in Pennsylvania, he had become passionately pro-Union, and he had carried those sentiments to California. He would have enlisted in a moment if not for her, and she felt guilty about that, too. She was a burden. He probably hated her for turning him into a shirker.

She was fighting back tears by then. Melanie had expected childish theatrics and shallow complaints, but most of what Sukey had said rang alarmingly true. Ty *was* different, disturbingly so. As for the war, Melanie subscribed to his paper, knew his views well, and agreed he must find it difficult not to serve. But never in a million years, she said, would he blame Sukey for that.

"He loves you dearly. As long as you need him—and you do still need him—his place will be here with you. He knows that and he wouldn't change it. Besides, he's doing more good with his paper, supporting the Union cause and raising money to pay for supplies, than he ever could as a soldier."

"But don't you see?" Sukey wailed. "I'm glad I'm keeping him home, because if he enlisted he could get killed, and I would lose him forever. I'm terrified the war will go on and on and they'll make him fight. But I shouldn't feel that way, Melanie. It means I'm a coward and a terrible sister." She burst into tears. "His whole life would be different if I didn't exist. He would be happy. Oh, God—I wish he would get disgusted with me and send me away. Then he could do what he really wants."

Melanie took the girl in her arms and murmured words of comfort. This wasn't just a youthful rebellion; it was confusion and conflict and torment. When Sukey finally stopped sobbing, she said gently, "Don't worry about losing Ty. My father says they'll need soldiers in California to defend it, so even if your brother enlists, he's likely to stay right here in the state. If you want him to be happy, stop trying to drive him away. It won't work. He'll only get more and more worried and more and more rigid. The best way to get what you want is to stop provoking him. Convince him he can trust you. Then, between the two of us, I'm sure we can talk him into sending you away to school."

Sukey rubbed the tears from her eyes. "Is that really true, Melanie? About soldiers being kept in the state?"

"Yes." She gave the girl a fierce hug. "Do me a favor, darling. Don't be in such a hurry to grow up. Believe me, it isn't all it's made out to be."

Chapter 13

A lex wanted to strangle Melanie's companion with his bare hands. They were riding together in a gig, Melanie doing the driving, and the bastard kept rubbing her back and fondling the nape of her neck. She didn't respond, but she sure as hell didn't fight him off, either. Alex thought darkly that if being mauled was the price she had to pay for obtaining the man's help, she should have found herself a better class of cohort.

He had been watching her for some four hours now, ever since well before dawn. Ned had gone to sleep by then, and Alex had taken over surveillance duties for the night. Melanie had slipped out of the house through the back door, carrying a small valise, dressed in the clothes of a mechanic or miner. She had hurried to a livery stable south of Church Street, emerging at the reins of the gig.

Alex had dashed inside and helped himself to a horse, lost her while he saddled and bridled it, but spotted her empty gig a minute later in front of a boardinghouse a block away. Almost half an hour had passed before she had appeared with her cohort in tow, and Alex preferred not to think about what they had been doing all that time.

The two were heading north now on a quiet

back road. It had been light out for hours and he didn't want to be seen, so he was following at a discreet distance. The ride had been unexpectedly pleasant—he was surrounded by rolling, oak-dotted hills parched gold by the summer sun, meandering streams and rivers, and pine-covered peaks—but hunger was beginning to gnaw at him, taking his mind off everything but his next meal. They finally came to what passed for civilization in these parts, a short stretch of road lined with one- and two-story buildings of wood or brick and stone, and stopped in front of a bakery. According to the sign on the post office, the town was called North San Juan.

Melanie remained with the horses while her co-hort went inside. He emerged with a paper sack and climbed back into the gig. Alex waited until they had driven away, then bought himself some breakfast. He caught up with them a short ways out of town. They had spread down a blanket at the roadside and were having a picnic.

He began to eat, grateful to put something in his stomach. Melanie finished her roll and started to get up, but the man pulled her back down and took her in his arms. Alex's jaws clenched in mid-muffin. It was all he could do to stand and watch stoically as the pair kissed passionately. Then the man pulled off her large, broad-brimmed hat and took down her hair, which tumbled wildly over her back and shoulders.

Alex gaped. It was chestnut-colored and curly, not dark brown with lush waves. He was too far away to see the woman's face, but she clearly wasn't Melanie. He had done it again. Followed the wrong person. He couldn't believe it.

He wanted to kick the nearest inanimate object at first, but quickly realized there might be a silver lining to this particular cloud. Within minutes, he was chatting amiably with the pair. He explained that he had gotten lost in the woods and stumbled upon this country road, then asked about the local geography and the prospects for finding gold. The girl did most of the talking, introducing herself as Mrs. Susannah Guthrie, but she was obviously Miss Sukey Stone and she was just as obviously running away from home. If Alex had been a knight in shining armor, he would have wrested her from the clutches of her alleged husband, a handsome but dim young fellow named Grant Guthrie, and hauled her back to town. But he wasn't, and, besides, she gave every indication of ruling their little love roost completely. So he continued to talk to them, and a few minutes later, armed with the stuff of final victory, he headed back the way he had come.

It was almost ten when he reached Nevada City. He returned the borrowed horse and strolled to the Stones' house, but no one answered his knock. When he reached his room and found Ned gone as well, he concluded that Ty and Melanie must have awakened to find Sukey missing and started combing the town for her, and that Ned had dutifully followed. He wasn't in the mood to track them down, so he did what any sensible, civilized man would do after hours of trudging through the back of beyond. He filled his belly and took a long, hot bath.

He returned to his room to find the door wide open and Ned pacing anxiously back and forth. The hackman saw him and froze. "Oh. There you are."

Alex rolled his eyes. "I seem to recall instructing you not to worry about me."

"Who was worried?" Ned turned away, muttering testily, "All the same, you might have left me a note."

"I would have, but I didn't have time," Alex said with exaggerated patience. "Sukey left too quickly. I thought it was Melanie—"

"So you followed her. You followed Sukey."

"Exactly. And I take it *you* followed Ty and Melanie when they went looking for her. I assume they're back?"

"Yes, and worried sick from what I could overhear. Where is the girl? Is she safe?"

But Alex didn't answer. He was already out the door, and there was a smile a mile wide on his face.

Melanie was sitting on the sofa in the parlor, brooding. She accepted a cup of coffee from Ty, then stared at it numbly. "I thought I was so clever—that I'd nipped her little rebellion in the bud—but all I seem to have done was convince her you would be safe if you enlisted. She never would have left otherwise, no matter how much she wants to give you your supposed freedom. I'm sorry, Ty. This is all my fault."

"Drink your coffee, Mel." Ty joined her on the sofa. "And stop blaming yourself. If it was anyone's fault, it was mine. If I hadn't drunk myself into a stupor last night, I would have been awake when you dragged her downstairs to talk to me. Her and her crazy ideas about me and women and the war . . . If I'd been sober enough to drum some sense into her, this never would have happened."

Melanie nodded, but she still felt guilty. When she had prattled about danger and heartbreak last night, Sukey must have pictured adventure and romance. She had emptied the metal box in which she kept her savings and taken Ty's gig from the local livery, so she had probably left the immediate area. Not a single person in town had seen her that morning and none of her friends knew where she had gone. Melanie was terrified for her.

"Look, she has a hot temper," Ty added wearily. "She'll probably just drive around in a pet all day, then saunter—" There was knock on the door. He bolted to his feet. "Maybe that's someone with news."

Melanie followed him into the hall. She somehow guessed it was Alex even before Ty opened the door. He strolled into the house without an invitation and nonchalantly looked around. He was dressed casually, in black trousers and a gray flannel shirt with the sleeves rolled up, and he looked splendid—relaxed, handsome, and virile. She caught a whiff of shaving lather and shampoo. He even smelled splendid. He grinned at her and she blushed, aware that he had caught her staring.

Ty regarded him warily. Even in friendly Nevada City, strangers didn't barge into your house as if they owned the place. "I don't believe we've met. I'm Tyson Stone."

Alex turned around. "I know. I also know where your sister is."

"Thank God. We were very worried." Ty forced a smile. "I'm obliged to you for coming over, Mr.—"

"McClure. Alex McClure." He waited a beat. "I see that the name doesn't mean anything to you. Melanie obviously hasn't discussed me with you."

"No." Ty looked at her in bewilderment. "Then you've met this man? Who is he? What—"

Alex cut him off. "Later, Mr. Stone. All you need to know right now is that the information about your sister will have a price. And that Melanie is the one—"

But he never finished the sentence, because Ty was charging him like an enraged bull. "You filthy bastard—"

"Ty, don't!" Melanie shrieked—but the warning came too late.

Alex grabbed Ty's arm before he could land a punch and somehow lifted him off his feet. He twisted through the air, his arms and legs flailing, and landed hard on his rump on the carpet, gasping as though he'd had the wind knocked out of him. He didn't look so much hurt as astonished. He was even bigger than Alex was, but Alex had flipped him like a flapjack.

Ty blinked and sat up. "How the hell did you do that?"

"I learned it in the Orient. The Chinese call it *gongfu*. It's a system of self-defense." He extended his hand and helped Ty to his feet. "I expect we'll be spending the next several days together. I'll teach you the basics if you like."

"Uh, sure." Ty looked befuddled. "What's going on here, Melanie? Who is this man?"

"I work for a consortium in Hong Kong," Alex said.

"That's the first I've heard of it," Melanie muttered. "A consortium of what, Alex? Criminal triads?"

He ignored her. "Melanie has some information I need," he said to Ty, "but she's been remarkably stubborn about providing it. As a result, I've been forced to watch her and follow her."

"And you saw Sukey leave last night," Melanie said. "You thought it was me and you tailed her."

"She's quick for a female, isn't she, Stone? I know which road your sister took. I know whom she's with. And I know where they plan to spend the night." He finally looked at Melanie. "Well, sweetheart? How much does your little friend mean to you? Do you tell me what I want to know or do I walk out the door?"

"Now wait just a damned minute!" Ty exploded. "You're not going to use my sister to blackmail Melanie. I'm getting the sheriff."

He started toward the door, but Alex grasped his arm with lightning speed and unbalanced him with a firm, fluid twist of his wrists. A moment later Ty landed on the carpet again, flat on his back this time. He tried to get up, then groaned in pain and lay back down.

Melanie knelt beside him, looking at Alex with daggers in her eyes. "You're a damned bully. You really hurt him."

"No, I didn't. He'll recover in a minute." Alex rested his foot lightly on Ty's chest. "I want you to listen carefully, Stone. Melanie is in serious danger. She could be hurt or even killed if I don't protect her. And I can't do that without the information she has."

Ty looked from one to the other. "Uh, Mel? Is that true? Are we in the middle of another of your adventures?"

"Even if we are," she said with a sniff, "I don't need anyone's help. I can handle the job on my own."

Alex calmly shook his head. "No. You're going to answer every question I ask and you're going to do it right away. Your friend Sukey is with a grown man, and he touches her every chance he gets. I saw the two of them kiss, and if they'd been any hotter or closer, they would have fused together. If you refuse to cooperate, you'll be responsible for getting the girl seduced."

Melanie was outraged. The man had no morals, no decency. All he cared about was advancing his own schemes. "*I'll* be responsible? What about you, you miserable villain? Obviously you knew who she was. You knew she was only sixteen. You should have brought her home."

"I told you yesterday morning, I'm not that

much of a gentleman." He smiled at Ty and removed his foot. "That was just before she slid her tongue into my mouth. I was in her bed at the time on the steamer, and we were both half-naked. So you see, we have a prior relationship. A very close relationship."

Melanie turned crimson. "It was a slip," she said in a strangled voice. "I didn't want to kiss him. I mean, I did want to, but I should have had more sense. He's a scoundrel, Ty. A criminal. That's the whole reason I came up here. Because he was following me and I needed some information you might have."

"I'm a trader and a free-lance investigator, and she doesn't hesitate to make use of me when it suits her. She knows I would never hurt her. Ask her who escorted her from Sacramento to Nevada City."

Ty cocked a stern eyebrow at her. "Melanie?"

"All right. He did, but—"

"Then I think you had better talk to him." Ty slowly got to his feet. "And when you're done, you can talk to me. I want to know how I fit into this little escapade." He put his hand on Alex's shoulder. "Believe me, it's only the latest in a long line of them. She has a talent for landing in trouble. Between the two of us, I trust we can extricate her from whatever mess she's gotten herself into, but my sister will have to come first. You can use my study. It's the room back there. I'll wait in the parlor."

Alex nodded and walked away. Melanie grudgingly followed, simmering with resentment and frustration. "Men," she grumbled. They always stuck together.

Alex preceded her into the study and closed the door, and she retreated to the opposite end of the room. If he thought she was going to jump and dance like a puppet on a string, he had another thing coming. "What was all that about a consortium?" she demanded. "Whom are you working for?"

"I'll tell you in a minute." He lazed against the door with such graceful male confidence that her breath caught in her throat. "Come kiss me good morning first."

Of all the orders he might have given, that was the last one she had expected, but she should have known better. The man was a blasted satyr. A thrill of excitement raced down her spine. And the condition, God help her, was contagious.

"I certainly won't," she said flatly. "Get on with it, Alex. Ask your damned questions. Sukey could be in danger. I don't have time to dawdle."

"When I first walked into the house, you looked at me as if you wanted to salt me and lap me up. Now that we're alone, your cheeks are flushed and your eyes are sparkling."

"Because I'm angry with you."

"And because you want me. Do you have any idea what that does to me?" He crooked his finger at her. "Come kiss me, Melanie. We're not going to talk until you do, so if anyone is wasting time here, it's you."

She was trapped. She glared at him. "Oh, all right! Throw your stupid weight around. See if I care." She stalked across the room and kissed him hard on the mouth.

She was about to back away when he grasped her wrists and pulled her arms around his neck. One hand plunged into her hair to tug her head back and the other dropped to her buttocks to fit her against his groin. Desire slashed through her at the feel of his arousal. He nibbled her bottom lip, and she made a helpless little mewl of surrender. It was hopeless. She couldn't think straight when he held her and teased her. He had taught her too much about pleasure, training her to expect it and crave it.

He kissed her with slow, deep thrusts of his tongue, branding every inch of her mouth, moving against her in sultry erotic circles that left her weak and yielding. The world began to spin, and she clung to him to keep from falling, rubbing against him and sucking and tasting him hungrily. The excitement was almost unbearable, the wanting even worse. She dug her nails into his shoulders, longing for the warmth of his naked flesh against hers, wishing he would caress her the way he had on the steamer.

Instead, he broke the kiss and eased her away. Her knees felt so rubbery she had to clutch his shoulders for support. Her body was trembling violently. Everything seemed unreal, shrouded in swirls of fog.

He cradled her head against his chest and massaged her back. His heart was racing and his breathing was fast and ragged. Just like hers. "I feel as if I've been flattened by an anvil," he said hoarsely. "And you? The way you're trembling . . . Are you all right?"

She looked up, fighting her way through the haze, trying to regain her equilibrium. "No. You shouldn't have kissed me like that—as if you own me. You know what it does to me. It isn't fair." She bit her lip. "You hold all the top cards. I can't even fight you, much less defeat you. I don't like that."

"I don't blame you. I wouldn't, either. But I wanted you so much I was going insane. Desire like that isn't an ace, Mellie. It's a damned deuce." He smoothed her hair, then tipped up her chin and looked into her eyes. "It's a consortium of trading companies. H. Fogg and Company;

Samuel Russell and Company; Dent's; Jardine, Matheson . . ."

"I see," she said, but she wasn't sure she believed him. Nobody had ever accused the big trading firms of being simon-pure, but they were all reasonably respectable, and Alex was anything but. "And what's their interest in the matter? Why would they hire *you*? Are you really some sort of detective? What do they expect you to do?"

He chuckled. "Oh, no, you don't. I might be willing to enlighten you eventually, but only if you're extremely cooperative. You can begin by explaining your involvement in this affair. It's only logical to assume that the tiger wasn't the first hollow object to leave China with something valuable hidden inside." He paused. "Let's see now. We've also lost a jade horse from the Ming period, a gilt bronze Buddha from the Six Dynasties, a golden stem cup from the Tang period, and a modern suite of pearl and diamond jewelry. A dozen items in all, Melanie, and every one a masterpiece. Don't try to tell me the necklace inside the tiger is the only one of those objects you retrieved, because I won't believe you. Your actions were too precise that day, too adroit. It was a familiar routine."

It was pointless to argue. His information was accurate, his logic flawless. She pulled out of his arms and crossed to the window. "So? What about it?"

"I'll wager all twelve of them were smuggled into San Francisco, and that you picked them up. Why? Who sent you? What happened to them? And don't tell me they were sold to help the wretched of the earth. I want specifics, including the names of your cohorts on both continents."

"I don't have any cohorts. I'm an eccentric heiress, remember? Nobody tells me what to do or questions my actions." She stared out the window, praying he would believe her lies. Her life's work was at stake. "I went into the curio business so I could retrieve smuggled valuables without arousing suspicion. I have no idea who sends them. I receive anonymous notes telling me they're coming. I use the money they bring to pay for my rescue work. End of story."

"*Stolen* valuables," Alex corrected. "The gold and ruby necklace inside the tiger wasn't any gift from the empress. Like all the other items I've listed, it was stolen by accomplished professionals."

Melanie's lips twisted into a contemptuous sneer. "Her husband can afford the loss. So can all the other late owners. I don't feel guilty about taking valuables from the profligate oppressors of this world and using them to do a little good. If they're your ultimate masters, Alex, you're working for bloodstained scum."

"They aren't. The taipans are." She heard him walk closer. "Your sentiments are very noble, but the situation is more complicated than you pretend. Don't insult my intelligence by telling me you work in the dark. The operation is intricate and highly organized. Given the slip you made yesterday afternoon, I assume your friend Shen Wai is involved. As you just said, your social position puts you above suspicion, and that makes you an invaluable tool. Obviously he talked you into aiding his cause. Now stop stalling and give me the details. All of them, my dear, because if you don't, your Chinese friend is going to live out his natural life in pain and deprivation."

Melanie paled and jerked around. The man was utterly immoral, as deadly as a viper. If kisses didn't work, he used threats. And if anyone could make good on them, he could.

She began shaking with fear and rage. "If you

so much as touch him, I don't know how or when, but I'll slit your miserable throat. And he didn't have to talk me into anything! I'm nobody's god-damned tool." She gulped for air and fought for self-control. "I started helping because he told me who I was. The granddaughter of a prostitute. My grandmother was raped when she was eleven—*eleven!*—then sold to a brothel to be used by men like my grandfather. My mother found her dead in her bed one morning, drenched with blood, but nobody cares when a whore is murdered and no-body cries when half-Chinese riffraff goes hungry. Mama was thirteen at the time. She had nothing. No one. So she fled to a brothel and sold her vir-ginity to the highest bidder, because it was the only way to survive. And then the horror began again—men abusing my flesh and blood. Using her sexually wasn't enough for them—they had to hurt her and degrade her, too. My father finally made her his mistress, but he wouldn't marry her. He was from a fine New England family, and she was only a half-breed bastard. So she was still a prostitute, wasn't she? And do you know some-thing, Alex? You're the same as my father and my grandfather and all those other men. You talk about passion and pleasure, but that's a pretty way of saying you want to spread my legs and take my virginity and make me into your whore."

Alex was utterly stunned. He had never imag-ined that Melanie sprang from such traumatic roots, never guessed she had such a personal mo-tive for doing what she did. It was obvious that she wanted to save lives, nothing more—and that she knew nothing about a larger picture that in-cluded the purchase and shipment of arms and the fomenting of a revolution. She didn't realize it, but her adored Shen Wai had used her very badly.

Almost as incredible, she was still a virgin. He

hazily recalled some banter about her virtue, but he had assumed they were speaking of her fidelity to Bonner, not her sexual purity. Perhaps he should have known better—he hadn't missed her flashes of shyness—but there was nothing naive about her seductive performance in his brougham and nothing innocent about the barbs she launched whenever he boasted too much about his virility. There was nothing unseasoned about her sweet hot mouth, either, or about her clever fingers and mobile hips.

It appeared he had her lively imagination and passionate nature to thank for those pleasures, but no woman developed skills to rival Delilah's without some prior experience, too. Still, he supposed he owed her an apology. He wasn't devoid of scruples, and he had always chosen women who played by the same rules he did. Mellie obviously didn't, but now was the wrong time to repent. When you had backed your opponent into a corner, you didn't step aside and let her slip away. You attacked.

He gave her a level look. "It's an interesting story, but it doesn't answer my questions. About the smuggling operation . . . Who are your contacts in China? What is Shen Wai's exact role? What happens to the curios after you retrieve them?"

Her face, previously florid with anger, grew ashen and pinched. "God, you're a bastard. You have no feelings. No morals. Not even a shred of simple decency."

"We're here to discuss you, not me." He folded his arms across his chest. Her words left him smarting with guilt, but he was afraid that if he showed any weakness or admitted to any regrets, she would dig in her heels and fight him until she dropped. "I suggest you start talking. And skip the lies and evasions, madam. My patience isn't unlimited."

Melanie looked into his eyes and saw only ice. Something inside her shattered, crumbling in the face of such inhuman ruthlessness. What was she going to do? If she spoke, he would destroy her life's work, persecute her beloved Shen Wai. But if she remained silent, Sukey might pay a price that would haunt the girl forever. Melanie would never forgive herself for letting that happen, and neither would Ty.

She couldn't decide. Either way, the consequences were unthinkable. She suddenly wanted to tear at her hair, to claw at her own skin. Tears welled in her eyes, and she hastily turned around. She couldn't stop them from rolling down her cheeks, but she didn't make a sound. She still had a little pride left.

Alex grasped her arms, and she flinched and went rigid. He forced her around, crushing her resistance as if she were a recalcitrant kitten. She stared at her toes, humiliated to the depths of her soul by her tears and her impotence.

He muttered an exasperated curse, then pulled her into his arms. She wedged her hands between their bodies and tried to push him away, but it was useless. Her arms wound up trapped against his chest.

"For God's sake, stop fighting me," he said. "You're only torturing yourself, and you can't possibly win."

She stood in his embrace, shaken and trembling, and silently wept. Neither of them moved for several seconds. His touch, when it finally came, confused her completely. It was unaccountably tender, a light and soothing caress of her neck and shoulders.

"Look, I'm sorry," he said in a husky, agitated voice. "I thought you were more experienced. That's how wonderful you are. How exciting. If your damned maidenhead is so important to you, I won't take it, but don't ask me not to make love to you. I can't help myself—not when you respond the way you do."

He paused for several moments, perhaps waiting for some reply, but she had none to make. She didn't understand him, didn't know what to make of his sudden gentleness. She only knew that his hands were charming her the way a fakir charms a cobra—calming her fears, dissolving her anger.

"About your rescue work," he continued softly. "I won't interfere with it, all right? I understand about your mother and grandmother and I admire you tremendously for what you do, but you'll have to find some other source of funds. Those profligate oppressors you mentioned sold their jewelry and antiquities to the trading houses I work for before they were ever stolen, and the houses sustained huge losses as a result. They hired me to put a stop to the operation. The empress's necklace was the bait. I've been following it since Peking, waiting to see in whose hands it would end up. So we come back to you."

Melanie sniffled a few times. There was no menace in the air, she realized, no aura of danger or deceit. Alex's role in all this was legitimate, then, and his sense of chivalry not entirely extinct. She felt a surge of relief. It was one thing to be attracted to someone like Alex—a woman couldn't control that sort of thing—but to respond heatedly to a coldhearted criminal, to actually enjoy his company, would have been weak to the point of disgrace. At least she wasn't a total fool.

Her body began to uncoil. It struck her that no male had ever told her he admired her work before, not even Shen Wai. Alex was one of a kind, far less conventional than the men she was accustomed to and less narrow-minded about the capabilities of her sex. She suddenly felt warm and safe in his arms. If only she could make him understand her feelings, the choice wouldn't be difficult at all.

She slid her arms around his waist, and he sighed and nuzzled her hair. "That's much better. Talk to me, Mellie. Tell me what's going on."

"I'll try." She snuggled closer and felt his manhood stir and harden. It was an excellent sign. "But Alex? Could I ask you a tiny favor first?"

He kissed her temple. "What's that, sweetheart?"

"That you won't use what I tell you against Shen Wai. That you won't harm him in any way."

He stiffened and frowned. "Not a chance. Absolutely not, Melanie. My orders are to punish the men involved in the operation. Ruin them socially or destroy them financially if I can't get them sent to jail. It's obvious Shen Wai is one of them. The ringleader on the California end of it, I suspect. He deserves whatever I mete out."

Melanie wasn't discouraged. Men could be stubborn when it came to what they saw as their duty. Sometimes a woman had to wheedle and entreat. "Even if the cause is a noble one?" she asked sweetly.

"Rescuing prostitutes and coolies, you mean."

"Yes."

"You give him the smuggled objects to sell, and he gives you back the proceeds."

"Only a small percentage. He uses most of the funds for his own projects."

"Projects of a similar nature to yours."

"Of course."

Alex knew the money went for weapons and rebellion, not saving lives, but he couldn't explain that to Melanie. She didn't trust him enough to take his word over Shen Wai's. "If what you claim is true," he said carefully, "I'll permit Shen Wai to make restitution. That's the best I can do."

"But he doesn't have that kind of money, Alex. He donates whatever he gets to our cause." She slid her arms from his waist to his neck. "Please try to understand. He was devoted to me when I was a child. He gave me the deepest love I've known. I couldn't live with myself if I caused anything to happen to him." She gazed at him imploringly. "Please, darling. Leave him alone. For me."

A half smile teased Alex's lips. "So I'm your darling now, am I?"

"Yes." She brushed her mouth across his, and his eyes grew smoky with desire. "But only if you promise not to harm Shen Wai. Shall I kneel down in front of you? Beg and beseech you for mercy?"

The thought of Melanie on her knees was more than Alex could endure. He swept her up in his arms, marched to the nearest chair, and sat down, settling her on his lap. She smiled coyly and began to toy with his shirt, smoothing the collar and fingering the buttons.

His manhood was aching so abominably by then that it was all he could do not to thrust himself against her like a rutting ram. "What is his safety worth to you, sweetheart? Your maidenhead, perhaps?"

Melanie saw the twinkle in Alex's eyes and knew she was being teased. "Oh, absolutely, but I know you wouldn't want to obtain that particular commodity via blackmail. You're much too impressed with your skill as a lover." She traced the outline of his upper lip with her finger. "You won't be truly happy until I pant that I can't resist you and beg you to take me."

He caught her hand and kissed her palm. "Now there's an appealing picture. Why don't you stop torturing me and bring it to life?"

"Because I'm not in a panting mood, only a pleading one," Melanie lied. Touching him—knowing how much she excited him—was as erotic as it was heady.

"A pity. Well then, since you're determined to deny me, why don't you tell me about the maps?"

"I don't know where they lead, only that it's probably in the gold country. That's why I came to Nevada City—because Ty was a miner once and knows the area well. I was hoping he could decipher them." She planted kisses from Alex's temple to his forehead. "You see how cooperative I can be when I want to? About Shen Wai—"

"I'll think the matter over and let you know," he said irritably. "Now stop nagging me, Melanie. And stop making up to me. Kisses won't get you what you want."

She broke into a smile. His heart was pounding wildly and his skin was hot and damp. "Won't they?"

"Very well, you seductive witch, you win, but only because I hate seeing you so distraught. But he'll have to stop his thieving and smuggling, do you understand me? The star on the cloth map—what does it indicate? A meeting place? A spot where something valuable is buried?"

Melanie burst out laughing. "You mean you don't know? You've been following me all this time and you have no idea what the prize is?"

"That's it. That does it." He reached down, pushed aside her skirts, and ran his hand up her leg. She giggled and tried to wiggle off his lap, but he wrapped his other arm around her waist to prevent her from leaving. She began to struggle in earnest then, but his hand continued its inexorable climb, easily defeating her efforts to dislodge it. She was rigid with shock by the time it slid into her open knickers and cupped her intimately.

"I know exactly what the prize is," he said. "This."

The shock began to fade. His hand felt so warm, so exciting. He stroked her gently with his palm, making her feel breathless and dizzy, and then slipped a finger between her nether lips and slid it lightly back and forth. She gasped and began to burn—on her palms and the soles of her feet, on her face and neck, and, most of all, on the swollen bud of flesh at the very core of her.

Ah Lan had mentioned a woman's pleasure, but she had never told her it would feel like *that*. She sucked in her breath. "Dear God, Alex, what are you doing to me?"

He fondled her belly and her silky curls. "We were discussing prizes. I was teaching you about yours. You might want to remember how vulnerable it is the next time you're tempted to tease me into giving you your way." He stroked her again, very lightly, then slowly withdrew his hand. "About that star on the map—what does it mark?"

"It's, uh, a large cache of gold." She shuddered, still burning from his caresses and shocked by her own reckless response. "You can't touch me there again. It isn't right. Only a husband should do that."

He laughed. "My God, not only a virgin, but a prude. What have I gotten myself into? Listen, sweetheart, you need to tell me about the man you sensed following you last week. Is he still out there? Did you feel him this morning?"

She accepted the change of subject without a peep. She knew Alex, and if she made a fuss about the liberties he had just taken, he would promptly take them again, simply to prove he could make her let him. "I was focused on Sukey, so I'm not sure. Still, the menace he radiates is so intense that I suppose I would have sensed him if he were close by, and I haven't felt a thing since yesterday on the steamer."

"Then we probably lost him in the crowd on the wharf. Or if we didn't and he learned our destination, it would have been too late for him to catch the public stage. It had already left by then. If we're careful, he won't pick up our trail, even if he traces us to Nevada City."

Melanie nodded. "I hope you're right. He must have learned about the gold, Alex. Followed me because he didn't know where it was buried. Either he doesn't have maps or he can't read the ones he has."

"And Shen Wai? Can he?"

"I assume so, but he's visiting the Comstock with my father. I was afraid if I waited for him to return, you would find someone to interpret the maps and get to the gold before I did."

"Your pursuer could do the same thing," Alex said thoughtfully. "I think you'd better tell me everything you know."

Melanie did. She had no choice. She had a deadly enemy out there, and Alex was her best protection. As for the gold, first she had to find it. Then she could worry about keeping it.

Chapter 14

~~~~~~~~~~

"Are you deaf? I said get out of here, you pigtailed heathens! Scum like you doesn't belong in here!"

Hsu Wing understood only one word of the hotel clerk's harangue—pigtail, an American insult—but he comprehended the man's contemptuous tone and dismissive gestures well enough. This ignorant, round-eyed devil was chasing him and his superior, Chung Chu, out of the establishment they had just entered. He reached into the billowing sleeve of his tunic, intending to avenge the offense with his knife, then thought better of it. The locals in a benighted backwater like Nevada City would probably string up a Celestial for a good deal less than slashing a white man's face, no matter how richly deserved the punishment was.

He and Chung Chu strode outside and climbed into their buggy. "Foul-smelling barbarian trash," Hsu muttered.

Chung, who was eight years Hsu's elder, smiled and said that patience came with age. Unlike Hsu, Chung had ice in his veins. The insults of some pale-skinned inferior didn't bother him. All he cared about was retrieving the gold.

Chung instructed Wang, their servant, to drive up the street, then added to Hsu, "Sooner or later we'll come to a Chinese shop or home where we can obtain the information we require."

The buggy wobbled and creaked its way uphill. It was the sorriest excuse for a vehicle Hsu had ever seen, but they'd had to settle for what they could get. Twenty people had wanted passage on Sunday's public stage, and with baggage, there had been room for only fourteen. Negroes, Celestials, and drunks had been sent to the end of the line.

Having no choice, they had decided to rent a vehicle for their journey, but no white man had been willing to accommodate them, and the Chinese livery had lacked anything suitable. They had finally spotted this buggy on the street and bought it from the blue-eyed rabble who owned it, paying him twice what it was worth. And then the damned thing had broken an axle north of Auburn, and it had taken a small fortune to persuade a local wheelwright to fix it. He hadn't hurried, either, finishing late the next morning. Hsu thought in disgust that they could have taken the Monday stage and gotten here almost as soon, and with less discomfort, too.

They came to Commercial Street, saw some Chinese shops down the block, and made inquiries, holding themselves out as wealthy gentlemen on a pleasure trip. Here, at least, they were treated with the deference they deserved. They quickly learned where Mi-Lan Wyatt's friend lived, but were told that the two had left town. The man's sister had run away from home, and Mi-Lan and her friend were pursuing the girl.

Their informants added two additional men, neither of them locals, had joined the pair. Because of the physical description Hsu and Chung were given and the contents of Mi-Lan's letter, they assumed that the men were Alex McClure and a comrade or servant. Hsu knew McClure by reputation, but Chung had actually met him. McClure was a man of his word, Chung said, and without the prejudice so typical of the English in Hong Kong. But he was also tough and clever, ruthless when he needed to be, and had powerful cohorts in a rival triad. Perhaps Mi-Lan and her friend were his captives and perhaps he had talked them into cooperating, but either way, extra prudence would be required.

In time, Hsu remarked to Chung, the group would find the girl and bring her home, then turn their attention to the gold. Luckily, the perfect spy existed in the person of Stone's Chinese servant Wong Suk-Ling, a young girl who could easily be persuaded to do their bidding. In the meantime, several of the local mandarins were vying for the honor of entertaining them. Hsu's mood began to improve. There were worse ways to spend a few days than being feted by men who esteemed you and enjoying the local women.

Melanie first noticed storm clouds on the horizon around two o'clock, after they had passed through North San Juan, but she paid them little heed. A shower occasionally wet down the pavement during the dry season, but it never rained hard. Their hired buggy was a covered one, so the discomforts of the journey would likely begin and end with the dusty, rutted roads and the bruises she would probably acquire from being squeezed and jostled by a trio of strapping men.

They were trading amusing stories to pass the time, each of them trying to top the other three. Ty, who had been so solemn the night before, was enjoying himself immensely, just as he had in the old days. So was Melanie, who had devoured every morsel Alex supplied, all of them from his years at a large trading firm. People said San Francisco was free and easy, but compared to Hong Kong, it was as tame as a day in the park.

The weather slowly worsened as they drove northeast. About two hours past North San Juan, thunder suddenly roared in the distance and lightning slashed the darkening sky. The tumult caused the horses to bolt forward, but Ned quickly controlled them. That was when Melanie remembered that the Sierra wasn't the coast. Clouds that passed harmlessly over the shore and valley could turn heavy and violent when they reached the turbulent mountain atmosphere. It began to drizzle, adding a dank miasma to the air.

Between the clouds and the rising elevation, it grew uncomfortably cold. She shivered and turned up the collar of her coat. Alex, who was telling a highly improper tale about the flagrant infidelities of a taipan named Dugan and the public revenge the man's wife had exacted, put his arm around her shoulders and pulled her against his chest. It warmed her up, so she didn't object.

"So there he was the next morning, naked as a jaybird on a cot outside his mistress's house, awake enough to know what was happening but too drugged to be able to move. He was covered with chicken livers, especially on his tenderest parts. It seems that his mistress had a prize bitch with a passion for"—he grinned—"for organ meats of all sorts. Someone let the dog outside, and she ran over to Dugan and began licking him vigorously. A large crowd had gathered round by then. Dugan's member rose like a breaching whale under the ministrations of the bitch's tongue. It was a remarkable sight—almost as if the beast had been bred to the task. Rumor has it that when the crucial moment arrived, some wag in the crowd called out, 'Thar she blows.' They later said—forgive my crudeness, Mellie—that the bitch gave better head than her mistress did."

Melanie laughed and blushed at the same time. "My God, you're lucky Dugan didn't kill you."

Alex looked astounded. "Kill *me*? Why me?"

"Because you arranged it. You know you did. Was the vengeful wife your mistress?"

He chuckled. "No, my former boss's. Charlie Burns. I mentioned him before, remember? He and Dugan were bitter rivals. Dugan used to beat her, so you can imagine how much I enjoyed orchestrating his humiliation. Although let me tell you, it was no easy job to find someone willing to train the dog. Dugan fled Hong Kong a few weeks later. His wife eventually divorced him. She's married to Charlie now."

"God, I envy you," Ty said dreamily. "Traveling all over the world, having marvelous adventures—"

"Of extremely dubious propriety, Ty. Just ask Melanie. I'm sure she'll be glad to expound on what an out-and-out bounder I am."

"Because women don't understand these things," Ty said. "It's obvious that if the other taipans engaged in smuggling, spying, and thievery, your boss had no choice but to do the same."

"I'd like to meet the man," Ned put in. "He's a shrewd one. I mean, Alex was only a clerk, and very young, too, but Burns recognized his talent right off. Taught him and promoted him."

"Thereby turning him into the remarkable master criminal he is today." Melanie burrowed her hand under Alex's coat and felt through his shirt for his medal. "Still wearing this, I see. Tell me, do you and your friends in the triad ever smuggle opium onto the mainland?"

"Triad?" Ty and Ned asked simultaneously.

Alex removed her hand and placed it on his thigh. "I was their partner in a few ventures. It's not something I can discuss." He gave her a reproving look. "And no, I don't. I don't approve of the opium trade."

"I'm amazed to hear it, seeing how lucrative it is. What about your life after you left Burns and Company? Can you discuss *that?*"

"Which aspect? The brutal assaults? The ruthless piracy? The looting and raping?" He circled her throat with his hands and looked at her through narrowed eyes. "The vicious strangulations?"

Ty began to laugh. "Close your mouth, Mel. He's only baiting you." He pointed up the road. "That's Camptonville, Alex, greatly diminished from its glory days in the early fifties, but we can still get a decent meal there. We'll have to be quick about it, though, or we'll lose the light before we get to Downieville. It's another twenty miles."

Downieville, a thriving town of thousands, was their destination. Sukey had told Alex that she and Grant Guthrie, the actor Ty had warned off, were on their wedding trip and planned to stay at a "nice hotel" there. The plushest was the St. Charles, so Ty thought they should check there first. Alex insisted that Sukey had the situation well in hand, but Melanie was still worried. She only hoped they found the pair before any real damage could be done.

As much as she enjoyed sitting in a comfortable chair and putting hot food into her stomach, she was relieved to get back on the road. It began to rain harder, turning the dirt into deep, puddle-pocked mud that slowed them even more. Their route ran parallel to the Yuba River, usually a tame stream in high summer but suddenly a churning torrent. Every now and then the skies opened up, releasing a furious and sometimes lengthy cloudburst. It grew so dark that when lightning split the sky, the whole world seemed to light up. The cover on the buggy couldn't protect them from such weather, and they were soon soaked.

To make matters worse, they were climbing through the most rugged terrain in the gold country now, thousands of feet higher than Nevada City. Each new downpour created waterfalls from out of nowhere, powerful gushes that raced through the craggy pine-covered mountains into the river below. It was spectacular country, but Melanie was far too frightened to enjoy it. The stage road wasn't a bad one, but she was grateful for Ned's skill. The horses were jumpy and clumsy. A lesser driver never could have controlled them.

Lightning flashed violently, and was followed so quickly by thunder that Melanie knew the storm must be right on top of them. Shaking a little, she cringed against Alex's chest. "I hate storms. When I was a child at sea, they used to strap me into a hammock. The ship would pitch and thrash helplessly, and so would I. I hated being confined— hated being trussed and closed up in that way. I still do. I always got horribly seasick. The ropes used to burn my skin."

He stroked her cheek. "I know. I remember what it was like."

"I would hear the men yell to each other. Scream in fear. And the sounds ... The shrieking wind, the water crashing against the deck, the masts cracking apart ..." Thunder roared in her ears, and she burrowed closer to Alex's chest. "Sometimes men died. Men who had been kind to me. I was the sailors' pet. Like a mascot. That was the worst part of all, Alex. The funerals. I like to think I can handle anything, but I can't handle this. I'm frightened. I wish it would end."

"Only a fool wouldn't be frightened." He hugged her hard, then added grimly, "I think we should stop at the next town, Ty. I don't know how Ned can even see in this weather, much less drive."

"Pure luck," the hackman muttered. "If I recall this road correctly, it only gets worse."

Ty confirmed it. "Especially after Goodyear's Bar. That's the only other town, Alex. The road climbs even higher, then plunges down to Downieville. It could be flooded or even washed away."

Alex asked how far Goodyear's Bar was. Ty pondered the landmarks and the bad conditions and guessed about an hour. "And I agree about stopping. It'll be pitch-black by then. Even if we continued, we would never get through."

Melanie looked up. "But Sukey—"

"Can take care of herself very well," Alex interrupted. "I told you that before. Do you seriously think I would have left her with that oily young idiot otherwise?"

"How should I know?" Melanie's worry and fear suddenly exploded out of control, slamming into the nearest available target—Alex's head. "From what I've seen, you'll do whatever you need to to get what you want." She pulled away from him. "You don't give a damn about anyone but yourself. Certainly not about Sukey, given the way you abandoned her, and not about me, either. You would leave me to rot if you had to choose between me and your precious gold."

"You know that isn't true—I've been risking my neck for you for the past two days—but I'm prepared to overlook the insult for now and let you apologize later on, when you aren't so overwrought." He looked at Ty. "Believe me, your sister can handle the man just fine."

"Whether she can or can't," Ty said, "we're stopping in Goodyear's Bar. We won't be much use to her dead—"

"Which is the direction we're headed in," Ned finished. "Nobody is lucky forever."

None of them argued. Tension filled the buggy as they crept toward Goodyear's Bar. They didn't need forever, only another hour, but there were times when a horse lost its footing or a wheel got mired and they were sure they wouldn't make it. Melanie held herself rigidly aloof the entire time, pretending Alex wasn't squeezed in beside her. When the lights of Goodyear's Bar came into view, she almost wept in relief. A minute later, they pulled up to the Pioneer Hotel, a well-built, two-and-a-half-story frame building where Ty had stayed in the past.

Alex unloaded the luggage and carried it inside while Ned and Ty saw to the buggy and horses. Melanie followed Alex, talking about how pleasant the place seemed until she realized he wasn't going to answer. The hotel was half-empty, so he was able to obtain a room for each of them. All four were on the second floor, Melanie opposite Ty in the middle and Alex and Ned at the far end. Alex registered, then picked up their bags and led the way upstairs. He unlocked Melanie's door for her, then coolly informed her that he was going to change and have a bite to eat. He didn't invite her to join him.

The male species, she told herself as she entered her room, was unfathomable. She had inflicted everything from sexual torment to a knife wound on the man, and what did he get into a sulk about? A trifling slight to his honor, murmured in a heated moment. It was incredible.

Ned and Ty came upstairs, but departed a short while later, no doubt to join Alex in the dining room. Melanie washed, pulled on a dry dress, and tidied her hair. She picked up a magazine, then put it back down. The men were having a fine time eating and talking, and thanks to Alex, she was stuck here alone in her room. It wasn't fair.

She finally went downstairs and peeked in on them. They were in a cozy booth at a table laden with snacks and champagne. She noticed it was set for four, not three, and hesitantly stepped through the door. The vacant spot was next to Alex.

Ty saw her and called her over. She squared her shoulders and marched to the table, sitting as far from Alex as she could. His expression was forbidding. Her heart began to pound in her throat. They couldn't go on this way, fighting a silent war. The trip would become a misery.

"Alex?" She put her hand on his arm. "Uh, about what I said in the buggy ..."

He turned and stared at her coldly. "Yes, Melanie?"

She flushed and removed her hand. "I'm sorry. I know you would protect me if I were in danger. I didn't mean to impugn your honor."

"But you did. A man gets tired of being labeled a villain. I admit I've used a heavy hand with you at times, but much less of one than most men in my position would have employed. Certainly I've never given you reason to think I would rape you, beat you, torture you, kidnap you, abandon you, or do any of the other contemptible things you've accused me of plotting."

His lecture left her awash in guilt. She *had* accused him of all those things, unreasonably so. She couldn't blame him for being annoyed. "I know. Please don't be angry with me. It's just ... you can be very intimidating at times. And my imagination has a way of running away with me."

"As does your tongue."

"I know. I'm sorry." She looked away. "I shouldn't have lost my temper, but I was worried about Sukey and the words simply slipped out. I just wish you had brought her back and avoided this whole mess, that's all."

He sighed, then stuck a finger under her chin and turned her to face him. "Maybe I should have, but Ty told us the whole story before, and it might be better that I didn't. Sukey has some growing up to do. The world is colder and harsher than she thinks. A brief adventure can be a good teacher."

"I agree," Ty said. "We'll find her tomorrow morning and bring her home. In the meantime, Sierra County isn't San Francisco. Nothing too terrible is likely to happen here."

"But that actor she's with—"

"Is completely harmless." Alex picked up Melanie's hand and brushed a kiss across her knuckles. "I'm sure of it, sweetheart. Now stop worrying."

The sensuous touch of his mouth raced along her nerves and warmed her up. It felt nice, but the warmth in his eyes felt even nicer. She moved closer to him. "But what if he's not, Alex?"

"He is. I'm so positive about it, I'll even tell you how I got my medal if I'm wrong." He filled her glass. "It's been a long, hard day. Have some champagne. Try to relax."

She sipped her wine, finally reassured. It would be a cold day in hell before he told her about that medal, so he must be certain he wouldn't have to.

"We were talking about your tiger when you came in," he continued. "Ty wants to have a look at it, and also at the cloth map. You did bring them along, didn't you?"

"Of course." She had told Ty about the maps and the gold that morning, but only briefly. They had been in too much of a hurry for a lengthy conversation, and the topic had never come up again. "Then you think you can help?"

"I can try," Ty said. "Alex was giving me some additional details just now. A hundred thousand in gold is a huge amount, Mel, too much to have been taken from rivers and streams. You said it was left behind in '50 or '51 by a small group of Celestials after about a year of work, so that rules out a quartz mine, too. There wasn't much hard-rock mining in those days, and given how expensive and complicated it is, only well-capitalized companies ever succeeded at it. That leaves dry diggings as the source of the gold. I assume the Chinese miners found some soft, rich leads near the surface, the type of rock they could work with picks and shovels. My guess is that the cache is down to the south somewhere. The geology is right, and that's also where large numbers of Chinese miners were looking for gold during the first few years of the rush. The same is true of the Mexicans, and they built *arastras* wherever they went."

Melanie nodded. Mineral-bearing rock had to be crushed before further processing, and the Spanish had long used horse- or mule-drawn stone mills called *arastras* for the purpose. "I see what you mean. The Chinese miners had to mill the gold in secret, so they needed a simple, effective method. They probably saw *arastras* being used and built their own in some out-of-the-way location."

"Yes. I know the area well, but if nothing on your tiger rings a bell, I have some material in my office we can check. I've been collecting it for a map of the entire state, showing geographical features and roads and trails."

They continued to talk, speculating about the

gold's exact location and planning a trip to retrieve it. The conversation was animated and friendly at first, but then Alex raised the subject of what would ultimately become of the cache and the discussion turned into a argument. Melanie wanted the gold for her rescue work. Alex planned to take a finder's fee and give the rest to the taipans as partial compensation for their losses. Ty wanted a fat percentage to go to the Union cause in return for his assistance. Only Ned remained above the fray. All he cared about was staying alive and getting paid.

Everyone's temper was a little short by the time they finished eating. They marched upstairs and gathered in Ty's room with the two maps. He studied them at length, then shook his head. "I wish I could picture the tiger flattened out, but I can't. It's nothing but a jumble of meaningless lines. I'm stumped."

"Then we're lucky you've been collecting those charts," Alex said. "In the meantime, exercise is better than arguing. How about a lesson in *gongfu?* I could show you some kicks and throws."

Melanie gaped at him. "You can't be serious, Alex. Your back is full of stitches. If you let Ty toss you around, they could open up."

"Stitches?" Ty repeated. "You've got them in your back, too? That must have been some earthquake."

Alex broke into a smile. "The earthquake had nothing to do with it. Mellie stabbed me on the steamer. But—"

"She *what?*"

"Right between the shoulder blades," Ned explained, "but it was only what he deserved, Ty. The thing is, if you try to seduce a wary female like Mellie, especially one who sleeps with a knife under her pillow, you're going to pay a heavy price when she suddenly wakes up."

Ty gave Alex a look that reeked of disgust. "Melanie was right about you, McClure. You're a damned scoundrel. Trying to seduce a sleeping virgin, for God's sake. It's disgraceful. Pathetic. Get out of my sight before I'm tempted to slug you."

"He would knock you cold before you could land a punch," Melanie pointed out.

"I know that. Why do you think I'm just standing here?"

Alex ran his hand through his hair. "Jesus, Ty, you can't seriously believe I knew she was a virgin! Hell, the way she—well, never mind about that. I made a mistake, okay? I've told her I was sorry."

"Really, Ty, it was all my fault," Melanie said. "I led him astray. He was very understanding about it, too. He still intends to seduce me, but he's willing to do it without ruining me."

"A true prince," Ty muttered.

"Oh, absolutely," Melanie responded. "Anyway, you know how I am about the sick and injured. After I stabbed him, I naturally started brooding about his wound. I badgered him until he surrendered unconditionally and let me clean it and stitch it up." She frowned at Alex. "Speaking of which, you've been awfully lively all day. Have you been taking your medicine?"

He scowled right back at her. "Don't nag me about it. It turns me into a bloody sleepwalker, so I left it in Nevada City. And don't nag me about the *gongfu,* either. The cut is closed already, but even so, nobody is going to toss me around. Ty and Ned can be partners. I'll demonstrate the preliminaries and talk them through the rest."

Melanie was glad to hear it, but she wasn't reassured about his back. Infection was too serious a risk. "Listen, Alex, I put a lot of work into that wound and I won't have it fester. I'm going to mix up a fresh batch of medicine, and you're going to drink it even if we have to tie you up and pour it down your throat."

"Not a chance," Alex said. "Not even if it's three against one."

In other words, he didn't care whether the medicine was good for him or not, he would fight off a whole brigade before he would swallow it. Melanie wanted to brain him, but she was also realistic. "Fine. Act like a thickheaded mule. Since we obviously can't force you, I'll mix up a topical ointment. I trust you'll do me the supreme honor of stopping by my room later tonight and allowing me to apply it." She stalked from the room before he could answer.

Alex laughed and closed the door. All in all, it had been a splendid day. He loved the way Melanie clung to him whenever she was aroused or frightened or upset. He never would have admitted it, but it warmed his heart when she fretted about his health. No woman had ever teased him more provocatively, and he had even forgiven her her insults, since worry about her friend had caused them. He couldn't wait to get her alone.

He turned to Ty, still smiling broadly. "She's incredible. Half angel, half witch. You can't imagine how much I'm enjoying this case."

Ty didn't smile back. "I doubt that the same is true of Mel. She came up here for my help, and I aim to give it to her. When you go to her room later on, I'll be right behind you."

If they were going to quarrel about Melanie's virtue, Alex preferred to do it in private. He looked at Ned. The hackman was sprawled in a chair with his feet on the bed, taking in every word. "Has it ever occurred to you that there are times when you should excuse yourself?"

"Nope." All the same, he got to his feet. "Believe me, Ty, you have nothing to worry about. He thinks he's running the show, but she's done almost exactly as she likes, right from the start. And even when he wins a round, he always backs right off. She's got him wrapped around her little finger, if you ask me." He walked to the door, saying over his shoulder, "If you want me, I'll be in my room."

Ty waited until Ned had closed the door, then said, "That's reassuring, but it doesn't change how she looks at you when you touch her, or the way she seems to crave your approval. She's infatuated with you. Fascinated by you. Leave her the hell alone, Alex. She wants a happy marriage and a flock of kids, and you can't give her either of those things."

"If she did, she would have them by now," Alex retorted. "Instead, she's broken five engagements in five years. She thinks she should settle down, but she doesn't really want to. That's why she likes *me*. I have no interest in marriage. That makes me completely safe."

Ty gave him a scathing look and delivered a sharp lecture about Melanie's childhood and the way she'd been treated by her father. Alex could see the effect that must have had, but not why Ty was so concerned. Her background had evidently led her to want the same things he did, so what was the problem?

"Mellie knows exactly what I am," he said, "and exactly what I can give her. Adventure and excitement. Physical pleasure. That's precisely what she wants, and if she weren't enjoying it, she would send me packing. Since I'm not going to take her to bed, I'm the perfect diversion. Years from now, when she's married to some banker or lawyer, she'll look back on me very fondly. She wouldn't thank you for interfering in her life, but I'm sure you know that. From what I gather, she was never very conventional, even as a young girl. We can argue all night, but in the end, she'll do exactly as she pleases."

Ty hesitated. "Well, maybe. But we've been friends for a long time, and you don't abandon your friends. It's my duty to protect her."

"From what, Ty? A broken heart? Unrequited love?" Alex laughed. "Believe me, she wouldn't have me if I got down on my knees and begged her. Now how about some *gongfu?* As I said before, it beats arguing."

"Sure. I'll get Ned." Ty opened the door. "With any luck, it will keep me from getting killed if I'm obliged to fight you."

Melanie mixed up a batch of ointment and some fresh liniment, then changed into a nightdress that covered her like a nun's habit and got into bed with a book. It was a memoir of the early rush, a topic that normally enthralled her, but she couldn't seem to focus on the words. Her thoughts kept straying to Alex. He was like the apple in the Garden of Eden—beautiful and tempting and dangerous. She knew better than to take another bite.

She could hear the men exercising across the hall—their raspy pants and hearty laughter and the soft thuds they made when they landed on what sounded like a mattress. She sighed. Men found pleasure in the simplest things. They were so much less complicated than women were. They didn't fret or brood, but seized whatever life offered. She wished she were more like them.

The session ended and footfalls filled the hall. Someone knocked on her door. She invited the caller in, then got out of bed to greet him. As she'd expected, Alex strolled into her room.

She was startled to see Ty walk in behind him, then guessed the reason for his presence and smiled. "Ah. Guarding my virtue, are you, Ty?"

"Maybe. Tell me something, Mel." He nodded at Alex. "If he asked you to marry him, would you say yes?"

She was so flabbergasted that her mouth dropped open. "Marry Alex? Are you crazy?" She giggled. "Good God, can you imagine what sort of husband and father he would make? Running off all the time, getting shot at and stabbed, being pursued by beautiful women . . . He would be even worse than Thomas was."

"I don't know whether to be relieved or insulted," Alex said cheerfully. "What did I tell you, Ty?"

"Then you're not in love with him?" Ty persisted.

"Of course not. You know perfectly well I'm immune. Anyway, I have more sense than to get mixed up with him. I learned my lesson on the steamer. He may think something more than doctoring is going to happen here tonight, but he's wrong." She studied him. "Ty is sweating and you're not, so I assume you behaved yourself just now. I mixed up some liniment in case you'd abused your muscles—"

"I didn't, but the buggy ride did. I ache all over." He smiled at her in a way that curled her toes. "If you're offering to give me a massage, I'm not going to turn you down."

Ty frowned. "A massage?"

"He's prone to severe spasms," Melanie explained. "Massages help prevent them. It's strictly therapeutic. Take off your shirt, Alex, and I'll—" She checked herself. "Uh, you can leave now, Ty. I don't need you to stay."

"You're sure. You don't mind being alone with him."

Melanie had mixed emotions. Alex would be forced to keep his distance if Ty was in the room, but she hated the thought of needing that sort of male protection. It was a moot conflict, though, because Alex's scars were all that mattered. "Not at all. I'll be fine."

"If you say so, but if you need me, you know where I am." Ty gave Alex a stony look, then left the room.

Alex stripped off his shirt and lay down on the bed. He knew why Melanie had told Ty to leave and felt such a surge of gratitude and tenderness that his throat tightened. He had forgotten how thoughtful she could be. A gentleman would have honored her wishes and kept to himself, but he didn't think he could bear to. He wanted her too badly. Besides, once he had shown her how much pleasure her body could give her, she would wonder why she had ever hesitated.

"Thank you," he finally said. "For, uh, for remembering how I feel about the scars. And for caring enough to send Ty away."

"You're welcome." She sat down beside him. "I'm going to remove the plasters. Quickly is best, don't you think?"

He agreed, tensing but not moving as she rapidly pulled them off. The wound, she told him, looked perfect. There was no swelling or pus, and the edges had knitted together nicely. She applied the ointment and fresh plasters, then matter-of-factly told him to loosen and lower his trousers. He had never obeyed a medical order more eagerly.

He felt the cold splash of liniment on his back, then the warmth of Melanie's fingers. The massage was exquisite, a marvel of comfort and relief, pleasure and relaxation. He lay quietly and savored every sensation, even his intense arousal. He could afford to be patient. There was only one way the evening could end.

Melanie's hands and arms soon grew tired, but she didn't have the heart to stop her treatment. One look at Alex's back and she had melted with renewed compassion. If it was energy she needed, his scars—and his bitter memories—were a potent fuel. Besides, he made the most appreciative little moans when she soothed him, and it was satisfying to give him relief. As for the other emotions that intruded—tenderness, affection, arousal—she told herself she could control them.

Still, when he murmured his thanks and turned over, she scrambled off the bed and scurried across the room. The farther away he was, the easier it was to keep a level head.

He tugged up his trousers and propped himself against the headboard. "Running away?" he drawled.

She didn't mind admitting it. "You bet your life I am. I have a healthy instinct for self-preservation. You're nothing but trouble."

"But I give you pleasure. How can that be a problem?"

She rolled her eyes. "Spare me the phony innocence, Alex. We've discussed this before. The things you want to do to me are wrong. Sinfully licentious."

"But we've done most of them already," he said with a grin, "and we're both alive and well. I doubt God is even watching us, much less planning to punish us, and neither is your father." He beckoned her over. "Come, sweetheart. You're more of a freethinker than that. What can possibly be wrong about two people enjoying each other for a few hours?"

Nothing at all, when he put it that way, but pleasure wasn't the issue. "No. I don't want to."

Alex gazed at her. Her cheeks were flushed and her eyes were feverish. Obviously she did want to. He was tempted to walk over and prove it, but something stopped him. The tattered remnants of his conscience, perhaps, or an inflated male ego that needed her to give herself freely for once.

Her expression grew strained and wary. She was evidently troubled about something, but he couldn't imagine what. "Sin can't be the real problem," he mused aloud, "because I've never observed a shred of guilt in you after I've made love to you. Chagrin that you responded to a scoundrel, maybe, but not guilt. Since we've established that I'm a decent fellow, what—" He cut himself off. Maybe it was her damned virtue again. "Mellie . . . I did promise you'd be a virgin on your wedding night, remember?" Unless you've just married me, he thought, and wondered where *that* notion had come from. "I, uh, I meant it. So if that's what's stopping you—"

But Melanie trusted him completely on that score. "It's not." She grimaced, then added, "Baring my soul to you is getting to be a habit by now, so you might as well know the truth. I'm afraid of getting in too deep. Feeling too much. I wasn't honest with Ty. It could happen to me, Alex. I find you far too hard to resist. And that isn't a good thing."

He swung his feet to the floor and leaned forward a little. "But why not? Making love is better when your emotions are engaged. Mine certainly are."

"Yes. I know. You're fond of me." She smiled wistfully. That was all he would ever feel—a sort of absent fondness. "But I don't want to fall in love with you. It would hurt too much."

"That's ridiculous." He grabbed his shirt and stood up. "We would stay together for as long as you like. When you're ready to settle down, you'll fall in love with someone more suitable and marry him, but in the meantime, I'm sure I could make you happy."

"But that someone won't be you."

"No. We both know that. I would be a perfect lover but a poor husband."

"And you won't mind it when I leave you?"

He shrugged. "It doesn't matter whether I would mind or not. I wouldn't have the right to object."

She felt as if a cold, hard weight had settled in the pit of her stomach. "You know something, Alex? You're hurting me right now. Your remoteness. The distance you put between us. I look at you and I see a stranger. Whenever you toss me a crumb about your past or your feelings, I pounce on it like a starving animal. It's humiliating. Do you never let anyone close to you, or is it just me you push away?"

A haunted, almost stunned look entered his eyes. He hesitated, then mumbled, "I did once. It was enough." He walked slowly across the room, then let himself out.

Chapter 15

$$\sim\!\sim$$

Ned pulled up to the St. Charles Hotel at twenty past seven the next morning, remaining out front with the horses while Ty, Alex, and Melanie went inside. Ty asked the clerk at the front desk if Mr. and Mrs. Grant Guthrie were registered there, saying he was Mrs. Guthrie's brother, adding that he'd ridden in from Alleghany to surprise her with a brief visit. The clerk beamed as he checked his book, murmuring how nice family reunions were. The Guthries were on the top floor, he said, in room 302.

The threesome went upstairs. Ty tried the door, found that it was locked, and knocked loudly several times. When there was no answer, he began pounding with the flat of his fist, his lips thinning with anger when the door remained firmly closed. He was so agitated that Melanie was afraid he would slam his shoulder into the wood.

"Allow me." Alex took out his picklock and slipped it into the keyhole. A moment later there was a soft click.

Ty flung open the door with so much force that it crashed into the chest behind it. A handsome young man was sitting up in bed—alone. He was heavy-lidded and tousled, as if he'd been roused from a sound sleep, but he also looked scared to death. Melanie followed Ty to his bedside. Judging by Guthrie's face, Ty wasn't the only party the young man had enraged lately. His left eye was spectacularly black-and-blue.

He raised his hands protectively. "Now, Mr. Stone—"

Ty yanked them back down. "You gutless little bastard . . . Where is she? Hiding under the bed? Concealed in the wardrobe?"

"No. She's not here. If you would let me explain—"

"Explain what?" Ty grabbed him by his nightshirt and lifted him off the bed. "That you ran off with a sixteen-year-old child? You should be charged with rape."

"But I didn't touch her." Guthrie cringed away, his lips quivering in fear. "I swear it, Mr. Stone. She told me you'd beaten her up—"

"She *what?*" Ty bellowed, almost beside himself now.

"She said you'd beaten her for coming in late. She showed me the bruises—"

"She fell off her horse last week, you idiot. Everyone in town knows about it, so why don't you?" The question was no sooner out than Ty exploded all over again. "She showed you the bruises on her hip and thigh? You saw her with her clothes off? Damn you, Guthrie—"

"She slid down her trousers and knickers for a minute. That was all. I hardly saw a thing. I swear it."

But Ty was in no mood to listen. He released Guthrie with a hard shove, then slammed his fist into Guthrie's face. If Alex hadn't grabbed his arm at the exact same moment, mitigating the force of the blow, Guthrie might have had a broken jaw to complement his black eye.

Alex continued to hold Ty in check. "Just take it easy, Ty. Killing the fellow won't solve anything. Let him explain what happened."

Ty nodded grimly and Alex released him. Guthrie gave Alex a pathetically grateful look, but there was no recognition in his eyes. If he realized he had met Alex in North San Juan, it didn't show.

Sukey had awakened him early the previous morning, he said nervously, with a story about how Ty had struck her. She had shown him her bruises and begged him to take her away, telling him she would run off alone if he didn't rescue her. When he had tried to suggest alternatives, she had grown hysterical. He'd felt he had no choice but to accompany her and protect her from the dangers of the road.

"And you believed her drivel about what a brute I am?" Ty asked incredulously. "You're a total dimwit, Guthrie. She's no better actor than you are."

"But she's so beautiful, Mr. Stone. And she acted so sweet and helpless, weeping and pleading and kissing me—"

Alex coughed loudly, putting his hands on Ty's shoulders at the same time. "Certain facts are best left unstated, Guthrie."

"Uh, right. Anyway, I finally remembered hearing about her accident with the horse, but not till we'd passed through Goodyear's Bar. So I asked her about it and she admitted the truth, and then I figured—" He looked at Alex. "Are you holding him real good?"

"Yes. Go on. But for God's sake, use a little discretion from now on."

"I'm doing my best. I figured—I assumed it was me she really wanted, that her story was just a scheme to get me to go away with her. So when we got to Downieville, I took just this one room, and she got really mad. And I got mad right back, because she'd dragged me all the way up here and I figured the least she could do"—he stopped and looked warily at Ty, but Ty merely glowered at him—"was, uh, be nice to me. So we were sitting in the dining room arguing about it, and some people came in—"

"What people?" Ty snapped.

"Circus people. Jugglers, acrobats, an African sorceress, an India rubber man, a bearded lady . . . They'd finished a performance in the park and stopped in for a bite to eat. Sukey went over to talk to them, ignoring me completely, so I got angry and went upstairs." Guthrie gingerly touched his eye. "And that's how I got this. I was sitting upstairs, minding my own business, when a whole bunch of 'em stormed into my room, and it belted me."

"It?" Alex repeated with a puzzled frown.

"The bearded lady. It had breasts, all right, but I'm not so sure it was a female. It was as hairy as a bear and twice as strong. You should have seen its muscles. Anyway, Sukey went off with them. Took the gig and stranded me here. The manager said they were worried about the weather. They were trying to make it to Sierra City so they would have less distance to travel today."

"Travel to where?" Ty asked.

"Quincy. They have a show there tomorrow."

Ty groaned. "Oh, hell, not Quincy. It's over fifty miles, Alex." He scowled at Guthrie. "Sooner or later we're going to track her down and take her home. If I were you, I'd be working in another town by then."

"Whatever you say, Mr. Stone." Guthrie edged further away, then added diffidently, "I guess you're not interested in my advice—"

"You're right. I'm not."

"All the same, if you plan to punish Sukey, or even just to yell at her, I'd wait till you got her away from those circus people. You're tough"—he gestured toward Alex—"and he's even tougher, but that bearded lady thinks it's Sukey's protector, and it'll leave both of you flat on the floor if you get it annoyed."

The road from Downieville to Sierra City followed the path of the Yuba River, a gurgling stream dissected by myriad waterfalls. The river ran through a deep canyon lined with vegetation, while the terrain beyond consisted of alpine meadows, evergreen-covered mountainsides, and soaring, jagged peaks. Ty always said it was the prettiest stretch in the gold country, especially as you approached Sierra City and the barren pinnacles and rocky granite ledges of the Sierra Buttes came into view.

It was a crisp, sunny day, perfect for enjoying the scenery, but Melanie found it hard to enjoy much of anything when Alex was jammed in beside her, acting as proper as an English butler. She only realized how warmly he'd come to treat her when he stopped doing it. His teasing smiles, protective embraces, and intimate tone of voice were gone now, and she missed them keenly.

The road was rougher and narrower along this stretch, but the area had gotten less rain the day before and was less muddy, so they made good time. Still, the minutes crept by like snails. Only the constitutionally chipper Ned was in a talkative mood, and after a few of his stories were met by near silence, even he gave up.

Then, about an hour into the trip, Alex finally strung more than half a dozen words together, asking Melanie if she had heard of the Taiping rebels, and if so, what she thought of their activities.

She didn't know which surprised her more, that he'd addressed her directly or that the question concerned Chinese politics. It was hardly a common subject.

The Chinese civil war had begun over a decade ago. She had a personal interest in everything that happened in the land of her grandmother's birth, so she could hardly *not* have heard of the Taipings. "Of course. I hope they succeed. The emperor is a depraved tyrant. I hear he's killing himself with women and drugs—that he may not last much longer. But even if he dies, the rest of the Manchu nobles are no better. They're corrupt and haughty, with no real interest in the people they rule. As long as they remain in power, there's no real hope of reform."

"Perhaps, but the leader of the Taipings is just as bad," Alex said. "He calls himself the Heavenly King, the Tien Wang, and he claims he's the brother of Christ, but his actions prove otherwise. He preaches sexual discipline and communal ownership of land, but he lives with dozens of concubines in incredible luxury, and his personal fortune is immense. The rebels have plundered and raped and killed. They've sacked native temples and destroyed sacred relics all over China. They're not saviors—they're fanatics."

"Spare me the propaganda of your masters the taipans," Melanie said scathingly. "They hate the Tien Wang because he deplores the opium trade and intends to end it, and they're terrified of losing all those profits. I'm not claiming the rebels are perfect, but most of what you say is ridiculously exaggerated. Besides, there was never a revolution without blood."

Alex looked down his nose at her. "Ridiculously exaggerated, hmm? I've seen it with my own eyes,

Melanie. The looting, the slaughter, the brutality . . . And when was the last time *you* were in China?"

He knew the answer as well as she did—when she was ten, before the rebellion began. "I don't have to go there to know the truth. I've talked to dozens of girls who were sold into slavery because of the emperor's negligence and greed. Imperial taxes are higher than ever, but he allows bandits to run rampant in the provinces and his own officials to bleed the peasants dry. He coddles Western traders, who exploit the Chinese people callously. Anyway, there's more to the revolt than the Tien Wang. He has able, honorable lieutenants. If there's excess, they'll correct it. That's more than you can say for the emperor and his Manchu thugs."

"The imperial government provides stability and control," Alex insisted. "Unlike you, I deal with its officials regularly, and most of them are competent and reasonably honest. If you think there's suffering now, what do you suppose would happen if a bunch of radical zealots like the Taipings gained power? The areas they rule are chaotic. The whole country would end up that way."

"You're a typical Englishman, terrified of real democracy. You'd rather put your faith in a corrupt monarch and a fossilized ruling class."

"And *you're* a typical American, in love with the idea of revolution."

They continued to argue, Melanie growing more heated with each contentious exchange while Alex got colder and more imperious. It was only when Ty glared at them and muttered that their yammering was giving him a headache that they retreated into silence.

The quiet lasted clear to Sierra City, where they stopped to make inquiries about Sukey. The town, a small one, had been destroyed by an avalanche in 1852 and only rebuilt in 1858, so there were only a few hotels to check at. The manager at the second one they came to, the Zerloff, recalled the circus people clearly. A pretty redhead had left with the group that morning, he said, driving a two-horse gig, accompanied by the troupe's bearded lady. He confirmed that the circus's next stop was Quincy, but said he didn't know which hotel the troupe planned to stay in.

The road to Quincy was a poor one. There were no diggings to the north, so there was little in the way of civilization along the route. Reassured that they were on the right track, they purchased the makings of lunch and continued on their way.

The area, a vast basin, was dotted with exquisite mountain lakes nestled in pine-covered hills, but Alex was in no mood to notice scenic beauty. By the time they stopped to eat, he was wishing he'd brought his medicine along. A good dose of the stuff would have knocked him cold, and then he wouldn't have had to think about the misjudgments he had made and the fact that he wasn't any closer to gaining Melanie's cooperation than he'd been in San Francisco.

He supposed he had his integrity—the integrity she repeatedly questioned—to thank for that. He hadn't felt right about seducing her into helping him, not if it would leave her hurt and unhappy, so he had sought to sway her with facts and logic. Unfortunately, she was so softhearted and naive, so full of faith in the vaunted people, that he'd barely kept hold of his temper. As matters stood now, he would have to ride roughshod over her in order to do his job. And that bothered him.

So did her coldness and silence. From the first moment they'd met, he'd sensed a powerful connection between the two of them, and it had grown stronger whenever they'd touched or talked. He had come to expect it, to like it, to find it soothing and oddly exhilarating. But it was gone now, and he missed it. He missed *her*.

When she finally spoke to him, a hesitant "Alex?" he felt such a burst of elation that he almost leaped like an excited puppy at the chance to converse. He stopped himself just in time. He was a man of wealth and power. He didn't grovel or snivel to anyone, least of all to a woman.

"Yes, Melanie?" he said politely. "Did you need something?"

"No. I just wondered ..."

But she didn't finish the sentence. He glanced at her, saw the anxiety in her eyes, and melted completely. "What, Mellie?" He twined a strand of her hair around his finger and gave it a gentle tug. "Tell me what's on your mind."

"The Taipings." She paused, still visibly uneasy. "I wondered why you'd brought them up. You have to admit, it's an odd topic for a drive in the country."

He surprised himself by how quickly he decided not to lie to her. He was tired of manipulating and outflanking her, he supposed, even when it was for her own good. All the fun had gone out of besting her, leaving only impatience to finish his job and a vague sense of guilt.

He braced himself for her anger and accusations, then admitted, "Because that's where most of the money from the sale of your smuggled valuables goes. Shen Wai buys arms and other supplies in America, then ships them to the rebels in Nanking. He was lying when he told you he uses the money for work similar to yours. I asked you about the Taipings because I wanted to know how you would feel about Shen Wai's activities. From where I sit, he's used you very badly and doesn't deserve your loyalty, although I don't suppose you believe a word I've just said."

On the contrary, his words were like the missing piece of a puzzle sliding into place. Shen Wai disappeared for days or even weeks at a time, never discussing what he did while he was away. More often than not, he was vague about the details of his rescue work. She knew he had cohorts, but he had never named a single one of them or confided the specifics of their activities. Now she understood his evasiveness.

She looked at Alex thoughtfully. "How do you know all that?"

"The truth is that I don't," Alex said, regarding her warily. "But it fits the facts I have. Weapons have turned up in the hands of the rebels after each major theft, and Shen Wai is the one who fences the stolen valuables."

Melanie replied that it fit the facts she had, too, then listed them. "But Shen Wai isn't what you think. He knows I support the rebels—that I would approve of what he's doing—so he didn't have to trick me into retrieving the smuggled objects. If he's kept things from me, he must have an honorable reason."

"I hope you're right. I know how much he means to you." Alex stared at the roadway. He had promised not to punish Shen Wai, but it would be hard to keep his word if the Celestial wounded Melanie's heart. "So we're at an impasse. We have different plans for the gold. Opposite views of the world. And it's not going to change. We're never going to agree about a damned thing."

Melanie wanted to say that they agreed about the pleasure they felt when they held each other, the fun they had gossiping and joking, and the closeness they shared when they confided secrets almost no one else knew, but that wasn't what Alex had in mind. "No," she said. "I suppose we're not."

Quincy, the seat of Plumas County, was situated in a charming valley at the northern end of the Sierra. The town contained numerous businesses and many fine houses, and while it couldn't yet boast of a school or a church, it did claim a fine new courthouse. On the green behind that courthouse, according to the clerk at Bradley's Hotel, the circus planned to perform the following day.

He added that the troupe had registered several hours before and was setting up tents for its sideshow. When Ty asked if a pretty young redhead had been traveling with the group, the clerk said he remembered the girl well. She and the bearded lady had been fast friends, and one of the strangest pairs he had ever seen, like Beauty and the Beast. He assumed she was still in the woman's company.

It was dinnertime and everyone was hungry, but they decided it was more important to run Sukey to ground than to eat. They carried their bags upstairs, then walked to the courthouse. But just as they turned toward the green, Ty stopped abruptly and gaped at something in the street. "My God, that's Colonel and Frémont."

Melanie peered around, looking for a distinguished gentleman. "Colonel Frémont? The former senator?"

"No. His namesakes. My new team. I bought them to pull my gig." Ty pointed at an approaching vehicle. "They're the ones right there, the big, strong chestnuts with the white markings."

He strode up to the driver, a plump gentleman in business attire. "Excuse me, sir, but are you with the circus?"

The man looked startled. "Good heavens, no. I'm a banker with Wells Fargo." He suddenly chuckled. "Why? Do I resemble someone who is? One of the clowns, perhaps?"

"No, of course not," Ty said. "I don't mean to pry, sir, but would you mind telling me where you got that gig?"

The man smiled in understanding. "Ah, I see, it's the vehicle you recognized, not me. I did buy it from someone in the circus, the bearded lady. I was standing in Bradley's Hotel, telling a friend that Quincy had grown so much that I needed a team and gig to get around, when she offered to sell me this one. She was a tough negotiator, I'll tell you that much. She held me up like a bandit, but I truly did need something soon, and it's a good little carriage."

Ty asked the fellow if a pretty young redhead had been anywhere about, and he nodded. "Yes. She was standing with the bearded lady. Now that you mention it, the creature might have been bargaining on the girl's behalf, because she handed the girl my money afterward."

"I'm her older brother," Ty explained, "and your team and gig used to belong to me. She took them without my permission. I wonder if could I persuade you to sell them back?"

But the banker firmly refused, saying he was sorry, but the team and gig suited him perfectly and he didn't want to part with them. Ty smiled at him through gritted teeth and wished him a pleasant evening. "I'm going to wring the little wretch's neck," he grumbled as the banker drove away. "Running off with that imbecile Guthrie was bad enough, but selling my new horses and my custom-made gig ..."

"She probably needed the money," Melanie said. "Actually, it was very enterprising of her."

"Enterprising, my foot! She should have thought about money before she left. If her savings weren't enough, she should have taken her jewelry along and sold that."

He marched onto the green behind the courthouse and looked around. Ned touched his shoulder and pointed. The bearded lady was emerging from a small tent in the sideshow area. While only a few inches taller than Melanie, she was as burly as a stevedore and very hairy. Ty gawked. Even Alex pronounced himself impressed.

Ty had no sooner informed her that he was Sukey's brother than she launched into a lengthy harangue, the sum of which was that he didn't understand the girl; that he had confused her, hurt her, and driven her from her home; and that he was a miserable wretch whose black character rendered him totally unfit as a guardian and shamefully unsuited for so noble a calling as publishing a newspaper.

Ty listened with a rigid back and a clenched jaw, grimly holding his tongue until the woman finished. Then he muttered, "I'll try to do better in the future. If you would tell me where she is . . ."

The woman eyed Melanie. "And who would you be?"

"Melanie Wyatt. I'm Sukey's friend, and I've been very worried about her."

"Umm. She mentioned you. Said you were a decent sort." She waved the men away. "I'll tell Miss Wyatt, but not the likes of you three. Now, shoo."

The men withdrew, Ty glowering and Alex and Ned fighting back laughter. Melanie listened to the woman's explanation with increasing dismay, reporting the results to Ty as they returned to the hotel. "The circus is staying here for two or three days, then going to Rabbit Creek. Sukey didn't care for their itinerary, so the bearded lady looked around for someone suitable to entrust her to."

"And found whom?" Ty asked irritably.

"An elderly minister named Archibald Hamilton. He's been touring the county, preaching in the local towns, but he's returning home to Oroville in the morning. The bearded lady assured me he was reputable and kind, but there is one small problem. He stays in the homes of the faithful when he travels, not in hotels or boardinghouses. She had no idea where they were spending the night. There must be a hundred houses in the area, and they could be at any one of them."

"It's almost dark," Alex said, "and the back roads here are little more than trails. A search just isn't possible."

The veins in Ty's neck bulged out. "So we'll have to go to Oroville. Oroville, for God's sake! Do you have any idea how far that is?"

"Seventy-five miles," Ned said calmly, "but it's all downhill, and it's a very good road."

"I don't care how good the bloody road is! It's seventy-five interminable miles. The blasted girl has us tramping all over creation. I have a newspaper to put out. Printing jobs to do, although if that bearded lady starts trumpeting what a villain I am, nobody will ever hire me again. I swear to God—"

"I told her it wasn't true," Melanie said hastily.

"—when I get my hands on the girl, I'm going to turn her over my knee and thrash her until her bottom is even purpler than Guthrie's eye."

Alex put his arm around Ty's shoulders. The gesture was a friendly one, but Alex's voice was pure steel. "No. It's one thing to lace into Guthrie, but you're not laying a finger on your sister. She's a female, Ty, a child. The two of you will talk things out and come to an understanding."

A flush crept up Ty's neck. "Sure, Alex. I was just blowing off steam. I wouldn't really hit her. I never have. I know this is partly my fault."

"It's been a long day," Melanie said. "Everyone is hungry, frustrated, and tired. I'm sure some food will improve our moods."

She was right. Dinner was excellent, or perhaps the amount of wine everyone consumed only made it seem that way. Alex arranged a poker game afterward, coaxing the other participants into letting her play. She bluffed shrewdly all evening and teased everyone who fell for it, especially Alex, but the men laughed so hard at one another's misfortune that they didn't mind losing to a female.

Alex gave Ned and Ty another *gongfu* lesson after the game broke up, inviting Melanie to join them and showing her some basic moves. To her astonishment, the techniques enabled her to put even Ty on the floor. They stopped around eleven, but only because they wanted to get an early start. She was full of energy, sure she would never be able to sleep. She'd had a glorious evening. She didn't want it to end.

Out in the hallway, she brushed Alex's hair back from his forehead and inspected his wound. "Hmm. All healed up. Come into my room and I'll snip out the stitches and medicate your back. If you ask me nicely enough, I'll even give you a massage, although I doubt that you need one."

Alex followed, fighting a silent battle with his conscience. After tonight, he wanted Mellie more than ever, but only a cad would have succumbed. On the other hand, who could really blame him if he did? She was beautiful and clever and vibrant, she'd teased him until he'd wanted to haul her to his room and rip off her clothes, and he'd been touching her, albeit purely for the purposes of instruction, for the past hour. Now he was sitting half-naked on her bed. Naturally his senses were wildly inflamed. A man had his limits, everyone knew that.

She doctored him with crisp efficiency and he responded in kind, playing the cooperative patient. The look he gave her when she finished could have softened the devil himself. "My back is throbbing. Aching. Nobody can soothe it the way you do. Please, Mellie, will you massage it for me? I'll be forever in your debt if you do."

She laughed. "You lie very convincingly, Alex. You should be in politics. I'll get my liniment."

He loosened his trousers and stretched out on the bed. Contentment washed through him, and then, when she first touched him, pleasure and relaxation. The room was quiet except for her grunts of exertion and his own low moans, and he soon drifted into a peaceful, almost dreamlike state.

The spell was only broken when she murmured his name. He opened his eyes and glanced over his shoulder. "Hmm?"

She smiled uncertainly. "I was wondering . . . If you lived in Scotland until you were ten or eleven years old, where did you get that accent?" Her touch lightened, growing more sensual. "Surely you didn't just knock about England after you ran away—not when you talk like an Oxford don."

He had the sense it was a test—that she wanted him as much as he wanted her, but only if he was willing to talk about the past. Although sex was a powerful inducement, he had kept his own counsel for so many years that he resisted. In the end, though, the need to reconnect, to reestablish the sense of union they'd once shared, was so urgent and intense that he changed his mind.

"From my grandfather. He was the one I ran to. He was minor nobility—a baron. He was determined to turn me into a proper English gentleman. His tutors and fancy schools changed me on the outside, but inside, I was still a Scottish hellion. I suffered through a year at Oxford, then ran off to sea. It was eighteen months before I saw him again. We argued about my future, but in the end, he accepted the choices I'd made."

To Melanie, that simple answer was as precious as a hundred diamonds. After tonight, she knew in her heart that she was never happier than when she was with Alex, talking and joking, and that every night could be as wonderful as this one if she played the game by his rules. A man wouldn't have hesitated for a moment. He would have grabbed what gave him pleasure. But no matter how unconventional she was, she was still a woman, and she needed more—Alex's soul as well as his body, for however long they were together.

She dug her thumbs into the small of his back and ran them up his spine, and he moaned softly. "So how did you find him? Or did you know all along where he was?"

"No. He was never mentioned at home, so I assumed he was dead. But then . . . I, uh, I told my stepmother about the incident with the gun. She searched through my father's desk and found my grandparents' address, then wrote them that she was sending me to their home in London. She told me exactly how to get there and scraped up the money to pay for it. My father would have flogged her if he'd known, so she literally risked her life to save me. She said she prayed my grandparents would take me in, but if they didn't, I wasn't to come back, because my father would kill me if I did, or I would kill him. And she was right."

Melanie shivered at the horror of that casual statement. "But they did take you in."

"Yes. I'm not sure why, but I suppose guilt had a lot to do with it. My stepmother had told them how much I'd suffered, but even before that, they'd had letter after letter from my mother, describing her life, begging for a reconciliation. My grandmother wanted to answer, but my grandfather refused to allow it. But she must have had a tiny streak of rebellion in her, because she secretly saved all those letters, and she gave them to me to read when I was sixteen."

Melanie asked what had caused the estrangement, and Alex explained that his grandfather, a devout Anglican, had been appalled by the idea of giving his daughter to a Scottish Calvinist minister whom he considered heretical rabble. Alex's parents had met in a museum when his father was studying in England, he added, and fallen madly in love, rendezvousing in secret when his grandfather had learned of the affair and demanded that it end. Faced with his intractable opposition to their marriage, the lovers had run away to Scotland together.

"So it was all very romantic," Alex finished. "From what I can gather, they were blissfully happy for the first year, and then I came along. You know the rest."

"Most of it," Melanie murmured. "Not all of it."

Alex turned over. Melanie was referring to the night he'd found the gun, but there was only so much a man could be expected to confide. "Yesterday, before I left your room, you asked me if I'd ever let anyone close, and I said, 'Just once.' I was talking about my mother, Melanie. She abandoned me when I was eleven, not six, at least in my mind, and it was the most painful thing I've ever experienced. I needed her in England, but she never came. And that's all I want to say about it, except that I left because I didn't want to cause you that same kind of pain."

An eerie chill raced down Melanie's spine. She didn't believe for a moment that Alex thought it was all in his mind. His mother had left him twice, the second time by choice, and it still hurt.

"No matter what I do, there's going to be pain." She extinguished the bedside lantern and lit a candle. A dim glow suffused the room. "If I have to suffer, I might as well have some joy first."

She stretched out beside him and he took her in his arms, stroking her hair as he cradled her against his chest. "You're sure?"

"My, but you're suddenly noble." She slid her hand down his chest to his belly, then inched it lower. His manhood was fully engorged, but far from feeling embarrassed as she had in the past, she found the shape and texture and size of him beautiful and fascinating. "Admit it, darling. You wouldn't let me leave even if I wanted to." She made slow circles with her thumbs on the sensitive head. "Would you?"

He was startled by her boldness, then amused. "Not now I wouldn't. What are you doing down there?"

"Educating myself." She explored him with her fingertips. "You're like silk and steel, Alex. So soft and hot and strong. Touching you excites me."

"That's nothing compared to what it does to me." He took her mouth, but there was no teasing this time, only deep, fiery kisses that made her tremble and burn.

He cupped her breast and stroked her with his thumb, but she could tell his attention was on himself, not on her—on what was being done to him. The world was a little hazy by then, but she hadn't forgotten the tricks Ah Lan had described. She circled the base of his member with one hand

and ran her fingers up and down his shaft with the other, and a feverish tension seemed to grip his body. He began moving in time with her caresses, writhing under her agile fingers, kissing her with a wild, almost helpless need. Greatly encouraged, she dug in her nails a little, gently raking him, and then teased and kneaded his most vulnerable parts.

He moaned and tore away his mouth. "God, Mellie . . . Where did you learn that?" The question was a ragged whisper.

"From a friend. I've never done it before. You're my first experiment." She nipped his lower lip. "Was it nice?"

Alex thought to himself that it was a damned sight more than "nice." It was ecstasy and torture and excitement so violent it hurt. "You know damned well it was." Her fingers grew more playful, and he thought he would die of frustration. "No." He groaned. "Touch me harder, sweetheart. I need it rougher when I'm this aroused."

She tickled his inner thigh. "When I feel like it, McClure. Now lie quietly. You're not in charge here."

"Whatever you say." Smiling now, he closed his eyes and let her do as she pleased. He recognized the techniques she was using—he'd had a Chinese mistress who had pleasured him this way—but Mellie's lovemaking, while less practiced, was ten times more exciting. She drove him and then withdrew, keeping him poised on the edge, until he was so mad with frustration and need that when his climax finally came he moaned her name repeatedly, and he'd never cried out that way in his life. Then he simply lay there, spent and panting and euphoric.

Melanie watched him a little warily. After George, she knew that a man could erupt with anger after he lost all control. But when Alex finally recovered, a slow, devilish smile spread over his face. "You have an interesting friend. Remind me to thank her when I meet her. Or is it a him?"

"Her. She's a madam named Ah Lan." Melanie explained about their friendship and the lessons Ah Lan had provided, then admitted with a blush that George had disapproved fiercely. To her relief, Alex seemed amused by the tale.

He unfastened her dress, and she shivered in anticipation. "As I've told you repeatedly, George is a pompous prig. He isn't remotely worthy of you." He pulled down her bodice, then dealt with her corset, taking full advantage of the fact that the laces were in front. Her nipples puckered and hardened as he casually brushed and rubbed them, and a familiar ache suffused her belly and loins. "For a maiden experiment, that went very well. You've got an amazing amount of raw talent." He stripped off her corset, then divested her of the rest of her clothing. "But to really perfect your skills, you'll need protracted daily practice." He gave her a lingering kiss. "And selflessly, in the interests of scientific inquiry, I'm willing to offer myself as a subject. But first . . ."

He pushed her onto her back with a playful arrogance that made her pulses race with excitement, then undressed and stretched out beside her. At first he simply stared, drinking her in with his eyes until she blushed and trembled. Then he caressed her with a warm, sure hand, stroking her breasts, her belly, her thighs, and finally her womanly mound. She went rigid, remembering the way he'd parted her and pleasured her, longing for him to do it again. But instead, his hand stilled completely.

He suckled her nipples until they throbbed, then raised his head. "I know how much you enjoy being teased, but I think we'll save that for the next time. You need to learn how much pleasure your body can give you, so you'll understand what I'm making you wait for. Just relax and trust me." He rubbed her gently and intimately with his thumb. "All right, love?"

"Yes. God, Alex ..." She clutched his shoulders and blindly sought his mouth. He kissed her with hot, slow, thrusts of his tongue, and a sweet, sultry submissiveness filled her body. Then he slid on top of her and probed her with his member, spreading her thighs to expose her completely, teasing the spot that made her burn violently. He stroked her harder and she shuddered. As his rhythm grew faster and his touch more intense, she felt a desperate, almost overwhelming craving. She had no idea what she needed, only that she wanted him to continue whatever he was doing. Moaning, she wrapped her legs around him and arched her hips so the contact would be closer.

His member moved lower, easing inside her a little, and she whimpered with excitement and frustration. She wanted him back where he'd been, and then she wanted him deeper inside her. But when she jerked up her hips, mindlessly offering herself, he abruptly pulled away. "That's enough of that," he muttered against her mouth, and slid off her.

She tried to pull him back. "Please, Alex. Don't stop. You can do whatever you want."

"Hush. Just relax." He gave her a searing kiss and slipped his hand between her legs. At first it was exactly like before, a light but firm stroking that left her flushed and gasping, but then he slid his fingers downward, eased one inside her, and moved it slowly in and out. She instinctively gripped it, matching its rhythm, but it wasn't enough. She moaned, thrashing helplessly against his hand, and a second finger joined the first, gently stretching her, driving her mad with longing.

His thumb finally grazed the spot she wanted him to touch, and a wildly erotic tension gripped her body, intensifying as he worked her harder and faster. The sensations were incredible, exquisite. And when her climax finally came, wave after wave of violent pleasure, she screamed and dug her nails into his back and wanted it to last forever. Finally, unable to bear any further contact, she pushed away his hand.

She snuggled into his arms afterward. "Thank you, Alex. That was—it was everything you said it would be." She felt sleepy and content, but also fascinated and a little embarrassed. There was so much she didn't know. "Would you mind if I asked you a question?"

He smiled. "You learn very quickly, love. We men can't refuse you women a thing at a time like this."

She swatted him playfully. "It's not about your deep, dark past, you wretch, at least not in the way that you think. It's just that Ah Lan once told me that she and her lover had pleasured each other five times in a single night, and I wondered if you'd ever done that with a woman."

He chuckled. "Not for quite a few years, but I could with you."

"How interesting." She mulled it over. "But would you truly want to? Because as much as I liked it, I wouldn't. Once was enough. I don't feel the slightest desire to repeat it."

"Because you're tired, and because it's only been a few minutes since your climax, but even so, I could make you want to again if I wished to, and quite easily. And the answer to your first question is yes."

"Oh, dear. I'm terribly sorry, Alex, but I'd rather go to sleep." But then another urgent question came to mind. "I was just thinking ... If, uh, if your member was moving in and out of me instead of your fingers, would I like it even more?"

Alex roared with laughter. "I don't know, sweetheart. Most women do, but some don't. I only know that I certainly would. I had the devil's own time stopping myself."

She remembered the way he had pulled away from her. "But you did." She hugged him hard. "You're very honorable. I would have let you, you know. I was absolutely frantic for you."

"And I almost took advantage of it. Believe me, it was a near thing, but I didn't want to get you pregnant, and my condoms were back in my room." He stroked her bottom, and a pleasant warmth curled through her. "I won't get that close again. It's much too dangerous."

She felt a wave of disappointment. "But it was so exciting, Alex. Couldn't we, please? Maybe just a little? I love the way you feel." Indeed, she could feel him again, hard and warm and fully aroused against her leg. She reached down and stroked him, and a flush of desire swamped her senses. "Good grief, I do want to. You were right. How amazing."

"Of course I was right." He pulled her on top of him. "But only for a minute," he muttered. He grasped her hips and directed her movements, and it was even more inflaming than before. She was so excited by the time he lifted her away that she thought she would climax within moments, but he slowed her down, sweetly teasing her, whispering that he wanted her to fight the pleasure and make it last.

He knew what he was about. It was bliss and torture, even better than the first time. When she finally returned to earth, she was so eager to please him back that she asked him to instruct her in detail, and she learned there were erotic tricks even Ah Lan hadn't mentioned.

They made love twice more that night. The third time Alex woke her out of a sound sleep and did things with his mouth that would have embarrassed her to death if she hadn't been in a misty dreamworld. Instead, she drank in the pleasure greedily, then did the same things to him. After the fourth time, he smiled and said they could set erotic records some other time—she had a long day ahead of her and needed to sleep. When she woke the next morning he was gone, and she thought she'd never felt so lonely in her life.

Chapter 16

Thomas Wyatt returned from Virginia City early Tuesday evening. He had found that his Comstock silver mines were producing exceptionally well and, with luck, would earn him and his partners millions by the time the leads played out. As a result, he was in an excellent mood.

His cheerfulness diminished sharply when he learned that his daughter had decamped to Nevada City on what sounded like a trumped-up pretext, but his annoyance didn't affect his appetite any, and the smells that emanated from his kitchen made his mouth water expectantly. Unfortunately, his normally stolid housekeeper fussed and dithered so much as he ate that the food went down like rotgut and grubs, prompting him to flee to his study as soon as he decently could.

He was writing to a friend in Hong Kong when Shen Wai poked his head around the door and coughed discreetly. Thomas waved him inside. Not two hours before, his old friend had been as exultant as he was, but now he looked oddly somber.

He sat down on the chair beside Thomas's desk. "I have some disturbing news, Captain. I arrived home to find my majordomo, Fou Ning, laid up in bed. He was severely beaten last Saturday by two men he identified as members of a Chinese triad."

Thomas had always liked Fou Ning. He was an intelligent man with a splendid ear for the latest news. "How is he? Do you have any idea what precipitated the attack?"

"He's bruised all over, with some broken bones, but luckily his mental faculties were undamaged. Dr. Chang thinks he will recover completely. As for the cause of the attack, only minutes before, Mi-Lan had called at my house. She was disguised as a male in order to evade pursuit, on her way to the Sacramento steamer. She asked Fou Ning to have a servant retrieve her luggage from your house and deliver it to the boat. Your gig was on the street outside, and she wanted it driven to the Mercantile Library. Fou Ning gave the appropriate orders shortly before she departed." Shen Wai withdrew some papers from his pocket and placed them on the desk. "She also left me an envelope. With her permission, Fou Ning scanned its contents after she left—a letter and two maps, all of the utmost importance. He was about to store them for safekeeping when the triad members stormed in. You might recall that he has what some call a photographic mind. The triad members seized the envelope and carried it off, but Ning reconstructed the contents as best he could. Mi-Lan's letter was originally in Chinese, but I've translated it for you."

Thomas picked the letter up, reading it with a mounting sense of shock and alarm. It was no secret to him that Melanie took troubling risks at times, and while he didn't like it, he had never tried to prevent it, either. He had long ago conceded that Wai had been justified in telling her about her past, and he knew that for both of them, the past demanded action. But now it appeared that Wai had involved her in criminal activities as well as charitable ones—that a man he trusted and respected had endangered her behind his back for personal gain. He was so enraged by Wai's selfishness and perfidy that it was all he could do not to grab him by the scruff of his neck and hurl him against the nearest wall.

He slammed the letter down. "Do you mean to tell me that you've embroiled my daughter in a smuggling ring? What in bloody hell were you thinking? Do you have any concept of how much danger she's in?" He didn't wait for answers, but continued furiously, "It's bad enough that she's being followed by members of a brutal triad, but now Alex McClure is after her, too. You've got friends in Hong Kong, for God's sake. You must know the man's reputation. Disguised or not, she'll never be able to lose him. He's a master of disguises himself." He leaned forward, a menacing look in his eyes. "You and your damned intrigues! I should kill you for this."

Wai reached into the sleeve of his tunic, pulled out a knife, and slid it across the desk. "You're right, Captain. Slash open my contemptible chest. Pull out my despicable heart. It's only what I deserve."

Thomas picked up the knife, walked around the desk, and hurled the weapon into the expensively upholstered seat of Wai's chair, right between his parted thighs. "Don't tempt me," he snapped. "I want to know what's going on here. And don't leave anything out."

"Of course not, Captain. Why else would I have come to see you?" Wai pulled out the knife and frowned. "That was not very good for my blade, not to mention your chair."

"Damn it, Wai—"

"Please calm yourself. I apologize a thousand

times for putting Mi-Lan in danger, but in all fairness, I must remind you that the *Aurora*—"

"Wasn't expected until Friday. I know that." Thomas flung himself back in his seat. "Well, Wai? What the devil have you involved her in?"

"Saving the Chinese people. Redeeming the Middle Kingdom. It was her fate." Wai tucked his knife back up his sleeve. "I'll explain in a minute, but first, may I offer you some reassurance?"

So it wasn't personal gain, Thomas thought. That was some small comfort. "Don't patronize me. Get on with it, man."

Wai blithely ignored the demand. "You're correct that McClure is dangerous, but in this case, it works to our advantage. He needs Mi-Lan to lead him to the gold, so he won't allow the triad members to harm her. Nor will he harm her himself, even for the purpose of extracting information from her. When it comes to his dealings with females, he is known to be . . . exceptionally chivalrous."

Thomas stared at him in disbelief. "Chivalrous? Are you deranged? Good God, Wai, the man is a damned Lothario. You know how impetuous Melanie can be. Hell, I've had to watch her like a hawk since she was thirteen. I suppose Ty will try to protect her, but they say McClure could give Don Juan lessons in seduction. I don't want to think about what Bonner will do if she falls into McClure's clutches before we can track her down and—"

He noticed his housekeeper hovering by the door and cut himself off. "Not now, Mrs. Dibble."

She wrung her hands together. "But Mr. Wyatt—"

He glared at her. "I'm busy. Your domestic problems can wait. Close the bloody door."

"But it's—it's about Alex McClure."

She was so deathly pale that Thomas reined in his fury about her snooping and nodded coldly. "Yes? What about him?"

"F-first Miss Wyatt went off, and then *he* showed up asking for her. I knew something was wrong when he—when he didn't come back, and, uh, when Artie crept in with Miss Wyatt's gown on. But he was so handsome and charming and clever, and I'm only a f-foolish female, so—"

"You're speaking of McClure? He was here in my house?"

"I-I think so." She began to sob. Thomas's fury gave way to astonishment. The woman never wept. She was as tough as a Mexican's mule.

Between her stammering and her sniveling, it took every ounce of patience he possessed to extract her story from her, and he lost no time in hustling her out of his study afterward. Then, scowling deeply, he slammed the door and returned to his desk.

"Do you know why she was sobbing?" he asked Wai. "Not because she believed Melanie's tale about Sukey being ill, or because she stayed in town when she should have accompanied the girl to Nevada City, or even because McClure tricked her into telling him Melanie's plans. Oh, no. She was crying because she was besotted with Dr. Samuel Seabury. She'd thought she made herself a conquest. And she was angry and upset that she'd been taken in." He ran an agitated hand through his hair. "If McClure can maneuver a stringy old bird like Harriet Dibble into doing his bidding, what chance does a green girl like Melanie have against him?"

"I believe you underestimate her," Wai replied. "Unlike Mrs. Dibble, Mi-Lan is accustomed to lavish male attention and will keep a level head. Though you persist in refusing to see it, her clairvoyance is as real as mine is, and it will help protect her. I nonetheless agree that we must find her as soon as possible." He paused, then added casually, "You haven't looked at the two maps yet. I'm afraid I couldn't interpret them. And you? Do you recognize any of the landmarks?"

Thomas absently glanced at them, then shook his head. It was only a moment later that he realized the significance of the question. "I can't believe it. My daughter—the girl you practically raised—is at the mercy of some debauched villain, and you're thinking about the gold. Give me back that knife. I'm ready to use it on you now."

Wai promptly did so, then raised his tunic to bare his chest. "I await my fate, Captain. Have mercy on my offensive flesh and dispose of me quickly."

Thomas muttered a curse and Wai smiled and looked at the floor. Both of them knew Thomas wasn't going to slice up an old friend. "Wipe that bloody grin off your face, you scoundrel. I want you to answer my questions and help me with my plans. What's all this about Melanie's fate and saving the Chinese people?"

Wai sobered, saying that the Taipings, though Christian-influenced mystics, had the Mandate of Heaven because their movement would lead to reform, and that he and Mi-Lan had to bow to the will of the gods. He described his smuggling and fencing operations, claiming that Melanie concurred with his views but knew nothing of his activities. She thought the gold, like the smuggled valuables, was intended for charity work, but in truth, the original miners were now rebel soldiers who wanted it used to buy weapons. But Wai insisted he had lied to her to protect her, not to deceive her. She would have insisted on helping him even more if she'd known the truth, and besides, she was a female, so his enemies would assume she knew nothing—unless she slipped and said otherwise. The less he told her, the safer she would be.

The longer Wai talked, the calmer Thomas grew. Wai was obviously telling him the truth, and after all these years, Thomas understood the depth of his friend's religious beliefs. Besides, Wai's reading of Melanie's position was likely accurate, at least insofar as her immediate safety was concerned.

As for the future, the two agreed they would have to follow Melanie's trail. Although the steamer didn't leave until four the next day, it would still get them to Sacramento and the stagecoach lines into the mining country sooner than going by horseback in the morning, and with any luck, they would find her before McClure relieved her of both her virtue and the buried gold.

Wai picked up his papers and tucked them back in his pocket. "The miners are old friends of mine. They assured me I would be able to interpret their maps, but who can be expected to make sense of memories of tracings? They look like scratches a chicken would make with its claws."

"Maybe so," Thomas said, "but I'll bet we could determine the location of the cache if we had accurate enough maps to compare them to. We could go straight to the gold that way. It would save us days." He frowned, thinking the problem over. "You know, Wai, it crossed my mind to ask Bonner to join the search. After all, he has a legitimate interest in Melanie's safety. But the existence of McClure complicates matters."

"You're afraid he might take what rightfully belongs to Bonner. But what Bonner doesn't know can't hurt him, Captain."

"My thinking exactly, but I've just realized that he might have the information we need. Suppose he commissioned maps for his land-grant cases? One of them could contain the very features we're looking for." Thomas paused. "Now that I consider the matter more thoroughly, I see that there's no real need to mention McClure's name, or even to tell George too much of the truth, given his feelings about Melanie's adventures. She's looking for some buried gold, and so are the triad members. That's danger enough to consult a devoted fiancé, don't you think?"

Wai nodded. "Absolutely, Captain."

Thomas and Shen Wai called on George at ten the next morning. He was poring over law books at his desk but professed himself delighted to see them. He hadn't yet heard from Melanie, he said, but hoped to receive a letter within the next several days. And Thomas? Had he enjoyed his trip? Were his mines as lucrative as everyone said?

Thomas resigned himself to talking silver, analyzing the boom in the Comstock and offering to sell George some shares in his mines. The fellow was his future son-in-law and the father of his eventual heirs, he reasoned, so it was all the same money in the end.

"But I've taken enough of your time with small talk," he finally murmured. "I'm afraid my visit has a more serious purpose, George. Both of us know what a handful my daughter can be, and—"

"Oh, God, what now?" George asked with a laugh.

"Just that Sukey Stone is as healthy as you or I. Melanie went to Nevada City for—let's call it a treasure hunt. During the early rush, some Chinese miners unearthed a fortune in gold, but buried it for fear that the white men in the area would rob them. They mapped the terrain carefully and returned to China, planning to come back for the cache when it was safe to carry it out." Thomas nodded at Wai, who was standing beside him with Fou Ning's maps. "Shen Wai was their friend. They recently sent him their maps and asked him to retrieve the gold on their behalf. Unfortunately, the maps fell into Melanie's hands while we were away. She left Wai copies, then took off after the gold. Obviously she sees it as a grand adventure. But the maps are very cryptic, presumably to provide as much security as possible. Melanie couldn't interpret them, so she went to Tyson Stone for help."

George shook his head, smiling ruefully. "I should have known. The trip was much too sudden. Excuse me for saying so, Thomas, but you've let the girl run wild." He sobered. "I won't do the same. One of these days her luck will run out and she'll get hurt. I hope she enjoys her little adventure, because it's the last one she's going to have."

"I'm afraid it's anything but little, George. The cache is worth a hundred thousand, at least. A Hong Kong triad learned of its existence and sent some men to find it. They stole the maps Melanie left for Shen Wai, but we doubt they'll be able to make any more sense of them than she could, or than Wai can, for that matter. We assume they plan to follow her to the gold, then steal it. In other words—"

"She's in a great deal of danger." George paled dramatically. "Dear God."

Thomas realized George's hands had begun to shake. The man was really distressed. "Easy now," he said. "They have no reason to harm her. All they want is the gold."

"But we all know what she's like. Stubborn. Reckless. She won't give it up without a fight."

"Which is why we hope to beat her and the triad members to the cache. Wai?" The Celestial handed George the two maps, and Thomas continued, "Wai's servant saw the maps before they were stolen and made these copies from memory. We know it's somewhere in the gold country, but that's about all. I was hoping you'd have maps of the area from your land-grant cases. That you could compare the two and determine the hiding place. Otherwise, we plan to start in Nevada City and try to pick up Melanie's trail from there. You're welcome to join us, naturally, but I know how difficult it is for you to get away."

"All the same, I'll do my best." George looked the maps over. "Hmm. I see what you mean by cryptic. I do have some charts of the area, but they're stored in my study at home. Can I keep these for a while? I have a client coming in soon, but I'll drive home after he leaves and carry out your comparison. I'll stop at the courthouse afterward and try to reschedule my cases. If you could return around two o'clock . . ."

Thomas nodded. One way or another, he and Wai would board a steamer at four that afternoon. What George told him at two would determine which one—the steamer to Sacramento and Nevada City, or the one to Stockton and the southern mines.

George ushered Wyatt and Shen Wai out of his office with a palpable sense of relief. The Chinaman gave him the chills. He was so damned quiet, as if he saw things other men couldn't. But that was impossible, George told himself. He had given a flawless performance just now. Far from suspecting a thing, Wyatt and the Chinaman had taken his trembling excitement for a lover's distress.

He told Sam he wasn't to be disturbed, then locked his door and pulled out his charts. He prided himself on his sharp memory and his keen eye for geography. If a match existed, he would quickly find it.

In fact, it was only when he realized that the lines on the first map represented streams and rivers as well as wagon roads and trails that he was able to select the proper chart, and even then, there were numerous discrepancies. There always were in a land as vast and poorly surveyed as California, and besides, Wyatt's map was only a copy of a copy.

The case in question had been a complicated one, he recalled, but one of his most lucrative. A few years before, when copper had been discovered thirty-five miles east of Stockton, every grant holder within miles, including his client, had laid claim to the strike. Always aggressive in such matters, George had gone after the gold in the foothills around Columbia and Murphys as well as the copper at the edge of the valley. In the end, he had won his client a share of what was now Copperopolis and some territory farther to the east.

Once again, he compared the Chinaman's map with his chart. There was no doubt about it. The gold was north of Murphys. All he had to do was find the geological features that matched the ones on the second map, and he would know exactly where to dig.

If he left this afternoon, he would be in Stockton by morning and in Murphys by nightfall, while Wyatt would have to start in Nevada City, two days behind him and probably more. Wyatt would never find maps as good as these, and without them, it could take him weeks to find the cache. But even a two-day lead would be long enough. There was no way Wyatt could arrive in Murphys any sooner, and the gold would be dug up, assayed, and sold by then. With a hundred thousand dollars, George thought, he could buy himself a whole new start—pay off his debts and use the funds that remained for his new investment.

Only one thing stood in his way—the possibility that Melanie would find the gold first—but it was a slim chance. The absence of legible maps would be a huge stumbling block. Indeed, with any luck, the whole bunch of them—she and her friend Stone, Wyatt and the Chinaman, and the Hong Kong triad members—would wander the foothills aimlessly. Even if they found the empty hiding place eventually, they would have no way of knowing when the gold had been removed. By the time they returned to San Francisco, he would be a wealthy man—and at long last, a free one.

Ty and Alex were sitting in the dining room of Bradley's Hotel on Wednesday morning, eating breakfast, when Ty rolled his eyes and pointed toward the door. "There she is. I was beginning to think she would never come down."

Alex turned and waved, smiling broadly when he caught Melanie's eye. The smile she gave him in return warmed his heart and lit up the room, but the pleasure he felt at her arrival turned to confusion when he noticed the enraged look on Ty's face.

"What's wrong?" he asked. "Why are you—"

"Because you're a damned bastard, that's why. Look at her, for God's sake. She would claw her way through an avalanche if you asked her to. Couldn't you have kept your trousers on last night?"

Alex almost told him to mind his own business, but a friend as old as Ty was entitled to speak his mind. "Calm down, Ty. I didn't do what you're thinking."

"Then it's only a matter of time. She's besotted with you. You won't even have to ask. She'll offer." Melanie was halfway to the table now. Ty glanced at her, then added in a low, heated voice, "You're wrong about what she wants. Before you accept, think about her life in San Francisco and compare it to what she would have as your strumpet in Hong Kong. If you have even a shred of integrity—"

He stopped in midsentence when she reached the table. "Morning, Mel." He forced an easy smile onto his face. "You should try the flapjacks. They're very good."

"Mmm. They sound wonderful." She slid in next to Alex. "I could eat a bear. Where's Ned?"

"Seeing to the horses," Ty answered. "We'll leave as soon as you're finished."

"Then I'll be quick." She hooked her arm through Alex's and cuddled close, then raised her chin to offer her mouth. "Hi there. Did you miss me?"

He dutifully pecked her on the lips. Ty watched them with a bland expression on his face, but Alex could sense the simmering hostility beneath the surface calm. "Hi yourself, lazybones. Of course I did. Are you packed yet?"

"Yes." She gazed at him adoringly. "I was worried that your cut might have opened during the night, but it seems fine. How can you look so fit and rested on so little sleep?"

He smiled and said it was a talent he'd developed at sea, but he was beginning to feel uneasy. Melanie was young and beautiful, a rarity in this tough male environment, and every man in the room was sizing her up. He could imagine what they were thinking, especially if they'd noticed the absence of a ring on her finger, and he didn't much like it.

Neither he nor Ty spoke very much while she ate, but she more than made up for it, chattering happily about the weather and the trip ahead. When she wasn't talking, she was worshipping him with her eyes. She seemed oblivious to the speculative looks she received and the scowls that crossed Ty's face whenever they touched or exchanged an affectionate glance, but Alex wasn't. He grew increasingly uncomfortable as the meal progressed, all but jumping to his feet when she excused herself to fetch her bags.

"I'll come with you," he said. "We need to talk."

She gave him a provocative look. "Talk, darling?"

To his disgust, his groin tightened fiercely. "Yes. Talk."

The minute they reached her room, she closed the door and threw her arms around his neck. "Last night was the most perfect night of my life. I missed you when I woke up this morning. The bed felt so empty and lonely." She moved against him and nibbled his bottom lip, and his arms went helplessly around her waist. "Have I told you lately that I adore you?"

The feel of her almost unmanned him. He wanted to loosen his trousers, toss up her skirts, and tease her until she trembled, but remembered Ty's words and put her at arm's length instead. "Yes, a few hours ago, but you don't have to say it when your behavior shouts it from the rafters. Everyone in the room could see it, including Ty. Especially Ty."

She looked puzzled. "So? I don't mind if he knows."

"Then you should. He's very protective of you. He wanted to castrate me."

"He'll get over it soon enough. He's not my keeper." She smiled uncertainly. "You sound upset, Alex. Are you annoyed with me for some reason?"

His temper began to unravel. How could she be so naive? "You're damned right I'm annoyed. You need to learn a little discretion. You can't act in a way that announces our relationship to the world, Melanie."

She massaged his shoulders seductively. "But why not, darling? Didn't your previous mistresses smile at you in public? Didn't they touch you and kiss you and tease you?"

"Of course they did, but they were from the Hong Kong demimonde." Her touch was pure torture. Scowling, he grasped her hands and put them at her sides. "For God's sake, stop that. You're not some cheap plaything. You're a respectable unmarried woman—"

"No, I'm not. Not anymore." She grinned at him. "You're worried about my reputation, aren't you? That's very sweet, but it's really not necessary. I've considered the matter carefully, and I've decided I don't care what people say or think— except you. As long as I can please you, I'll be happy." She sank to her knees and fingered a button on his trousers, and his loins began to burn. "It's going to be a long trip, Alex. Why don't you let me—"

"No, damn you!" Suddenly furious, he yanked her to her feet and shoved her away. "Stop acting like a two-dollar whore. It's vulgar and offensive."

Melanie went dead-white and backed away from him. She was utterly stunned. She was sure Alex wanted her—his arousal was glaringly obvious—so why was he so incensed? Why had he begun to castigate her the moment they'd reached this room? Wasn't she giving him the exact relationship he wanted?

She was so bewildered by his angry tone and

rough treatment that it was a few moments before his actual words sank in, and then every ounce of pride she possessed went straight to her backbone. "I'm very sorry, Mr. McClure, but I suppose it's in my blood. I come from a long line of them, you know."

He reddened. "Hell, Mellie, I didn't mean to—"

"As for what I just offered to do, you didn't find it vulgar or offensive last night." She raised her chin. "If I remember correctly, you moaned and writhed and screamed, and then, about an hour later, you begged me to do it again."

"I know. I'm sorry. It was a foul thing to say. You were only doing what I taught you to do." He turned toward the window, but not before she saw the flush on his face deepen markedly. "That's the whole point. You were right on Monday. I'm turning you into my whore. Taking what I want on my own selfish terms and cloaking it with pretty words. It has to stop. It isn't right."

Her anger gave way to renewed confusion. None of this made sense. He'd been relaxed and affectionate downstairs. Why had he suddenly changed? "But why not, Alex? You make me happy. I don't want to leave you. Whatever happened to staying together and giving each other pleasure until I was ready to settle down?"

"It won't work." He opened the curtains and stared outside. "For one thing, I'm not a saint. I want to have sexual relations with you, and if we keep sharing a bed, sooner or later I'm going to do it."

Melanie wasn't deaf and blind. After spending the night with Alex, she understood that very well. "I know." Blushing, she added softly, "I want to please you, Alex. You can have me whenever you want me."

He jerked around. "Have you lost your mind?

No decent man would marry you if I took you. For God's sake, Melanie, do you have any idea what your life would be like in Hong Kong? You're used to moving in the highest social circles—"

"Society bores me to death. I wouldn't miss it a bit if I gave it up, not that I can see why I would have to."

"Then it's time you woke up from the dreamworld you're obviously living in. You're accustomed to the finest treatment wherever you go, but nobody bows and scrapes to a mistress. It would be one thing if you had a husband to provide a veneer of respectability, but you don't. You would be young and unmarried and alone, beyond my ability to protect you from slights and snubs." He took a few steps forward. "You would be a kept woman and everyone in town would know it. You would be shunned by polite society, condescended to by shopkeepers, pursued by rakes, and gossiped about by everyone. I refuse to let that happen."

The picture he painted was so absurd that Melanie almost laughed. "Kept, Alex? Are you serious? Good grief, I'm the heiress to a huge fortune, and my trust funds make me wealthy in my own right. You know as well as I do that money buys respect. If I decide I want a husband, conformable or otherwise, it will buy me that, too." All the same, honesty compelled her to admit that some of what he had said made sense. "Still, discretion would make things more pleasant, I'll grant you that much. I should probably hire myself a spinster aunt and a large staff. Set myself up as an eccentric heiress and businesswoman. I do have some experience with the role, you know." She smiled, well-pleased with the plan. "I'll continue my rescue work, of course. As for you and me, people will look the other way as long as we're reasonably circumspect. They always do, if the lovers are rich and powerful enough. Things will work out perfectly."

Alex shook his head. "You're forgetting one thing. We would be in Hong Kong. There must be people there who knew your parents—who would remember what you came from. I don't care how rich you are, you'll have too many marks against you. Society will tolerate only so much, and it won't accept the bastard daughter of a half-Chinese whore if she runs her own household and warms some rakehell's bed."

The smile faded from Melanie's face. Alex was probably right. Even with all her money, the combination of sexual impropriety and low blood would bring her down. She would be snubbed by the social elite and relegated to the Hong Kong demimonde.

And then she smiled again, because none of it mattered a bit. "I really don't care. I would have the two things I want most, you and my work. I'm sure you have wonderful friends, and that some of them have mistresses, and that I would enjoy their company immensely. As for insolent clerks and oily Don Juans—"

"Life isn't a goddamned fantasy," Alex said impatiently. "The world is a hard, cruel place. It would hurt you every day. Believe me, you would wind up caring like hell—and you would hate me for it."

She folded her arms across her chest and prayed for patience. "If you're finished telling me how I would feel—"

"Somebody has to, since you don't have sense enough to figure it out on your own."

"God, but you're arrogant and stubborn. For heaven's sake, Alex, you know what I came

from—a ship and a series of mining camps. The
life you think I need—"

"Is the only life you've known as a woman, so
don't tell me you wouldn't miss it. You're not an
unruly girl anymore, running wild in the damned
wilderness. You're rich and famous and indulged." He picked up her valise and handed her
her carpetbag. "We've argued for far too long. I
had no business asking the things I asked. It was
some sort of temporary insanity." He took her
arm. "Come along now. We have to leave."

Melanie suddenly felt cold and frightened. "But
Alex—"

"I said come along, Melanie. I'm much too fond
of you to ruin your life."

He dragged her toward the door, but she dug in
her heels and resisted fiercely. "If you care for me,
then let me stay with you. I'll be miserable if you
don't. I love you."

He stopped and sighed. "You only think you do,
because of the pleasure I've given you. You'll forget me soon enough."

She was so enraged by that statement that she
whacked him with her carpetbag, slamming it
against his thigh with all her might, but tears were
running down her cheeks. "Stop telling me what I
think and feel, damn you! I'm not some innocent
little chucklehead. I've lost count of the number of
proposals I've had, but I didn't want a single one
of those men the way I want you. I do too know
what love is, because you made me feel it." She
began to sob. "Please, Alex. Let me stay with you.
I swear I'll make you happy."

"Hell, Mellie, don't cry. Not over me." He set
down her valise and put his hands on her shoulders, then said softly, "It's better to end it now,
especially if you truly love me. One of us has to
be sensible, and since I'm older and more

experienced ..." He dropped his hands. "I'm sorry, but the answer is no. That's final."

Melanie felt as if Alex had thrust a knife into her heart. So this was love. She'd been right to try to avoid it. It left you exposed and raw and bleeding.

Chapter 17

〜〜∽OO∽〜〜

Watching Ty and Alex after she went downstairs, Melanie quickly figured out where
Alex's attack of conscience had come from, and
she wanted to throttle Ty Stone for sticking his
nose where it didn't belong. Then Ned noticed the
tension between Ty and Alex and began needling
them gleefully, and things went from bad to
worse. She wound up sitting between Ty and Ned
during the trip to Oroville, but she would have
ridden atop the buggy if she could have, just to
avoid contact with the whole male species.

As for Alex, he was the worst one of all. Here
she was, hurting abominably, but at least she was
trying to be civil, attempting to converse pleasantly about politics with Ty and Ned. And what
was he doing? Brooding. Carping about Ned's
driving. Offering pearls of alleged wisdom in a
clipped, superior tone when he bothered to speak
at all. An hour into the trip, she finally snapped
that if giving her up had put him into such a sour
frame of mind, perhaps he should reconsider. He
stiffened and apologized, then lapsed into total silence.

They stopped to stretch their legs and water the
horses half an hour later. Two long days of travel

had wearied both the humans and the livestock, but luckily, it was a warm, clear day and the road was in excellent shape, permitting a rapid rate of speed and frequent breaks. After the second stop, Alex began talking again. During the third, when Melanie said she wasn't hungry, he coaxed her into eating some lunch. And during the fourth, which was halfway to Oroville, he started telling her tales from his schooldays, trying to cajole a smile out of her.

He finally succeeded with a story about taking revenge against a brutal headmaster by sneaking an opiate into the man's port during his meeting with an important benefactor, causing him to wobble and stutter like a sot. Though she appreciated Alex's efforts to cheer her, she was also a little resentful. She was aching inside and he was telling stories—to amuse her, it was true, but he had recovered much too quickly. She wanted him to suffer as much as she was.

Still, the ride was more agreeable without everyone sniping and brooding, and the second half of the trip passed more quickly than the first. They stopped to make inquiries about the Reverend Archibald Hamilton when they reached the outskirts of Oroville, a mining town on the fringe of the gold country. A blacksmith they spoke to knew him well, telling them he had come there from the States two years before to live with his wealthy sister, a recent widow. He preached throughout the surrounding counties now and was a popular figure in the area, much esteemed for his kindness and common sense.

The smithy gave them directions to his house, a two-story frame building on a sizable lot on Montgomery Street. A few minutes later they knocked on the door. A tall, thin man with wild white hair and a beard to match answered and invited them in. After looking them up and down, especially Ty, he said in a ringing tone, "Aha! The plot thickens. I'm Archibald Hamilton, and I'll wager you're Tyson Stone. Am I right?"

Ty backed up a step and regarded the minister warily. Melanie had the feeling he was bracing himself for another tongue-lashing. "Yes, Mr. Hamilton." He introduced Melanie, Alex, and Ned, then added, "I don't know what my sister told you about me, but—"

"Only that you're the most wonderful brother in the world, and that if you bar her from your home and never speak to her again, it will only be what she deserves." Hamilton led them into the parlor. "Come in, come in. Have a seat. Make yourselves comfortable. I'll get you all some sherry." As he bustled about, he continued, "I had a feeling you would manage to track her down, although she claimed it was impossible. She sniffled all the way from Quincy, you know. I've never known a female with so many tears in her. I was planning to take her home tomorrow morning, but she was afraid to go." He gave Ty an artless look. "It seems she flouted your orders, destroyed your reputation, and sold your team and gig. Those are grave transgressions to be sure, but hardly worthy of banishment and eternal silence. Wouldn't you agree?"

Ty laughed. "I'm not so sure, Mr. Hamilton, but I have a feeling you're about to tell me that God smiles upon the merciful."

"That He does, son, that He does." The minster passed out the sherry and sat down. "I have to admit, the engaging little baggage vilified you very impressively at first, but it wasn't hard to get at the real truth of it. I believe the longer she was away from home, the more lonely and frightened she became, although she was taking care of herself very well. She's exceptionally resourceful for a girl her age. In any event, I suppose she ran into me just when she was ready to confide in someone."

"After some delicate and clever prodding on your part, I'll bet," Melanie said, thinking Hamilton was everything a clergyman should be.

"Could be, could be. Ty, you'll be gratified to know you've grown a great deal wiser over the past few days, as well as kinder and more honorable. I believe she's ready to do whatever you say, not that your plans are necessarily the best for all concerned. But let me begin at the beginning."

Hamilton explained that Sukey had initially spun the same outrageous tales that she'd told the bearded lady, but either the minister had been shrewder than the circus performer or Sukey had been less convincing, because he had been dubious from the start. Today, as they'd driven to Oroville, she had confessed her sins and poured out her heart, relating the story of her life and asking his advice.

"But I told her I was in the business of listening, not judging," Hamilton finished, "and that until I'd heard your side of it, Ty, I could hardly give her guidance. I was hoping to speak to you when I brought her home, assuming you were agreeable." He smiled. "They say I have a talent for counseling people. How about it?"

"I'm willing to try. I've never claimed I was perfect, only that I was doing my best." Ty drained his sherry, then stared into his lap. "But my best was a poor thing at times. I treated Sukey as too much of a child. I worked so hard and worried so much that I made both of us miserable. But I was terrified of failing. She was such a huge responsibility, and I'd had ... rather a misspent youth."

"You'll have to tell me about it. I'm always on

the lookout for material for my homilies." Hamilton stood, then boomed toward the hallway, "You can come out from behind the door now, Sukey. I promise you your brother won't bite you."

Melanie barely had time to wonder how Hamilton had known Sukey was eavesdropping when the girl peeked anxiously around the door. Ty got to his feet and held out his arms, and she burst into tears, barreled into the parlor, and flung herself against his chest. She sobbed that she was sorry and asked if he could ever forgive her, but he was already stroking her hair and murmuring how relieved he was to see her.

Hamilton was beaming when the pair finally separated. "Excellent, children, excellent. Run along to the kitchen, Sukey, and fetch some of my sister's apple cake. I'm sure your brother and his friends would enjoy having a bite to eat while we sort out our plans."

Sukey rubbed her eyes and trotted off, and Hamilton and Ty sat back down. The minister promptly invited everyone to dine and spend the night, but there was only one spare bed in the house, and Melanie wanted Ty and Sukey to have as much time as possible to talk. She insisted that she, Alex, and Ned should go to a hotel while Ty remained at the house, and Hamilton finally agreed. Since the buggy barely held four, much less five, Ty offered to take Sukey home on the public stage, leaving the gig for the other three.

Everything was settled by the time Sukey returned with a tray of cake. She was smiling by then, and as irrepressible as ever. "So who are your two friends, Mel?" She pointed to Alex. "And what was he doing in North San Juan? Not looking for gold, obviously."

Melanie took a piece of cake. "His name is Alex McClure, and he was following you, but only because he thought you were me. And that's Ned Jones. His . . . assistant."

Looking pensive, Sukey held out the tray to Ned and then moved along to Alex. "You were following Mel?" She stared at him in fascination. "Why? Does she have something—" Her gaze jerked back to Melanie. "Good grief, he's the one you told me about, isn't he? The one who's thrilling and dangerous and disreputable. What is he doing here?"

Melanie paled a little. "It's a long story. I'll tell you about it when we get home."

But Sukey showed no signs of hearing. She was too busy gaping at Alex. "Heavens, he's handsome. Even better-looking than Grant."

He smiled at her. "Thank you, Miss Stone. It's a pleasure to see you again. Believe me, you were wasted on the likes of Guthrie. I suppose you chose him because you could control him so easily, but if you're ever tempted to run away again, I hope you'll select someone more interesting. More worthy of your beauty and intellect."

"Don't put ideas into her head," Ty muttered.

"And charming into the bargain," Sukey said. "Gee, Mel, no wonder you were smitten. Are you still, or have you gotten over him?"

Melanie tried to hide her feelings, but it was hopeless. Her throat got tight and her eyes filled up. Knowing she couldn't speak without crying, she simply shrugged.

Sukey's gaze returned to Alex, her eyes narrowing ominously. "You hurt her, didn't you? You hurt my friend."

"Not on purpose, but this is hardly the time or place—" He suddenly yelped in pain, because Sukey had plunged her hand into his hair and yanked viciously. "What in bloody Christ! Uh, excuse me, Reverend. What do you think you're doing, you little wildcat?"

Sukey glared at him. "Taking a strand of your hair, you contemptible bounder. You'd better make things right with Mel, do you hear me? Because if you don't, I'll put a spell on you that will—"

"A spell?" Ty interrupted with a laugh. "What a brilliant idea! He fully deserves it, Suke. Tell me, have you been studying black magic during your adventure?"

"I'm beginning to feel a certain sympathy for Guthrie," Alex grumbled, rubbing his head. "If you were even half this much trouble in Downieville, young lady . . ."

"The African sorceress taught it to me," Sukey told Ty. "She was best friends with the bearded lady. It was to use on you if I wanted, but I wouldn't have, not ever. It was too awful." She glared at Alex again. "But it's not too awful for *you*. I'm warning you, you'd better fix things up with Mel or I'll make you . . . You won't be able to . . ." Blushing, she glanced at the Reverend Hamilton, then muttered, "Your, uh, your potency will vanish completely, that's what."

Alex broke into a grin. "Is that right! I'm terrified, Miss Stone. I beg you, spell out your demands in more detail."

Sukey tossed her hair. "You won't be laughing after I cast my spell. I know about men like you. Your male powers are highly important to you."

A loud chuckle erupted from across the room. "They're important to all of us, my dear." Hamilton walked to her side and held out his hand. "Witchcraft is very un-Christian, Susannah. I couldn't possibly allow it. Give me the gentleman's hair."

Sukey looked mutinous, but she wasn't prepared to gainsay a man of the cloth, especially one who had assisted her so gallantly. "Very well." She opened her fist. "I probably wouldn't have done it anyway. The other ingredients in the brew are too disgusting."

Hamilton plucked up the strands of hair and gave them to Alex. "It appears that Ty and Sukey are not the only people here who could benefit from my services. If you and Miss Wyatt have a problem, I would be happy to help."

Alex smiled politely and shoved the hairs in his pocket. He wasn't impressed by the outlandish threats of an unruly little chit, and he didn't have any need of Hamilton, either, at least not in his capacity as a samaritan. "I appreciate the offer," he said. "Maybe I'll be in touch."

But there was no "maybe" about it. He knew what he wanted—Melanie—and he knew what he meant to do—marry her, because it was the only honorable way to have her. The only problem would be talking her into it.

Alex was standing outside Melanie's door, wrestling with a troubled conscience and a bad case of nerves. It wasn't fair, what he was about to do, but what real choice did he have? She'd flirted with him outrageously during dinner, whispering what she planned to do to him when she got him alone, touching him furtively under the table to emphasize the point, and quite naturally he'd responded. By dessert he'd been hot enough to set his chair on fire.

In other words, she was intent on seducing him, and he was only too wiling to be compromised. He'd known the timing wasn't right for a proposal, that the longer she wanted him and missed him the better his chance of success would be, but his passions had gotten the better of him. So he had told her how much he cared for her and asked her to marry him, and just as he'd feared, she had turned him down flat.

It wasn't enough that he craved her tenderness and adored her wit, or that they excited each other wildly in bed. She wanted eternal devotion. Undying love. No barriers or reservations whatsoever. And he couldn't give her those things.

Still, he wasn't about to let her go. He was too unhappy without her, and the same was true of her. So for the second time that day, he had tried to talk some sense into her about what sorts of relationships were acceptable in this world, but she'd refused to listen. If he had decided to maneuver her into doing what was best for her, well, what other option was left to him? Like any female, if her pleasure was intense enough and her need was great enough, her emotions would take over, she would give him what he asked, and that would be the end of it.

But when he raised his hand to knock on her door, he found that it was shaking with nerves. He'd never doubted his talents as a lover before, but Mellie was different. For one thing, she was a virgin, and for another, he was achingly anxious to please her and make her happy. He grimaced. Right at that moment, he could have used her friend Ah Lan at his side, whispering the deepest secrets of the Orient into his ear.

Melanie was sitting up in bed, staring dejectedly into the candlelit dimness, when someone knocked on her door. Her heart leaped into her throat. She knew it must be Alex, but she didn't know whether to welcome a visit or dread one. She had teased him half to death during dinner, made him want her so much he'd proposed, then refused him when he'd admitted he didn't love her. He'd become exasperated with her, even angry, and she couldn't really blame him. It wasn't unreasonable to want a man's love, but only a shrew would try to tempt him into betraying his sense of honor.

She got out of bed and let him in. He entered the room and closed the door. He was wearing a sashed dressing gown and an unreadable expression—his poker player's face, she thought. Another speech was probably in the offing, similar to the one that morning, the same as the one after dinner.

Without a word, he lifted her into his arms and carried her to the bed. His heart was pounding fiercely and he was shaking a little. It wasn't a lack of emotion she'd seen in his eyes, she realized, but the exact opposite. He was stiff with tension but trying not to show it. That was only to be expected in a man like Alex. He hated displaying anything he considered a weakness.

It was obvious why he had come. After all, a man didn't carry a woman to bed just to chat with her. So if he was tense, it was because she had pushed him into this, because he had deep reservations and was forcing them aside.

Her throat got even tighter. Torn between guilt and desire, she couldn't get a single word out. She raised her hand and stroked his cheek, and he looked into her eyes. She didn't try to hide her feelings. As for Alex, there was heat in his gaze now, not just strain and doubt.

"This morning before we left . . ." He spoke in a soft, hoarse voice. "You said I could have you whenever I want you. I want you so much it's killing me, Mellie, but at dinner tonight . . . You were annoyed with me. You resented the way I lectured you. So I thought maybe you'd changed your mind."

She shook her head. Guilty or not, she loved him desperately, and she knew that anything that bound them closer together couldn't possibly be wrong. "No. I haven't if you haven't." She reddened and looked downward. "I mean, if you're sure you really want to, Alex. I know you have your conscience to answer to."

Alex threw back the covers, settled her gently on the bed, and sat down beside her. He would have preferred not to talk about his conscience, but he had set his course of action and wasn't going to be swayed. "I look at you, Mellie, and my conscience doesn't stand a chance." He kissed her on the forehead, then smiled at her. "It will all work out. Let's not think about it right now."

Melanie pushed away the obvious—that they would have to think about it eventually, and that working things out required one of them to give in—and hesitantly smiled back. She trusted Alex completely and wanted him with all her heart, but she was suddenly a little nervous. She'd heard about this deflowering business from Ah Lan, and it wasn't always pleasant.

"Yes. All right." She touched his arm. "I do love you, you know."

"Yes." He removed a metal tin and a small bottle from his pocket and placed them on the bedside table. "I don't deserve that, but I'm very grateful for it. I'm going to make you happy, sweetheart. I swear that I will."

He kissed her on the mouth, sweetly rather than passionately, then removed her nightdress and his own dressing gown and pulled the covers over the two of them. He was naked and very aroused, and when he stretched out beside her and took her in his arms, she realized he was still shaking. She put her arms around his neck and clung to him. They were lying side by side, touching along the whole length of their bodies, and his hands were on her buttocks, pressing her against his manhood. The knowledge that he would soon be inside her increased her anxiety, but it also made her tremble with a longing that she'd never experienced before.

He began to kiss her, slowly and tenderly at first, then with mounting passion, sliding a hand between their bodies to caress her belly and breasts. As always, she drank in the taste and scent and touch of him, but there was a heady difference now. She was used to his raw physical hunger, but he was burning with intense emotion, and it was more potent than the strongest aphrodisiac. Her anxiety faded. Her longing intensified.

His mouth moved lower, licking a sensitized nipple . . . nipping it just hard enough to send an erotic hint of pain sizzling through her . . . suckling it gently and then more roughly to intensify the pleasure. She massaged his neck and shoulders, needing to touch him wherever she could reach. Her excitement mounted as he tasted her other breast, then slipped his hand between her legs and intimately teased her. She moaned and raked her nails down his chest, then found and grasped his member. But before she could caress him, he pushed away her hand and tumbled her onto her back.

He straddled her, looming above her, supporting himself on his elbows. "It would be better if you didn't touch me." His voice was strained, but he was smiling slightly. "I want to go slowly, love, and if you excite me too much, I'll never be able to do it."

His manhood was lightly grazing her, providing much too tempting a target. She wasn't at all nervous now, merely aroused. Smiling coyly, she captured him in both her hands and began to fondle him.

"Oh, no, you don't." With dizzying speed, he pinned her arms above her head, then regarded her with mock sternness. "If you try that again, I'll bind your wrists with my sash and tie them to the headboard. Do I make myself clear?"

"Perfectly, Alex. You'll render me helpless and do whatever you want." She looked at him from under her lashes. "Is that supposed to be a threat? Because if you want the truth, it sounds wildly exciting."

His lips quivered helplessly, and his sternness gave way to laughter. "You're right. It does. So we'd better save it for another time, because I have to keep some semblance of control here." He sobered. "Have pity on me, Mellie. I'm very nervous about this. I don't want to hurt you, but I might not be able to help it. In case you didn't notice, I'm finding this business of making love to a virgin extremely unnerving."

She ran her toe up and down his leg, utterly relaxed now, thinking him the most wonderful man in the world. "I have complete confidence in you, Alex. I'm sure it will be splendid."

He rolled his eyes. "There's nothing like a little extra pressure. If you want splendor, you're going to have to lie as quietly as you can and let me arouse you. You can't touch me back. I need to keep a cool head."

"A cool head, eh? Now there's a tough pun to resist." Grinning, she went limp. "Very well, Alex. I'm your willing slave. Show me the moon and the stars."

"Well, hell, Mellie, if I was worried before ..."

"Hush." She looked at him with her heart in her eyes. "I love you. I want us to belong to each other. Everything you've ever done to me was perfect. This will be, too."

It was just as she expected. Alex was gentle, passionate, and controlled, kissing and caressing her until she begged him to let her touch him back, then stroking and probing her with his tongue until she writhed beneath his mouth and whimpered incoherently. When he finally moved away and reached for the tin he'd brought into the room, she felt only fierce love and frantic anticipation.

He took out a condom and put it on, then unscrewed the bottle beside the tin and poured a fragrant amber liquid into his palm. He was soon teasing her with oil-slick fingers, stroking her most sensitive flesh one moment, easing in and out of her to open and stretch her the next.

She shuddered. The hot, slippery feel of him was driving her mad. "Dear God, Alex, if you don't stop that—"

"I'm finished, love. You're ready. Try to keep still." He put a pillow under her hips and parted her thighs, then settled himself between her legs. She felt him enter her, taking her very slowly, repeatedly pulling out and then easing deeper inside her. It felt strange to have him penetrate and fill her, but she decided she rather liked it.

He stopped after a few minutes, his body stilling completely as he kissed her savagely and teased her skillfully with his fingers. Pleasure exploded into feverish longing. She began to move against his hand, needing him to touch her harder and come deeper inside her.

Alex was frantic himself by then. The last thing he wanted was to stop. Mellie was sweet and tight and exciting, a mixture of innocence and worldliness so potently sensual that his schemes were hanging by the merest thread. But if he gave up now—if he didn't strike while he had the advantage—she would never give in. He would ruin her life. Destroy her. Lose her forever. The thought was so chilling that sanity finally returned.

He knew she was on the edge of her climax. He could feel it in her hunger and wildness. He grasped her hips to stop her from thrashing and tore away his mouth. "Mellie . . . Tell me how much you want me."

"You make me frenzied. Desperate." Melanie was so aroused she could barely talk, much less think lucidly. She tried to move against him but he wouldn't permit it. "Please, Alex. Don't tease me. My whole body is on fire."

"Then you'll do whatever I say. Give me whatever I want."

She didn't understand what he was asking, or why he sounded so strained. "I don't . . . Do what? Give you what?"

"Anything. Everything. Do you love me enough to agree?"

She shook her head in confusion. "In bed, you mean? You know that I do. What do you want that I haven't done?"

"Nothing. Not in bed. That's the one place we're perfectly matched." He withdrew a little and looked at her with grim determination. "I was talking about marriage, Melanie. You're going to wed me before we return to Hong Kong. I insist on it."

Melanie's head cleared at a rapid rate of speed. Alex had gotten her into the most vulnerable position imaginable, then pounced like a tiger. Not only was his timing extremely odd; his methods were arrogant to the point of tyranny. "You do, do you? How interesting. Tell me, why are you asking me again? And why now?"

"I'm not asking you. I tried that and it didn't work, so I'm telling you." He moved gently in and out of her, smiling now. "Say yes, love, and let's get on with it." He caressed her breasts, massaging her nipples in the way she liked most. "I'm at the end of my tether here."

She shuddered. He was arousing the most delicious sensations imaginable in her belly and breasts and the intimate core of her, but they weren't going to change the feelings in her heart. Her answer was still no. She wasn't going to marry a man who didn't love her.

But even so, of its own accord, her body was moving in response to his thrusts. She closed her eyes as the pleasure swamped her senses. On the other hand, she thought hazily, there was nothing to prevent her from fibbing. If she said yes, he would stay. Once they had finished, his scruples would become irrelevant. She would be ruined, thank God, and able to live her life the way she wanted.

She crossed her fingers behind his back. It was only three little letters, after all.

"Yes," she whispered.

He grunted his satisfaction and began to make love to her again. Between his torrid kisses, his playful fingers, and the feel of him inside her, she forgot everything but the need to give and receive pleasure. And then he probed deeper and harder, and pain slashed through her loins. She flinched and he retreated at once.

She permitted several such forays, then frowned at him. "I'm not enjoying this at all, Alex. I think you should stop fiddling around and get on with it. Do it like the plasters. Quickly is best."

"And I was sure that taking you slowly would work. Good Lord. Instructed by a virgin. I'll never live it down."

"I won't tell a soul." She managed a smile. "It *is* my body. If it's going to be ravished, I should get to say how."

"You have a point, love. Hold on tight." She

clutched his shoulders, and he gave a powerful thrust and drove himself inside her. Then he stayed where he was, stroking her hair and panting a little but otherwise remaining motionless. "Are you all right? Should I leave you?"

Melanie's heart was racing and her skin felt clammy, but the pain was almost gone and an aching tenderness had taken its place. "I'm fine. I've never felt so close to anyone in my life." She wrapped her arms and legs around him and held him tight. "You feel wonderful. I could keep you here all night."

"Who wants to go?" Watching her face, he slowly pulled out of her, then eased himself back inside. "Ah. Paradise regained. I can't possibly feel as wonderful as you do."

But he was wrong. He did, especially when he began to arouse her again. Gentleness turned to passion and passion to raw wild need, until she was crying out with every hard, deep thrust of his member. Her climax was long and intense and moving, but for her, his was even more splendid, from the heat in his voice as he moaned her name to the possessive way he took his pleasure to his sweetness and trust when he finally went slack, then nuzzled into the crook of her neck.

She tenderly stroked his back. "Don't you dare fall asleep on me. You're far too large. Think of the headlines. 'Heiress Squashed to Death After Illicit Tryst.' "

He rolled onto his back and pulled her against his chest. "Is there any soreness, Mellie? Any discomfort?"

"Just a little." She teased his nipples, then fingered his medal. "Make that '. . . After Illicit Tryst with Murderous Triad Member.' If you're asking if I'll want you again tonight, the answer is probably yes."

"Probably, love? Come now, be honest. You can't stop touching me. Can't get enough of me. I only asked because I wondered if I should refuse you for your own good."

She pinched his thigh. "God, you're an arrogant devil."

"Ouch. Not really, but I do enjoy teasing you. It makes you even hotter for me, as impossible as that might seem." He closed his eyes, looking vastly content. "You were wonderful, sweetheart. Marriage is looking more agreeable all the time. I don't know the procedures for a quick wedding in this state, but I expect the estimable Mr. Hamilton could tell us. We'll visit him first thing tomorrow morning."

Melanie had hoped to delay this conversation indefinitely, but Alex was forcing her hand. Either they settled things now or he would drag her before a preacher in the morning. "I know I said yes, but it was only a word, and you blackmailed me into saying it. I've told you how I feel. Nothing has changed."

He opened his eyes and smiled indulgently. "Of course it has. You have to make an honest man of me. You can't give a man your maidenhead and then refuse to wed him. It's—it's immoral, that's what it is."

"I don't care. Just listen to me, Alex." She expected him to argue, but he simply nodded. "The intense passion you feel won't last forever, and if there's no deep and abiding love to replace it, you'll feel restless and trapped. Either you'll stay with me and resent the loss of your freedom, or you'll wander the way my father always has and feel guilty about abandoning me. Either way, both of us will be miserable. I simply can't have that. I love you and I'll be your mistress, but I won't tie you down. Marriage is out of the question."

Alex pulled himself up and eased Melanie into the crook of his arm. She'd never stated her feelings so explicitly before, but he'd heard enough from her and Ty so that everything fit together and clicked into place. With any other woman, if he had maneuvered her into agreeing to marry him, the combination of promising him her hand and giving him her virginity would have stopped her from backing out, but Mellie was unique. He couldn't fault her for her reluctance. He *had* blackmailed her, and her fears were understandable.

"The things you're afraid of won't happen," he said quietly. "I'm very fond of you, Mellie. Surely you must know that. I can't imagine we'll ever bore each other. I want you with me in Hong Kong as much as I've ever wanted anything, but it can't be as my mistress. I couldn't live with myself if I exposed you to that. You love me, so marry me and stop worrying about the future."

"But how can I?" It was a cry from the heart, confused and forlorn. "You don't love *me*."

His own heart lurched painfully. "Please try to understand. It's not that I don't want to. I simply can't."

Melanie had experienced pain in her life, but never like this. The rejection was agonizing. Excruciating. She tried desperately not to cry, but couldn't help it. "I know." She buried her face against his chest. "I don't evoke those sorts of feelings in you. But someday you'll meet someone who does, and you won't want a wife around to complicate matters. Mistresses are so much easier to dispose of."

Alex felt like the blackest villain in hell. Melanie's voice was an anguished whisper, and his chest was wet with her tears. He hated being the cause of such suffering.

He held her close against him. "Please don't cry. You're completely wrong. It's me, not you. It's as if—as if there's a wall between me and the world. It separates me from the rest of humanity. I put it up a long time ago and now ... I can't seem to tear it down."

He began to shake. He had never said those things aloud—had barely even said them to himself. "I think it began when my mother died. Died physically, I mean. When the beatings began. After the first few times, when I realized they weren't going to stop, I tried to harm myself. I ran into a wall at top speed. Teased a horse into biting me. Climbed a tree and made myself so dizzy I slipped, but the branches broke my fall. I wasn't supposed to go near that tree, and my father whipped me viciously for it. That was the first time my mother came. She begged him to stop, but he screamed that she was a demon I had summoned from hell to save me and whipped me even harder. So she vanished, but she returned later on, when I was alone in my room."

Alex fought for air. He felt cold and sweaty and nauseated. And then Melanie straightened and kissed his cheek, and gently massaged his neck, and miraculously, the feeling began to fade.

A minute or two went by. "Did she speak to you?" Melanie finally asked. "What did she say?"

"That she loved me and she was sorry she'd had to leave me. That I was a good boy. That my father had a sickness of the brain that couldn't be cured. I was to obey him, but it was best not to let myself feel anything toward him. I did try, but I couldn't help misbehaving—and hating him for his cruelty. She told me I should leave my body while he was beating me, that if I tried hard enough, I could float to the ceiling and escape the pain, at least for short periods of time. And she was right. I learned to do it."

He shuddered violently. "But it was the trick of a demon, Mellie, or it could have been. As a child, I was never sure who or what she was. Who or what *I* was. She always came after the worst beatings to comfort me and urge me to go on, and in between, I used to ache for those visits. I never—I never courted torture just to see her, not in Scotland, but there were times when I came very close."

Melanie had forgotten her own pain by then. Alex's suffering was ripping her in half. His memories haunted and tortured him so! If she hadn't been so desperate to understand him, she would have stopped him. Instead she murmured, "That's only natural. She was all you really had."

"No. The night I found the pistol . . . I pressed it against my temple. To this day, I don't know whether I would have pulled the trigger or not, only that my mother appeared and stopped me. She told me to turn to my stepmother for help. I'd refused to let myself love her, but I knew she was a good woman. God knows where I would be without her."

"So you went to England. You once said you needed your mother there, but she never came."

"Yes. I'd been torn from everything familiar, and everything I did was wrong. My looks, my accent, my manners, the things I'd been taught in school . . . Even when I tried my hardest, the other boys beat me and teased me. My tutors and my grandparents criticized and corrected me constantly. I'd never felt so lonely or inferior in my life. I wanted my mother desperately. I used to pray for her to come, to plead with her and make bargains with God, and when she didn't . . ."

His voice trailed off. Melanie gazed at him. His

eyes were glazed with pain. She could guess what had happened next and it filled her with horror. "You misbehaved. You tried to provoke such a severe beating that she would have to appear."

"Yes. I, uh, I skipped my lessons. Sassed my grandmother. Defied my grandfather. He didn't want to paddle me, not after seeing my scars, but I gave him no choice. I cursed him while he was doing it, trying to bait him into losing control, but it didn't work. It was just an ordinary beating, the kind boys get every day. Painful but restrained." He stared blankly into space. "It was a turning point, Mellie. I behaved after that. I studied and I learned to fit in. But something inside me died that day. I knew my mother was gone forever, and I couldn't bear it. I didn't want to need that way again. To love that way again. To hurt that way again. And I never have."

Melanie's eyes filled with tears. She stroked Alex's cheek, very tenderly. "You don't have to need me, but if you could love me, I swear to God I would never hurt you. And I would never, ever leave you."

"I know." He kissed her back, growing hot and tumid as the embrace grew increasingly passionate. "The wall is still there," he murmured against her mouth, "but when I hold you this way, I want it to go away. Believe me, I do." He left her in order to protect her, then pulled her fully on top of him. "Be patient with me, sweetheart. Give me time."

Melanie felt closer to him than ever, but his confession only confirmed her fears. "I'll give you as long as you want, and I won't press you or complain, but I won't marry you, either. Not if you can't love me."

Alex hadn't put himself through hell in order to

be denied. He grasped Melanie's hips and thrust himself inside her. She was his now, and he meant to keep her. "The hell you won't," he muttered, and kissed her deep and hard.

Chapter 18

~⟨◯◯⟩~

Melanie and Alex arrived in Nevada City late Thursday afternoon, strolling up to the Stones' house arm-in-arm. Their argument of the previous evening was forgotten now, or at least pushed to the backs of their minds. Alex believed Melanie would eventually see reason and do things his way, and Melanie believed the reverse. Behind them, Ned was unloading Melanie's bags, but they paid him no attention. They had spent a glorious night together in bed, and nobody existed but the two of them.

They walked inside, pausing by the door to kiss. Melanie heard voices coming from the parlor, most of them male. She wasn't surprised that the Stones had beaten them home. They had gotten a late start.

"It sounds like Ty and Sukey have company," she said. A vague sense of uneasiness filled the hallway, but she was too wrapped up in Alex to speculate about the cause. "I suppose we should say hello."

"All right, but only for five minutes. Then I'm taking you to dine and to bed." Alex draped his arm around her shoulders. "Or maybe the other way round."

They strolled into the parlor. To Melanie's delight, the visitors turned out to be her father and Shen Wai. The entire company was poring over some maps and charts that were spread out on the table in front of the sofa. She sniffed appreciatively. Suk-Ling was putting out supper on the sideboard, and everything smelled delicious.

Melanie broke into a smile. "Papa! Wai! Welcome home. It's so good to see you."

Everyone looked up, startled by the interruption. Melanie was about to ask Thomas and Wai how their trip to the Comstock had gone when Thomas bolted to his feet. He glared at Alex, then began bellowing like a trumpeting elephant.

"Get your hands off my daughter, you scabious bastard! I swear to God I'll kill you!"

Alex nudged Melanie away and held up his hands. "Easy now, Mr. Wyatt. I don't want to have to hurt you—"

"You took her, didn't you! You seduced my daughter!"

"Yes, but I plan to—"

"I knew it! Damn you!" Thomas gave Alex a look of pure hard rage, then charged forward and began circling him on the Brussels carpet.

Alex's guard went fully up, but his posture remained defensive. "Calm down, Mr. Wyatt. I've asked her to—"

"I'm going to beat the bloody tar out of you, McClure. And then, when you're senseless on the floor, I'm going to slice off your lecherous balls."

Alex's jaws clenched. "Look, you obstinate blockhead, I adore her and I want to marry her. She's the one who—"

"And you think I would give my daughter to a debauched bloodworm like you? I'm going to slit your lustful throat. Cut out your depraved heart.

Chop you in tiny pieces and feed you to the local curs."

"You think so?" Alex beckoned Thomas closer with a taunting crook of his finger. "Fine. Go ahead and try, old man. In deference to Mellie, I'll even let you live."

Melanie rolled her eyes. Thomas and Alex were two of a kind and an even match, but a fight was utterly ludicrous. "For pity's sake, you two—"

Without looking at her, Thomas roared, "Stay out of this, madam. It doesn't concern you."

"He's right," Alex said. "Sit down, Melanie."

"My own future doesn't concern me? Excuse me, but no arrogant males are going to—"

"Ty!" Thomas snapped his fingers. "Carry her to the sofa and keep her there. I don't want her hurt."

Ty looked at Melanie and shrugged helplessly. Melanie shook her head in exasperation and sat down on the sofa. At least Alex's back was more or less healed.

She pecked Wai on the cheek. "Pigheaded fools. With any luck, they'll knock each other cold. God knows they deserve it."

Wai's lips twitched. "Be tolerant, Mi-Lan. Sometimes we men have a need to fight. I'm relieved to see you looking so well. Tell me, do you have the wooden tiger?"

She gestured toward the hall. Ned had set her bags by the door and departed, presumably to drop off the rest of the luggage at the boarding-house and return the buggy and horses. "It's in my valise. I'll get it when this show is over."

Alex and Thomas were cautiously stalking each other, feeling out strengths and weaknesses. As Melanie watched them, another wave of danger rolled through the room, leaving her puzzled and a little tense. Logic suggested it had something to do with the fight taking place, but her instincts said otherwise.

Alex feinted and withdrew, and Thomas did the same. Thomas's leg shot out, but Alex danced out of reach. Then Alex tried a kick, but Thomas was just as nimble. The pair fenced this way for several minutes, slowly circling each other, looking intently for openings. Finally Thomas lunged forward, captured Alex's arm, and tried to hurl him to the floor, but Alex answered with a grip of his own and successfully parried the attack. Both men staggered but neither one fell.

Each looked at the other with dawning respect, evidently realizing that he was dealing with a fellow expert in the art of *gongfu*. For the next several minutes, they took turns trying to kick or fell each other, always in vain. But far from angering or frustrating them, their failures seemed to intrigue them. The fury in Thomas's eyes gave way to concentration, the derision in Alex's to calculation. When the first successful blow finally came, a deceptive and powerful twist that landed Alex on the floor, Thomas actually cackled in delight.

"So you don't want to hurt me, eh? So you'll let me live, will you?" Thomas gave Alex a scornful kick with the side of his boot, and not a particularly gentle one, either. "Get up, you arrogant puppy. Show me again how ferocious you are."

Alex cursed and got to his feet, and a minute later Thomas was on the carpet and Alex was doing the laughing. The battle intensified after that, the blows and falls coming more often as each man struggled to defeat the other. Ten minutes went by, then twenty. Both were panting and sweating by then, hurling out colorful but good-natured taunts as they maneuvered for position and meted out punishment. They seemed to be fighting for sport now, not for blood, and having themselves a whale of a time. They were so closely matched that Melanie began to think they would go on forever.

And then Thomas managed an especially effective throw and Alex crashed violently to the floor. He lay gasping and inert for several moments, then tried to get up. But he winced with the first small movement, cursing softly as he lay back down. "I give up," he muttered. "You win, Wyatt."

"You're bloody right I do, you two-bit Don Juan." Thomas pulled a knife out of his boot and crouched down on his haunches. "Now where should I begin?" He touched the blade to Alex's throat. "Here?" To his chest. "Here?" To his crotch. "Or here?"

Alex turned as white as a ghost and stared at the ceiling with glazed eyes. Melanie knew of only one thing that could make him act that way, and it wasn't the fear of death. Besides, her father's eyes were twinkling. He wasn't remotely serious.

She jerked to her feet and bolted forward. "Don't jostle him, Papa. He has a problem with his back—"

But Thomas wasn't listening. Grinning from ear to ear, he tucked his blade under Alex's collar and slashed downward, ripping the shirt from top to bottom. By the time Melanie reached the pair, Thomas had shoved the shirt aside and was holding the knife to Alex's heart. And then he looked at his victim's chest.

Appalled, he pulled away his knife. "Jesus, McClure. What in hell happened to you?"

To Melanie's amazement, Alex actually answered, in a calm, steady voice that held no trace of anger or embarrassment. "It's a souvenir of my childhood, Mr. Wyatt. My father used to beat me."

Thomas rocked back on his heels. "Whip you

senseless, you mean. God, what a bastard he must have been."

"Yes." Melanie knelt down by Alex's side. "The beatings damaged the muscles in his back. They're prone to spasm now." She tenderly brushed the hair off Alex's forehead. "Should I get my medicines, darling? Give you a massage?"

He smiled wanly. "Maybe later, sweetheart. It wasn't a bad one. It's already easing off."

Thomas kept staring at Alex's chest. The scrutiny made Alex uncomfortable, but far less so than before. The past was losing its awful power.

Thomas's gaze finally settled on the medal around Alex's neck. "The Eternal Brotherhood, eh? Ty mentioned something about that." He smiled mockingly. "A man with such dangerous friends should fight better, McClure. You were easy pickings."

"The hell I was. I just landed the wrong way. I was gripped by a spasm and I couldn't move for a few seconds." Alex cautiously sat up and pulled the sides of his shirt together. "If it weren't for my damned back, you wouldn't have stood a chance. I'd have made mincemeat out of you."

"Only in your fondest dreams," Thomas retorted cheerfully. "I've been traveling for four straight days and I was close to exhaustion. I would have finished you off in the first ten minutes otherwise."

"For heaven's sake, you two, stop rattling your sabers," Melanie said with a smile. "You can hold another match when you're both rested and healthy." She stroked Alex's cheek. "Can you get up, darling, or will you need some help?"

"Melanie." Thomas tucked his finger under her chin and turned her to face him. "You keep calling him darling. You never called Bonner that, or any of the others who threw themselves at your feet, and you never cooed at them that way, either. I doubt you ever loved them, but Ty says you love McClure. Is that true?"

"Yes, Papa."

"I see. And he wants to marry you?"

Melanie sighed and got to her feet. The whole lot of them would gang up on her now. "Yes, Papa, but—"

"Then you have my blessing." Thomas stood and stared down at Alex. "Your reputation precedes you, McClure. From what I've heard, it isn't an admirable one, but I'm going to be honest with you. I wasn't enthusiastic about a single one of the others she said she'd marry, but I find myself liking you very much. The truth is, you fight damned well—clean and hard and shrewd." He paused. "Melanie needs a firm hand, we both know that, but I also expect you to give her her lead and treat her with gentleness and understanding." He held out his hand and helped Alex to his feet. "Agreed?"

Alex nodded. "Of course, sir. I would treat her like a queen if she would have me, but she won't. She has some crazy notion of coming to Hong Kong and living as my mistress. I believe she thinks her own background should make that acceptable to me, but if anything, the reverse is true. I can't protect her from gossip unless she marries me." Alex smiled at her tenderly. "Maybe you can talk some sense into her, Mr. Wyatt. I've failed completely so far. She's the most perfect woman I've ever met and I wouldn't change her a whit, with one exception. She's willful enough to try the patience of a saint."

"And Alex is no saint." Melanie squared her shoulders. "Besides, he doesn't love me, Papa. I refuse to tie him down."

"Doesn't love you?" Thomas repeated in astonishment. "Are you deaf, girl? He says he adores you. Wants to treat you like a queen. Thinks you're well-nigh perfect, for God's sake. Of course he loves you. Only love is that blind."

"No. Desire is, too. Don't forget, Papa, I've seen you when you're hot for a woman. You would crawl through broken glass for her at first, but it never lasts. Alex is fond of me and he wants me, but I need more than that. You can badger me all you like, but I won't marry him."

"Of all the romantic claptrap . . ." Thomas glowered at her. "Unlike most females, you have a brain in your pretty head, so kindly use it. Alex is wealthy and handsome and intelligent. He'll give you fine children. He's obviously besotted with you, so I don't want to hear any more drivel about not marrying him. You've given yourself to the man, so you'll bloody well have him, and soon. You have no good reason to refuse. It's nothing but maidenly nerves and childish stubbornness."

He turned to Alex. "We attend Mr. King's church in San Francisco. The First Presbyterian. Will that suit you?"

Alex knew he should agree and leave it at that. Wyatt, after all, was on his side. But he was also being extremely unfair. "It will suit me very well, but give me a little time to bring Mellie around first—to convince her we would be happy together. She isn't some silly female with no sound reason for her feelings, sir. Forgive me for being blunt, but she's afraid I'll turn out like you. Wrapped up in my business affairs, always running off on some new adventure, treating my children with an absent sort of affection when I notice them at all. My scars go very deep, and they've left me . . . less human than I would like to be, and she fears that. But she also has scars of her own, and they've made those fears even worse. And you're the one who put them there."

Thomas's face reddened with outrage. "That's ridiculous. I love the girl. I want what's best for her. I could have sent her to my family or left her with servants—it's what other men in my position would have done—but I kept her with me. I protected her and indulged her."

Ty was quick to challenge him. "Only because Wai badgered you into it. And sending Mel to Boston was never a serious possibility, Thomas; you know as well as I do that your father cut you dead when you refused to join his legal firm. Nobody is saying you treated her cruelly or failed to provide for her, only that she needed you to be both mother and father to her, and you couldn't or wouldn't do it. And then there are your women. She's watched you pursue them, enjoy them, and discard them almost all her life. What do you suppose that's taught her about men and whether she can trust them?"

"So I'm a villain. A monster. I've ruined her bloody life." Thomas stalked to the sideboard and poured himself a brandy, his fury prompting a terrified Suk-Ling to scurry to the nearest corner. "Well, damn the lot of you. Damn the things I've done for you."

Tension filled the room. Everyone stared at Thomas, speechless in the face of his rage. Melanie felt a rush of guilt. There was no denying Thomas's patience and generosity, especially to the Stones. Ty was obviously thinking the same thing, because he reddened and hung his head.

Shen Wai finally broke the silence. "There's some truth to your accusations, Ty, but it's not the whole truth."

Ty grimaced. "I know. Forgive me, Thomas. We owe you more than I can repay."

Thomas didn't reply, just belted back some brandy.

"You certainly do," Wai said, "but it's not what I was referring to. Captain, I know I have no right to speak of your most private feelings, but I find that I must." He turned to Melanie. "Mi-Lan, you must understand . . . Your father runs from one unsuitable woman to the next and one adventure to the next because the demons inside him will not let him do otherwise. He loved your mother deeply. He's never forgiven himself for failing to marry her. He's never forgiven himself for her death."

A twisting pain tore at Melanie's gut. "Which I caused. I'm sorry, Papa."

Thomas looked up. He was sober and pale, as if all the anger had abruptly drained out of him. "No, Mi-Lan. I planted you inside her. It was my fault she died. Now you're all I have left of her. I swear to God I love you, but sometimes— sometimes it hurts like hell to look at you."

"I understand." She reminded him of what he'd loved, which was sweet, and what he'd lost, which was bitter. "You've given me an uncommon amount of freedom and denied me nothing. I'm sorry if I was ever ungrateful. I have nothing to complain about and a lot to be thankful for. Alex and Ty meant well, but—"

"They were more right than wrong. I've always known how much you missed having a mother— that you looked to me to take your mother's place—but I couldn't do it. Or wouldn't, as Ty says. After all, it was so easy not to, Melanie. I was a busy, important man, and nobody expected more of me than I was already giving." He paused. "Not even Shen Wai or Ty's mother. Not really." He drained his glass, then continued, "But they hoped I would do more, and I should have tried to. Tried harder. I apologize for failing you, my dear. Alex, I think, will do better. If you make me a grandfather, I promise to try to redeem myself with the next generation."

"Alex is a good man in the ways that truly matter," Wai added. "He will never disdain you for your past, Mi-Lan. He will never try to break your spirit. He will never ask you to be something you are not. You should trust him when he says you will make each other happy."

There was another strained silence. This time it was Melanie everyone watched, but she couldn't get a word out. She was at war with herself. Her head told her one thing, her heart another. And then Alex put his arm around her and murmured that his back was beginning to ache, and all that mattered was easing his pain.

She helped him to the sofa and got him settled, then brought him something to eat. He thanked her with a kiss, then said gently, "We'll resolve this later, all right, love? I wasn't given a deadline to conclude this case and return to Hong Kong, so we've got plenty of time to sort things out." He pointed to the maps spread out in front of him. "Speaking of which, it's time we laid our cards on the table and got on with finding the gold. Ty? Wai? Have you figured out where it's buried?"

"North of Murphys, probably," Wai replied, "but I won't be certain until I see the original maps. Mi-Lan? Can you fetch them?"

Ned was back by then, eavesdropping shamelessly from the doorway. Grinning, he carried Melanie's bags into the room and she pulled out the tiger and the cloth map.

Wai studied the two items, then chuckled. "A very fine spot. Excellent *feng shui*. If I had seen these maps, I would have recognized it at once. The use of the tiger was particularly ingenious. It's hollow, you see. It tells me that the gold is not in the ground, but in the cave below."

Thomas walked over and sat down, wineglass and supper in hand. His good humor evidently restored, he ruffled his daughter's hair and gave his old friend a quizzical look. "But Moaning Cave is eight or ten miles south of Murphys, Wai."

"There's a second cave in the area, Captain. A whole series of them, in fact. A Celestial discovered them in the early days of the rush, but kept them a closely guarded secret. My people used them as a place of refuge against white men who meant to harm us."

"So you know and you didn't tell me. Now why doesn't that surprise me?" Smiling, Thomas turned to Alex. "I hear you're working for some of the big trading companies. What's your exact role in all this? What are your objectives?"

Everyone ate supper while Alex and Shen Wai discussed their activities and their motives. Melanie listened avidly, learning what she'd assumed, that Wai had deceived her for the most honorable of reasons, and that her clairvoyance hadn't played tricks on her after all. She announced that someone besides Alex had indeed been following her—the triad members—and unless she missed her guess, they were here in Nevada City.

"And very near this house," she added. "I felt it when I first walked in, and later, when Alex and Papa were arguing. It was a sense of uneasiness, but it didn't seem to connect to their fight." She frowned. "How odd. It's completely gone now."

"Maybe it's not odd at all," Alex said slowly. "We were discussing the location of the gold. If our enemies were watching the house and heard us talking, they've learned where the cache is by now. They have no further need to spy on us or follow us." His eyes jerked to the sideboard. "Ty, your young Chinese servant—she seems to have disappeared."

"I'm sure she's somewhere about," Melanie said. "She was one of my girls, Alex, a fourteen-year-old child sold into prostitution by her father. I had her trained as a housekeeper and sent up to Ty. She can't be mixed up with a criminal triad."

Ty asked Sukey to search the house, then added, "Mel didn't sense the triad members before we left Nevada City, but they were on the steamer and they knew her destination, so they must have arrived here after we left for Downieville. Anyone in town could have told them we were looking for Sukey, so all they had to do was wait for us to return. Given how long we were gone, they had all the time in the world to learn that Suk-Ling worked here and threaten her into doing their bidding."

Shen Wai concurred. Even a stalwart like Fou Ning had been frightened by the pair, he said, so little Suk-Ling wouldn't have stood a chance. Sukey returned a minute later, confirming that the girl was gone. "And she's taken what little she owned from her room. She must have betrayed us and run away."

"She's probably with one of her Chinese friends," Ty said. "I'll have to find her and bring her home. I doubt there's any danger—the triad members have gotten what they wanted—but I'd welcome some help all the same. Ned? Thomas? Will you give me a hand? Maybe Alex and Wai can settle their differences while we're gone."

The three men armed themselves and left. The rest of the group continued to talk, turning to the subject Ty had alluded to. Who had the strongest claim to the cache of gold and the empress's necklace? What would become of Wai's illicit operations?

After a crisp lecture from Alex, Shen Wai and Melanie conceded that they had no real right to the jewels. They had been stolen from Jardine, Matheson and legally belonged to the firm. Besides, Alex's reputation as an investigator would suffer profoundly if he didn't find the necklace and return it, and neither of his opponents wanted that.

The gold was more problematic. Alex insisted that his employers deserved recompense for the losses Wai had caused them, and Wai answered heatedly that his allies had mined the gold, legally owned it, and had the right to spend it however they wished. Melanie suggested her own pet project as a philanthropic compromise, but the two men were riding the high horse of principle and ignored her completely.

Then Alex began to negotiate, laying other issues on the table. The stealing and smuggling had to stop. The arms shipments had to end. Otherwise, despite his feelings for Melanie, he would be forced to take action against Wai and his cronies— actions that were bound to distress her. She would hate him, refuse to marry him, and regret it for the rest of her life. And it would be all Wai's fault.

Wai finally chuckled and shook his head. "All right, you English bandit, we'll make a deal. I wouldn't want to ruin Mi-Lan's life, after all."

"Don't put it off on me," Melanie said hotly. "I keep telling you, Wai, I'm not going to marry him unless—"

"Oh, for heaven's sake, be quiet," Sukey interrupted. "Of course you are, Mel. Everyone knows it but you. Now stop meddling and let the two of them come to terms. They're having a fine time haggling, can't you see that?"

"Well done, my dear," Alex said. "Perhaps you're not such a terror, after all."

Sukey giggled and Melanie crossed her arms in front of her chest and glared at all three of them. "Fine. Horse trade to your hearts' content. But I meant what I said, Alex. I won't have you, not on your terms."

Alex leaned over and murmured in her ear, "You damned well will, madam, but in the meantime, I'll content myself with making you want me. I can't wait to get you in bed. You're going to claw me and writhe beneath my body and whimper for me to take you, all night long."

Melanie blushed, but she also answered in a clear, tart voice. "I'll look forward to it, Alex. If you're lucky, I'll even return the favor. Now stop bragging and get on with your negotiating."

Laughing, he turned back to Wai. "You raised a hellcat, my friend. There's no bargaining with her, but perhaps you and I can teach her the meaning of the word 'compromise.' I'll begin by admitting that your politics are your own concern. I'll even confess that my future wife has swayed me a little in that regard. Things will never change under imperial rule, and perhaps the stability isn't worth the oppression. The Taipings, for all their bloody excess, represent hope, and it's possible they can learn to govern. So you can buy and ship as many arms to the rebels as you like, but not with my clients' money. No more stealing from the trading houses. In return for leaving the rest of your operation alone, I want the cache of gold."

"I'll give you a third," Wai said.

"Half," Alex insisted.

"Done."

Melanie beamed at Alex. He had actually listened to her. He had put morality above his business interests. "You know something, Englishman? There's hope for you after all."

"Enough to marry me?"

"Could be, especially if you give me a cut of the gold for my girls. And not a pittance, either."

He looked amused. "How about ten thousand from each of us, Wai? Do you suppose that will get her off our backs?"

Wai nodded and Melanie fetched some champagne. Five of her twenty would go to Ty for the Union, she decided, and she would keep the other fifteen. The group was toasting its newfound harmony when Ty, Ned, and Thomas returned with a red-eyed and shaken-looking Suk-Ling.

"They stormed in here and threatened the poor child with everything from rape to torture to death," Ty said. "Swore they would kill me and Sukey if she didn't spy for them and keep quiet about it. They left town about thirty minutes ago on muleback. I suppose they want to get there as soon as possible, and mules are surefooted even at night."

Sukey moved to the girl's side and took her arm. "Come, Suk-Ling. You've had a horrible few days. Let's get you safely to bed." Suk-Ling began to sniffle, and Sukey led her out of the room.

Alex quickly raised the subject of how soon they should follow, asking Wai how easy it was to find the cave. "Not easy at all," Wai replied, "at least not in my day. The grass in that area was very high, and it concealed the entrance to the cave. It was difficult to spot even when one had directions, which I doubt these triad members do. I doubt anything has changed, because the cave would have been discovered by white men years ago if it had." He paused. "We're all very tired, so it would be unwise to hurry after them. Besides, after so many years, few if any of the original Chinese miners probably remain in the area, and the ones there now are unlikely to know about the cave. I believe we can safely leave in the morning."

Everyone agreed, deciding that mules would be the surest, quickest way to travel, especially since Wai knew shortcuts that would take them off the stage road. Ty wouldn't be joining them, though, and neither would Sukey. He had a newspaper and pamphlets to put out and was sure Sukey would offer to help. She had admitted on the way to Nevada City that she was tired of traveling and looked forward to being at home.

"Then Mr. Hamilton was helpful?" Alex asked. "Sukey is more tractable now?"

"Yes, and I'm more reasonable, I hope. We plan to stay here for the time being, but she may go to school in Benicia this fall. If she does, I imagine I'll enlist. We'll see."

Alex sighed. "If only Mellie were as sensible. We'd be married in no time."

"Speaking of sensible, Alex," Thomas said, "is that back of yours going to survive two days on a mule?"

"It will have to. Melanie won't be left behind, nor should she be, and I won't let her go without me." He put his arm around her. "I trust you'll take good care of me, love. Keep me from slowing everyone down."

She smiled sweetly at him. "Of course I will, darling, providing you stop talking about marriage."

"Fine. No more talk. I'll stick to action."

Thomas looked at the pair approvingly. "You know, Wai, I think he's just what she needs. Tolerant but protective. Just look at the difference between him and Bonner. The man wouldn't even postpone a few legal cases in order to join us, and he disapproved of Melanie's whole adventure in the first place. I wonder if he even tried to get away, and how thoroughly he really checked his maps. You're well rid of him, my dear. I admit I felt a little sorry for him at first, losing you to Alex, but no longer. He doesn't deserve you."

Melanie shook her head in bemusement. "Wait a minute, Papa. Do you mean you consulted George before you left? What did you tell him? And what's all this about his maps?"

She was even more confused after her father reeled off the facts. "But Papa, George keeps his maps in his office. You know how organized and meticulous he is. He wouldn't move something as important as his maps around, not when he and Sam use them all the time. So if he told you the maps were in his house, he must have been lying."

"And Bonner had Fou Ning's sketches for several hours," Alex said thoughtfully. "I'd wager your Comstock mines against my Hong Kong shipping interests that he's having financial problems, Thomas." Alex listed the reasons he thought so, adding that Bonner had once lamented that his marriage to Melanie wouldn't give him control of her fortune, at least in California. "Maybe he didn't come along because he wants the gold for himself. He might have checked his maps as soon as we left, realized the cache was near Murphys, and lied to us about nothing matching up. He probably figures he can get to the gold before we do."

"Which he will," Wai said, "and if he digs deeply enough, he'll hit limestone. But he'll have no way to know that it's the roof of a cave rather than solid rock."

"Do you mean to tell me that George was after

my money?" Melanie asked indignantly. "That he never really loved me?"

"Not just your money," Alex said. "Your body, too." He grinned at her. "I can't fault the man's taste."

Chapter 19

⌒〜⦿⦿〜⌒

George checked his map for at least the sixth
time, then frowned. This was definitely the
spot. The two outcroppings of rock were up to his
right and the stream was down to his left. The
three large trees, all live oaks, grew in a triangle
directly in front of him, and the row of smaller
ones, sycamores, was behind him. According to
the star, the gold was smack in the middle of this
meadow.

He leaned on his shovel, panting from his exertions. He had set up camp on Thursday, pitching
his tent by the stream, and started digging at once,
moving outward from the position of the star.
Now, a day and a half later, the meadow looked
like a gophers' playground and every muscle in
his body ached. Hundreds of pounds of gold,
whether loose or crated, couldn't sink or shift
without a trace, yet he had found nothing. He was
beginning to think it was gone—that someone had
stumbled across it years ago and removed it.
Either that, or it was buried deeper than he'd
managed to excavate.

He was staring moodily into space when he noticed some figures off to the east, above the outcroppings of rock. They were coming from the

direction of the nearest road, a rough-hewn trail that ran north from the town of Murphys. They dipped below the peak of a hill, then reappeared. As they angled closer, he could make out two men on mules and a third driving a team pulling a dray.

Their arrival here was peculiar. Few men seemed to use that road, much less veer off the trail to this deserted meadow. One of the intruders spotted him and pointed. After a brief pause, the trio changed direction, heading directly toward him.

He saw their style of dress and tensed. They were Chinamen, possibly the triad members Wyatt had mentioned. George dropped his map and shovel. With a racing heart and a trembling hand, he took out his pistol and held it at his side. It was a fine new six-shooter, and highly reliable.

The men kept coming, stopping about thirty yards away from him. The one driving the dray was in the middle. He yelled something at George in Chinese, gesturing for him to go away. George was badly frightened, but he grew a little bolder when he noticed that none of them was holding a weapon. Not even the best revolver in the world could turn a one-eyed man into a crack shot, but at least he was armed. If these men were triad members, they would also possess weapons, but it appeared they had stowed their arms away.

He pointed his gun at the group. "Get out of here! This is my meadow!" He waved it vigorously toward the road. "Go back where you came from, you yellow savages!"

Far from obeying, the three squawked at him and gestured in a threatening manner. George's fear increased, but so did his determination. His life was a living hell. The gold was his only salvation. These triad members wouldn't have come all this way for nothing, so the cache must still be present. He didn't care if it was buried halfway to the land of their birth, he meant to have it.

Still, he was a gentleman and not a killer, so he gave them a final warning. He discharged his gun harmlessly into the air, then pointed it straight at their heads in what he hoped was a menacing manner.

The next thing he knew, two of the Chinamen were thundering down on him, their mules running faster than George had believed the creatures would move. Panicking, he fired at the pair. They kept coming, bending low over their mules' necks to protect themselves. He fired again—and again. Something slammed into his body and a hideous, agonizing pain shrieked through his core. Gasping for air, he fired yet again, then glanced downward. A knife was impaled in his chest and blood was soaking his shirt. Retching, he discharged his sixth and final round. And then something hit him violently between the eyes and he crumpled to the ground.

Hsu Wing dismounted from his mule, pulled his knife out of the white man's flesh, and cleaned it off. Chung Chu did the same, wincing as he wiped his blade on the dead man's shirt. "My arm was hit, but not badly." He directed Wang, their servant, to bring him their medical kit, then shook his head in distaste at the pale, blond corpse at his feet. "Someone so inept with a firearm shouldn't brandish one at all. He should beg for mercy. He would still be alive."

Hsu frowned at that. "You have much too generous a nature, I think."

Chung shrugged. "As I've told you before, killing often creates more problems than it solves. Besides, a hostage is always a useful thing." He picked up the dead man's gun, a fine one, and also a paper that was lying on the ground by his head. "Hmm. A copy of the treasure map. I wonder who he was and how he knew of the cache."

"Not a faithless associate of Alex McClure, surely. He looks too soft. Perhaps an acquaintance of Mi-Lan Wyatt or Tyson Stone who learned of the gold and betrayed them." Hsu pointed toward the stream. "Look. The one-eyed barbarian was camping down there. His possessions will bring us a few extra taels that we won't have to share with our associates."

Wang trotted up with the box of medicines, and Hsu treated and bandaged his superior's arm. He was proud of his skill at the art of healing. Wang, meanwhile, was digging a grave a few yards away. The area appeared deserted, but it was foolish to leave a dead body unburied. Corpses drew coyotes and other scavengers, and the creatures' feasting could attract unwanted attention. Wang dragged the body to the grave, then covered it with dirt and tossed the white man's shovel on top.

Chung pronounced himself fit enough to search for the cave, so the three men split up. Each took a different section and rode methodically back and forth, stopping now and then to poke at the ground. They weren't discouraged when success didn't come quickly. Suk-Ling, the serving girl, had heard talk about a whole series of caves, so they were dealing with something large. The entrance could be a sizable distance from the star on the map.

After an hour or so, Chung called to his countrymen and pointed to the three oaks, indicating that they should rendezvous there. "It occurred to me," he remarked to Hsu a minute later, "that it's always an advantage to know the whereabouts of one's enemies. It's a long and arduous trip from Nevada City, so this is the earliest Mi-Lan Wyatt and her party are likely to arrive. I'm going to send Wang back to town to watch for them. He can follow them if he sees them and report to us on their activities. If they seem to be headed our way, he can ride ahead and warn us."

Hsu nodded and Wang rode away. Hsu and Chung continued their inspection, trekking the area for several hours more with no success. Hsu grew frustrated and increasingly testy. It was getting cold out and he was growing hungry.

He finally waylaid Chung and grumbled, "There must be a better way. I know the cave was a secret even many years ago, but someone in the town may remember it. It will be dark soon, so we might as well stop looking and talk to the local Celestials."

Chung agreed. The two men stopped by the dead man's camp to collect his valuables, a sturdy horse and wagon, and some new camping supplies, and returned to Murphys, where they quickly found a buyer for the lot.

After enjoying a sumptuous dinner, they waved some money around and interviewed the local miners. Nobody knew about the cave, or admitted that he did, except a drunken old man who said the entrance was by the stream. He confided that he'd killed a local mandarin in a fight once and, fearing for his life, had fled to a small cell that no one else knew about. He described its location, claiming he had hidden there while a lynch mob set traps for him. If the stream hadn't dripped into the cell and provided him with water, he added dramatically, he would have died by the time everyone decided his actions were in self-defense and his friends could call out the good news to him.

It was an entertaining tale, but Hsu and Chung put no credence in it. They had searched the area thoroughly, and the entrance wasn't there. Besides, the stream was downhill from where they knew the cave to be. It couldn't possibly drip inside.

Chung was philosophical over the setback while Hsu was impatient. They returned to their hotel to wait for Wang, but several hours passed before he appeared. Mi-Lan Wyatt and four men had arrived at dusk, he reported, going directly to the Sperry Hotel, the finest one in town. They had registered and dined there, and then all but one of them had gone upstairs. This final man, a Celestial, had left to make inquiries among the locals, presumably to seek information about their own activities. Wang had tailed him all evening, ultimately following him back to the Sperry.

Between Suk-Ling's report and Wang's description, it was easy to identify the four men. They were Alex McClure and his companion, the former acting affectionate and possessive toward Mi-Lan Wyatt; Mi-Lan's father, Thomas, a one-time resident of Hong Kong who had a formidable reputation in his own right; and the shrewd and dangerous Shen Wai. It was a daunting group, one that Hsu and Chung had no desire to confront openly. Unlike the dead man, they were skilled fighters, and there were four of them to their own three.

That being the case, the gold was far too bulky to steal from under their enemies' noses, even by means of an ambush. They had made a connection here, a dealer in jewels and other valuables who was willing to exchange the gold for gemstones after a visual assay, but even the most cursory inspection took time. They would have to gain it with cleverness and stealth, using violence only as a last resort, because Chung was firmly opposed to harming McClure. He liked and respected the Englishman, but even more to the point, McClure was most likely seeking the gold on behalf of the Eternal Brotherhood, and if he died, it would become obvious who had killed him. Chung wasn't about to enmesh his triad in a blood feud with a powerful rival like the Eternal Brotherhood, not if he could help it. They needed a plan of attack.

Then Hsu suddenly remembered something that had happened late in their search, when he was peevish from failure and anxious to depart. "I was near the top of the slope. My mule insisted on walking down to a large and thriving oak. There was some tall grass beneath, and it was green and tender despite the summer drought. Perhaps it was being watered by an underground stream."

"The stream the old man spoke of. A different one from where the dead man made his camp."

"Yes." Hsu paused. "If his tale was true, the entrance to the cave would be somewhere nearby."

"But even if we go there at dawn and find the gold immediately," Chung said, "we might not have time to load it and cart it to town before our enemies arrive. If they spot us, or if Shen Wai learned about our connection here—"

"They might be able to take the gold away." Hsu smiled coldly. "Then we'll have to see to it that they're otherwise occupied, won't we?"

* * *

Melanie, Alex, Ned, and Thomas passed the evening playing poker, waiting for Wai to return from his reconnoitering. Melanie lost heavily, something she blamed on her lack of concentration. Fear had slashed through her the moment she had entered this town. Alex had quickly spotted the source and discreetly pointed him out to the others. He was a Celestial, apparently a servant, and, according to Wai, fit Fou Ning's description of one of his attackers.

This same man had watched them during dinner. Melanie hadn't seen him, only felt his aura—and then she had felt it diminish, presumably because he was tailing Shen Wai. Wai was armed and on his guard, but that hadn't stopped her from fretting about him all evening.

She was greatly relieved when he strolled through the door unharmed. Two gentlemen had made inquiries about the cave that evening, he reported with a chuckle, receiving one lead, a true but improbable story that they had refused to take seriously because it came from a drunken old man. Since they had failed to locate the gold and spirit it away, the trio had but one option left. They would have to attack, either to force the group to disclose the location of the cave or to steal the gold once it had been recovered. Either way, the group would have to watch their flank from now on.

Melanie glanced at her father. In deference to his sensibilities, she and Alex had slept in different houses in Nevada City and in different rooms last night in El Dorado, but she was too fearful now to worry about propriety. "I'm the logical target," she said. "I'm a female, so they'll see me as the most vulnerable. They could try to break into my room and take me hostage."

"So you want Alex there." Thomas cocked an eyebrow at her. "Strictly for protection, of course."

She blushed. "Not just for protection, Papa. I admit that I miss him."

"Promise me you'll marry him, my dear, and you can have him in your room. Otherwise you'll be stuck with me."

Alex stood. "I'm not going to blackmail her, Thomas. Come along, Mellie." He glanced around the room as she moved to his side. "We'll see you all at breakfast. Seven o'clock, shall we say?"

"Hell, Alex, you're never going to bring the girl to heel if you give in to her that way," Thomas grumbled. "Use what you've just been handed. Make her pay for her pleasures with a trip to the altar."

Alex regarded him soberly. "We're in a dangerous situation. The triad members will do whatever they need to to get the gold. One or more of us could get hurt or even killed. I'm not going to spend what could be my last night on earth playing games. I want to be with your daughter."

Thomas rolled his eyes. "An impressive speech, but wildly overblown. We outnumber them, Alex. They can't find the cave without us. Their associates chose them to come here, so we can assume that they're cool and shrewd. They're brutal when necessary, I admit, but they don't kill indiscriminately or Fou Ning would be dead now, and so would Suk-Ling. They won't be foolish enough to start heaving around hatchets."

"Especially given that medal you wear around your neck," Wai added. "If you turned up dead, your cohorts would reason out what happened and take revenge, and nobody in his right mind starts trouble with the Eternal Brotherhood if he can possibly avoid it. It's theft and kidnapping we have to worry about, not murder, and I agree with

Mi-Lan. She's the likely target. She should avoid her own room."

Alex knew that their arguments made sense, but he still felt damned uneasy. "I agree, so she'll stay in with me. She's my responsibility now, Thomas, not yours."

Thomas finally conceded the point. "Very well, Alex, you win." He waved the pair toward the door. "But don't keep each other up all night. You'll need your wits about you in the morning."

The couple promised and left the room. Under normal circumstances Melanie would have objected to being termed some male's responsibility, but the world had begun to vibrate and darken all around her, especially after Wai had returned, and the independence she had always insisted on seemed unimportant now.

She was shaking by the time they got into bed. Alex slipped on a condom and took her in his arms. He was physically aroused, but he didn't attempt to make love to her. "I don't flatter myself that you're trembling with passion, love. What's wrong? Is the menace very near? Very strong?"

"There is no menace," Melanie said hoarsely, "and in a crazy way, that's what makes it so frightening. What I've sensed all evening isn't danger, exactly. It isn't even fear. It's more like worry. A nameless dread. A terrible anxiety. I'm exhausted, but I feel as if I'll never sleep again." She bit her lip. "I'm not making any sense, am I? I'm sorry, Alex."

He rubbed her back. "Easy, love. I think I understand. You're saying it's something new. Something you've never encountered before. You don't know how to interpret it."

"Yes. Except . . . it's floating all around me, throbbing like some kind of living creature. And I have the sense I'm going to lose everything I want and love because of it." She clutched at him fiercely. "Especially you. I can't stand it, Alex. It's smothering me. Driving me mad." She pressed herself against him. "Make love to me. Make me stop thinking. Make the dread go away."

Alex knew what she was feeling because he'd experienced such sensations himself. When terror was all around you—when your life seemed to hang in the balance and all you could do was wait—you looked for any relief you could find. Some men drank, some men fought, and some sought refuge in a woman.

In his younger days, he had tried all three, and none of them had been worth a damn. Drink had clouded his mind and fighting had tired him out. As for sex, it had left him feeling restless and empty. There had been lust but no tenderness. Physical relief but no solace. He had never had the right woman.

Melanie was moving against him now, but he doubted she was finding much pleasure in the act. There was a convulsive wildness in her body, but none of the intense sensuality that he always found so erotic. Compassion surged through him, making him feel as if someone were squeezing his heart and soul. He wanted to care for her, to chase her demons away. He desperately wanted to be the right man.

He nuzzled her throat and face. "Easy, sweetheart. I promise I'll make it better. Just try to relax." He eased her onto her back and covered her with his body, then gently entered her. But when he started to make hot, slow love to her, she tried to hurry the pace, panting into his mouth and thrusting against his groin.

He pinned her beneath his weight to keep her still. "Not like that, love. It will only upset you more. Follow my lead and let me give you the things you need."

Melanie barely heard him. She was so distraught that she twisted against him in a helpless quest for oblivion, but he firmly took control, sweetly but insistently gentling her until she responded to his sheer male power, murmuring words of comfort until the madness subsided and a yearning submissiveness took its place. He was all fierce heat and tight control at first, but after two nights apart, they wanted each other too feverishly for prolonged love play. Their lovemaking was swift and passionate after that, but it was also full of feeling.

She fell into an exhausted sleep, waking a few hours later to the feel of Alex's mouth on her womanhood. Their lovemaking was much gentler this time. He had never been so tender and giving, and it made her feel beautiful, precious, and cherished. She responded by putting all the love she felt into the way she touched and kissed him. The pleasure they shared was exquisite, but more like a warm and soothing bath than a raging inferno.

He cuddled up behind her after his climax, fitting himself to her shape. "Ah. The tension is finally gone. That's good." He yawned. "Sometimes I astonish myself with the magnitude of my own talents."

"Obviously I bring out the best in you." She smiled sleepily and squirmed backward, snuggling as close to him as she could get. "I love you so much I could burst, Alex. I feel warm and safe and content. I wish we could stay this way forever. I've never been so happy in my life."

"Neither have I." He tucked his arm around her waist. "I was an old man at eight, but you make me feel young again, Mellie. Carefree. Drunk with the pleasure of life. I never imagined all that was possible."

"I'm glad," she murmured, and thought wistfully that at least she had made him feel something new and special, even if it wasn't love.

Chapter 20

Melanie didn't know which to trust: the deserted, bucolic countryside or her own deep fears. Nobody had attacked them as they had traveled from Murphys to the cave site. They hadn't seen a single soul. But the presentiment of danger had grown steadily stronger as they'd ridden along, until she'd decided that the triad members must have found the entrance to the cave and secreted themselves inside.

Shen Wai was down on his hands and knees now, searching through the tall grass for the waft of cold air that emanated from the cave's entrance. "Ah. Here it is. It's almost completely overgrown. We'll have to clear away the grass and dirt in order to get inside. Believe me, Mi-Lan, nobody has disturbed this place in years."

"I can see that, Wai. I suppose I'm just irrationally anxious." Melanie knew she could be overly imaginative, but still, the aura was chillingly intense here.

Wai and Ned worked while she, Alex, and Thomas stood guard, positioning themselves in a circle around the large old oak that shaded the cave's entrance. The rolling nature of the countryside demanded special vigilance because somebody could lurk behind a hill and burst upon the scene without warning. But nobody did.

Wai called her over as soon as he and Ned had finished, holding a lantern into the chasm so she could peer inside. The first few yards were a downward ramp, and then a series of steps had been chiseled into the stone. She shivered at the inky dankness of the place. It reminded her of the bowels of her father's ship.

Wai saw the haunted look on her face and patted her shoulder. "So you still hate small, confined places, hmm, Mi-Lan? Perhaps it would be best if you stayed outside."

"Yes." She straightened, then held out her palms. "See, Wai? They're damp just from looking, and my stomach is tied in knots. There's no way I could actually go down there."

Alex and Thomas walked over to inspect the gorge, and Wai took out a ball of string and tied one end around the tree. "If my calculations are correct," he said, "the spot marked by the star should be on the other side of that hill. Once we find it, I can measure the distance and the angle from this tree. With luck, I'll be able to duplicate the route to the gold down in the cave."

The group started toward the hill, walking with their guns drawn and their eyes roaming the landscape. Melanie was so convinced that someone was waiting on the other side of the hill that she almost fired when they reached the crest. But nobody was there.

Wai pointed toward the left. "There's the section we want, Captain, between the two stands of trees. Someone has dug up the entire area."

"Bonner, undoubtedly," Thomas said. "Alex was right. The bloody fool must have wasted the last two days here."

Melanie felt a surge of anger, then pity and deep

distaste. It was sickening that George had stooped
to such perfidy, pathetic that he'd fallen so low.

They made their way down the hill. A coyote
was digging in the dirt, but he ran away when he
saw them coming. A shovel was lying nearby, and
they walked over to inspect it.

Judging by the indentation in the ground, something had been dragged to this spot—the spot
where the coyote had just been digging—from a
short distance away. There were brownish-red
smears along the route, on the clumps of over-
turned grass.

"Those are bloodstains," Alex muttered. "This is
a grave."

George's grave. Melanie felt it in her bones.
Blanching, she turned into Alex's arms. Her stomach was heaving and her eyes were hot with tears.
"You said they wouldn't kill, Papa. And Wai—you
said it was only theft and kidnapping we had to
worry about, not murder. You were both wrong."
She began to tremble. "Oh, God, Alex. I want to
go home. I don't care about the gold."

Alex lifted her into his arms. "I'll take her back
to the mules and give her some water while you
check this out, Thomas. Ned? Would you ride
shotgun?"

Ned nodded and Alex started up the hill.
Melanie put her arms around his neck and buried
her head against his chest. "But Alex . . . Your
back . . . I should walk."

"It's fine. Let me carry you, Mellie." He kissed
the top of her head. "There's so little else I can do
for you. I'm sorry. I agree it was almost certainly
George. I know you still had some feelings for
him."

"Yes." Little more than a week ago, she had
been wearing George's ring. She had held him and
kissed him. The contemptible things he had done

since didn't change that. "I just wish—if he needed money, he should have asked me for it. He would still be alive."

"He couldn't bring himself to do it, sweetheart. He didn't see you as a partner. As someone to confide in. As someone to share his struggles. He thought of you as an inferior, and a man like George doesn't ask his inferiors for help. You aren't to blame for his death."

Melanie relaxed her grip on Alex's neck and gazed at him solemnly. "Is that your way of telling me that you do see me as a partner, Alex?"

"I don't know. Maybe." He stopped and frowned. "Yes. I do." He looked bemused. "And the amazing part of it is, I never expected it to happen, not with you or anyone else. But I met you and the world began to change." He kissed her gently on the mouth. "I'm profoundly grateful, Melanie. You have no idea how it makes me feel— that there's a person on this earth whom I can trust completely."

He carried her to the tree and set her on the ground, then fetched her canteen from her saddlebag. The sense of menace here was stronger than ever, but when Alex said such beautiful things to her, all she could think about was saying them back.

She pulled him down beside her. "I'm profoundly grateful to you, too, Alex. You treat me like a man. Not even my father or Shen Wai—"

"A man? Good God, I hope not." He took her in his arms and kissed her a little less gently.

She nuzzled him back. "Don't tease me about it, darling. It's very important to me—that you respect what I do and listen to what I say."

"I would be a fool not to. You're very intelligent." He kissed her again. "And very beautiful." And again, with unmistakable passion.

Ned snorted derisively. "If I have to be subjected to your billing and cooing, I want a share of the gold. It's enough to make even a strong man lose his breakfast."

They ignored him. Melanie needed physical comfort, and Alex wanted to provide it. They were still locked in an embrace when Melanie felt something cold splash onto her head. She thought it was water at first—Ned's idea of a joke. But then a wave of dizziness hit her and something strong and medicinal invaded her nostrils. She and Alex lurched woozily apart. The last thing she saw was Ned collapsing to the ground in front of her, his unfired pistol dropping from his hand as he fell. And the last thing she felt was a foul-smelling cloth closing over her face.

Hsu and Chung worked silently and efficiently. In under a minute, McClure and his cohort were tied to the tree and Mi-Lan Wyatt was slung over Hsu's shoulder. He carried her into the cave while Chung led the way with a lantern. Their plan, to don clothing the color of foliage and hide in the oak with an agent that would render their enemies insensible, had worked perfectly. As Chung had predicated, the group had eventually split up. Inevitably, their guard had begun to drop. But the two Celestials had expected the opening to come a little later, when some of group entered the cave to search for the gold while the others remained on patrol. Fate, they decided, was with them.

The old man had been very precise about the location of his secret cell. It was to the right, he'd said, through a long and narrow passageway, beyond some twisting formations that looked like a dead end. Hsu and Chung found he had been accurate, as well. There was so little room in the passage that Hsu barely managed to carry Mi-Lan through. The circular space at the end was also very small, only about six feet across. The water the old man had spoken of bubbled from a crevice several feet above the slanted floor and flowed out into the passage.

Hsu set Mi-Lan down, tied her hands behind her back, and propped her against the wall. He and Chung didn't leave the formation immediately, but stopped in the middle of the passage. The girl would awaken soon. She couldn't be permitted to escape. Chung took some blasting powder out of his knapsack and the pair went to work.

Alex's eyes fluttered open. Everything was dim and blurry, and his back and arms ached so fiercely that he yearned for unconsciousness to reclaim him. And then he remembered Melanie.

He jerked fully awake, screamed out her name, and looked around frantically. He was flush against a tree, and his arms had been yanked backward and pulled around the trunk. His wrists were bound with rope and attached to something else—someone else, he realized, on the other side of the trunk.

He yanked hard and heard a low groan in return. "Ned? Is that you? Can you see Mellie?"

"No. They must have taken her," Ned said thickly.

Alex thought he knew about fear. He had lain spread-eagled on a bed waiting for the crack of a whip, reefed a sail in a violent storm, and even run from a spray of bullets. But the piercing terror that shrieked through his mind was worse than all those things combined. "We've got to get Thomas and Wai." Thunder roared inside the earth. "Jesus Christ, what was that?"

"It sounded like an explosion," Ned said. "From down in the cave."

"Yes. They must have taken her inside. I don't know what they're doing down there, but we've got to get help before they come out. On the count of three, Ned, all right? One, two, three . . ."

The two men screamed repeatedly. But just as Thomas and Wai broke over the crest of the hill, two Celestials emerged from the cave with drawn pistols. One dashed over to Alex, the other to Ned. The first fired two rounds into the air, perhaps a signal of some sort, and then crouched by Alex's side and held a gun to his temple.

Alex recognized him at once. Chung Chu. Given his extensive contacts in Hong Kong, it probably wasn't surprising that he would know one of his adversaries, but his identity was a stroke of good luck.

"So we meet again," Chung said calmly. "How is your back, McClure? Have my father's treatments helped you any?"

Alex tried to hide the relief he felt. Chung Chu seemed the same as before, a man of measure and logic, but relief was a weakness the Celestial would disdain. He forced a smile onto his face and answered Chung in his own language, Cantonese.

"Yes. He has excellent fingers. A deep knowledge. I hope to enjoy his treatment in many future times." He paused. "A girl was here. Where—"

"Never mind that. She'll be fine—if you cooperate. Now be silent." Chung reached under Alex's shirt for his medal, fingered it for a moment, and then called out to Thomas and Shen Wai, also in Cantonese, "Stop right there. Throw down your weapons. All we want is the gold. Do as you're told and you won't get killed."

Thomas and Wai stopped, but they didn't lower their guns. Wai was the one who answered. "I don't believe you. You've killed a man already with your knives, and you'll kill us, too. Your promises mean nothing. We knew your victim, and you didn't even have the decency to bury him deeply enough to keep the coyotes away. We had to do it." Wai squared his shoulders. "You can kill our friend or shoot at one of us, but I promise you, you'll be dead before you can get off a second round."

The Celestial pushed up his sleeve. A blood-stained bandage was wrapped around his arm. "The dead man fired at us. We were forced to defend ourselves. I apologize if the grave was too shallow. It wasn't intentional." He nodded at Alex. "McClure and I are old rivals, but friendly ones. He has powerful connections, Shen Wai, and I have no desire to begin a feud. Still, I'll have to kill him if you try to resist. Now drop your weapons and no one will be hurt."

Wai and Thomas lowered their arms, but their weapons stayed firmly in their hands. Chung stood, still aiming his gun at Alex's head. Alex noticed that his hand was as steady as his tone. He took a chance on speaking.

"Chung Chu is man who keeps his word. Obey him."

"When he tells me where my daughter is," Thomas replied, in much better Cantonese than Alex's.

"Mi-Lan is imprisoned deep inside the cave," Chung said. "Without our help, it could take you days to find her. Kill us and you might get the gold, but some of you will die along with us." He looked at Thomas. "Including your daughter, Wyatt."

Thomas and then Wai tossed their guns to the ground and raised their hands. It was the logical course of action, but Alex was still sweating with relief. He didn't give a damn about the gold. All he cared about was getting Melanie out of that cave, and the sooner they all cooperated, the quicker he could do it.

Chung ordered them to stand by Ned, then picked up their guns. As he was tucking the weapons in his pockets, a third man arrived in a mule-drawn dray, the same one who had tailed them the previous evening. He ran off the group's animals, then untied Alex and Ned.

Chung's other compatriot lined up the four captives by the cave, handling them with deliberate roughness. He wanted to punish every one of them. Alex could see it in his eyes.

Chung didn't object to the abuse, but gave the group instructions in a cool, authoritative voice. They were to go inside, locate the gold, and set up a chain to carry it out. When it was stacked in the dray, they would be shown where Mi-Lan Wyatt was.

"We set off a small blast," Chung added. "Rubble is blocking the passage to her cell. It's very narrow, with room enough for only one man to work there. You can choose who will free her. The others will be tied up."

Alex struggled to keep the worry off his face. He told himself that Melanie hadn't been harmed in the explosion, because if he had let himself believe otherwise, he might have become violent and gotten people killed. He prayed she was still unconscious from the anesthetic, because he knew how terrified she would be if she wasn't, trapped inside a cold, black cell. He wanted her out of there, and now.

He started to talk in Cantonese, struggling with every word. "We obey you, Chung. Free the girl. She's frightened. No tricks. I promise."

Chung shook his head. "No. No offense, McClure, but only a fool would tempt a dangerous tiger like you. She's safe for the time being. She'll stay there until we have the gold."

Alex tried again, asking for less. "The girl is my wife soon. I worry. Walk me to the cell. I talk to her. Calm her. No rescue, I promise. Only after you have the gold. Please."

The man's cohort had been silent until then, but now he laughed. "The famous Alex McClure, begging us for favors. How amusing. Get down on your knees and beg us harder, McClure, and maybe we'll let you speak to her."

Alex didn't think twice. He sank to his knees. But before he could say a word, Chung motioned him back up. "My apologies, McClure." He gave his compatriot a hard look, obviously annoyed by his outburst. "My assistant has an unusual sense of humor. He wasn't serious. I'll grant your favor, but I'll also take the precaution of tying your hands behind your back before we enter the cave. And afterward, you'll have to be the last one on the chain, nearest the entrance to the cave. You know I have little use for killing, but if I lose sight of you for more than a few minutes at a time, I'll have to find you and shoot you. No second chances."

Alex nodded. Chung was obviously in charge here, and he could be trusted to do exactly what he said. "Thank you. You have my debt. I remember back in Hong Kong." He turned his back and offered his hands.

"I know you will," Chung replied with a chuckle, and tied him up.

Melanie awoke to find herself sitting in icy water, surrounded by total darkness, her hands bound painfully behind her back. The cold, the smell, and the jagged feel of the walls told her she was deep inside the cave.

She began panting and shivering fiercely. She could handle being imprisoned, but not the blind horror of her underground jail. There were monsters all around her, the ones from her childhood, and she was no less terrified because she knew they weren't real. She bit her lip and dug her nails into her palms, trying to get her emotions under control.

It was hopeless. The fear overwhelmed her. It left her trembling with panic and powerless to move. But one thing terrified her even more than blackness and confinement did, and that was churning, icy water—the water of a violent Pacific storm. In some small corner of her mind, she understood that the water in this cave must come from a harmless stream, that it couldn't possibly crash in and attack her, but she kept feeling it lash her face. In the end, it was the fear of drowning, or simply of the water, that finally yanked her to her feet.

She stood paralyzed, too frightened to explore, too petrified to feel her way to the exit. Tears filled her eyes, but she fought them down. Her father always told her not to cry. It was pointless, he said. It only made things worse.

She sucked in her breath, then slowly released it. She was a woman now, not a child. If she was going to survive this private hell without going mad, she would have to fight down the panic she felt. She blanked her mind, breathed deeply, and counted backward from fifty. The panic subsided a little. But the moment she finished the exercise and took a hesitant step sideways, it returned in full measure.

Somebody called her name—not Melanie, but Mellie. She thought it was a hallucination, that she'd conjured up Alex out of sheer desperation, but he began talking to her in such bad Cantonese that she knew he had to be real. She lacked the imagination to dream up such sentences.

His presence calmed her at once. She was safe now. He was going to rescue her. "I'm here," she yelled back in English. "Oh, God, Alex, you've got to hurry. It's horrible in here."

"Talk Cantonese, Mellie. There's a guard. A fair man. I know him in Hong Kong. He wants news of what we say. The door to the cell is closed. A trap. No rescue now. First they own the gold. We find it and carry it to a wagon. I know you're frightened. Be brave. We work fast. Rescue soon. I promise."

It was the tone of a man who was desperately worried and trying not to show it. Melanie didn't want him to know how terrified she was. It would only distress him more.

"You speak the worst Cantonese I ever heard," she said. "I'll be fine, Alex. I love you."

"I know." He hesitated, then added in English, "I think of not having you with me and—" There was a low thud. He grunted and coughed. Obviously he'd just been punished. "I go now." He was back to Cantonese. "Return soon."

"I'll wait right here," Melanie called back. It was a joke, a feeble attempt to assure him that her spirits were high and her fears were under control, but if he heard her, he didn't answer.

She told herself it wouldn't be long before he returned, an hour perhaps, but she was in the middle of her worst nightmare, and the strength he had managed to instill faded very quickly. It was exactly like last night—the awful anxiety, the nameless dread—but ten times worse, because the cave was all around her. It took every ounce of courage she possessed not to exhaust herself by sobbing or screaming. She kept the monsters at bay by filling her mind with numbers, saying them and picturing their shapes as she counted back from fifty repeatedly.

Still, she couldn't drive out the feel of the water. She could hear it trickle in, but she didn't understand that it wasn't flowing out until it rose above her ankles. She remembered that Alex had said something about a door being closed, about a trap. He must have been trying to tell her that the triad members had sealed off the cell, that it would be useless to try to escape. And now not even the water could get out.

The pain in her feet was excruciating at first, and then, mercifully, they went numb. But the water kept climbing higher, renewing the icy torture. She realized that if she could locate a shelf or ledge, she might be able to lift herself out of the water. She somehow managed to overcome her fear and the deadness in her feet and turn toward the wall. Then she dragged herself sideways, probing the cave with her body. There was no ledge, but one part of her prison was a little higher than the rest. She finally discovered a slight depression in the wall and braced herself against it, conserving some of her strength. Those were small triumphs, but they kept her going.

She repeated her exercise again and again. She kept telling herself Alex would return soon. Her spirit held steady, but as the water inched toward her hips, her stamina began to fail. She was drowsy and physically exhausted, as if someone had given her a powerful drug. Her knees kept buckling, and it got harder and harder to summon the energy to lock them back in place. She finally decided it couldn't hurt to sit.

She slid to the floor, shivering violently as the coldness closed around her. The water almost reached her nose, but she straightened her back and stretched to her full height, and it sank to the level of her chin. But it kept rising, and her strength kept declining, and Alex still didn't come. Her head drooped down, but she sputtered and jerked it up. The water rose higher, and she mustered the last shred of her strength and struggled to her knees. But finally, inevitably, it was simply too hard to keep fighting. She closed her eyes and slipped beneath the surface.

It was lovely down there. Beautiful and bright and warm. She saw a pair of figures in the distance, shadowed by brilliant light. They were smiling at her, walking toward her. She didn't recognize the one on the right, but she had to be an angel. She was very tall, with long platinum hair and a beautiful face.

She knew the one on the left, though, and smiled a smile of pure, fierce joy. "Mama! Oh, Mama! I love you so much. I'm so happy to see you." She wanted to run to her mother's arms, but couldn't move.

Her mother smiled back. "Ah, Mi-Lan. You've grown into such a beauty. Such a wonder. Someday you'll come to me, but not today. Go back."

Melanie felt bereft. "But, Mama . . . It's so peaceful here. So beautiful. I want to stay with you."

"And you will someday, when the time is right. But it's too soon for you now, my child. You must go back."

Then the second woman spoke. She had an English accent and a voice that sounded like music. "Alex is calling to you, my dear. Listen. Can't you hear him? You can't leave him yet. It would kill him. Go home to him now. And when you see him, tell him this. We can only come when the need is desperate. And it wasn't in England."

"You're his mother?" Melanie asked. But the women had vanished, and the water was dark and frigid again, and she was frantically clawing her way to the surface.

"Melanie! Answer me, damn it." Alex was lying on his back. The blade of his hatchet was wedged against the wall of rubble, and he was kicking at the end of the handle with all his might. There was a space between the top of the wall and the roof of the cave, large enough to wedge his lantern into but much too small for him to fit through. "Melanie!" he screamed. "You have to answer me!"

He kicked again and again, insane with anguish and fear. Water was seeping through the wall. He hadn't seen it the first time he had come, but it had to be three feet high now, a bloody lake of the stuff, and Melanie was trapped in it. Maybe drowning in it. He couldn't endure the thought.

He yelled to her again, begging her to answer, smashing his heel against the hatchet at the same time. There wasn't enough room in the passage to swing the tool with any force, so he'd been reduced to using his foot. The muscles in his back clenched viciously with every new assault. Carrying twenty crates of gold and quicksilver amalgam had taken its toll. Still, he kept pounding with all his strength.

Then Melanie finally spoke, and tears of relief filled his eyes. Her voice was so weak that he almost didn't hear her over his shouting and kicking, but at least she was still alive. He stopped to make out her words.

"Alex . . . I'm so tired. I'm trying, but I can't . . ."

"Hold on," he screamed. "The passageway to the cell is walled up. I'm breaking through the wall at the bottom so the water can drain out. It won't be long." At least he prayed that it wouldn't. "The triad members—they got the gold, but nobody was hurt. This will be over soon, Mellie, I promise."

"Thank God. But it's so hard . . . I'm so cold . . . I can't . . ."

"I love you, Mellie. Hang on a little longer, okay? Can you do that, sweetheart?" The words were punctuated by kicks. The rubble was heavy and very thick.

He had told her what she most wanted to hear, but she didn't answer. She was obviously clinging to life by a thread. He was terrified she would drown before he could save her. He didn't know how, but he had to keep her going.

"Mellie!" *Wham.* "I'll tell you . . ." *Wham.* ". . . about my medal." *Wham.* "I know . . ." *Wham.* ". . . you want to hear the story." *Wham.*

"Your medal?" she said. Her voice was noticeably stronger.

He murmured his thanks to God and started talking, kicking at the wall after every few words. "Yes. Don't talk again unless I ask you to. You need to conserve your strength. I was working for Charlie Burns, darling, smuggling goods past the Chinese customs. Candy, cotton, salt, tea—"

"Opium?"

"I told you not to talk. Yes, that too. I didn't like it, but I admit I smuggled it in those days. My ship was attacked by pirates from the Eternal Brotherhood."

He finally breached the wall, making a hole about two inches in diameter, and water began shooting out. He worked frantically to enlarge it, trying to will away the pain, to escape in his mind to some distant place. "There were eight of them. One was very young. A boy of about thirteen. I later found out that it was his first raid. They were better fighters than we were, but we had more men. There was a fierce battle. The fighting was hand-to-hand, mostly. A knife or hatchet here and there. It was a chaotic scene."

A large chunk of limestone gave way, and the water poured out faster, soaking him. "Someone flung the boy over the side. I saw him sink beneath the surface. The bay was stained with his blood. I convinced myself that we were winning. I thought about the boy and decided I could be spared for a few minutes. He reminded me of myself at that age. So young. So desperate to prove his manhood. So I jumped in to save him."

Another big piece of limestone came loose and the whole middle of the wall crumbled down, taking the lantern along with it. Alex bolted to his feet, twisting in agony when a muscle in his back tightened savagely. But he somehow managed to catch the lantern in midair and save the flame from going out.

"The water, Alex . . ." Melanie choked out. "It's going down. Thank God. You saved him?"

"Yes." He leaned against the side of the cave for a moment, panting from his exertions, waiting impatiently for the contraction to ease. "But I miscalculated. I was our best fighter, and when I left the battle, our enemies got the upper hand."

Alex's back was still clenched and his breathing was still labored, but he couldn't make himself wait a moment longer. He stepped over the rubble and stumbled down the passageway. "My actions should have cost us dearly. But the boy's father was leading the raid—he was the head of the triad—and when he saw me in the water, holding his oldest son, he called off his men. And I called off mine."

Alex reached the cell at the end of the passageway. Melanie was sitting on the floor, shivering and hugging herself. She looked bedraggled and exhausted—all except her eyes, which gleamed with love and adoration. He was beside her in two quick strides, kneeling so hastily that another spasm slammed into him.

Melanie saw him flinch, spotting the pain in his eyes only moments before he masked it and stiffened. The sob of need and relief that was rising in her throat died in a fraction of a heartbeat. She'd thought she was too cold and weary to move. She'd been so desperate to escape this awful cave that her lover had become a heroic savior in her eyes, almost a god. But in that brief fragment of a second, everything changed. Alex was simply a man, an incredibly valiant one, and that was better than a god any day of the week.

She leaned toward him, feeling eerily stronger and warmer, cursing the ropes that prevented her from holding him. He only went quiet and still that way when he was in the grip of a spasm, and she wanted to comfort him. "You were going through hell out there, weren't you?" she asked softly. "The pain must have been awful, but you didn't let it stop you. That's courage, Alex. When you're human and you suffer and you rise above it. And you've been doing it all your life." Her eyes welled up and her voice grew hoarse, but she refused to let herself lose control. "I knew I was lucky to have—to have even a small part of you, but I didn't realize just how lucky. You're the most magnificent man in the world."

Alex straightened the instant he possibly could, very gingerly. While he was moved by Melanie's words, he was also highly embarrassed. He didn't feel he deserved them.

He quickly cut through the ropes that kept her prisoner, then took her in his arms. She was alarmingly cold. For several long seconds he simply held her and warmed her, stroking her back, nuzzling her hair, assuring himself that she was real and safe and *his*.

Finally he murmured in her ear, "Courage is being trapped in a horrible nightmare, the way you just were, and conquering your panic and fear. And hell is realizing how much you love someone and being terrified you're going to lose her. If anyone is lucky, I am."

Melanie hugged him fiercely and finally allowed the tears to fall. "I was afraid I would never hear that from you, Alex. Maybe we're both lucky." A shiver racked her body. The unnatural burst of strength was fading now, and the cave was suddenly closing in again. "Please, Alex, just lead me out of here. If I could lean on you a little—"

"I'll carry you."

"But your back—"

"Will be fine as long as I don't move the wrong way." He handed her the lantern, lifted her into his arms, and carefully got to his feet.

Melanie quashed the urge to object. Alex knew his limitations, and, besides, if he wanted to be tender and valiant, she meant to enjoy every moment in his arms.

She snuggled against his chest. "So what finally happened?" she asked. "Between you and the leader of the raiding party, I mean?"

He chuckled. "You expect me to finish the story, do you? I'm not so sure that I should. It's a secret, you know."

"You're a tease, Alex McClure." Melanie was smiling herself now. "Out with it, you wretch. You trust me completely, remember?"

"So I do, my love. So I do." He paused. "We made a deal, Mellie. We sold the goods and divided the profits between the triad and the trading firm. It was an act of unacceptable leniency on his part to stop fighting, but he loved his son, and his men were well-paid never to speak of what he'd done. It was an act of negligence and stupidity on my part to save the boy, but my men were equally well-paid never to speak of what *I'd* done. So both our reputations were saved."

"And the medal?"

"He gave it to me as a token of his friendship. I wear it to remind myself of the value of humanity—and also because it's saved my life on more than one occasion. And now it's just saved yours, although I can never tell him what happened. He swore me to secrecy about the incident."

Melanie reached for the medal and fingered it. A quiet euphoria was setting in. Alex loved her, and the world was a bright and beautiful place, even in this dank and awful cave. "But it didn't," she admitted. "Save my life, I mean, although the story captured my interest and gave me strength. I couldn't have left you. I had to survive. Your mama ordered me to. I was surprised by her platinum hair. I thought of her as dark, because you're so dark. But you have her height and beauty."

Alex stopped dead in his tracks. His heart jumped erratically. It was too much to hope for, too much for God to give him—not only Melanie, but a miracle that joined her to the most profound experience of his life. "Then you saw my mother. She came to you in the cave."

"Yes, and my own mother, too. I was drowning, and they saved me." Melanie repeated what the two women had said, explaining the part about England in a soft, impassioned voice. She could feel Alex's emotion and wanted him to understand how deeply she shared it. "Your mama wanted to come to you, darling. I'm sure of it. I could tell how much she loves you. But there are obviously rules about such things, and they prevented her from seeing you."

Alex mumbled a quiet thank you. "It's, uh, it's a comfort, Mellie. To know she didn't want to leave." He started forward, only to stop as the light from the entrance to the cave came into view. "But it doesn't matter the way it used to. My mother was right when she said it would kill me to lose you. Not physically, but in every other way that counts. The wall I put up—it protected me from my own emotions. And then I met you, and you started chipping away at it. Last night and earlier this morning—I felt it dissolving. And just now . . ." He grimaced. "There *was* no wall. I felt everything. It was agonizing. And if I lost you—if I love this way and have it taken away again—I would put the wall back up and nothing would knock it down. I would be too afraid to expose myself to any more pain. It scares me to be this defenseless, but you're worth it. Loving you is worth it, because you bring such incredible joy into my life. Will you marry me now?"

It was the most wonderful proposal Melanie had ever received. "Of course," she said.

Alex kissed her, then carried her out of the cave and into the light.

Epilogue

San Francisco
September 1861

Mrs. Hall McAllister, San Francisco's society queen, had proclaimed it a perfect match, and society had emphatically agreed. Melanie Wyatt was the city's darling, of course, but she was also a real handful. They had always said it would take an exceptional man to tame her, and Alex McClure was exactly that man. A wealthy trader and a dashing detective, he was also the handsome grandson of a genuine English lord. Their romance, sighed the ladies, was as thrilling as any novel.

Everyone knew the story by now. Melanie, who was generous to the point of recklessness when it came to the poor, had learned of a fortune in buried gold and rushed off to find it. But the adventure had almost cost her her life, for she'd had a trio of dangerous rivals.

The first had been Alex McClure, who had contracted to return the gold to the Hong Kong trading houses to whom it rightfully belonged. The second was a group of Chinese criminals who meant to steal the gold for their triad. And finally, there was George Bonner, Melanie's perfidious fiancé, who had learned of the cache from her own lips, and rather than helping her retrieve it, had attempted to snatch it for his own use.

Instead, he'd been killed in a fight with the triad members, and nobody had mourned his passing. Events had unmasked him as an incurable speculator with huge debts who was marrying Melanie for her money. But where Bonner had been a scoundrel, Alex had proven to be honorable and brave.

He had fallen in love with his beautiful rival at first sight, he'd admitted; and even if he hadn't, he would have protected her. As a gentleman, he could do nothing else. His principles had led him into a trap set by the triad members and lost him any chance at the gold, but they had also gained him a bride. For not only had he saved Melanie's father and her beloved Shen Wai from possible murder; he had also rescued the lady herself from certain death.

The most difficult task of all, however, had been to win Melanie's heart. Though Bonner was a villain, she was distressed over his death and in no fit state to be wooed. But with her father and her friends championing Alex's cause, her gratitude and high regard had turned to love, and she finally had consented to wed him. After a ceremony at Mr. King's church, they were husband and wife, and blissfully happy.

That was the official story, anyway, and if some of it fell into the category of twisting the facts to put the best possible slant on things, the most important part was true. The bride and groom were indeed blissfully happy. They had never doubted that they were deeply in love, but each had wondered if the other was capable of compromise. In the weeks before the wedding, they had learned that the answer was yes.

Now, after a reception at the Oriental Hotel, they were drinking champagne in the Wyatts' parlor, discussing their future with the only people who knew the truth about their past. They would live in Hong Kong, where Melanie would continue with her charity work, Alex would concentrate on his trading business, and neither would become embroiled in politics. Both wanted children, three of them at least, and they intended to begin that pleasant project at once. As for Alex's detective work, he would take the cases that intrigued him, and Melanie would function as his partner to the extent that it was safe for her to do so.

Alex pulled his new bride onto his lap and playfully nuzzled her neck. "If you want the truth, my love, I hope you'll be so absorbed in me and our children that you'll lose all interest in adventuring. It would spare me a great deal of worry if you did, because I have the feeling that your definition of safe is considerably broader than mine."

She gave him an innocent look. "You have a point, darling. Of course, being a husband and father, if one does it correctly, is as demanding as being a wife and mother, so the absorption will work both ways. Where you'll find time to wander around the Orient, carrying out investigations, I simply can't imagine."

"Alex will make the time," Shen Wai said with a laugh. "And I suspect that you will, too, Mi-Lan. As your Christian bible says, leopards don't change their spots. The risk can be minimized, however, if your home and your place of business have the proper *feng shui*. I'll visit you very soon to make an inspection."

Thomas nodded thoughtfully. He had decided to spend a part of each year with his daughter and her family. "I believe that I'll join you, Wai. I'll need your advice on a favorable site for my house there." He glanced at Ned. Alex had asked the hackman to remain in his employ as an assistant at his trading firm, and Ned had accepted. "It's a glorious city, Hong Kong. You'll enjoy living there, Ned."

"I'm sure you're right, Mr. Wyatt, but that's not why I'm going." Ned grinned at Alex. "You've gotten me used to a certain level of excitement in my life. I figure I'll have to follow you to Hong Kong to keep it."

"Hong Kong," Sukey repeated dreamily. "It does sound exciting, and romantic, too. I would love to visit you all someday, and perhaps even stay for a few years." She paused. "Gee, Mel, with all those children you plan to have, you'll need a nanny eventually—"

"But it won't be you," Ty interrupted. "Not until you're through with your schooling, Suke."

"I meant after that," she said. She was entering the girls' academy in Benicia next week and had thoughts of attending college. "I'd be a wonderful nanny, don't you think so, Alex? I could teach your children all sorts of interesting things, like how to drive a team, how to work a press, how to cast a spell . . ."

Alex groaned and rubbed his head, and Sukey burst out laughing. "Well, maybe not the last one, though witchcraft is a fascinating business. I hate to give it up."

"But you will," Ty said.

"I suppose I'll have to. You would worry if I didn't, and we can't have *that*." She sobered and touched her brother's arm. "In truth, I'll be worried enough for both of us. I swear to you, if I could cast any spell I wanted, I'd hex every rebel in the South to keep them all away from you."

Ty gave her a fond smile. "That's one spell you

have my full permission to cast, not that I'll need your help. I'll be fine. That's a promise."

For a few moments, nobody spoke. Ty planned to enlist in the army after Sukey began school, and despite his show of confidence, everyone was as worried as his sister. After the Battle of Bull Run on July 21st, the nation had quickly realized that the war was going to be longer and bloodier than anyone had imagined. The Union had lost that day, sustaining nearly three thousand casualties. When the president had called for more volunteers, Ty had decided to join a Pennsylvania regiment.

Sukey hadn't objected; she had come to understand that a man like Ty had to fight for what he believed in, not just from the safety of California, but as a member of the Army of the Potomac. He would have felt like a coward and a hypocrite otherwise, and that was the last thing she wanted for her brother. But it wasn't an easy thing, to send someone you loved to war—and with a smile.

Still, she tried her best. "I know you will. After all, Melanie says so. Just this afternoon, she was telling me about a vision she had last night. You were fighting in a great battle, the last one you took part in. She sensed danger but not tragedy. Isn't that right, Mel?"

Melanie nodded. She'd never had a vision of the distant future before and didn't quite trust it, but there was no reason to mention that. "Yes. I couldn't see you, Ty, but I knew you were there, and that you survived. It was very vivid. It makes it easier to leave here—to know that I'll see you again someday."

Better a good sign than a bad one, Ty thought, not that it really mattered. As much as he wanted to live, there were causes worth dying for, and the Union was one of them. But they had gathered to celebrate love and marriage, not to talk about the war, so he opened a fresh bottle of champagne and filled everyone's glasses.

"Since I'm destined to survive," he said lightly, "allow me to propose a toast. I suggest that we meet in Hong Kong when the war is over to celebrate all our achievements: my sister's increasing knowledge, Ned's rise to taipan, my own promotion to general, the birth of at least two children"—he winked at Thomas and Wai—"and maybe even another wedding or two." He raised his glass. "To Melanie and Alex, and to our reunion on . . ." He thought for a moment. "It's best to err on the side of caution, I suppose. Let's make it the first day of '64."

Everyone drained their glasses and said it would surely be sooner. Then Alex stood, taking Melanie with him. "And now, if you'll excuse us . . ."

"I've never consummated a marriage before," he murmured as he carried her upstairs. "I intend to savor each moment to the hilt."

She rolled her eyes. "That's all you men ever think about. Staking your claim. Stamping your ownership."

He laughed. "Actually, I was thinking about making a baby, my love. Correct me if I'm wrong, but I believe a condom would interfere with the process."

"Oh," she said, and blushed. She looked forward to that part herself. Life, she thought, had never been sweeter, and she and Alex had never been happier. *If only Ty weren't leaving next week . . .*

Alex seemed to read her mind. "I know," he said softly. "I'm concerned about him, too. I feel as if I've known him for years, not just weeks. But you have to trust in your own visions, Mellie. After all, they didn't steer you wrong with me, did they?"

The fear began to fade. Alex was right. A vision that strong just had to be true. Ty would survive. "No," she murmured against his mouth. "They didn't."

Wyatt Tyson McClure was conceived that very night. Years later, his father would jokingly tell him it had taken five attempts and the endurance of an ox to accomplish the feat, but his mother knew better. It had happened the very first time. She had felt it in her bones, and she was never wrong about things like that.

Author's Note

Dear Readers:

Runaway Bride is the first book in a series set in the 1860's which feature paranormal elements in their plots. As you've just learned, clairvoyance figures heavily in the first tale. Now I would like to tell you about the second, which revolves around time travel and telepathy.

The novel takes place near the end of the Civil War. Tyson Stone is in Washington, D.C., working as as undercover agent in the fight against Confederate sabotage. His current assignment: to investigate a beautiful woman who has appeared from out of nowhere. But Sarah Maravich isn't a spy. She's a straightlaced historian from our own future on a top-secret mission to the past, and things have gone dangerously awry. She's landed in the wrong time; her orders prevent her from explaining who she really is; and the man holding her prisoner is the most formidable opponent she's ever faced—as well as the most attractive.

I hope you'll enjoy reading the book as much as I enjoyed writing it!

Avon Romantic Treasures

Unforgettable, enthralling love stories,
sparkling with passion and adventure
from Romance's bestselling authors

FORTUNE'S FLAME *by Judith E. French*
76865-8/ $4.50 US/ $5.50 Can

FASCINATION *by Stella Cameron*
77074-1/ $4.50 US/ $5.50 Can

ANGEL EYES *by Suzannah Davis*
76822-4/ $4.50 US/ $5.50 Can

LORD OF FIRE *by Emma Merritt*
77288-4/$4.50 US/$5.50 Can

CAPTIVES OF THE NIGHT *by Loretta Chase*
76648-5/$4.99 US/$5.99 Can

CHEYENNE'S SHADOW *by Deborah Camp*
76739-2/$4.99 US/$5.99 Can

FORTUNE'S BRIDE *by Judith E. French*
76866-6/$4.99 US/$5.99 Can

GABRIEL'S BRIDE *by Samantha James*
77547-6/$4.99 US/$5.99 Can

Avon Romances—
the best in exceptional authors and unforgettable novels!

MONTANA ANGEL   **Kathleen Harrington**
77059-8/ $4.50 US/ $5.50 Can

EMBRACE THE WILD DAWN   **Selina MacPherson**
77251-5/ $4.50 US/ $5.50 Can

VIKING'S PRIZE   **Tanya Anne Crosby**
77457-7/ $4.50 US/ $5.50 Can

THE LADY AND THE OUTLAW   **Katherine Compton**
77454-2/ $4.50 US/ $5.50 Can

KENTUCKY BRIDE   **Hannah Howell**
77183-7/ $4.50 US/ $5.50 Can

HIGHLAND JEWEL   **Lois Greiman**
77443-7/ $4.50 US/ $5.50 Can

TENDER IS THE TOUCH   **Ana Leigh**
77350-3/ $4.50 US/ $5.50 Can

PROMISE ME HEAVEN   **Connie Brockway**
77550-6/ $4.50 US/ $5.50 Can

A GENTLE TAMING   **Adrienne Day**
77411-9/ $4.50 US/ $5.50 Can

SCANDALOUS   **Sonia Simone**
77496-8/ $4.50 US/ $5.50 Can

Avon Regency Romance

SWEET FANCY
by Sally Martin   77398-8/$3.99 US/$4.99 Can

LUCKY IN LOVE
by Rebecca Robbins   77485-2/$3.99 US/$4.99 Can

A SCANDALOUS COURTSHIP
by Barbara Reeves   72151-1/$3.99 US/$4.99 Can

THE DUTIFUL DUKE
by Joan Overfield   77400-3/$3.99 US/$4.99 Can

TOURNAMENT OF HEARTS
by Cathleen Clare   77432-1/$3.99 US/$4.99 Can

DEIRDRE AND DON JUAN
by Jo Beverley   77281-7/$3.99 US/$4.99 Can

THE UNMATCHABLE MISS MIRABELLA
by Gillian Grey   77399-6/$3.99 US/$4.99 Can

FAIR SCHEMER
by Sally Martin   77397-X/$3.99 US/$4.99 Can

THE MUCH MALIGNED LORD
by Barbara Reeves   77332-5/$3.99 US/$4.99 Can

THE MISCHIEVOUS MAID
by Rebecca Robbins   77336-8/$3.99 US/$4.99Can

America Loves Lindsey!

The Timeless Romances
of #1 Bestselling Author

KEEPER OF THE HEART	77493-3/$5.99 US/$6.99 Can
THE MAGIC OF YOU	75629-3/$5.99 US/$6.99 Can
ANGEL	75628-5/$5.99 US/$6.99 Can
PRISONER OF MY DESIRE	75627-7/$5.99 US/$6.99 Can
ONCE A PRINCESS	75625-0/$5.99 US/$6.99 Can
WARRIOR'S WOMAN	75301-4/$5.99 US/$6.99 Can
MAN OF MY DREAMS	75626-9/$5.99 US/$6.99 Can
SURRENDER MY LOVE	76256-0/$6.50 US/$7.50 Can

Coming Soon

YOU BELONG TO ME	76258-7/$6.50 US/$7.50 Can